Mum

without you I wouldn't
be the person I am today
thankyou for showing me
who I truly can be

Ricky

Designated: QUARANTINED
Ricky Cooper

Draft edited by TGC editing.
www.tgcediting.co.uk

Final editing by Torchbearer editing
www.torchbeareredits.com

If you want to get in touch.

Find me at my website http://ricky-cooper.co.uk/
Find me on my page https://www.facebook.com/R.C.books
E-mail me at ricky.author_cooper@yahoo.co.uk

Dedications

For me, this book has been a wild untamed rush, but one that could never have happened if it was not for my fabulous Beta readers and friends.

Mary Philo, Monique Happy and Mark Lewis, Sarah Peace and Shannon Sharpe, not forgetting, Justin Gowland, Christopher Levdahl, December Maglior, and Tom J Leeland and my advisor and long-time friend and brother Norman Meredith.
Without all of you and the help and guidance you all gave so freely, this would be one very rough book.

A massive thank you also goes out to my author friends and supporters, especially my co-writer Tania Cooper, author of the excellent *The Broken* series, and with whom I am currently writing the Paranormal Romance series Heaven's Scent.
Tony Baker, friend, confidant, surrogate brother and author of the outstanding *Surviving the Dead* series, as well as Darren Wearmouth, author and advertising extraordinaire. His advice on advertising and publication methods, are invaluable to any budding or active writer.

In addition, I owe a massive debt of gratitude to the stalwart Andy Shaw BRMC (Ret) and Lee McEwan BRMC (Ret) Their advice, help, and none too gentle honesty has been a boon to this writer and his work. I have no doubt at all that without their careful and honest reading of the coal rough drafts, this book would be nowhere near the polished piece it is today.

Finally, my ever-supportive family.
If I was to be without any of you, well, I—for one—would not exist, and like me, this book would never have been possible; I love you all from the bottom of my heart and owe a debt I can never repay.

Glossary of terms

UKSFC: United Kingdom Special Forces Command

HLC: Heavy Load Carrier

T55-GA-714A turbo-shaft: Engines mounted into the CH-47 Chinook helicopter

L96A1: British Infantry sniper rifle

Detonator/Det cord: A type of multi yield explosive used in various sectors of civil engineering and the military. It comes in a reel that can be cut to length as needed and can be detonated by either a time/length based fuse or radio detonator.

Sco19: Designation for British Specialist Armed Police

Russian Phrases

Skoroy brata: *See you soon, brother.*

Proshchay staryy drug: *Good-bye, old friend.*

Svoloch: Scum (or similar)

Debil: Moron

Ublyudok: Mother fucker (or similar)

Zarazhennyy: Infected

Glupyy ublyudok: Stupid bastard

Der'mo, Demony: Shit, Demons

Psikhopat: Psychopath

Vy gnilostnyy lezhal meshok s gryaz'yu , ya budu imet' svoy grebanyy golovu: *You putrid sack of filth. I will have your fucking head.*

Voz'mite moyu zhenu i doch', on moy: *Take my wife and daughter; he is mine.*

Operational Phrases

E6: Cleanse order given to soldiers and personnel for the area to be sterilised.

T.T.O.R: Time to Operational Readiness.

I.C.O.4: Infected Control Order Four.

S.A.U: Specialist Assault Unit (pronounced saw)

Previously in Designated

With the decimation of the original teams in Afghanistan and Russia, and rapidly rising casualties in all theatres, Broadhead is forced to expand its field of operations.

America has long since gone dark, suffering the brunt of the initial outbreaks, leaving them little more than a collection of closed communities, sheltering within bases and bunkers throughout the United States. Carl and the special response team have been dispatched to offer whatever aid they can and to see if anything can be salvaged.

China has gone dark. With zero communication in or out of the People's Republic, everyone is left to guess as to the fate of the one point three five billion people trapped within the borders of a dead country.

Amidst it all, ghosts from Derek's past begin to surface. Ridgmont, Derek's former commanding officer, comes calling in search of blood. The loss of his son during a botched operation twisted his mind beyond all logic as he focuses his misplaced rage on Derek.

With the formations of new teams, Derek finds his position and role changing; new ranks are levied and bodies mount as Ridgmont circles and the Infected begin to threaten hearth and home.

1

Standing in the biting wind, the entirety of Broadhead's tactical units waited. The door to the admin building swung open as Colinson and Baker strode out of it, their mutually grim expressions saying everything, even before Derek began to speak.

'Briefing, Hall B—now!'

The teams filed off towards the briefing hall while Baker and Colinson stepped back into the admin block.

'So, Baker, how we going to play this?'

The A4 sheet sat on his desk, a mass of information crammed onto its pale white surface.

'You think it's legit?' Baker quietly muttered, answering Colinson's question with his own.

Colinson shrugged, his shoulders tugging at the seams of his shirt. Breathing sharply out of his nose, he pushed away from the table edge and walked to the window. 'No reason to think it's anything but, although having said that, we can't trust anything that's come through the UKSFC. So I don't know what to think.'

Derek nodded as he leant against the doorframe, his arms across his chest. 'All this shit started because his mob was passed over in favour of us; fucking arrogant little twat.'

Baker's voice rose with each word as he slowly began to lose his temper. Slamming his fist into the wall, he all but bellowed the final word. A loose file box clattered to the floor beside Colinson as the vibrations shook the wall.

Shaking his head, Colinson stepped over to the floor-mounted safe and knelt, his fingers dancing over the keypad as he tapped in the sixteen-digit alphanumeric code. The sheaf of pages in his hands slipped into the blank folder in the overstuffed safe.

Pushing himself to his feet, Colinson turned and clasped Baker's shoulder, nodding towards the door.

'Well, there's fuck all we can do here. Let's go and brief the others; see if we can make head or tail of what the hell we are going to do.'

****

Baker, Kingsley, Rawlings, and Bolton stood at the entrance to Hangar Three, the rain lashing about their still forms as the main doors slowly pulled apart. The CH-47f-HC6 Chinook stood before them, its silent shrouded form imposing even in the cavernous hold surrounding it. Baker stepped forwards, his boots echoing in the vast area that seemed to want to eat him whole.

'Oi, Bakewell!'

Derek stopped mid-stride as the voice echoed across the girder-laden roof; his helmeted head pivoted in search of the plaintive voice. Kingsley and Rawlings entered the hanger, fast on Baker's heels. Bolton hung back, his small frame crouched beside the entranceway, weapon pulled tight to his shoulder as he let the thermal optics illuminate the area. His eyes tingled as he stared into the telescopic sight. The dancing waves of blue and black blended seamlessly as the multi-coloured human forms that were his teammates flickered through his field of vision.

Kingsley and Rawlings moved up beside Baker, rifles pressed to their shoulders as Baker still searched for the source of the voice.

'Over here, you twat!'

Baker's head pivoted to the open ramp way of the Chinook; silhouetted within it stood the smirking form of John Davies.

'Didn't think you'd get away with it that easily, did you?'

Baker shook his head and made his way to the base of the stairway as a puzzled Kingsley and perplexed Rawlings stood rooted to the spot, rifles held limply in their grasp. Davies grinned at the bald, bearded Welsh man stomping up the steps of the aircraft. A wide grin broke his features as he came level with Team Two's commander.

'What in God's name are you doing here, you English twonk?'

Davies chuckled as he motioned behind him. 'Ain't just me here, big man.'

Looking over Davies' shoulder into the slowly brightening interior of the HLC helicopter, Baker met the heavy gaze of the entirety of the second team. Shaking his head, he shoved Davies in the shoulder and entered the plane.

'Damned English pup can't even be left behind without showing up.'

The chatter died out as the two T55-GA-714A turbo-shaft engines fired. Their roar seeping into the hold dulled, but only slightly, by the metal skin of the aircraft. Kingsley pulled a spare Norwegian jumper from his kit bag at his feet, folded it into a sloppy pillow, and shoved the waded, bunched material behind his head as he listened to the growl of the engines vie for supremacy against the birthing of mother nature's storm child.

Rain lashed the night's sky, turning the crisp, frozen ground into a mire of slush and mud. The thick, heavy wheels tossed up a freezing spray of grit and semi-frozen dirt as it taxied out onto the runway. Baker watched as one of the ground crew was pelted by the tyres' cast off; the crewman stoically ignored the semi-frozen lashing as he skilfully guided the lumbering craft to its take-off position.

Shifting in his seat, Baker looked about him then at Rawlings, who sat with his rifle cradled in his lap. The L96A1 long rifle bounced as the muscles in his right leg began to tremble; the caffeine roaring through his system brought out every nervous childhood tick he had fought so hard to control all his adult life.

Baker watched as his long-time squad mate and friend toyed with one of the .330 Lapua rounds his rifle fired, the pointed and bevelled cylinder rolling across his knuckles, gold-tinged yellow light dancing across his face as the glimmering shell reflected the glow from the lights above them.

His left eye began to twitch, seemingly winking of its own accord as the overdose of highly caffeinated coffee flooded his alcohol-addled system.

Baker forced himself to look away; the worry tugging at his mind was going to get him nowhere. Setting his sights on the viewing port opposite, he watched with an idle curiosity as the pole lamps ringing the base slipped away behind the veil of autumnal rain; the hazy misting curtain of droplets swirled in the down blast of air from the rotor blades as the aircraft lifted its ponderous bulk into the water-drenched, inky blackness of the sky.

****

A black square slipped open and ropes spilt from the hold as, one after another, the team slid to the floor. With practised ease, they moved away, weapons ready as the rain lashed at their shifting forms. A sharp motion from Baker, and Davies peeled off leading Reiley, Jones, and Hamilton into the writhing wall of water. Baker pushed forwards, the rain lashing about him as he swept his rifle in a smooth arc covering the area to his front.

'Rawlings, Bolton—find a high perch; give us some cover.'

Baker watched as Rawlings and Bolton moved off into the burgeoning wall of water. Baker and the remaining contingent from Team Two made their way forwards. Rippling pools of water rolled away from their falling feet as they made their way across the black tarmac surface of the road. Kingsley's eyes closed to little more than

5

slits as he gazed through the hazy blur of water and ice; the haze-ridden darkness shifted before them as the eight-foot-high chain link fence of their objective appeared from the shadows.

Dropping to his knees, Kingsley slid forwards. The reinforced kneepads of his combat trousers scraped over the floor as he spun, his back coming to rest against the fence as Baker planted his booted foot in his cradled hands.

The muscles of his shoulders bunched, the steel-like tendons snapping taut as Kingsley heaved, propelling Baker upwards. The fifteen-stone soldier left the floor, water cascading off his form as he curled his fingers over the top of the fence; with the grace of a cat, he landed, tucking his body into a tight roll as he absorbed the impact through his legs.

Baker rose to his feet, moving with practised ease through the pooled shadows cast down between the pole lights of the gravelled path beside him.

Dropping back to one knee, he slowly eased open the top of one of his vests pouches. The coiled spool of detonator cord felt like grease-covered string as he wove it through the links of the chain and padlock holding the gate closed.

The sharp crack was swallowed by the pounding rain about them as the low-yield cord detonated, the chain clinking to the ground as its links tore apart. Baker reached out as Kingsley grabbed hold of the gate from the other side, both men heaving it aside with the muffled squeaking of wheels. Baker shook his head, pea-sized droplets flying forth in a sparkling halo of water.

'Echo Two, Echo Two. Echo One. Infill completed.' A soft double-click echoed in Baker's ear as he waited for Davies' reply. *'Roger that, Echo Two in position, no movement within perimeter.'*

Baker sent a double-click through the radio as he waved Baxter and Clarkenwell forwards, the two soldiers skimming past their commander, the gravel beneath their feet barely making a sound as they ghosted by.

Kingsley appeared from the shadows as Baker reached the door. His chocolate-brown eyes seemed to glow as he dropped to one knee; with a nod of his head, Baker watched as Clarkenwell twisted the handle on the door and pushed open, flattening himself to the wall at the last second. Baxter, his LMG pulled tightly to his shoulder, rushed past him, sinking into the pitch-black corridor and vanishing from sight.

****

Rawlings watched the stark-white forms of his comrades and friends disappear into the building, the rain plastering his already soaked ghillie suit onto his prostrate form. He shifted his sight picture onto the right hand side of the building as he felt the rain ease slightly, the incessant pounding dropping to that of a spring shower.

'Thank Christ for that; Damned rain was doing my nut.'

His sardonic quip went unanswered, the constant pattering of rain on grass his only answer.

'Oh Two, what? You ignoring me now? Bolton?'

Silence greeted his questioning; the pattering of rain seemed to call out to him as his hackles rose. Slowly, his hands left the rifle's stock, sliding over the slick, wet grass towards his sidearm, the pistol lying mere centimetres away on the waterlogged ground beside him.

'Don't.'

The voice was cold and calculating with no trace of emotion in the single word. Pushing the cold and callous warning aside, his hand still made its slow journey towards the handgun.

'I wouldn't if I were you, buddy; you won't make it. Your spotter saw sense—just give up.'

7

The cold steel of the man's weapon pressed into the folds of Rawlings' ghillie suit, worming its way through the dense fibres to the nape of his neck. The cold kiss of the steel muzzle made Rawlings tense involuntarily, stilling his movements instantly.

'Good lad. Now, hands out to your sides raised off the floor, shoulder level.'

Rawlings did as he was told; slapping wet footsteps drew his attention as he saw Bolton lifted from the floor, his hands trussed behind him. Flicking his gaze forwards, he calculated how long it would take him to roll and bring his weapon to bear; he tensed his body to do just that, his hips shifting ever so slightly. He rolled his shoulders and was about to move when black leather filled his vision and his entire world went dark.

'Told you not to move.'

****

Davies crouched at the corner of the building, water dripping from his rifle's silencer as he watched the irrepressible fluid shift along the lip of his helmet. The glimmering liquid coalesced into hanging globules, and then with all the grace of a parachuting hippo, fell to earth, bursting against the top of his gloved hand.

Rising silently from his crouched position, he began to skulk forwards, the low-hanging windows beckoning him and his three men. Davies lifted his gloved hand towards the reinforced, mesh-laced windows when his eyes snapped shut, blinded by the sudden light

The windows shone. Shaking his head, glowing afterimages remained in his vision, the swirling formless shapes dancing across his eyes as he forced himself to gaze into the room beyond the glass. He bit down hard onto his bottom lip as he watched ten black-clad soldiers converge on the four men inside the building. Pushing himself back from the window, he motioned to the others to back up as he scurried into the welcoming arms of the shadows.

8

****

Baker's teeth ground together as he watched them close in, the Heckler and Koch MP5SDs they carried never wavering. Baker slowly raised his hands to shoulder height and a soft grin played over his features as he watched Baxter and Clarkenwell switch from target to target, their weapons held ready.

'Stand fast and lower your weapons.'

The voice came out slightly muffled, spoken as it was, through the Nomex balaclava covering his captor's features. Baker cast an appraising eye over the men before him, their matte-black uniforms devoid of any identifying markings. The Gerber tactical daggers held inverted on their chests and the Sig-Sauer 9mm pistols in hard-shell drop leg holsters gave Baker pause. His eyes drifted to the top left pocket on their battle vests.

As his gaze alighted on the woven black thread of the dagger inside the conjoined and inverted V's, his blood ran cold.

'Do as he says. Baxter, Clarkenwell, lower your weapons. Kingsley, you as well; this lot don't fuck about.'

The black sergeant grudgingly let his weapon drop, the rifle bouncing against his frame as it hung on the three-point tactical sling that snaked its way around his body.

'They who I think they are?'

Baker simply nodded as he watched the soldiers approach; with one smooth motion, the operative unsheathed his knife and slipped it behind the Cordura sling across Derek's chest, then with a short, sharp, flick of his wrist, cut the weapon free of Baker's body. A heavy clatter echoed around the empty building as his weapon hit the hard, unforgiving concrete.

The sound echoed around him as it was answered by the heavy

metallic clunk of its brethren as they were sent crashing to the floor. Baxter, a pain-filled wince riding through him, watched as his weapon collided with the unyielding ground. Staring at the impassive eyes of the operative before him, he spoke.

'I hope you're going to pay for me to have the sights fixed and the barrel re-blued.'

Baxter's sarcastic comment was met with a clenched fist slamming heavily into his solar plexus.

****

Bolton's hands were tucked behind him, the steel scaffold pole cold against his skin. The winter's chill seeped through him as the metal's water-etched surface sucked at his skin, the ice clutching at him as it tore at his flesh. He winced when he moved, the sharp bite of the icicles' teeth snipping lumps from his palms as he flexed his fingers.

The operative before him held out a cigarette. Bolton let a small, derisive chuckle echo through his throat as he leant out, his lips parted slightly to clasp the filter. The soft paper and cotton tip stuck to his chapped lips as he settled back on his haunches. The yellow, flickering dance of the lighter in the operative's hand stung his eyes as he sucked at the processed stick of tobacco.

'So, Bolton, where are they?'

Bolton blew the blue, tar-laced smoke from his nose as he looked at the shadowed face in front of him. Its hawk-nose sneer made his hands itch with the desire to smash it from this world.

'Who?'

The sneering face creased with anger as Bolton once more drew in the nicotine-drenched smoke.

The face's fists clenched, the watery blue eyes dancing with a

10

barely suppressed rage. The glittering stain of manic psychosis pranced just out of reach as they bored into Bolton.

'The rest of your team—Davies and the others!'

Bolton's smirk sent ash trickling down the front of his rig as he stared back at the face in front of him.

'Oh, I thought you meant your wife and daughter. I was going to say they're down the road in the Premier Inn; didn't know your kid was into anal.'

A brick-sized fist crashed into the side of Bolton's head, sending him sideways. His hand squealed as his flesh ground against the pole, blood seeping from around the flex cuffs. Shaking his head, he pulled himself back onto his knees, blood trickling down the side of his face as it gently pulsed from the rippled tear in his hairline. Relaxing his lips, he let the cigarette's smoke fill his lungs, the burst of nicotine calming his nerves as he steeled himself for his next reply.

'Okay, you got me; your mother was there too.'

His head snapped left as a boot tore into him, the ridged, grit-covered sole tearing into the side of his face; a trail of torn skin and soil-filled grazes covered his jaw and cheek bone as he once more levered himself onto his knees.

'I am going to ask you again; where are they?'

Bolton spat the snapped cigarette away, blood trickling from his torn lip. He ran his tongue over the centimetre-deep tear, the taste of copper filling his mouth as his own blood coated his tongue.

'Okay, sorry. I meant to say we're all meeting up down there; Davies has gone to get the beer. Then we're all going to sausage slap the three of them!'

His head snapped backwards, a deep metal-filled thrum filling the

11

air as his head hit the pole; stars filled his vision as another punch landed, sending him sideways into the floor. He struggled onto his knees again, blood pouring from his nose and face. He felt the sting of freshly opened flesh as his eye began to swell; hawking up a mix of mucus and blood he spat it on to the floor.

'You don't like me, do you, James?'

Bolton winced sharply as he smiled, watching the watery blue eyes as they drank in the sight of his battered face.

'Shit, whatever gave you that idea? I love everyone—just ask your mother and daughter; hell your wife is so "loved" that she's taken more of a pounding than Omaha Beach on D-day.'

The sharp toe of a boot slammed into the side of Bolton's head, his vision swam as he forced himself to stay upright.

'Who gave you the call?'

Bolton's lip twisted as he smiled, blood pooling in his mouth.
'I think his name was Sook jit; oh and that's pronounced, suck shit.'

The dancing ballet of psychosis edged ever closer to the pair of pale, watery blue eyes as he heard the clenching of a gloved fist.

Bolton spat out a molar, a twisted blood-covered smear of nerve and gum trailing after it.

'One last time, where is Davies and the rest of your team? You know I don't like hurting you like this; it's too... messy, doesn't get you anywhere.'

'You don't like hurting me? Is that why they're doing it? Then again, your wife had some wild ideas... those I liked. This... I could take it or leave it.' He pitched sideways, his eyes going dim, the sound of leather on flesh filling the air as the three men around him beat him into submission.

12

****

Rawlings staggered along, his hands held clasped behind his back, the flex cuffs biting deep into the flesh of his wrists. A sharp shove between his shoulder blades sent him staggering as he fought for purchase on the rain-slicked tarmac. He raised his face to the rain as he finally lost his footing and fell to his knees, the hard shell of his kneepads clacking off the water-laden surface.

A muffled grunt caught his attention. Glancing to his left he watched the battered form of his long-time friend and squad mate fall in beside him, blood oozing from his nose and lips as his head hung limply against his chest.

'James, bro, you okay?'

Bolton's one good eye cracked open, a roguish grin flourishing on his rapidly swelling features.

'They got nothing.'

He tried to wink, only to find his swollen cheek and brow too painful to move. Rawlings heaved as the tattered and torn left side of Bolton's face fell into view. The light played off the shimmering mess of torn skin and flesh cut so deep that the sinew and the shadowed glinting of bone teased Rawlings' closed eyes, the hot sting of tears burning their way through.

****

Baker marched out of the building, Kingsley at his side. The sloshing footsteps of Baxter and Clarkenwell followed in their wake.

'You ready?'

A soft chorus of affirmations graced his ears as well as a solitary static-filled double click. A smile teased his lips as he stoically walked towards the blurred shapes ahead, his mind whirling as he

13

began to cycle through all the options before him.

****

Davies watched through the scope of his rifle as Baker and the others were pushed towards the group waiting in the centre of the car park, their captors grabbing hold of their shoulders and forcing the four men to their knees. With a short motion of his hand, Davies sent Hamilton and Jones through the shifting shadows as he rose to a hunched crouch and made his way slowly forwards.

The illuminated sights of his optics settled on one of Broadhead's captors. A smooth flick of his thumb set his weapon to automatic. He watched as the black-clad soldiers moved into position around Baker and the others.

His finger grazed the trigger; the need to open fire was stronger than anything he had ever felt in his ten years as a soldier. Grinding his teeth together, he watched as a cadaverous shape appeared behind Rawlings and Bolton. It moved between the black-clad troopers who were standing over the two kneeling soldiers like a pair of daemonic watchdogs.

He wanted nothing more in the world than to clamp his finger down on the trigger, unleashing a storm of death upon those who would cause his friends and family harm. But he knew that for all the good it would do, it would harm those he wished to save tenfold. In an agonising moment of visceral self-betrayal, he pulled his finger out from the trigger guard and watched the events unfold.

Baker stared with contempt and hatred at the man responsible for the deaths of many he had held dear.

The twisted, smirking visage of the blonde man was like a knife twisting in Baker's very core. The molten seeds of rage burned deep in his soul. He shook and twisted his shoulders, his flesh tearing as he tore at the flex cuffs binding his hands behind him. The hot, coppery smell of his own blood wafted up from the wet floor beneath him as it poured from his ripped skin, soaking the sleeves of

14

his jacket and pooling in the fingers of his gloves.

Motion in the corner of his eye distracted him from his own rage. He watched Kingsley rise, his movements almost feline as he sprang from his knees and launched himself forwards. A glimmer of wet, carbon-fibre-infused plastic ended Kingsley's efforts as the stock of a weapon crashed into the base of his skull. Like a marionette with no strings, Kingsley slumped to the floor, blood seeping in a thin, diffused halo about his head as the flesh began to bleed.

'Valiant effort, but alas it was too little too late; once again, Derek, you have fallen short of the last hurdle and failed as you always do.'

Ridgmont slowly stepped forwards, his face now lined and creased, no longer the pale young officer Baker had known twenty years before.

'Why me? Why us? All we've ever done is our job. I can't be held accountable for the actions of others. You know this isn't the way an officer does things. Hiring killers... what, are you a coward?'

Ridgmont's features contorted into a feral snarl as he reeled from the barbed words.

'You have the gall to call me a coward? Me, the man who pulled you from the fires of hell itself. It is you who are the coward, sir, not me!'

He gesticulated wildly at Baker, the nickel-plated 9mil in his hand glinting in the cold moonlight.

'Pulled me from the fires of hell? You were the one who sent me in there—me and the rest of Charlie Company! How many of your men died? How many of them begged you to send in armoured support while they were cut to ribbons in open ground? Men with families, men with mothers and fathers; sons and daughters.
'Begging, all of them begging you for help while those around them died, including your own son. And you call me a coward;

you're the one who marched your men into the meat grinder, all for a handshake and a lump of tin.'

Ridgmont's eyes went dark as he stepped back, reeling from Baker's words as the bound and kneeling lieutenant carried on.

'I was there. I saw him pulling his own men from the field through a hailstorm of lead. I watched as he took round after round and still pulled two of his command team to safety.

'Do you know what he said to me as I sat there trying to stop him from bleeding out? Do you know what he said as his blood slipped through my fingers? "Tell my father I'm sorry." His dying words, Ridgmont, were not some grandiose platitude or heroic statement; they were nothing more than an apology to the man who had sent him to his death.'

Baker glared. Ridgmont's lips curled into a venom-filled smile as he stared into the eyes of hatred. Lifting his pistol, he weighed the implement of death, letting it float in his hand as he brought it to bear.

'Thank you for sharing that with me. I appreciate the words but, alas, it changes nothing.'

He levelled the pistol at the back of Bolton's head.

'And here we have it, Derek, another man's blood on your hands.'

Baker threw himself forwards, black gloved hands pulled at his combat suit, holding him down. He watched, his heart clenching as Ridgmont's finger tightened on the trigger. Bolton looked up into Derek's eyes sensing the sands of his life slipping through the hourglass and smiled.

'Chief, kill this cunt for me.'

His left eye exploded. The 9mm hollow point destroying the left side of his head as it carved its path through his very being.

The echoing crack of the pistol rolled across the empty grounds around them as Bolton's body slumped forwards into a puddle of brain and bone. Baker rocked on his knees as he watched the steaming pool of blood and brain matter slowly ooze forth. Rawlings knelt, his body quivering as he stared at his friend and partner. Tears cascaded down his face and his hands turned blue as he strained to break the reinforced plastic that bound him.

****

Davies watched as the gun bucked in Ridgmont's hand and Bolton's lifeless body tumbled forwards. He closed his eyes and replayed the scene in his head. Moving his eye back to the scope, he saw Baker slump back, his backside coming to rest on the heels of his boots while Ridgmont sneered; his eyes glazed with a psychotic lust as he stared at the shattered remnants of Bolton's skull.

Shifting his grip, Davies wrapped his index finger around the trigger and squeezed.

****

Baker hit the floor as Davies' three-click warning buzzed in his ear. The two men either side of Ridgmont dropped; the left side of both their heads vanished in clouds of gore and fragmented Kevlar. Gunfire erupted all around, the hectic staccato chattering of Hamilton's Light Machine Gun ripping the rain-lashed night to shreds as the muted pops of the MP5SDs surrounding him answered the call to war. Baker rolled forwards. Dragging his knees to his chest, he pulled his arms down past his posterior; the flex cuffs scraped over the back of his legs as he pulled them up over his boots. Jumping to his feet, he leapt forwards. Rain pounded into his eyes as he roared, his voice strangled and coarse, reaching out with his bound hands.

Ridgmont curled his fist into the collar of Rawlings' uniform, simultaneously drawing the duel-edged dagger from its sheath on his calf. The seven-inch blade glowed dully in the diffused silver light of the moon. The dagger's pointed blade rose in a slow arc. Baker lunged forwards, his blood running cold as he watched the razor-fine edge scythe its way across the pale skin of Rawlings' throat. The soft, tender flesh parted and blood surged forth, coating his rapidly paling skin in a red sheen as it flowed across his chest, soaking into his tunic.

Baker fell to his knees as Rawlings tipped forwards. Clamping his hands down on Rawlings' neck, Baker could do naught but watch, helpless as his friend's blood seeped through his fingers, the glowering form of Ridgmont towering over them. With the screams of the wounded and dying echoing through his mind, he stared into the darkening eyes of his friend.

Rawlings managed a half smile as he wrapped his hand round the back of Baker's neck and pulled him closer. He shook as he lifted his weakening form from the floor, speaking in a liquid-filled whisper. Flecks of blood speckled Baker's skin as the last words of a dying man met his ear.

Rawlings' slack form weighed heavy in Baker's arms as he slowly lowered him to the cold, wet ground. A burning tear rolled down his cheek as he stared at the sightless eyes, the shine and mirth replaced by the soulless, flat gaze of death.

Baker sprang to his feet, Rawlings' blood still wet on his hand, and snatched his sidearm from the holster on his thigh. The chequered grip squelched against his blood-slicked palm as his head snapped left and right, searching for the man who had callously ripped away the lives of his men.

Baker launched the pistol at the floor, its synthetic grips cracking as it bounced off the unforgiving surface.

'Fucking coward!' he screamed. The chill air was forgotten as he watched the glowing rays of dawn cast their reproachful gaze upon the scene that lay before them.

He bellowed with rage, his voice echoing into the wilderness. As he fell once more to his knees, a deep-seated seed of hatred bloomed within his heart.

2
February 9, 2013
Hamworthy Barracks
Poole Harbour, Dorset

A vibration pulsed through Derek's leg as his hand slipped through the flap of his thigh pocket and pulled his mobile free. He stared at the screen, his thumb pressing down on the accept icon so hard that the screen became a multi-coloured pool of flickering pixels.

Stumbling to his feet, the voice on the phone filled his ear. He pocketed the mobile and sprinted towards his Jeep, the battered vehicle still only a dark spot on the concrete slipway.

'Where the fuck d'ya think you're going, Baker? This ain't finished yet.'

The confused and anger-slashed words of the instructor filled his ears as he ran across the sand, feet slipping through the grains as he struggled to keep his footing.

'My wife's having my kid, Barklay. I don't give two shits if this isn't finished; I'm going.'

The irate instructor threw his fins and mask to the floor. The rest of the team looked on, their faces twisting into amused smirks, watching Barklay begin to turn beetroot red.

'I don't give a flying fuck, Baker; while you're here, you're on my turf and under my rule.'

Baker continued running as Barklay bellowed after him. Derek leapt over the railings and onto the slipway.
'Go fuck yourself.'

****

Rain lashed the windscreen as Baker roared down the dual carriageway. The lampposts shimmered as he flew past, pushing the already complaining engine further toward death as he stamped the accelerator into the floor.

His mobile danced over the dashboard as he rapidly slew into the outside lane and flew through the exit onto the M27. The signs for London, Southampton, and Winchester snapped past his uncaring eyes as he ploughed ever onwards.

Snatching up his phone, he jabbed at the answer button and set it to speaker. Holding it against the steering wheel and with the windscreen wipers rattling, he strained to hear.

'Cherry, where are you mate? Janet is going nuts here, and they can't delay much longer. This tot is on its way with or without you, man.'

The phone slipped from his grip, bouncing off his knee. He snatched at it as it tumbled away.

'Fuck it all to hell.'

Baker reached fruitlessly for the phone as it slid past his feet. Glancing down, he dove for it, the slim casing slipping in his grasp as he glanced up again, looking through the steering wheel at the set of lights shooting towards him.

Yanking the wheel left with a panicked curse, he slewed across three lanes of traffic before managing to gain control again. Horns blared as Baker's Jeep roared onwards, the phone clutched loosely between his thumb and forefinger.

****

Janet screamed while nurses hurried around her. Her hair hung lank down her sweat-soaked face as she struggled against the rapidly shortening contractions.

Davies stood with the phone to his ear, unsure of what to do while Anna sat next to Janet's bed.

'Where the bloody hell is he?'

Davies shrugged as he stared at Anna, unsure of what to say.

'About fucking time you sorted that out. What the hell are you doing? That refresher course was supposed to be done at twelve so you were back here in case this actually happened, which it is by the way, and can I say staring at the growler of my boss' wife ain't exactly something I had in mind to do today.'

Baker's harried reply made Davies wince as he pulled the phone away from his ear; his eyes danced between Janet and Anna while a nurse rapidly pulled the thin cotton sheet back over Janet's legs. Her withering glance at Davies made him shrink away slightly as Anna smirked at him.

'Look, buddy, just hurry up, okay...?'

Davies was cut short. Janet screamed as the contractions hit her full force.

****

Baker tossed the phone back on the dashboard and turned off onto the M25, aiming his violently shaking Jeep at the M4 towards Heathrow Airport.

'Fuck it all. Come on... fucking move, you twat.'

Baker swerved round the truck and veered off onto the M4.

'I'm coming, baby. I'm coming.'

****

22

'He's on the M4, so I don't know what else to tell you.'

Janet groaned again, the pain shooting through her as the midwife scribbled on the clipboard in her hands.

Janet's knuckles turned white as she clutched at the railings of her bed, her words muffled as she tried to talk through the Entenox tube in her mouth. The potent mix of gas and air dulled her pain-frazzled senses to the point of uselessness.

A sharp spike of searing pain lanced through her as her contractions flared once more. Tears rolled down Janet's face while she slumped back into the sweat-soaked pillows, sobbing softly to herself.

'I don't know how much more of this I can take; if he doesn't get here soon, I'm going to divorce the bald bastard—baby or not.'

****

Baker's Jeep tyres squealed against the wet tarmac as he pressed the brake pedal into the floor. His weight and momentum drove him against the seatbelt, causing a vicious red weal to rise from the skin along the side of his neck.

With an energy born of fear and excitement, he dragged the seatbelt from its clip, all but ripping it from its mounts in an overzealous attempt to extricate himself.

The door crashed against the frame as he slammed it shut, and he sprinted through the lightning-streaked deluge. He felt the water seep down his legs, soaking through the heavy woollen socks that clung to his feet like a second skin as they slid along his sole, bunching below the instep of his foot as he skidded over the ridged and buckled paving slabs around the entrance to the hospital.

He flew through the hospital's doors, his feet sliding under him as he slammed into the reception desk. He dragged himself from the floor, pulled his hand over his bald scalp and forehead, and wiped the rainwater from his eyes then looked at the bewildered girl in front of him.

'My baby's having a wife.'

His words tumbled in a sodden stream of babbled confusion as he tried to drag his thoughts into order. His mind sagged into a pile of wet mush when the girl in front of him giggled.

'Sorry, my wife is having our baby.'

The receptionist smiled, tapping at her keyboard while glancing up at Derek's wide, over excited eyes.

'What's her name?' Derek frowned, unable to recall the name of the woman with whom he had shared his entire world; finally, after a frantic bundle of seconds he spoke.

'Janet, Janet Baker.' For an eternity, Derek waited as she tapped at the computer keyboard.

'Maternity ward...'

Derek scowled at the overtly obvious statement.

'Floor two, room 631.'

Before the words had fully left her mouth, Derek was sprinting towards the stairs. He ploughed into the doors, sending their heavy, fire-resistant panels slamming back into the concrete walls.

Janet watched through bleary, pain-filled eyes as her husband staggered into the room. His sodden and strung-out form filled the room as he strode towards Janet's bed, the soles of his boots squeaking on the linoleum-covered floor.

A weary, pain-stretched smile filled Janet's face as she slowly reached towards Derek, curling his fingers through hers. Baker dropped into the vacant seat at her elbow.

With careful, almost delicate slowness, Derek lifted the slim, clear oxygen tube from the bedside and set it out of reach as he leant against the rubberised mattress.

'I got here as quickly as I could. I... I'm sorry I wasn't here.'

Janet winced as she tried not to laugh; Derek's rain-drenched beard teased at her skin as he kissed her hand. Sorrow and elation danced in his eyes in a swirling vortex of indecisive emotion. Janet slowly eased her fingers from his hand, running her slim, slightly shaking digits over his cheek as she spoke.

Her breathing was shallow and tenuous. She shifted her head, trying to set the two nasal vents in a more comfortable position.

Derek leant in carefully, lifting the pipes from behind Janet's ears, which allowed her to position her head more comfortably before setting the tubes back.

'Thanks, and don't feel bad; I wasn't alone. Besides, there is little to stop a Baker when they want out of somewhere.'

Derek couldn't help but chuckle; his lips brushed Janet's pale skin as a small, almost gentle tapping filled the room.

Looking up, they smiled at the dark-skinned nurse who walked in. The stark-white bundle in her arms glowed in the light streaming through the doorway.

'You must be Derek?'

Baker nodded. Her flat-soled shoes whispered as she walked. Passing the baby to Janet, she turned toward the new father.

'This young lady gave us quite a fright; thought for a while there we were going to have a few problems.'

Seeing the look of worry and fear that crawled over Derek's face, the nurse smiled. Patting his forearm, she moved by to check on Janet's vitals.

'Don't look so scared. It was nothing we weren't prepared for... just a few opening night jitters. Janet's blood pressure dropped a bit and the little one there needed a bit of a hand coming into the world. As I say, nothing to worry about. We will be keeping them both here for a week or so to make sure nothing else happens.'

She glanced at Janet and winked, drawing another weary smile from the new mother.

'Thanks, Shanice.'

Shanice smiled as she reached the doorway. Her hand closing over the frame, she looked over her shoulder at the new trio.

'No worries, love; give us as shout if you need anything or hit the buzzer there. I am just down the hall and will be here in a jiffy.'

With that, she was gone, leaving the newly minted parents with the one person they never thought they would be holding. Derek's eyes burned with the question that he wanted to ask.

'It's a girl.'

His face burst into a cheesy grin as he reached out, and Janet slipped their daughter into his hands for the first time.

'She's beautiful, just like her mother.'

Janet snorted as she watched him peer closer at the sleeping form in his arms. Glancing up, he smiled, the condescension in his wife's eyes making him chuckle as he gently bounced his daughter.

'Derek, I look like I've just gone thirty rounds with a rabid chimpanzee and have been molested by a gang of drunken Polish dockers. So please do not call me beautiful right now, or so help me,

26

I will pull your bollocks off.'

Derek all but choked on his laughter as he stared at Janet supine on the hospital bed.

'Whatever you say, gorgeous. Whatever you say.'

3
March 2013
Broadhead Memorial Garden

Baker sat overlooking the parade ground, his back to the rose garden and the eight hundred and ninety-seven marble posts within it, the brass plaques shining in the sun with as much lustre as the day they were laid in place. He knew that behind him were two more with names from a list stretching back hundreds of years. They had died for little more than one man's jealousy and grandiose sense of self-importance.

Baker had no doubt that he was the focus of the man's ire and rage and was, in the other man's eyes, responsible for the death of his son. That did not change the fact that two men who hadn't deserved to die now lie dead. Turning his head, he looked at the three-foot-by-three-foot brass plate that marked the entrance to the gardens shimmering in the afternoon haze. His reddened and tired eyes drifted over the copperplate letters, reading the flowing script as he had many times before.

"Many great things are simple and can be expressed in single words:
Freedom, Justice, Honour, Duty, Mercy, Hope."

Etched beneath it all was the unit's insignia—the winged arrowhead. A symbol of the combined forces unit: the paratroopers' wings from the SAS insignia framing the edges, the SBS Spartan sword set in the arrow's centre, the Queen's crown beneath it and edged in by a curling line of parchment with the unit motto flowing across it.

Until Death.

Despite the passage of time, the changing face of war and men that wage it, one constant remained… the red arrowhead, the unit's namesake. Derek glanced down at the post beside him; the name was meaningless now, the man and his legacy long since taken by time.

Just another man from another time who, like him, had answered the call and paid the final price.

The marble bench chilled his buttocks as, with a deep, drawn out sigh, he lifted the manila file and flipped it open. His eyes danced over the lines of closely printed script. Again and again, as the words tripped and stumbled through his mind, the names of men and women he had trained and fought beside scalded his heart.

Beside each moniker, the three-lettered abbreviation that he loathed with his very soul was set, its scarlet letters glaring at him from the cream pages he clutched in his hand.

Rubbing his eyes, he sighed, wondering just how many more names were going to adorn the lists. How many more pillars added to the garden before the problems of tomorrow became the solutions of yesterday.

Baker residence
Northeast London

'Last words are for fools who haven't said enough.'

Davies sat in the deckchair his eyes shielded from the glare of the sun. Baker cast a sideways glance at John then turned back to snapping the caps off the bottles of lager sitting on the draining board in front of him.

'What you on about?' Baker asked in a slightly cautious tone while taking in the seat next to him.

Davies chuckled as he took the bottle from Baker's outstretched hand, wiping away the ice cool layer of condensation before lifting it to his lips.

'It's something Rawlings said to me once when I asked him what his favourite last line was; a Karl Marx quote was the last thing I was expecting.'

Baker smirked as he thought through a similar conversation he and Rawlings had once had, holed up together in an observation post in Afghanistan almost eleven years before.

'It's not too surprising, to be honest. Rawlings was a rather deep man when you got past the sarcasm and ascorbic wit.'

Baker lifted the bottle to his lips as he watched Janet play with the gurgling bundle of arms and legs that was his three-month-old daughter.

'You know what Rawlings said to me right before Ridgmont vanished?' Baker suppressed the rising urge to break something as the bubbling cauldron of hate and pain boiled in his gut at the mention of the now rogue colonel.

Davies shook his head as he idly watched Anastasia throw a ball for Kingsley's yapping spaniel, its lopping stride making its ears flap and bounce as she raced after the ball. His eyes tracked the straw-coloured canine as it scooped the ball into its mouth and raced back to Anna, dropping the sodden tennis ball in her lap.

'The cheeky fucker pulled me close, lifting himself off the floor and whispered "Happy New Year's."'

Davies almost choked on his drink as Baker spoke, spindly lines of pale white foam dripping from his nostrils as the fizzing carbonated alcohol fought for a way out.

'Seriously?' Davies quizzed as he wiped the dripping foam from his chin. Baker smirked and nodded as he drank deeply from the bottle in his hand.

'Yep.' his reply coming in a short gasp as he rapidly swallowed the mouthful of lager. John shook his head and set his now empty bottle down on the table between the two chairs.

'Should've seen it coming, really.' Baker laughed, his voice tinged with a deep regret. All he had left of one of his oldest and closest friends were reminiscences; the fickle mistress of his memories, and through it all he knew, if they were allowed to, even those would be lost over time.

Kingsley dropped to the floor, his dreadlocks bouncing off his shoulders as he thumped against the hardwood decking, bottle in hand.

'Ay up, lads.' He spoke choosing to ignore the fact that Baker had jumped slightly at his appearance. He shifted, his legs stretching down the steps of the decking, flip-flop covered feet nestling in the green grass of the lawn. Leaning backwards, he set his elbows against the smooth, dark timber, the bottle still held loosely between his fingers.

'You hear about the new acquisition?'

Baker glanced down at his friend, his curiosity mildly piqued. 'Which one?' Kingsley lifted the bottle to his lips before replying. 'Armoury.' Baker nodded before consciously realising Kingsley couldn't actually see him nod.

Davies glanced quizzically from one man to the other as he listened to Baker's reply.

Kingsley stood up. 'Want another?'

Baker chuckled as he drained the last of the amber liquid and tossed the bottle into the bin.

'Sure, bottle opener is on the drainer.'

'So what's this new acquisition then?' Baker smiled at the look on Davies' features. His lined and battle-worn face torn between annoyance and a childlike eagerness to know.

'Secondary sidearm… Anna recommended it. Seems the Russians have been having a lot of trouble with the "Newer" Infected. Same problem the Yanks had in Vietnam with the introduction of the old style 5.56.'

Davies nodded. 'You mean with the whole Viet Cong getting hit a couple of dozen times and getting up again.'

Baker nodded and carried on speaking. 'Anyway, it's one of the latest Smith and Wesson revolvers, fires either a .410 shotgun shell, 45ACP, or the 45 Colt round. Despite the six-round maximum capacity, this thing is like holding a cannon in your palm—blows holes through just about anything.'

Davies snorted derisively. 'I doubt that somehow. Nice gun though. Seen it before.'

Baker grinned at Davies. 'Thought you'd say that; you know this is the one favoured by Floridian alligator hunters.'

32

Davies' eyebrows rose as he thought through the implication of Baker's words. 'No wonder they call it the Governor.'

Baker grinned as he pushed up from the chair and went down the four steps to his lawn; the bottle hung limply from his fingers as he made his way towards the barbecue. The scent of sauce-covered steaks wafted over him as he reached forwards, lifting the top cover clear. Smoke swirled up, filling his throat as he wafted his empty hand to clear his vision.

Setting his drink down on the tray table to his right, he picked up the oak-handled tongs. Reaching forwards, he slid the stainless steel plates of the flat-headed tongs along the grill, watching as the steaks lifted and bulged. He gingerly flipped the inch-thick slabs of meat over, listening to the hiss of melting fat as it dripped free and landed with an oily splat atop the glowing coals.

A slim arm encircled his waist as a miniature hand batted at his shoulder; he smiled as he felt Maria's petite fingers ensnare the cotton of his tee shirt. Shifting the tongs to his other hand he twisted, lifting Maria from Janet's arms and bouncing his little girl on his forearm as her hands closed around the collar of his shirt. A soft yawn left her as she nestled against his chest.

'Looks like she just made herself at home.' Derek smirked as Janet lay her head on his shoulder. 'How long you got free?'

Baker's shoulder sagged as he set the steaks onto the waiting plate and turning, his daughter slumbering against his shoulder, cast his gaze slightly downwards, his eyes locking onto Janet's. The drifting swirl of fear, pain, and sheer fatigue weighed heavy in his eyes. Lifting her hand, she traced her fingers along the edge of his jaw.

'We don't know; none of us do, with the way things are...'

He trailed off as he set the platter down on the garden table. A lump caught in his throat as he turned, his eyes scanning the chairs set around the table. His friends and teammates stood, despite the two empty seats none of them dared go near. The hand-carved names on the backrests were enough to deter them all. Baker let his eyes trace the scrollwork, the hours he had put into carving the twenty-two original seats and the seven additions that adorned his garden. Swallowing hard, he brushed his lips against Janet's forehead and moved past her.

'I'll put Maria to bed; the monitor is on the table.'

Janet smiled at him as he spoke. 'I know, you Muppet; I put it there, remember?'

Derek smiled and walked away, passing Kingsley and Davies as they made their way towards the table.

****

Derek sat, leaning forwards, his elbows resting limply on his knees as he stared out over his garden… from the carefully crafted borders that scalloped the lawn's edge to the centre rock garden and its sprawling range of miniature mountains.

His soul weighed heavy, pulling him down into the decking beneath his feet. He felt… tired; tired of living in a world filled with death and people so foul that they felt the need to inflict the most grievous of harm upon those they had never even met. Tired of the need for men like him, the ones who put themselves in the way of those willing to harm others in the name of misguided fanaticism and xenophobic hatred. The ones willing to lay down their own lives to protect their fellow man.

A soft snort left him as he pondered the words bouncing in his skull—a few measly lines from the lips of a man more world weary than he.

"Derek, nothing in this world can show the true nature of man better than war and nothing in nature wages war on its own kind, other than man; so, by our own nature and design, man is destined to exterminate itself and has done so ever since we crawled out of

the swamp. You, me, and what we do is all that people have done for thousands of years—police the edges and skim off the crap that floats to the top. Sometimes I wish something would come along and give us all a good dose of chlorine and be done with it. Fuck natural selection; this damned gene pool went stagnant years ago."

A soft, sad, and weary smile tugged at his lips as he watched the wind stir the branches of the small conifer trees standing sentry at the foot of his lawn.

Janet stood, leaning in the doorway of their French windows, watching her husband. She idly toyed with the simple band of gold that encased her finger, turning the smooth polished surface over the soft skin of her finger. She stood vigil as he sat. Something tickled her mind as she watched him, a feeling so faint and brief that it was gone in seconds… like smoke through her fingers as she reached out to grasp it. The cold touch of the unknown rippled down her spine and she shivered. Hugging herself, she stepped out onto the deck and padded quietly towards her husband.

Her soft steps kissed his ears as she moved closer. Dragging his hands over his unshaven, weatherworn features, Derek spoke.

'I don't know if I can do this anymore.'

Janet froze, her feet stiff and cumbersome as her legs wobbled, leaving her teetering on the precipice of what lay before them. She shuffled forwards, her words falling dead as she tried to piece together some semblance of a normal thought.

'Do what?'

Derek clambered to his feet, his body a dead weight as he forced his world-weary frame to its full six foot three inches. His eyes bore into her, their hollow, empty gaze eating through her.

'I thought I could stop this, keep it in check, just push it under the carpet and go on like it never happened. But I can't; I can't keep pretending I'm okay.'

35

Janet just stood, watching and listening as he spoke, his gaze never leaving hers. Her heart trembled with fear, willing him not to utter those few words that she knew would bring her whole world crashing down around her.

'Every time we go, someone comes home in a fucking box. I used to be okay with it, squash it down, and push it away. Thinking of you made everything okay again. Thinking of how life could be without all this shit in the way. You, me, and Maria. But...'

He trailed off, his mind awash with the dancing images of places long past and faces just gone. Janet took a tentative step forwards, her slim hands reaching for him, he stepped away as her fingers brushed him. She left her hand lingering in the air for a moment before slowly letting it drop.

'It just doesn't work. Nothing works anymore; every time I close my eyes, I get the same damned nightmares. I put on a face when I wake up, pretend everything is going to be all right, that I can keep going; but I can't keep it on anymore; it hurts to wear it. It feels like I'm a stranger in my own damned skin. I just don't know who I am anymore.'

Janet rapidly closed the gap between them, ensnaring him in a grip that only a band of iron could surpass; slowly Derek sagged, his body thumping into the railings behind him as he slid towards the floor.
'I... I... I just don't know if I can carry on. I don't know if I can trust myself to keep you safe; whatever I do, I know it's going to be the wrong choice... I... I just can't face it; I can't.'

Tears began to roll down his cheeks as he slowly crumpled under the weight of his own fears and doubts. He fell against Janet as he let it all pour forth. The loss of two of his oldest friends, the tipping point for all that he bore, his life choices like the weight of the world on Atlas' shoulders. Janet held her husband close, his body shaking as the tidal wave of fear, inadequacy, and shame poured over him.

In her heart, she knew the man before her would do all he could to keep her, their daughter, and anyone else around them, no matter who they were, safe from harm; but at that one singular moment she realised just how much he was giving up to do it.

Broadhead Armoury

The armourer grinned at the men as they stood in a rather impatient line whilst he dished out their latest acquisitions one soldier at a time. The compact clamshell holsters hugged the contours of the revolvers like skin. Jones lifted his, testing the weight in his hand. A soft scratching filled the air as he dragged the ballpoint pen across the pale yellow sheet of paper.

Nodding to the armourer, he picked up the weapon and left the low-lying brick building by the only other door available.

The gun sat in the small of his back, the hard-shell holster nestling against vest. Jones looked up, catching Baker's eye as he stepped out of Colinson's office. Baker's face all but bubbled as he waged war with the mix of rage and sadness, fighting for control as he looked up at Jones. They shared eye contact for a second before Jones nodded and walked away.

A high-pitched wail broke the silence. Jones cursed and sprinted after Baker; the siren meant one thing and one thing only, both men sharing a mutual dread at the thought of what lay ahead.

4
April Twenty-eighth
Central Middlesex Hospital

Janet stared around her, her daughter clutched to her chest as she sprinted through the corridors of the building; a heavy weight lay on her thigh as she ran.

The Sco19 officer bellowed down the corridor as Janet ran; her lungs burned, drawing her to tears with pain. Her teeth felt like bitter shards of ice-cold glass as she sucked in deep, lung-scalding gulps of disinfectant-tainted air.

Maria's plaintive wailing echoed off the walls as she squirmed in fear of the noises around her. Bullets flew past Janet's ears, the screams and garbled cries behind her snapping dead as the rounds found their marks. Looking to her right, she stared at the blood-spattered and sweat-stained form of Kevin as he held the shocked and quivering form of another nurse. The young girl's eyes were glued open with fear as she stared at the wall, driven beyond hysteria.

'Go! Fall back to the roof; a helicopter is waiting!'

The black-clad police officer pushed past them as he slapped a fresh magazine into his weapon and continued to fire, dreading the paperwork that was coming with it, if he lived that long.

He slowly began to walk backwards, his rifle snapping from target to target. Kicking out with his left foot, he watched as the magnetic locks holding the doors open died and the fireproof wood and plastic crashed together. The doors reverberated in their frame as body after body crashed into the solid sheet before them.

The officer peered through the eight-inch wide slit of reinforced mesh safety glass, his eyes tracking back and forth amongst the sea of faces.

The strutting, slathering form that greeted his gaze smiled as it watched the face behind the glass. The blood-laden sneering visage bent low, his head jerking from side to side like a bird's as he skulked closer to the window. The snapped, yellowing splinters of its nails scraped over the stippled, blue plastic coating the door as it pressed its face tight to the glass.

Saliva stained the transparent surface as it licked along the pane, tracing the outline of the officer's face with a viscous red-tinged, mucosa-filled sludge.

A cold reptilian look of calculation simmered in the eyes, holding the officer's vision. He watched, almost mesmerised as its gaze slowly dropped to the right side of the window. The officer's eyes followed the invisible line as he turned his gaze to the wall beside him. His head moved of its own volition as if his own sense of free will had deserted him, replaced by the machinations of something far more sinister than that which stood before him beyond the hospital door.

A dull clunk issued from somewhere in front of him as his eyes latched on to the grey plastic and chrome box on the wall; the splay-fingered indented image of an adult hand glowered back at him. His vision went blue as the emergency fire doors swung inwards. Turning his head once more, he came eye to eye with the grinning cat-eyed form in front him; its stained, gore-covered lips pursed in a mocking kiss.

'I want my mum,' was all he had time to utter before the grinning, bloodstained, Infected launched itself at him in a cackling gaggle of limbs and teeth.

Broadhead Operations Centre

'We have a job, people; the virus has infected three floors of the Central Middlesex Hospital.'

Baker's gut clenched tight as his body went cold. Colinson's words rang in his ears as he thought back to the conversation he'd had with Janet three days before.

****

They sat around the table in their kitchen, steam curling up between them from the mugs they clutched in their hands, the silence stretched thin like a layer of butter over too much bread. The strain of its tension mounting as Janet stared at the scarred wood of the solid pine table.

Her eyes tracked the swirls and twists of the timber's grain as it wormed away from her. Slowly, she looked up into the eyes of her husband; a soft smile danced in them as he looked back at her before it faded away, any attempt at conversation lost.

The silence was broken by the chirping burble rolling out of the radio that sat on the far edge of the table. Janet hurriedly pushed her chair away and stood, muttering quickly about needing to feed Maria. Baker sighed deeply; he knew something was wrong. Things hadn't been right for almost a month, even before Maria's birth. Things had taken a sudden twist; something had changed, not only in their relationship, but in Janet herself. And if he was to admit it, himself as well.

Baker sighed as he lifted the mug and emptied its contents down his throat before rising from the table and walking across the kitchen to the sink. The cold water shocked his skin as he rinsed out the cup, his hand gliding over the inside of the ceramic mug as a soft squeak issued up from inside of it. The skin of his hand tugged at the glazed surface of the pale blue vessel. He emptied out the water and turned off the tap as he set the dripping mug on the draining board.

41

Turning, he walked out the kitchen; his booted feet thumped against the floor as he walked towards the front door, the sound echoing back of the near deathly silence that had enveloped their home in the last four months. He stopped momentarily and quietly looked in through the gap between the door and doorframe leading into the small room where his daughter slept. He silently watched the suckling form of his daughter as she drank, her fingers wrapped in Janet's shirt, the nub of her mother's nipple clasped between her lips.

Janet looked up and saw Derek watching. A wan smile crossed her face as she locked gazes with him. Quietly, she beckoned him in and watched as he stepped softly into the room.

'I am working at Central Middlesex for the next three weeks. Not sure how my hours are going to play out, so I am going to take Maria with me.'

Derek nodded as he smiled down at Janet. 'Okay, darling; no problem.'

Baker turned and left the room. Janet watched, tears stinging her eyes as he walked away—no goodbye, no parting kiss, nothing. He simply left. With a heavy heart and a deep feeling of dread, she knew something had irrevocably changed and it wasn't for the better.

****

Baker felt his stomach lurch and his inner equilibrium twist like a snake in a whirlpool as his mind bounced itself back to the here and now, his mind flaring like a comet ploughing into the sun. He fought the need to vomit as he nodded grim-faced at Colinson. The man's question drifted out the door into the cold light of day long before Baker's mind even registered he was being spoken to. Colinson motioned for Baker to hold off as the other team commanders filed out of the room. Baker stopped and turned, walking back through the rows of chairs until he stood opposite Colinson.

'You okay?'

42

Concern tinged Colinson's voice as he spoke, watching Baker for any hint of falsehood or avoidance that may have wormed its way into his reply.

'Fine.' Baker's voice was flat, emotionless, the normal jovial inflection in his accented tones gone. It left his voice a dull, monotone parody of itself. Colinson's hackles went up as he gauged Baker's reply.

'Well, that's a load of crap! What's going on?'

Baker didn't bother to avoid the question; he simply let it crash over him and ignored it completely. He knew that Colinson was reading him like a badly written children's book, but at that moment, he just didn't care.

'Nothing.' Again, his voice was as flat as a sheet of polished glass. Colinson nodded; he could see Baker was stonewalling and no matter how he phrased a question, it wasn't going to be answered any time soon. Changing tactic, he grimaced inwardly as his professor's nasalised tones invaded his mind.

Now remember, David, if you can't get into their mind with kindness, there is always the proverbial sledgehammer of reverse psychology that we know as blunt-force nastiness.

Colinson shrugged off the subconscious lecture and ploughed on.

'Derek, I need your head in the game; this isn't a simple smash and destroy. There is a high civilian population in and around that hospital. A lot of lives depend on us keeping our heads together and getting this done quickly. I can't send you in if you're not one hundred percent. I need to know your shit is squared away; we don't need another Panjshir.'

Baker's eyes flared red as those words left Colinson's mouth. His feet shifted as he prepared to lunge, then before he could register what was happening, he was staring at the ceiling. Colinson's blonde-haired head peered down at him over the top of an

43

outstretched hand.

Baker slapped the hand away and pushed himself to his feet, his eyes burning with undisguised rage. Colinson stepped forwards, his open-palmed hands slamming into Derek's shoulders. 'What the fuck is wrong with you? Come on, damn it, tell me. You're a god damned SAU operator; fucking act like it!'

Derek bounced off the wall, file cabinets clanking from the force of his impact against the plasterboard.

Baker's eyes blazed as he stared at Colinson, his teeth clamped together so tightly his gums were slowly starting to bleed. He shook with rage and self-loathing. He was angry not only with himself but also at life and his situation. The problems between him and Janet that, for all his rumination and late night pondering, he could not understand. The widening gulf between them that he couldn't—no matter how much he tried—find a way to bridge.

'You want to know what's wrong? You really want to know what's wrong? Well, I don't fucking know; I ... do ... not ... know.'

Baker smashed his fist into the wall, his hand crashing through the paper-backed plasterboard. Flecks of pink coloured powder floated through the air. Wrenching his fist from the wall, he stared at the blood dripping from the creases of his fingers as it slowly pulsed from his knuckles. He flicked his hand, watching as the red globules of ruby coloured blood arced and splattered across the dull-grey painted plaster of Colinson's office wall.

Colinson observed the unfolding situation silently as Baker vented his anger. He looked on with impassive eyes as Baker rinsed the plaster from his torn knuckles in his office sink. The chilled water gushed from the tap, splashing in a never-ending torrent over the ripped and slashed skin. With utter indifference, Baker slowly picked the pieces of stained gypsum from between his fingers.

Droplets of his blood slipped free of his skin, falling into the water, twisting through the flow as they stretched into a diluted mist of blood. Their once ruby red forms lost as the water pulled them apart. Its unfeeling form decimating their tender morphing droplets as it swirled around the white porcelain sink.

'Feel better?'

Baker snorted at the question. 'Not particularly, I know for a fact that my knuckles will be the size of a midget's balls by tomorrow.'

Colinson smiled wanly. 'Not what I was asking and you know it. What's going on between you and Janet? You were both fine at the New Year's party.'

Baker winced at the memory. He turned to face Colinson, a dull lifeless smirk playing across his features. 'Then, mate, you're not as good of a skull scooper as you think you are. Shit hasn't been straight between me and Janet since before the baby was born; and to be honest, bud, I don't know if it ever will be again. I just don't know how to fix it. Fuck, dealing with a dozen Infected in nothing but a mankini and armed with a damned tooth pick would be easier than figuring this shit out.'

Images of the party danced through Baker's mind despite how he longed to forget that night. The party itself had gone down brilliantly; the events after had been some that the unit wouldn't easily forget. Returning with two men down was never an easy thing to witness, especially for the women. Their expectant gazes were some that would haunt Derek for as long as he remained bound to the earth. The looks on their faces as they watched them walk away from the rain-slicked parade grounds and the sudden shattering of all their worldly dreams as they saw the two black rain-drenched bags atop the chromed steel gurneys.

'Honestly, I don't know what it is. It's not baby blues or anything like that; Janet has been to see the postnatal nurse and all that crap. It's just something has changed with us, and I can't for the life of me figure out what it is; it's driving me nuts, Dave, it really is.'

Colinson nodded as Baker spoke. Lifting a box of cigarettes from his shirt pocket, he pulled one out before offering the open packet to Baker. It took a lot of willpower for Baker to refuse, but he did. Shrugging, Colinson slipped the now closed packet into his shirt pocket as he picked up the polished-steel Zippo lighter. A soft click issued from his hand as he flicked open the petrol-filled metal lighter and ran his thumb over the striker wheel. Light flared over Colinson's features as the shard of flint sparked against the bevelled disk.

Smoke curled from his lips as he drew deeply from the cigarette before speaking again. A cloud of blue-tinged smoke issued from his mouth, then with a soft, contemplative tone he spoke.

'How you been sleeping? Both of you, not just yourself.'

Baker laughed sardonically. 'What's that when it's at home? Look, Dave, this isn't the time to do this shit. We make it back in one piece, we can sit down and talk as long as you want.'

Colinson sighed as he weighed up the words he was about to put forth.

'Derek, you're grounded; until I can do a full evaluation or you're cleared by Conerly, you're off the duty roster. It's not something I wanted, but I can't have you in the field like this. Richards and Stabbler are going in with Team Three. I am sorry, mate, but that's how it is.'

Baker stopped his movements as he listened to Colinson. Turning, he glared at his friend and fellow officer.

'My wife and daughter are trapped somewhere in that hospital— the hospital where my daughter was born; nothing is going to keep me away.'

Derek continued to hold Colinson's eyes as the man slowly mulled over Baker's words.

'I'm sorry, Derek, but the decision is final. Until you're cleared, you're shelved. Combat operations can—and do—go on without you.'

Baker's jaw clenched, then without saying a word, Baker shoved Colinson's office door open and walked out. Sighing, Colinson sunk into his office chair. With a deep sigh soaked in regret, he cursed, tossing the small steel lighter across his desk and onto the floor where it lay glinting in the afternoon sun.

'Fuck it!'

Central Middlesex Hospital

Janet watched as the woman pushed herself tighter and tighter into the corner, the screams of the Sco19 officer slipping through the halls rending the last of her tattered psyche to shreds.

Kevin had a hand clamped tightly over the mouths of the two children he held in his lap, their prepubescent arms wrapped about his slim middle. A soft shushing emanated from him as he watched the blurred, shadowed wraith on the other side of the frosted glass. The hushed feral, almost primal sniffing echoed through the now empty corridors as it ferreted out its prey. A small squeak issued forth from Maria as Janet pulled herself away from the slowly encroaching pool of viscous blood creeping its way towards her.

The silence was broken by a soft, almost gentle sound. Janet glanced up at the window, the figure now gone. Her brow furrowed deeply as the sound grew. It coalesced into a soft roar as it slowly inched its way towards the cowering clutch. Setting Maria down as gently as possible, she watched for any sign from the blissfully unaware form that she was about to stir, then once satiated, she leant her head to the floor and peered over the red mire.

The glistening pool of shimmering red reflected a sight that she wished could be purged from her mind the moment she saw it.

Roysten, the forty-three year old senior nurse, was knelt, his staff shirt stained a russet red in the steaming, rapidly congealing pool emanating from the dismembered remains. His tongue slipped over his lips as he sucked the life-giving fluid from the linoleum tiles; he sucked greedily at the still warm fluid as it slid over his chin and fell in a pattering rain only to return again as he ventured forth. Snatches of sinew clung to his balding scalp as he leant down, his head seemingly swallowed by the hollowed remains of another hospital worker.

The corpse's face, too decimated to be recognisable, stared at the ceiling, its jaw locked open in a scream that would forever echo in eternity. A dull glow emanated from its mouth as Roysten dove once again, pushing aside the veil of offal and organ matter.

The former nurse paused momentarily; his head cocked to one side as his eyes shone with confusion. Reaching in, his torn and twisted nails scraped at the inside of his own mouth before returning with the offending object. The small steel slither glimmered in the harsh halogen light as he pulled the pin from the side of his mouth. Staring at it, he momentarily sucked on the steel needle before casting it aside and diving once more into his liquid feast.

Janet slowly pushed herself upright. Her face was an incomprehensible mask as she once more picked up Maria and cradled her child. Kevin stared at her for any sign or inclination as to what she had seen as Janet slowly began to rock back and forth, her knees pulled up tight together as sheltered her sleeping child. The woman in the corner began to groan, her low-pitched mewling whine echoing through the dank quiet of the room.

Kevin looked at her and growled a low, semi-muffled curse.

'Shut the fuck up, you bimbo; want to get us all killed?'

Her head lolled like a cut marionette. The line of speckled saliva hanging from her lips made the children in Kevin's grip squirm and cry in fear. Their hot tears cascaded over his fingers as he hurriedly pushed them behind him and told them to be quiet. Stroking their hair, he looked down into two very frightened faces.

'Hush now, it's going to be fine. I promise.'

The children gazed up at him, their faces full of fear and insecure trust in the man before them.

'Kevin, what are you doing?'

Janet had stood, fishing a heavy-grade cardboard box from a shelf and settling Maria on top of the pile of sterile white blankets within it before pushing the sleeping babe onto a shelf just above her head.

49

'What I have to.'

The whole conversation had taken place in a whispered instant as he crossed the seven feet to the woman and knelt in front of her. Her moaning grew in frequency and pitch the closer he drew. Stuffing his morals and Hippocratic Oath into a box, he reached forwards, placing a hand on the woman's chin and one behind her head.

He tilted her head back and gazed at her eyes. The glassy, dilated pupils and blood-tinged whites told him all he needed to know. In a sudden and vicious move, he severed her spine. The audible crunch of shattering cartilage was muffled by his body and arms as he all but set her head in reverse.

Relinquishing his hold on her head, he watched her body slide sideways. With a gentle care shown only to those destined to die, he lay her out on the floor, resting her now disconnected head on one folded arm.

Turning to the children in the corner, he smiled. Lifting one extended finger, he pressed it to his pursed lips, and then pointed to the woman on the floor.

'Sleeping.'

Both children nodded and continued to huddle in the corner. Turning to Janet, he flicked his gaze to the door then back to the woman; in a slow and deliberate motion, he tapped the bottoms of his eyelids. The silent signal told her all she needed to know. The woman had somehow contracted the virus. Mouthing a thank you, Janet stood once more and stretched, pulling the box containing her infant daughter from the shelf and setting it gently on the floor.

Kevin reached out, shifting the now dead woman slightly and searched any exposed areas of skin. Lifting the tight ringlets of hair from the back of her neck, his gaze alighted on six viciously deep and angry-looking welts; the oozing and broken dermis was a livid blue-tinged red. Letting them fall back into place, he stood and sat down next to the two children again.

Looking around him, he took stock of the contents of the small utility room and smiled. He turned his gaze to the youngest of the pair. 'Want to play a game?'

The girl nodded, her blonde bob bouncing as she demonstrated her enthusiasm.

'Okay, I want both of you, while sitting here, to look around the room and find as many things beginning with the letter M as you can.'

The children grinned, their slight fidgeting forms diligently scanning the room for anything with the letter M printed on its surface.

Their eyes peered with an innate level of curiosity only known by the young—the ones who thirst for the unknown and the sense of wonder anything new brings. Kirsty sat with her hands curled beneath her buttocks and her legs folded under her. Her bottom lip curled over her lower teeth as she gently chewed at it in intense concentration. Thoughts of their missing parents were pushed aside for the moment as the children gazed about them in search of their wayward letter.

Kevin slipped across the room, hunched over like a demented crab. His trainer-covered feet uttered the slightest of squeaks as he pushed himself into a sitting position next to his fellow physician. Janet leant over, whispering from the corner of her mouth as she watched the shadow image playing across the floor, its flat ghost-like form slipping over her feet as it wormed its way under the door.

'How'd she contract it?'

Kevin's face dropped, his head falling backwards into the stack of plastic containers; liquid sloshed against the sides of the ten-litre jug. It made him shiver slightly as the cold filtered through the semi-transparent surface. His brow furrowed as he turned and looked at the jugs behind him. The industrial cleaner shimmered in the low light as it rocked back and forth, trapped inside its plastic prison.

The printed label pasted across its flat, lifeless surface made him cringe. His eyes roamed its glossed surface as he took in the coloured symbols before him. The small yellow circle made his eyes widen slightly as he looked at the hand inside it, the small test-tube suspended over it, and the droplets falling towards the black silhouette, slowly eating their way through its shadowed form.

The words burned themselves into his eyes as he read them. *Caution: Corrosive.* Scooting over, he made Janet frown as he forced her to move. Maria whimpered from within her cardboard cot, her small form squirming against the bundles of plastic-wrapped cotton. Janet's soft voice rolled its way over the small bundle of softly gurgling life as she gently stroked the silken strands of her daughter's hair. Janet smiled as her hand passed over the smooth, warm skin of her daughter's head.

'There were small lacerations to the back of her neck, just below the base of her neck, and running down between her shoulder blades.'

His whispered words sent a small shiver down Janet's spine as she glanced at the children, still diligently searching the room.

'They going to find anything with an M on it?'

Kevin smiled at Janet's question, a sly grin forming on his aquiline features. 'Nope; nothing in here with an M on it.'

Despite the situation and the noises filtering their way through the door, Janet found herself chuckling at the naivety of the two children. Her head cocked to the side in a moment of clarity as she gazed at the slim form of the girl.

'Kirsty.'

The child turned and looked at Janet, her deep brown eyes locking

52

on to her own as the young waif gazed at her with a look of fearful questioning.

'Yes?'

Her voice was demure as she stared at Janet, her fingers plucking at the hem of her loose-knit woollen jumper. The bunched curls of coloured yarn were stained with crusted spots of drying blood. Her eyes betrayed her mounting fear as one small finger picked at the scabrous encrustation that clung to the hem of her jumper.

The flakes of dried blood fluttered free as her peach-coloured nail picked at it; lifting her fingers, she moved the encrusted nail towards her lips intent on ferreting out the clotted life's fluid from beneath her nail.

With the reflexes of a steroid-infused cobra, Janet lunged, seizing the girl's wrist. The extended finger was mere millimetres from her mouth. Lucy stared at the woman clutching her wrist with a terrified mix of confusion and pain as Janet slowly pulled her hand away from its former destination.

'Now, sweetie, you know that's not a nice thing to do. You don't know what you have gotten on that jumper; come with me and we will get it all cleaned off, okay?'

The girl began to pull away, uncertain of Janet's intentions as she tried to guide her towards the industrial cleansing wipes stacked neatly on one shelf.

'Kirsty, I promised your mummy I would look after you and I keep my promises.'

Kirsty stared at the twinkling set of emerald green eyes; the look of honesty and assurance that her intentions were pure were all but impossible for the child to miss. With a gentle tug of her arm and raised finger to her own lips, telling the girl to remain quiet, Janet guided the child to the waiting boxes of industrial clinical wipes.

5
Central Middlesex Hospital
S.A.U Team Three: Insertion

The wind whipped around them, snatching at their clothing in its vain attempt to ensnare them in its vaporous grasp. Richards watched the roads below snake their way through the city like ribbons of white-darted black silk; a smirk wormed its way across his features as he glanced around the open cabin of the helicopter.

'Walters, Sooker—I want you two on point; Walters you're with me and one section. Sooker, you're with Hawk and two section. Patterson, who's covering who? It's your call.'

Andre Patterson glanced about the cabin; his team was sitting, relaxed and ready as they winged their way towards Middlesex Hospital. His mind was awash with a myriad of thoughts as he weighed up whom to send with whom. Even if he split them directly down the middle, one section was going in a man down. Biting at his bottom lip, he closed his eyes and leant his head back as he began to speak.

'Token, King, Lucas, and I are with Richards. The rest of you are heading in with Hawk. That sound good to you, Rook?'

A curt nod greeted Patterson's query.

'Lincruster, you sit tight with the whirly bird.'

She flashed a quick thumbs up as she slid the helicopter through the north London skyline.

'A-Okay with me, Big Dog; mama bear gotta look after her little cub, after all.'

Rook grinned as he looked at Hawk. 'You okay there, brother?'

Hawk simply nodded as he stared at the bulkhead in front of him, his face a picture of impassive stone as he listened to the chatter around him. Token glanced at the American in front of him, the man's eyes a blur of cold anger and sadness; reaching out, he held out his hand to the man. 'Glad to be working with you.'

Jonathan 'Hawk' Stabbler glanced up and stared at Token, the young black Ghanaian's hand floating in dead space before Stabbler nodded and looked away. He let his hand drop slowly back to the fore-grip of his weapon. He was proud to be where he was, proud of his heritage, but also proud of being a British citizen and the first of his family to reach a level only ever dreamt of by others.

A tap on Token's shoulder drew his attention to the man on his left. Turning, he saw Richards leaning towards him, head cocked against the wind slashing at the open doorway.

'Don't think anything of it, buddy. Hawk's not one to pal up easily with anyone, especially not since Africa. It's not you personally, but we lost a lot of good friends there. For him, it's still a fresh wound and people of your "ethnic" persuasion bring a lot of bad memories out of him. Like I say, it's nothing personal; he just needs to get his shit together, that's all.'

Token nodded; he understood the situation. He didn't like it but he understood it. Turning away from Richards, he glanced at Carlstook. The man's face broke into a grin as he fished out the rabbit's foot he kept on a chain around his neck, Token grinned as Carlstook held it out for him. Taking it, he lifted the small appendage to his lips and kissed it.

'I cannot believe you still have that thing, my friend.'

Frank laughed, his whimsical chuckle making the others smile as he tucked away the disembodied appendage.

'Mate, I wouldn't get rid of this for all the tea in China; not that China's sending anyone any tea at the moment. If it wasn't for you braining that rabbit, we would have been dead out in the Hebrides by

55

now. You can bet your arse I am keeping this close to my heart.'

Token smiled, his brilliantly white teeth glimmering in the sunlight as it snatched its way between the buildings.

'Forty seconds, gentlemen.'

Patterson banged on the bulkhead, letting Lincruster know they had heard her. With a heavy-booted kick, he shoved the rope from the doorway as the helicopter settled into a hover over the roof of the hospital.

'You all have your orders; get it done and get home, ladies.'

He let his hand ensnare the rope, and with a Tarzan-esque swing of his legs, slid down the thickly woven yarn to the floor below. Several soft thumps followed as Token, King, Lucas, and Walters slid down behind him, all five men dropping to a knee with weapons raised and ready as Rook finally made his descent.

The rope slapped to the floor, its sloppy coils falling like limp spaghetti over itself as the clamp snapped open. Lincruster banked the chopper away as the first insertion team made their way to the rooftop stairwell.

****

Hawk watched intently, his fingers fiddling with the bunched ring of dog tags in his suit's pocket. Each one slid over the length of curled wire, clanking with a soft, muted *clink* against the others as he fed them through his fingers one by one. Carlstook stepped up next to Hawk, his hand clutching the overhead handle as he watched the side of the building flash by in front of him.

'How we playing this?'

Hawk let the bracelet of tags fall to the bottom of his ballistic suit's pocket once more before pushing himself to his feet.

'Same as we always do; go in shooting and don't stop until the Infected are dead, we run out of ammunition, or we go down.'

Carlstook shrugged as he let his hand fall from the ceiling grip and hopped out of the helicopter before its skids fully made contact with the tarmac of the car park.

Running forwards, he lifted his weapon to his shoulder as he dropped to one knee and fired three well-placed bursts, dropping the three Infected charging at them from the hospital foyer. Rising to his feet, he headed forwards in a hunched run, weapon swivelling from target to target, taking the outer foyer as the rest of the section made their way forwards.

'Magazine.'

He let the polymer magazine fall into his hand, his fingers dancing as he plucked a fresh one from the pouch on his chest and slotted it into place. The switch took all of three seconds as he once more sent rounds down range.

A sharp call went out as he saw Sooker slip past him, his gun spewing brass as the belt-fed weapon chewed its way through the string of glittering death.

The floor was awash with the dead by the time they moved off. A soft cackling echoed through the corridors, leading them to the open doors of the triage centre.

Cautiously, Sooker stepped towards the door, his feet foraging below him for any spot of the white tiled floor not covered in blood, excrement, or torn flesh. The soft splash of liquid rose up from the floor as he stepped through the puddles of bile and blood as he made his way towards the triage nurses' office.

Frank slid in beside him, his shoulder thumping against the hollow panel wall as Sooker gently edged the door open. The hushed silence cracked once again as the cackling laughter oozed its way out of the doorway. A stream of bile and offal-infused blood flowed over their boots as both men edged closer to the threshold of the room.

Carlstook's eyes widened as he beheld the sight before him. The child sat atop the desecrated corpse of the triage nurse, her pre-pubescent hands clutching the woman's entrails like string as she pulled them from the woman's disembowelled corpse. A wet splat echoed about the room as the child heaved one crimson-smeared blue slab from the woman's chest. The lung landed with all the grace of a dead walrus, sending a rippled geyser of blood into the air that coated the child's hair and face.

The spattering red droplets elicited another raucous cackle from the blood-smeared babe as she dived forwards once more and tore free the woman's heart. She lifted the oozing organ to her lips and licked along the rippled surface before sucking greedily at one of the entangled ventricles, biting through its rubbery hide as she drank greedily from the entrapped life-giving fluid.

Sooker turned away, his face green and pallid as he vomited over his boots. Revulsion and disgust poured from him in equal measure as his stomach evacuated its content. Carlstook clamped his teeth together as he fought the need to vomit. He settled the red dot of his rifle's optics on the child's chest, and then with an almost whimsical note, he whistled.

Her red, blood-crazed eyes snapped to his. The rubber-like twang of snapping arteries filled the air as they tore free and sent an arching spray of crimson fluid across the wall as Carlstook fired.

The child's head snapped back, crashing into the wall. Her chest erupted in a halo of blood and flesh as the bullets tore through her. With a soft, gentle thump, she tumbled back onto the table, her eyes forever locked in a feral glare of hunger as she came to rest in the crook of the nurse's arm, her long silken blonde hair lying in clumped matted lumps across her face.

****

The stairway was dark; the light of the door had long ago given up any pretence of even trying to illuminate their path as they wound their way deeper into the twisting corridors of the hospital. The damp air stank of mould; the clammy moisture-drenched air sucked at their lungs. The cold, rotting taste of stagnant water filled their mouths as they pushed on.

Rook held up a closed fist as he began to ease the door ahead of him open. A soft thump rolled up the stairwell as he connected with the door. Leaning into the thick slab of fireproof wood, he pushed and the door opened another inch; grinding his teeth together, he shoved harder and, to his chagrin, gained naught but another inch.

'Son of a bitch.' Letting his rifle hang, he pushed it onto his back as he grasped the leading edge of the door with both hands and pushed against the doorframe with his foot.

'Token, get a drone in here and see what the hell is blocking this door. I have a feeling I know what it is; just see if you can shift it.'

The miniature helicopter leapt from Token's palm as he sent it through the gap Rook held open, a soft electric whine filling their ears no louder than the buzzing of a gnat as it flitted past Rook's face.

Token stared at the screen as the small bug-like copter relayed all it saw with clarity. Suppressing an acid-filled cough, Token quickly panned the micro camera away from the pile of carrion at the foot of the door and sent the craft zipping down the hall. He glanced up to the top right of the screen, the digital readout displaying twenty-eight minutes and thirty seconds of flight time remaining as he gently guided the craft round a corner.

He quickly sent it zipping towards the ceiling as three dozen Infected fell upon the twisted remnants of one of the porters. The man's hand reflexively opening and closing as one gore-smeared nurse began to gnaw her way deeper into the soft flesh of his forearm, her teeth sending a jittery vibration through the severed limb's fingers as she tore its meat from the bone.

Token gently slipped the Nano UAV forwards a mere inch from the ceiling as the carnival of consumption continued on below. He once more reached the haven of its starting point and Token slipped his hand into the gap, between frame and door, and let the flying camera drop sedately onto his palm before slipping it into the padded case on his thigh, the screen module slipping into the pouch in the small of his back.

Rook cast a glance at Token as the Ghanaian began to speak, his words spiced with the lilt tone of his accent even as he whispered.

'We have, at the very least, a dozen Infected… quite possibly more; and yes, Mr Rook, it is most definitely what you thought it was.'

With a sigh, Rook tossed his head towards the gap, nodding. Ibrahim lifted his weapon's sling from around his torso and handed it off to Lucas as he lowered his limber frame to the floor and began to ease himself through the ever-expanding gap between the door and frame.

With a guttural grunt, he wormed his way through the gap; his muffled curses died on his lips as he came face-to-face with what was blocking the door. The smell of excrement and offal made him wretch as he pushed himself clear of the doorway.

Gingerly, he reached out his gloved hand and grasped the man's lab coat. With a soft squeak of cold flesh over linoleum, he pulled the technician clear of the door. The man's head thunked against the cold floor as he let go of the hem of his lab coat.

Stepping away from the mangled corpse and the streaks of blood and excrement marking the body's passage, he reached out and pulled the other clear of the doorway.

Her head lolled on the smashed remains of her neck. The split and cracked remains of skull left little need to ruminate on how she died. The pair of curved surgical scissors in her hand made Token pause; he glanced from the woman's hands to the deep lacerations in the man's chest and stomach.

'Who killed whom?' His self-rumination broken by the heavy thump of Rook's staggering form and the crunch of the stairwell's door as it swung inwards, smashing into the wall with a heavy, reverberating crunch of plastic on wood.

Their blood froze in their veins as the echoing crash of their entrance was answered by the guttural screaming cries that rolled their way; the ululating wall of noise roared down the corridors towards them, washing over them like the Red Sea of the Old Testament. The cacophony rose as the pounding of feet swept over them. Kweku's head snapped left as he caught his rifle and brought it to his shoulder just as the first galloping shadowed form broached the end of the corridor.

'Rolling fire, advance and engage. Walters, Lucas, Patterson—rear guard. Fucking move.'

They moved down the corridor, their bodies hunched and low as they let loose a volley of rounds into the charging Infected. Rook bellowed as he felt a searing pain flare through his shoulder. His right arm fell to his side, numb and useless. 'Fuck it!' he growled as he let his rifle drop.

The sling snapped taut as the weight of the weapon crashed against his collarbone. He clenched his teeth to the point of shattering as he twisted his now useless shoulder and pulled the pistol from its holster on his chest.

His eyes caught the glinting of polished steel as he moved. Releasing his grasp on his pistol, he left the weapon half in its holster and gritted his teeth once more as he grasped the protruding steel rod, his hand folding round the semi-flat handle of the surgical scalpel; then with a sharp intake of air, he ripped it from the blood-infused rent in his shoulder.

The in-rush of air was like ice water in his veins. As he pulled the offending item from his person, it sent squirming lances of lightning-like pain through him, their shivering forms racing through his arm and chest. He gasped, tears stinging his eyes as he let it clatter to the floor and once more drew his pistol.

6
Hospital: Interior: Floor Two

The corridors lay heavy upon them, their floors choked with overturned gurneys and beds; their dismembered occupants strewn across the floor like the tantrum-thrown parts of a child's doll.

Hawk stared at the battered and torn body in front of him, its baldhead split open like a crushed orange. Scanning the floor, he followed its outstretched arm, tracing its slim, pale length to the diminutive hand clutching the cold steel pole. His eyes locked onto the bag atop the drip stand, the half-empty bag lying like a dead fish against the cold melamine floor; he involuntarily sighed as he saw the printed lettering staring back at him. His lips moved as he softly sounded out the word to himself, *Cyclophosphamide*.

His head fell forwards slightly and tears stung his eyes as images of his father danced in his head—his smile as he grinned at the camera, despite the pain lancing through him as the cancer throbbed in the back of his skull; his glittering eyes that sung with the sadness of someone who knew their time was quickly running out, but despite all this, the one thing he would always remember was the slim, clear plastic tube that wound its way up his dad's arm and under his hospital gown, feeding him the clear liquid that was killing and saving him all at once.

He felt the tears roll down his cheeks as he remembered his face the day the doctors told him he could never have children again. He felt himself slide slowly into the smothering embrace of his own mind as a hand landed on his arm. Hawk jerked out of his reverie as the last image of his father danced is in his head. His open, vacant eyes and partially opened mouth as he gazed out the window of his hospital room; muttering a wistful goodbye, he turned to Carruthers, the soldier's questioning gaze tracing the pale lines of streaked tears running down his ruddy features.

'You okay, Hawk?'

Stabbler nodded as he turned and set off down the corridor, his shoulders hunched low as he panned his weapon across the corridor.

The corridor branched ahead of them; with a wave of his hand, he sent Carruthers and Carlstook down the left hand fork, while he and Hampson took the right. Sooker glanced about him, a tinge of nervous apprehension worming through him as he knelt, exposed and alone at the intersection.

****

Janet's head swivelled as she heard the hushed rattle of automatic gunfire roll through the silent corridors of the hospital. She shivered as she heard the guttural bellowing of dozens of Infected as they streamed past the door.

The children clung to her sides, their heads buried into her slim form as they tried to blot out the unearthly howls beyond their hidden bastion. Kevin shot an agonised look at the door as several Infected bounced off the panel of reinforced glass; he physically winced as stars of glistening red blood shot over the rippled surface of the meshed glass.

His gaze travelled to Janet's as she cradled the two children against her. Maria, swaddled in her woollen blankets, lay blissfully unaware in the impromptu cot. A soft burble of incomprehensible words drifted out her as she clutched at the edge of her blanket, small, toothless gums smacking gently together as she shifted in her slumber.

Janet stared at her child as she moved, a silent prayer drifting over the slumbering babe, begging her to stay quiet as the march of the damned continued outside their door.

Broadhead Barracks
Officers' Housing

Baker paced, his fists clenching and unclenching as he growled out his fear—fear at his inability to help his wife and child, fear that he was finally starting to lose his edge, fear at the world outside his door and the turmoil writhing through it; and above it all, fear at losing not just his life, but all he ever held dear.

He stopped in the centre of the room, his mind a whirling maelstrom of loathing and anger. His hands balled again as he resumed pacing. Turning, he stormed across the room, his fists smacking at the sides of his head as he bellowed in rage. He snatched his rig from the cot in his office, crashed through the door, and sprinted down the corridor, his eyes wild with fury.

Susan stepped into the corridor, her arms a mass of neatly typed and stacked papers. She grumbled to herself as she turned, staring into the onrushing path of a man possessed; in a whirl of fluttering paper and indignant squeals, she crashed into the wall as Baker charged through her, the clacking of quick-release buckles echoing in his wake.

Dazed and confused, Susan began her arduous task of collating and collecting her fallen paperwork, the pages rasping through her fingers as she plucked them one by one from the floor. Colinson watched with consternation mingled with acceptance and anger as Baker sprinted past his office door. Stepping forwards, Colinson walked briskly to his door and knelt, scooping up scattered sheets of paper. Susan looked round; Colinson's charcoal grey-clad form filled her vision as she reached out, her eyes avoiding his as she lifted the papers from his grip.

David smiled as he watched the worry etch itself through the corners of her eyes. A soft shimmer of hopefulness wormed its way through her as David began to speak. 'He will be fine, Susan; don't worry about a thing.'

The air was crisp and bitter as Derek jumped through the open door of his Jeep; his chest rig thumped and bounced against him as he viciously twisted the key and shoved the vehicle into gear. In a hot squeal of burnt rubber and a burst of smoke, he flew from the motor pool and out the gate. He drove as if Satan himself had come to collect, weaving through the backcountry roads as he made his way towards central London.

Central Middlesex Hospital
Exterior: Main Entrance

Bodies lay strewn in the carpark as Derek slid to a halt, the wheels of his Jeep squealing as he tried to meld the brake with the vehicle's floor. A heavy clunk rolled up from below him as it rolled over the shredded head of a dead nurse. Her skull collapsed, sending shattered pieces of skull and shredded flesh splashing ahead of him in a glistening halo of shimmering blood and cranial matter.

He stepped out of the Jeep, his feet sliding in the mashed paste of the deceased nurse's head as he lifted his rifle from the rear of the vehicle; he grit his teeth, his hand closing over the pistol grip as he lifted the unloaded weapon from the back seat of his vehicle. A dull semi-metallic clunk echoed through the empty carpark as he opened a box of 5.56 mm ammunition. He glared at the G36C in the passenger seat and ground his teeth together as he laboriously loaded the magazines in his ballistics vest. Finally, Derek slid the magazines into the pouches on his vest. After ten agonizing minutes of tedium, he rolled his shoulder and settled the weight of the general-issue Benelli M4 Super 90 between his shoulder blades. Then with the echoing clack of the assault rifle's charging handle rolling across the body-laced carpark, he sprinted for the front doors of the hospital.

Baker smashed through them like a runaway locomotive, his eyes shining with an uncontrollable, almost fanatical need to wrest his wife and child from the grip of whatever calamity had befallen them. Raising his booted foot, he kicked in the door to the triage room. It swung back on noiseless hinges, slamming into the wall with a *thunk* that echoed through the waiting area; it rolled over the walls and chairs, swelling over all in its path like waves over sand. His gaze travelled over the shattered skull, halo of pulped brain matter, and the minuscule corpse it accompanied as he stepped into the room.

Derek's eyes lingered on the torn and ravaged face of the nurse, her eyes locked in a screaming excitation of pain and horror as the shattered corpse of the child lay dead in the nurse's eviscerated chest cavity.

His weapon dangled from the one point sling as he stepped over to the hospital staff rota plastered onto the dry-wipe board. He scanned the board for anything showing any sign of his wife. His heart clenched in on itself as he thought of her and his daughter. His hand dropped to his thigh, brushing over the chequered pattern of his pistol's grip. His fingers brushed the tactile sides of the weapon as he stared at the dead child and her unwitting carrion bed. Shaking himself from the stress-induced stupor, he turned and felt the weight of his shotgun tugging at his back as he stepped into the waiting room. The scent and tang of fresh blood and excrement settled on his tongue as he stopped, finally taking note of the abounding destruction.

Chairs lay askew, cast aside as people fled in terror from the crazed and enraged forms of their Infected friends, family, co-workers, and patients. He stepped forwards, looking at the splintered and smashed remnants of the concrete and bolt housings that had been torn from the floor in a crush of fleeing bodies. Kneeling, his gaze travelled towards the doors he had entered through; the pulverised remnants of a human hand lay caught in the gas-powered pneumatic hinges of the door. The soft hissing of the closing door belied a far more sinister note as the brushed aluminium ground against the shattered wrist bones of the severed appendage.

The grating of metal on bone flowed to his ears as he watched the door pull the hinge shut. Turning his head to the left, he studied the rest of the room, taking in the splayed arms and pool of congealing blood slowly seeping out from beneath a toppled vending machine to the butchered remains of a staff porter. The man's tear-drenched face dangled from the remains of his torso where it hung swinging against the twisting column of his own spine.

Baker shook his head in wonderment, struggling to fathom what had possessed the seasoned hospital worker to try to clamber through the smashed window of the double doors; but as he knew all too well, in the grips of man's primal fight or flight instincts, common sense had little to say when it came to a person's method of escape.

Hospital: Floor Two

Rook crashed through the door, his back slamming painfully into the floor, his battle vest lost somewhere in the twisting corridors, torn from his body by the writhing Infected now astride him. He smashed his knees into the small of its back, sending the screaming rage-filled face past his head and into the floor. He rolled backwards, his curled legs slamming into its neck as he sank his weight into the fragile cartilage beneath him. The crunch of smashed bone reverberated through his body as he brought his gun to bear on the door in front of him.

Token stumbled through the door a second later, his flailing form besieged by the screaming, bleeding, rage-drenched contents of the upper children's ward. He swatted and punched at anything he could reach as they tore at his clothing, their prepubescent hands torn to shreds as they desperately tried to tear their meal from his flesh. He ensnared the waving locks of one child and, with a vicious wrench of his muscular arm, tore the child from him, its tortured screams filling his ears as he cast it aside. The sound of tearing silk filled the room as its scalp tore free.

Token spun, sending himself back-first into the square steel frame of the nearest bed. The crack of snapping bone met his ears; the slim arms encircling his throat went slack as all life left them. Spinning on his feet, he swung the clump of hazel hair up into his hands; the dripping lump of flesh on the end was warm against his gloved hand.

Turning to face the charging, scalped form of the Infected child, he sidestepped and wrapped the child's own hair around its throat. The pumping blood oozed down the back of its head as its eyes bulged in their sockets. Rolling his hand, he pulled ever tighter, watching as the skin of the girl's cheeks turned a deep purple. Then with the squeaking of its bare feet ringing in his ears, it went limp. Chest heaving, blood slowly worming its way out of his broken nose, he sank to the floor. The dull crump of dead flesh hit the tiled floor as he let the hair fall from his grip.

69

A look of detached surprise wavered over the men's faces as Token pushed himself into a sitting position against one wall, his breathing heavy and ragged as he listened to the gunfire rattle through the hall. Walters, Patterson, King, and Lucas stormed through the door, bullets smacking into flesh as they tried to push back the tide of Infected bearing down upon them. Slamming the door shut, Walters took aim as the Infected smashed themselves upon its flat, glossed surface.

'Well, we're stuck.'

Patterson turned and looked at Rook, a look of quiet puzzlement passing over his face.

'Rook, where's your rig?'

The former division operative smiled, a sharp wince running over his face as the broken remains of his third and fourth ribs ground against each other. A sharp hiss of pain-flushed air left him as he pushed himself into a higher sitting position.

'To be honest, Andre, I have no idea. If I were to guess, the rig, my rifle, and all of my spare ammunition and radio are somewhere back in the main corridor.'

Andre sighed as he walked over to his section leader. He knelt and poked his extended index finger into Rook's ribs. He watched Rook's face contort, a fresh wave of nauseating pain rolling through him as Andre kept on with his 'inspection'. Lifting his free hand to Rook's shoulder, he pulled the torn flaps of his suit aside and looked at the hole in Rook's skin.

Reaching into a pouch on the front of his rig, he pulled out a trauma pad. The length of high-tensile gauze clutched in his hand, he pushed the Celox-infused pad against Rook's shoulder as he wrapped the bandage over the wound. Pulling tight, he threaded it through the pressure bar and pulled. A muffled whimper of pain left Rook as the pressure built, sending shocking waves of pain through his torn muscle. Snorting out through his nose, he nodded at Patterson and closed his eyes as he pulled again, wrapping the bandage back on itself and sending the pressure ever higher.

A soft plastic click emanated up from Rook's shoulder as Patterson clipped the end of the bandage into place.

'That should see you until we can get exfil; just don't do anything stupid, okay? And pray to god, or whoever the fuck collects your ticket, that it,' he pointed to the freshly covered wound, 'isn't Infected, and I don't mean MRSA.'

Rook smiled as he fished in his thigh pocket for a cigar. 'Andre, if it comes down to it, I'll clock myself out rather than turn into one of those fucking things.' He motioned towards the door with his unlit cigar. 'By the way, chuck me your coms; I got to relay into Hawk, let him know what the hell's going on.'

7

Hawk's radio buzzed, his ear itching from the burst of white static; lifting his hand, he rubbed at the inside of his ear, trying to scrape away the maddening tickle that was pushing at the roots of his ear.

As he strained to listen, a familiar voice filtered through the wall of hissing electrical buzzing. Flicking away the flakes of congealed soap clinging to the tip of his gloved finger, Hawk pressed against his throat microphone, opening up the channel. His eyes widened as Rook relayed the situation of his team.

'Fuck it all to hell. Okay, brother, sit tight; if you can push to the evac, Kingfisher should be there.

'Hold position there, we are closing in on the source here. Collared a live ward manager. I will radio through if I come up with anything concrete. Keep it on a swivel, okay? See you on the other side.'

Stepping through the heavy double doors in front of him, Hawk swept the torch beam across the rows of beds; blood stained the loose-woven blankets and heavy cotton sheets. He stepped forwards, a soft wet tapping emanating up from his foot. Glancing down at his boot-covered feet, he watched as the ever-expanding ripples rolled through the slowly congealing pool of blood. A frown crossed his features as he lifted his foot and stepped over it, dropping to one knee besides the nurse's station. The flickering glow of the computer monitor reflected off the one-way glass set into the wall. The light bounced across Hawk's crouched form, casting a dancing hunched shadow across the floor.

'Sooker, on me. Hampson, Carruthers split left. Carlstook, dig in and cover the doors; we haven't got long here and need to find the heart of this bitch and rip it the fuck out.'

They split off, heading deeper into the ward. A soft mewling drew Sooker's attention as he slowly advanced into the second section of the ward. Beds lay strewn across the floor, their mattresses and blankets tossed aside like fallen trees in a forest; stepping over the claret-stained bedding, his footsteps as silent as falling snow, Sooker peered into the gloom. Motioning with one hand, he beckoned Hawk forwards. As silently as a stalking shadow, he appeared at Sooker's side. Tapping his ear gently with his index and middle finger, Sooker shifted and motioned towards the far corner of the ward. Hawk nodded, lifting his rifle to a tighter position as he stepped to the side and watched Sooker continue forwards.

Slowly and with infinitesimal care so he didn't disturb the steel sliders of the privacy curtain, Sooker pulled. As the curtains parted, both men felt their gorge rise. Hunched in the decimated remains sat a woman, her withered form sleeved in the bile and blood of those she had been feasting upon. Her soft, toothless gums sucked at the flayed strands of skin and flesh as she tried to prise it from the bone. Empty bowls, canisters, and packets lay strewn over the floor, their contents long since consumed in the burning need for sustenance. A dark viscous brown sludge flowed from the woman's hunched form, staining the back of her hospital robes.

The stench was overwhelming, filling their olfactory sense to the point of bursting. Pulling his battered and weatherworn Shemag scarf from around his neck, Hawk wrapped the patterned band of cloth around his face in a strident attempt to block out the vile odour.

Her sallow skin slipped and flapped against her age-withered frame as she pulled at the pallid dead flesh of the patient in her grip; the man's vacant, dead form lolled limp and lifeless as it jolted and bounced against the floor with each tug the woman made. She pulled as her lips and gums closed on the string of cabled muscle and skin; a soft, slick *pop* issued up from her wanton face as the lump of dead meat finally pulled free. Flicking her head back, the tousled curls of her blue-rinsed hair bounced against her age-lined face as she swallowed. The bulbous pustules covering her lips and face made her flesh shiver and move as she pushed the lump of meat around her saliva-drenched mouth.

Strings of the glistening, clear fluid ran from the corners of her mouth, coalescing in thick ribbons as it dropped from her chin to land with a wet plop on the front of her hospital gown.

****

Janet's head snapped up as the blood flashed over the window; the glistening spray cast a red-hazed shimmer over the walls. The children burrowed against Kevin and Janet, their shifting forms warm against them as they hid from the muted gloss of incandescent red smears sliding down the walls. A face crashed into the window, blood bubbling from its lips as it was crushed further and further against the glass. A small childlike groan rose from it as it began to slide, a weak and pitiful sound that made Janet want to weep. A sudden and almost violent squeal of flesh on glass made them all flinch; a soft whimper of fear boiled up from the girl in Janet's lap. Glancing to her left, Janet watched the softly moving figure of Maria as she shifted in her sleep, her infantile lips clapping together softly as she dreamt. Reaching out, Janet smoothed Maria's downy hair over her scalp as she gently shushed both children, praying they both stayed quiet.

Kevin edged the boy from his lap, setting him gently on the floor. The boy whimpered as he met the cold concrete of the floor, his hands clutching at Kevin's stained and torn lab coat; the fear and need for physical comfort was oozing from the child like water from a slowly dripping tap. Pushing the boy's clutching hands gently away from him, he stood and crept to the door, his hunched form looking like an amorphous crab as he slowly slunk towards the door.

Janet's sharply hissed and panic-edged call gave him pause as he reached out towards the door. His hand hung in the air mere centimetres away from the brushed steel handle of the storage room's door. His fingers brushed against the cold, lifeless steel bar. The cold crept through his fingertips and seeped deep into his knuckles, sending a wave of pain through his fingers as he curled his extended digits around the handle. He slowly pushed down on the handle; the bolt slid back millimetre by millimetre as he edged the handle down ever further. Clutching the steel bar in a death grip, he pulled the door towards him, his eyes pushed shut so tightly they began to ache from the self-imposed pressure. Kevin stepped to the side and peered through the ever-widening gap in the doorway.

The hand shot forwards, its long, slim digits closing around Kevin's neck; his eyes bulged as he felt the warm grasp of the Infected tighten on his throat. Kevin threw himself forwards, the Infected growling as he kicked the door shut behind him. Kevin cast his gaze backwards just as the door swung closed. His eyes begged her to remain silent as she held her hands fast over the children's mouths. She watched her friend and colleague disappear, the door slamming shut on him and their friendship like the lid on a coffin.

The warmth of its skin unsettled Kevin the most; he had expected the cold touch of death around his throat, not the warm supple grasp of another human. He thrashed violently as the distorted, pustule-covered face of his fellow human snapped down at him. Clumps of flesh and offal hung from its teeth; the squirming tendrils slithered over Kevin's skin and his gorge rose, bursting from his mouth in a fountain of bile and stomach acid. The Infected woman recoiled as the caustic mix of his lunch and bodily fluids scorched her already battered airways.

Her face twisted as she clawed at her throat, the stale flaking dregs of the hospital's re-heated shepherd's pie encrusting her lips. Thin red lines trailed down her constricting neck, the misted bile and stomach acid scouring the inside of her oesophagus, sealing the walls of her throat together like paste over paper. His mind boiled in his skull as he ran through the entirety of his self-defence training. Curling his fists, he let his thumbs jut outwards as he drove them forwards, smashing them into its eyes. Her ocular balls burst as he pushed forwards with as much strength as he could manage. He felt the lenses crumple as his thumbs carved their way forwards; the aqueous humours oozed over his thumbs as he continued to push.

A sharp jet of warm clear gel shot over his hand as he clasped the sides of her head and threw his weight sideways. Her screams echoed down the hall as his thumbs dug deeper inside her skull. He jerked his head from side to side as her hand clawed at his shoulders and chest. Her pain-drenched flails doubled as he forced his thumbs past the soft, porous sheath of bone in the back of her eye sockets.

His nails grated against the sides of her eye sockets as he pushed, shards of bone snatching and pulling at his already torn nails as he rolled his body over; with an almost primal growl, Kevin drove her head into the floor. The dull crack of her skull echoed like a popping eggshell as he crushed it against the melamine-covered concrete.

Kevin flopped back, his heels digging painfully into his backside as he tried to pull his legs from under him. His hands sank down, the grit and broken glass from the wall displays scraping at his skin. He snatched them up, fear coursing through him as he looked at his hands covered in the bloody remnants of the dead Infected's eyes. He tentatively reached forwards, peeling the smeared remains of the Infected woman's eye lens from the end of his thumb, the thin membrane sheet slid from his finger like a piece of plastic, cold and slippery to the touch. Reaching into the remains of his coat, he pulled out a bottle of disinfectant gel and squeezed; the cold, viscous fluid dribbled into his palm as he emptied the entire bottle. The cooling tingle settled into his hands as he smeared it over them, desperate to get the layers of filth off his body.

His eyes strayed from their task, his panicked, fear-laden stare travelling over the prostrate form mere feet away; the soft twitching of its feet sent a rhythmic squeak down the hall. Bile danced in Kevin's throat as he gazed at what he had done; the leaking mire of cranial fluid and pulped brain matter slowly inched its way towards him. It was as though the fluid was calling out, screaming at him for an explanation as to why he had, for the second time that day, desecrated his Hippocratic oath and taken another life.

Janet slowly eased the door open; the soft hush of the draught excluder seemed to tear at her ears as it invaded the soft silence that now fell over their sanctuary. She let her eyes drift, her mind soaking in all that lay before her. Turning, she ushered the children into a corner, desperate to keep them from seeing the tableau that awaited the unwary.

Pulling the door closed behind her, she reached out, setting her hand on Kevin's shoulder. His hands were still pawing and turning as he smeared the gum-like paste of blood, tissue, and disinfectant gel across his rapidly reddening skin.

'Kevin?' Her feather-light, encroaching whisper drew his eyes to hers. The shock-filled orbs of fear filled her vision as she took a soft but firm hold of his shoulder and elbow. With a gentle guiding tug, she ushered him to his feet, pulling him back into their small cocoon of chemical-filled safety.

****

Hawk lifted his rifle, settling the glowing red dot of his rifle's sight on the side of the woman's head, then with a smooth curl of his index finger, fired. The side of her head opened up like a piñata, sending waves of glistening bone and brain spattering against the curtains surrounding her bed. Her withered body sunk like a string-less puppet, the off-white curls of her age-frayed hair soaking in the swamp of blood and filth that surrounded her.

'Mark location so we can dispose of this crone.'

Sooker nodded as he pulled a waterproofed map of the hospital from his thigh pocket. Grease pencil in hand, he flicked it over the surface before setting the folded map back in his pocket.

Hawk turned and walked back to the front of the ward, his weapon held low and ready as he made his way towards the remaining members of his fire team.

'Right, boys, let's get out of here; I've had enough of this place.'

The television in the corner of the ward fizzed as the static burped at him. Turning, Hawk pushed and prodded several of the buttons before the frothing ball of white noise finally ceased. He turned, his feet sliding over the detritus covering the floor as a calm, cultured voice filled the room, stopping him in his tracks.

His skin stung as a wave of fear rolled through him, the words burrowing into his skull as he listened to words he had longed to forget.

Turning to the wall-mounted television, he saw the fear-licked face of the Prime Minister as he read from the auto-cue in front of him.

'Again, I repeat, The United Kingdom is now under quarantine; all flights inbound and out bound are cancelled indefinitely. Use of deadly force has been authorised and will be used as necessary to prevent anyone gaining entry into or to prevent those trying to leave the country. We will not accept the risk of spreading the Virus that has so afflicted our nation any further and as such, emergency protocols have been implemented.

A curfew is in full effect as of seven o'clock tonight. Anyone on the streets after 7:04 who is not required to be there will be detained without question.

We are now as a nation in a state of national crisis. All measures detailed in the crisis packs issued are in full effect. We ask you—the people—to see us through this. Do not let anyone inside your home for any reason unless they are police or military personnel with full identification. Do not break curfew for any reason.

Should you see anyone with any of the symptoms described in your packs, do not approach them. Do not make contact. Do not allow them inside your residence or place of business. Keep them away from your children. Activate the personal locator alarms; they will alert the police or military in your area and they will deal with them immediately.

We will overcome this, we will prevail, and we will, as a nation, survive.'

Hawk stared at the black cube on the wall for several minutes as the bead in his ear barked and screamed at him.

'Fuck that noise; we're leaving.' Stabbing at his throat mike, Hawk bellowed out a call.

'Rook, Patterson, anyone, come back.'

Patterson's breathless voice seeped through him as he listened. Biting his lip, Hawk kicked open the ward doors, firing from the hip as three Infected launched themselves at him.

'Hawk, we're almost at the roof. The place is a mess. There is no one left that hasn't been Infected; if there are, we can't find them. We're bugging out. See you at the evac.'

With that, Hawk's bead fell silent as he sent his boot into the face of another Infected.

'Sooker, Carlstook, punch a hole; we are getting the fuck out of here. They can glass this place for all I fucking care. I am not losing another home to the fucking things.'

He slammed the butt of his weapon into the screaming face of another Infected hospital worker; its forehead crumpled as Hawk turned the hot caustic fluids glistening in the air as he sprinted to the corner of the corridor.

****

'Fuck, fuck, fuck!' Rook's shoulder screamed at him as he hobbled alongside Patterson, his good arm looped over the man's shoulders as he was all but dragged along. The wailing roar of two dozen enraged Infected washed over them as they dodged and ducked, flailing arms and leaping bodies passing mere millimetres from them as the rest of the team fired mercilessly into the undulating horde about them.

'What the... shit!'

Token's semi-girlish cry echoed back to them as a screaming form threw itself at him. Lifting his weapon, he kept his finger on the trigger as he guided the screaming, blood-splattered form over his head. He ejected his magazine as he brought his weapon down, swinging it out on its sling into the face of another Infected as he pulled a fresh magazine from his rig. He felt the magazine click home as he lifted the weapon once more to his shoulder.

'Fuck you.' Walters slid forwards on one knee, the toe of his left boot sending glass shards spraying about him as he ducked. Pushing back up to his feet, he continued to run, a cone of orange-tinted death leaping forwards as he fired.

Jabbing his weapon forwards, he lodged the glowing barrel into the mouth of an Infected. The stench of hot flesh pervaded his nostrils as the barrel melted the back of the man's throat. Squeezing the trigger once more, Walters watched the back of the man's head explode in a blossoming spray of glimmering red droplets. With a strength driven by his need to live just one more day, he lifted the lifeless lump of flesh from the floor and charged forwards.

He swung the body like a shield, using momentum and sheer physical mass to swat aside all in his path. The loafer-covered feet of his shield quivered and kicked as they skipped over the mass of tangled wires and metal beneath them.

Reaching the stairwell, he smashed the door aside, sending several of their snarling besiegers over the stairs' railing, their twisting screeching forms clawing at the air as they plummeted to the cold concrete below.

Dropping to his knee, Walters spun, hugging the doorframe as his teammates sped past him. Hot brass pinged off his face as it clattered against the doorframe and the scalding discoloured cylinders scorched his skin in a dis-jointed pattern of mottled red welts.

'Go! Make for the rendezvous; I'll hold the line. *Go!*'

Walters squared his shoulders as the last member of their small fire team flew past him. Slipping a fresh box of ammunition from his hip, he linked the belts together just as the last of it clattered through the receiver.

The walls lit up with the streaming shadows of the dead and dying as the Infected pressed in upon him, their rage all-consuming as they descended upon his quickly weakening position.

****

Baker heard the heavy chatter of the belt-fed weaponry; its clattering echo slithered through the corridors, a withering bass line to the Infected chorus that lifted like the song of the damned from the very bowels of the once vibrant hospital. A bastion of health and vitality now home to the carnivorous legions of Satan's army of the damned.

Shaking his head, Baker let his rifle swing up onto his back, the last of his magazines falling to the floor with a dull clunk. The heavy clack of shells in a slide filled his ears as he pulled the shotgun from between his shoulder blades.

Levelling the weapon, he pulled its stock tightly to his shoulder; as he rounded the corner, his chest swelled as he bellowed out his wife's name. Baker's voice echoed down the corridor and a deep-throated growl returned to him; its disembodied form wormed its way across the walls as he pushed through the flapping double doors of the hospital ward. Swinging his aim, he fired. The growls' master fell to the floor, a smoke-withered hole the only reminder of its once human face.

The ejected casing curled past him as the spent shell was tossed from the gun, the heavy scent of cordite filling his nostrils as he pushed forwards. Three more empty casings tumbled to the floor in quick succession as the bodies of Infected fell. Baker's singular goal gave him a cold, calculated purpose until he was more machine than man; his mind was set in its task as he carved through all in his path.

He careened through the doors on the other side of the ward, their handles sinking deep into the walls as he sent them fleeing from his path. In a spray of bone and buckshot, the Infected lay at his feet in a pale, bleeding imitation of life. As the shotgun chambered another

81

round, he pulled a strip feeder from his pack and held it ready. The length of reinforced nylon was light in his palm as he pushed the magazine trap open and slid the cartridges home.

He slipped the tube into the pouch on his thigh as he moved onward, his speed never faltering as he cleared the corridor. He stopped, cocking his head to the side, mouth open slightly so he could listen clearly without his breathing rasping through his ears.

****

The heavy, thumping blast of a shotgun made the children whimper with fear. Janet gently ran her hands over their hair, the soft soothing motion making them both relax as they curled themselves against her.

Maria began to whimper, the soft mewling cry drifted up from the box she was ensconced in. Nudging the two children towards Kevin, Janet stood and gently lifted the softly wriggling form of her daughter from the padded warmth of the box.

Maria's head nestled gently in the crook of Janet's elbow as she slowly rocked her into a fitful calmness. Her small fists clutched at Janet's shirt as she stared at her mother, the bright iridescent blue of her eyes shining with a trust that danced and flirted with the furtive incomprehension only born by the new life that she was.

'Daddy will be here soon; now be a good girl for mummy.'

Janet lowered her head and brushed her lips against Maria's forehead. A soft, clutching hand traced itself against her jaw as Maria reached up, her tiny fingers grazing over the soft skin of her mother's chin.

Staring at the door, Janet felt the tears well up behind her eyes as the thumping blasts continued to echo.

'Come on, Derek; where are you?'

Derek threw himself forwards, rolling over his shoulder as he sent the Infected reeling. Curling up to his feet, he brought the gun to bear, tearing a fist-sized hole through the leering blood-smeared form in front of him.

A black rod of plastic filled his hand as he fed another tube into the shotgun's receiver, pushing the shells forwards. He kicked, sending the two prepubescent Infected forms in front of him sliding backward. Their screeching flailing bodies tore the legs from under another as Derek finished re-loading his weapon. The bolt shunted forwards as he lifted it back to his shoulder. The ear-shattering report rang in his ears as he stalked forwards once more.

'Janet!' His voice echoed down the hallway as he continued to fire, drowning out the roar of the weapon as it spat flying pellets of death. He ducked once again, sending the white-coated form of another hospital worker into the wall, a stomach-churning crunch echoing up from the floor as its weight shattered its neck. He felt it fall as he fired, the dull clunk of its feet against the cold floor punctuating his passage as he moved on.

A plaintive cry greeted his ears as he moved through the corridor. The soft, lilting voice scythed through the fog that crowded his mind; the voice was all too familiar to him.

His eyes narrowed as he pulled the shotgun tighter to his shoulder, his ears picking the sounds apart as he searched for the source. His eyes darted left where the drained, lifeless body of an Infected woman lay, her head crushed. Pieces scattered about her in a halo of bone and flesh. His eyes scanned the area as his mind tore the scene apart. Body and mind turning and twisting, he cut his way through the crush of Infected towards the body. The woman's head had melded with the concrete, crushed like a melon under a wheel.

His gaze travelled over the filth-encrusted skin of her cheeks to her eyes; they sat in her sockets, the destroyed orbs little more than puddles of mush.

His head screamed at him to stop as he emptied the magazine. The bolt locked home as the final cartridge spun free, the twisting vapour of burning paper and gunpowder drifting past him. He slipped the weapon from its sling, swinging the butt of it into the face of an Infected. Blood and flesh coated the heavy rubber pad. As he drove the Infected backwards into the wall, a crimson red spray coated the once cream paintwork as its cranium collapsed. The smell of charred flesh and steaming excrement filled his nose as he surveyed the scene about him.

The gathering pack of Infected advanced, wary of its prey. Their bodies vibrated with barely suppressed energy as their muscles quivered in anticipation.

Rolling his neck, Baker shook loose the tension as he shifted his shotgun onto his back once more. The heat tickled his spine as he set it between his shoulder blades. Reaching down, he let his fingers graze over the fluted pommel of his knife. The crenelated grip skimmed his fingers as he slowly pulled it from the sheath in the small of his back. At the same time, his left hand closed over the textured grip of the pistol on his thigh.

His mind swirled as he evaluated the dozens of possibilities. His eyes settled on the door twelve feet behind the mass of slowly encroaching flesh. He slowly slid his right foot back as he settled his weight lower. His muscles coiled like steel cable as he readied to make his move. The Infected screamed; turning they yowled and bellowed as they began to fall.

Baker swung his arm up, his blade covering his wrist as he moved forwards, the slide bucking as he squeezed the trigger. His aim snapped from target to target as they began to panic; Baker's eyes snapped up as the moving wraith-like shapes at the end of the corridor began to turn. The lancing tongues of fire leapt forwards as they moved. Their haze-laden black forms shifted and morphed as they advanced, cutting through the wall of flesh.

'Foxtrot Seven, that you?'

A quick sharp double click slithered through his ear as he pushed through. The blade in his hand scythed forwards, the flesh beneath parting like an overripe peach, the slick claret waterfall poured forth, dousing his forearm in a frothing wave of cloying syrup. Baker pushed forwards, bulling his way past the last remnants of opposition as they were cut down by the shadowed bodies behind them.

Ignoring the calls and shouted questions, Baker lifted his foot and sent it slamming into the door just above the handle. The frosted meshed glass split and cracked as he sent the door swinging back into the room.

****

Janet clutched Maria tightly to her chest as the door flew inwards, shards of plastic-coated wood showering her in a rain of jagged splinters.

A small squeak of alarm left the bundle in her arms as she pushed herself tighter into the corner. Flapping and flailing, Janet reached for anything that she could use. The cold smooth metal settled into her grasp as she pulled it from the shelf, smashing the capped end against the corner of the shelf. She pushed it forwards, her index finger curling tightly over the top of the nozzle as she sprayed her would be attacker. The fine white mist clung to their clothes as she emptied the canister; the thin foam of condensed vapour rolled down their leg. An arm curled over her shoulders and they were pulled forwards. Janet railed and bucked as she smashed the empty container against its head; the dull *thunk* of metal bouncing off plastic filled her senses.

'Janet, stop! For crying out loud, Janet, stop for a second and look.'

Kevin's plaintive pleadings bled through the wall of haze surrounding her as she continued the frenzied assault. Her eyes swam with fear and anger as she tried desperately to focus on the shadowed image before her. His hand clutched at her back as the blade fell to the floor. The cloying, viscous remnants of Infected blood smeared over her clothes as he pulled her close.

His voice shattered her resolve, crushing walls and defences beneath a tide of overwhelming fear as she crumbled. Her knees buckled beneath her, and she slid to the floor, her body turning against his as she held Maria against her.

'We have to move. Evac is on the roof; they are holding but can't keep on station for long.'

His words hung harsh and heavy as he pulled Janet's quivering form to her feet. Kevin's fear-struck eyes locked onto his as he watched Derek lift her from the floor. Baker's eye quivered as Kevin filtered through his peripheral vision, his hands wrapped tightly around those of the two children; their frightened whimpering filled the room.

'Come on, you skinny bastard; pick the kids up and fucking move.'

Patterson growled at the red-faced form struggling to pull along the two children. A snarl snatched at his face as he levered Rook into a better position.

'Oh for fuck's sake, Token, take the girl. You, Skinny—whatever your damned name is—pick the boy up and fucking move it.'

Kweku scooped the girl from the floor as he ran; her writhing, screaming form beat its minute fists against his muscular frame as he lifted her free of the bonds that bound her to the floor; her balled fists crashed against his helmeted head as he pulled her tight to his body. He could feel her heart pounding in her chest as she moved against him, her hands searching for any semblance of purchase as she was jostled and bounced by Token's sprinting form.

'Hold on tight, little one; this is going to be very loud and very scary.'

Token swung his weapon up, the stock braced against his upper arm. He gritted his teeth as he struggled to keep the barrel straight. The girl buried her head against him as his rifle chattered, the staccato popping filling her ears. She cried, her stifled sobs rolling through Token as he struggled to keep her from falling free of his grip.

****

Baker never once let up, his grip chaffing at Janet's skin as she stumbled and tripped along in his wake. Her mind tumbled and reeled as she struggled to fathom the man before her when she compared it to the man she knew as her husband. He pulled her through a turn that would have made a rally driver falter as he skirted the reaching arms of an Infected. Without a second's pause, he aimed and fired, sending the hollow-point round through its skull in a burst of blood and crushed bone.

He jabbed his fingers against the call button of his throat mic, his breath coming in an even, un-faltering wave; his eyes scanned the corridor ahead as he continued to run.

'Kingfisher, you there?'

The line crackled slightly as the connection opened, the static fizzing away as Lincruster's stout Scottish brogue filled his ear.

'Aye that we are, Cherry Pie. On station and ready to exfil; Hawk and the boys are on board and holding the wolves from the door; Echo Ten is pretty battered but he held them off long enough to secure your exit.'

Baker pushed Janet round a corner, his fist flying outwards, slapping an Infected into the opposite wall as it lunged towards her.

'Can the crap. We need a quick kill fire mission on Hawk's last known position before pick up. We are getting fucking swarmed!'

The line went dead as he lifted his pistol once more; the slide clacked back and forth as he drained the magazine. He ejected the magazine and without so much as looking, reloaded the weapon.

The heavy snarling whine was his only warning before the windows splintered, the walls bursting like an overstuffed piecrust as the high-velocity rounds tore through the concrete and plasterboard. Baker snatched a glance to the right as he sprinted forwards, his path cut clear by the scything wall of lead as Hawk unleashed the full fury of the M134 mini gun mounted to the doorframe.

The malicious grin cutting itself across Hawk's face made Baker's stomach clench. He had seen it all too often on the face of other operators—the unbridled need to satiate the clawing seed of vengeance that was eating away at him. Baker pulled Janet to the floor as the rounds arced over their heads, the men behind him falling into a huddled mass. Token's arm snatched out, pulling Kevin to the floor just as the wall around him disintegrated into a cloud of crushed masonry and plaster.

'Fucking twat is going to get us all killed at this rate.' Baker jabbed at the call button once more, his anger bubbling through the calm façade he had built about himself.

'Lincruster, get that trigger-happy prick off the mini-gun, he's almost cut us in half twice.'

The heavy throated whine stuttered to a close as Hawk was pulled away from the weapon. Baker stared around him; the devastation wrought by his manic, unfettered rage was staggering. Derek's mind soaked it all in as his eyes scanned the scene ahead. The walls sagged and slumped as their weight tore them loose. Jagged misshapen holes rent by the sheer weight of the metal cast forth sent arcing shafts of watery noonday sun filtering through the dust as Derek's booted feet pulled him through the human mire beneath them.

Janet's trainer-covered feet sucked and slapped as she was pulled through the ankle high sea of dispossessed flesh. She kept her eyes fixed on the back of the automaton with her husband's face as it pulled her over the ventilated remains of someone she had only hours before been working alongside.

She staggered her hands, clawing at the back of her husband's vest as her feet became ensnared in the thick, rubbery coils of intestine and bowel. They wormed their way around her as they tried to pull her under, their coiled lengths reaching up from the abyss below. The roiling core of hot, steaming, foetid foulness pawed and grasped at her legs as they tugged at her skin in their urgent need for her living warmth.

Blood soaked into the heavy suede of her trainers, its viscous warmth sliding between her toes as she kicked and slid through what was left of patients and staff alike. The conglomerate of people no longer separated by the barriers that held apart the living, they twisted and boiled in the unbridled unification brought upon them by one man and the weapon he had wielded.

Janet's feet once more left the floor as Derek pushed her through the stairway door; Maria's plaintive wailing echoed off the flat, featureless walls. Janet turned her hands, smoothing the downy hair of her daughter's head as she looked back at the man she thought was her husband. His crouched form rifled through the crumpled ball of webbing and mesh; its matte-black form shuffled and twisted as he spoke.

'Patterson, take the package to the roof; I'll hold the door and work my way back.' He shoved Rook's now empty vest into the man's chest as he reloaded the few remaining speed loaders for his shotgun, the pouches on his hips weighing heavy with the weight of Rook's unspent ammunition. 'Take care of this next time; we can't afford to replace them or you.'

Rook grunted as the harness pressed painfully against his chest, the heavy plastic and steel buckles digging into his bruised flesh. Token slipped past, the girl still clutched tightly to his chest as his feet pounded against the concrete steps of the stairwell. The child's eyes locked onto Derek's so briefly that he barely registered the glance, her bright blue orbs bleeding into his mind as he watched them filter past one by one. His shoulder burnt with the exertion as he unloaded his weapon, sending a wall of swirling pellets into the stumbling enraged mass as they bore down on the doorway. The heat rushed towards him as the snarling, snapping wall of limbs and teeth hurled themselves forwards.

Baker stepped backwards, his feet kicking free the small wooden chock that had held the door open; his ears pricked as the rolling echo of metal on concrete wormed its way up to him. Dancing shadows slid over the walls around him, the dull yellow light of the setting sun streaming in through the still open door one floor below. Baker turned, his feet thumping against the plastic-edged steps as he threw himself up the twisting lengths of the staircase.

8

The Infected's breathing fell in long, smooth pulls as he slammed through the door, weapons trained on his sprinting form, their aim unwavering. As he headed for the helicopter, the hot and heavy impact to his chest was something he had never felt before. A snarling growl left him as he cursed, his voice hoarse as it left his mouth. Blood welled in his throat, pouring over his lips as he continued to run. An unintelligible stream of blood-flecked curses left his lips as his fingers closed over the body in his path. His fist rose, slamming into Baker's back; they staggered, Baker's feet skipping as they fell forwards, hands scrabbling at the gravel beneath them as he continued forwards on all fours.

The Infected bucked, his body going numb as another hot stream ran through him. Sparks flew through his eyes as a dozen more passed through his fragile form, sending sizzling bolts of white-hot energy lancing through his mind.

He watched, hands clawing at the grit-laden surface as Baker leapt forwards, his feet thumping against the sheet steel. A wall of darkness ate away at the edges of his vision before blessedly consuming him completely.

Baker turned his hand slipping into the Cordura loop besides the door. His eyes watched as the body fell, blood pooling beneath it. He stepped up from the skid of the rapidly rising helicopter as the roof was slowly consumed by the baying hoard of Infected. Weapons chattered beside him as they leapt, fingers clawing at the skids, curling over the smooth powder-coated surface before being torn free under their own weight. Their bodies tumbled free, falling back into the uncaring arms of gravity, its pull enveloping them completely as they hit the concrete below.

'Lincruster, let's get out of here. I have had enough of this place.'

Derek dropped into one of the canvas-webbed seats, the frame groaning slightly under the sudden weight. With slow infinite care,

Derek peeled the blood-drenched gloves from his hands, pulling them inside out as he crushed them within his fist.

Staring out the doorway at the crimson halo slowly seeping along the gravelled roof, Derek sent the heavy gore-laden lumps of Cordura and Kevlar spinning through the air, landing with a silent thump on the corpses of the Infected below.

Janet watched him from the corner of her eye, the lines of his face deepening as he sagged in the chair beneath him. Each deep line weighed heavily on her as she saw the strain on him for what it really was; slowly, she edged her hand forwards, her fingers tracing over his as she edged it ever forwards.

Without so much as a sideways glance, Derek curled his fingers through hers as he clasped her hand tightly within his. The look that ghosted within his eyes made her pause, her hand tightening within his as she edged herself closer. Janet moved against Derek as she let her head slowly fall sideways, her blonde hair tumbling in waves over his form.

She sat in complete silence, resting against his shoulder; her breathing was slow and even as the torrent of fatigue she had held at bay collapsed over her, drowning her in its all-encompassing blanket of muscle-draining weight. Derek's eyes flickered down to his daughter, her small, fragile form cradled against her mother's chest. Her pale blue eyes travelled over his worn and weary face, from the coarse, black curls of his bearded chin to the strained and tired ghosts behind his eyes.

Her hand reached out to him as he leant forward, the slim stubs of her fingers trailing their way through his beard as Janet sat up slightly; her fingers twisted and wound their way through the briar that clung to his skin, the heavy, coarse hairs making her eyes widen slightly at the next sensation. Derek smiled slightly as he watched her face fill with an inquisitive light as he let her hands explore this newfound thing before her.

Lifting his daughter from Janet's diminishing sleep-soaked grasp, he set her gently in the crook of his arm as she continued to tug and grasp at the mane of coarse black hair surrounding his lower jaw.

9
May 2013
Downtime

Colinson stared at Derek, the lines in his friend's face deep and dark, fatigue stitching itself across the field commander's visage like threads through a tapestry.

'I'm putting teams one through three on leave; four will take point with drone support elevated to level-four containment protocol. Kweku is heading up the overhaul of all the quadro-copter systems and the mini quads.'

Derek stayed mute, his mind blank as he fought to keep himself upright.

Colinson's level gaze left little room for negotiation; Derek simply nodded and made a weary and bedraggled march from David's office.

****

Heat scalded his skin; flakes of dead skin swirled in the water beneath him as he scraped at his reddening hide. The coarse weave of the double-sided sponge scraped away the layers of filth that coated the slowly scorching flesh. He ran the coarse lump of lifeless sea sponge over the dirt-encrusted slab of his abdomen, watching as the water swirled around his feet. Lumps of clotted blood fell as he leant forwards, his forearms pressing against the wall. The chill of the tiles bit into him as he let the water pound down upon him.

Tears burnt as he screwed his eyes shut, willing the images away but still they danced, piercing all in their wake as they cackled and tumbled across his mind. The screams of the dead and dying filled his mind as images of embittered souls poisoned beyond all recognition tore their fellow man limb from limb, bathing in their blood as they set upon them in a bid to satiate their lust for food.

Baker looked down at his closed fists, nails biting into his palm as he balled his hands ever tighter. He grunted in pain-fused anger, smashing the flats of his fists against the solid, unyielding wall in front of him. He beat his fists against it again and again, the lifeless slab of concrete and tiles reverberating with each violent blow.

Derek slumped, the pain sapping the life from his mind as it slowly began to eat away at the daemons that tormented him, their laughter fading as the pain flooded through him.

Baker's mind dropped into a silent vacuous well as two slim arms ensnared him, their bands of warmth sliding over the goose-plucked flesh of his body as a pair of pert breasts pressed against his back.

The water ran between them, sliding along their skin gently. She pulled him closer to her; Janet slowly caressed his slick glowing skin, slim petite hands running over Derek's chest as she leant her head against his back. The thumping of her soulmate's heart filled her as she drank in his warmth.

Baker turned, his hands sliding over her shoulders as she looked up at him. Water-drenched trails of her hair clung to his heat-flushed skin. As his hands grazed over her arms, Baker felt his heart flutter, his soul relishing the feel of her tender skin beneath the calloused and torn skin of his palms.

Slowly, with a tenderness he rarely showed, Derek traced his lips over hers. His eyes slid closed, her scent and taste filling all as he gently traced his fingers along her spine. His touch left a glowing trail of fire that spread through her, filling Janet with an irrepressible urge as Derek cupped her firm buttocks, lifting her from the tiled floor.

Janet's legs closed round him as she threw her weight against the warm pillar of strength clasped so closely to her loins. Her lips closed over his as they fell against the smooth, cold marble. Fevered tongues danced, their embrace all consuming, ever tightening as they held each other. Derek's fingers traced the crease of her backside as he felt himself grow, the warmth of her sex hot against his stomach as she ground herself against him.

The searing heat of her inner core seeped forth as she bosomed against him, her breathing drawing deep as she clutched at his flesh.

Breaking away, Baker traced a path down her neck, his teeth nipping at her skin as they joined; frantic panting filled the room as he felt Janet engulf him, her sex swallowing him whole as she tossed her head back.

Sparkling pearls of dancing light flew from her hair as Janet raised her pleasure-soaked face to the falling wall of water, heat bouncing over her closed eyelids as she felt Derek move within.

Her mouth opened, a strangled gasp leaving her as Derek lowered his mouth, the soft pink nub of her nipple caught between his lips as he thrust into her. His teeth tugged at the sensitive bud as he pushed himself ever deeper into Janet's wet, silken folds. She writhed as he moved within her, her core igniting as she felt Derek slip ever further into her very being.

Janet felt his fingers dig into the supple flesh of her buttocks as he speared into her. Janet gripped him, completely drawing him in as she tensed, squeezing his tender rod as he filled her once more.

Her legs slipped from around his waist as he released, her hands splayed against the wall as she turned. Janet's slim, toned legs spread as he entered her once more, her head dropped as she gasped, her voice lost in the deluge of pleasure as her breath heaved with every thrust. Derek clasped her hips in his hands, her buttocks slapping against him as he drove forth once more, driving himself deep into her embracing warmth.

The sound of their wet bodies colliding filled the space entirely. She screamed as Derek thrust forwards, driving himself into her entirely, his throbbing member delving deeper into her all-encompassing core. A growl slipped from deep within his throat as

96

he drove into her, his body coiled like a spring, his buttocks tensing as his body burned with desire.

Janet shuddered in her climax, her silken folds clasping Derek's pulsing rod as her back arched, driving him over the edge. The growl pouring from him turned into a guttural roar as he released, sending his spreading warmth deep into her.

They sank to the floor, his member still encased in her warmth as they lay entwined. She slid off of him, her body rolling over the cold tiles as she curled in closer, resting her head against his chest as he kissed her wet hair.

'I love you, you know that.'

She nodded, strands of her flaxen hair clinging to his skin as she pulled him close, her emerald eyes locking with his as she gently kissed him. She rolled away from him, rising from the cold, water-drenched floor. A soft squeak flirted with his ears as he watched her slip slightly, his body tensing as he readied to catch her. Her backside swayed in front of him as she walked towards the misted glass panel door. She glanced over her shoulder, a mischievous sparkle in her eyes as she winked at him before disappearing through the swirling wall of steam.

He watched her go as he pushed himself into a sitting position, raising his face to the wall of water as it beat down upon him. He opened his mouth, feeling the hot droplets strike his tongue and teeth. His head dropped back against the tiles with a clunk, the mild flare of discomfort making him shiver. He pushed himself up from the floor as he spat out the lukewarm water. Running a hand through the briar that covered his lower jaw, he couldn't help but grin; even after the events of the previous twelve hours, she had still found it within her.

A chuckle left him as he reached for a towel; a thought striking him as it slithered across his mind. The images of a much younger woman clasped around his waist as they made love for the first time in the locker room of his old secondary school, the push button showers dancing to their rhythm as they let themselves drift on the currents of their adolescent desires.

Gemma Robinson. A smile tweaked Derek's lips. She always was a bit more outgoing than the others at that school were. Shaking his head, he wrapped the towel around his waist and stepped from the bathroom.

Janet glanced up from the bed, her nubile body glistening with the silver glaze cast over her as moonlight streamed through the open window. She shivered as the soft kiss of the warm spring winds washed over her; a smile curled her lips as she crooked a finger, beckoning Derek to her. Fire danced in his eyes as he took in the winsome sight that lay upon his bed, the curves of her lithe form drawing him in as the towel fell from about his waist.

He crawled across the satin sheets as he made his way to her. Janet's eyes widened as she watched him, the muscles bunching and curling as he crept like a cat across her body. Her eyes traced every contour as she let her fingers wander across his sculpted form. She felt the pull of his chiselled body as she slid her hands down his back. Digging her nails into the firm flesh of his thighs, she smiled as he let out a short surprised gasp.

As their lips met once more, the spell was shattered as red lights danced over the monitor on the bedside cabinet, the plaintive wailing of their child cast asunder any chance of once more uniting as a couple.

Derek sank to the bed with a soft mirth-laced sigh. 'I guess twice was too much to ask for.' Janet traced her index finger over his abdomen, flicking the end of his diminishing erection, making him jump as she lifted her hand away.

'It's nice to know you can still stand ready when called though. I was beginning to think I would have to throw grenades at you for the rest of my life, just to get some attention.'

Derek snorted, laughter bubbling up from his stomach as he

98

pulled on a pair of jockey shorts, the form-fitting boxers leaving little to the imagination.

'You get comfortable while I see what our darling bundle of joy wants.'

Derek moved towards the door; Janet watched his backside as she stretched, her toes curling as she let her body work itself loose. Derek watched her from the corner of his eye as she relaxed into the memory foam mattress, her nude form silhouetted against the light of the moon.

'Damn, I am lucky.'

His softly muttered comment drifted through the room as the door whispered shut. Janet smiled as she muttered a lilting reply to herself, sinking deeper into the sheets.

Derek lifted Maria from the cot, her tear-stained face flushed beetroot red as she continued to cry. Cradling her against his shoulder, he bounced slightly on the balls of his feet as he softly whispered, trying to calm his fretful daughter. Derek's mind cycled through all the possibilities as he continued to move about the small room, his fingers stroking the crown of her head as she continued to cry. Discarding one problem after another, his nose twitched, the scent of warm excrement pervading everything as he felt the heat radiate through his hand.

'Ah, should have really checked there first, hey sweetie?'

Padding across the room, he laid her down on the high-sided table, the pop studs on her baby grow snapping open as he pulled with one hand. Dropping his right to the drawer next to his hip, he pulled out a bottle of talcum powder and a clean nappy as he held Maria's legs up. With smooth practised movements, he discarded the soiled nappy, wrinkling his nose at the smell as he dropped it into the bin by his foot. The wipes were cold and damp to the touch as he lifted her bottom slightly, wiping away the dark brown smear covering her pink cheeks.

'How can one baby produce so much crap? What does your mother feed you when I ain't here?'

Maria wriggled at the sound of her father's voice, her still pink-tinged face crinkling as she yawned, the reason for her crying already forgotten as she gazed at the face above her. A soft burbling gurgle left her as she felt herself move. With a tender, practised motion, he wiped her clean, the soiled and stained wipes joining the nappy at the bottom of the bin as he slid the fresh nappy into place. A small white mist enveloped her nether regions as Derek peppered her bum and legs with a dusting of talcum powder, a soft sneeze drifting up from his daughter as she wrinkled her nose.

Lifting his child free from the confines of the table, he carried her drowsy, sleep-limp form to the cot; setting her down gently, the brush of his lips across her forehead made her stir as he whispered a soft goodnight. As he stood once more, he flicked his hand across the mobile perched over her, setting the mass of floating cartoon animals spinning as the lullaby filled the room.

The door to his bedroom clicked shut, the silent soft-close hinges dampening the sound to a dull clunk as the flat panel door connected with the frame. Stripping his boxers off, Derek tossed them onto the stool in front of Janet's vanity table and slid beneath the covers. A slightly irked smile tweaked his lips as he gazed at the softly snoring form of his wife, her legs tucked up as she curled into the duvet, pulling it tight around her as she slept. Derek slid into the bed, his arm snaking its way over Janet's soft, flat stomach, the rippled reminder of their daughter's recent entry into the world etched into her skin. His fingers traced the lines radiating over her sides, the soft yet jagged lines covering her like the claws of a tiger.

Laying his head down, he kissed her shoulder before closing his eyes and edging slowly into a fitful sleep.

Monmouthshire
Wales

The ground swallowed him whole as he dropped, the slick walls around him flashing past in a blur of bouncing torch light, the dazzling display of stroboscopic light making his stomach jerk slightly.

'I cannot believe you talked me into this.'

A deep rolling chuckle echoed up from below him as he dropped to the floor with a *thunk*, his feet shooting from under him, showering the other with a spray of ice-cold water as they laughed.

A sharp groan issued forth as his coccyx collided with a ridge of wet granite. The cave stretched, the hollow black maw drinking in the beam of his helmet-mounted torch as he gazed from one side to the next. His footsteps echoed around them as they ventured further into the twisting cave system.

'Okay, huni, you got your locator on?'

She stared at him, the pale yellow glowing halo of light making her squint as she listened to his reply echo off the walls around them. His words reverberated through the air until they chorused through the air, filling the silent cavern with a rolling wall of babbling voices; their formless words making her skin tingle as she looked about her.

His voice held a slight tremor as he replied, the words clipped and quick as she took his hand and pulled him further into the cave. A small smile slipped across her features as she led him through the slowly encroaching maze of tunnels, all the while the trembling in his hand and voice grew.

'Alexander Richards, you're not scared, are you?'

A flicker of pride-stung annoyance crossed his features as he pulled his hand away a little too sharply, leaving Susan more than a little perturbed. His eye caught the look as it skated through hers, the mixed pot of anger and worry, coupled with the slighted hurt of a lover on the cusp of scorn.

Pushing his male pride aside, Alex sat his backside into the soupy mess of silt and ice water in the bottom of the small cavern.

'Truthfully, more than a little. I don't do tight spaces very well. I have had ways of dealing with it. But this… it's a little more than I am used to.'

She looked at him, her head cocked slightly to one side as he spoke. The look on her face was a mix of annoyance and empathy. She reached out a hand and pulled him to his feet, the water pattering to the floor as it slid from the seat of his heavy reinforced caving suit, the coarse fabric grating slightly against his skin.

'Do you want to head back?'

His face held a dark look of determination as he squeezed her hand slightly, the simple act of assurance and comfort saying infinitesimally more than words ever could. Nodding, Susan turned, letting his hand fall from her grip as they pushed on. Their lights danced over the walls, the shimmering pools of white glazing over the crevices and crags as they moved on in the system.

'So tell me, wonder woman, how does a desk jockey go from punching a keyboard all day to sliding through the cracks and crevices of nature's stone innards?'

Richard's eyebrows rose as she simply shrugged, her reply short and tart on her tongue.

'Why do you have a job that involves, guns, bombs, and making things explode?'

Alex smirked, stepping forwards and running his hand over her

102

backside as they neared the connecting tunnel. Crouching low, he swallowed slightly, his mouth as dry as sandpaper; he fell to his hands and knees and began to crawl.

'That is a very good question. I couldn't stand them as a kid—too noisy and cumbersome, but I guess once you try something and find you're good at it, well you can't see yourself doing anything else.'

A soft chuckle echoed off the walls as he realised just what Susan had done, turning his own question against him and finding her answer in him.

10

Bude, North Cornwall
Cory Farm, Stanbury Cottage

The soft crunch of gravel filled their senses, the warm scent of
powdered stone and warm soil soaking their minds as they made
their way to the small beachside cabin. The low veranda sat warm
and enticing as they made their way forwards. The hushed almost
scrupulous movements of the waiting staff was the only thing to
break the silence as he hurried ahead of them, their cases held in his
hands as he scampered up the small ramp and to the door.

Stopping at the foot of the non-slip ramp, he smiled; the soft
tugging of his lips at the corners of his mouth made his eyes twinkle
as she stared up at him. The vibrant hue of her eyes made him feel
like a small child as she brushed her hand over his. Leaning down,
he cast a soft, fleeting kiss over her cheek. Turning, he made his way
back to the car and the two black plastic crates perched on the back
seat. They sat heavy in his hands as he carried them to the cabin, his
booted feet thumping against the slate tiles of the veranda as she
turned, her chair hissing slightly as it skimmed against the sand
under the wheels.

The sparkle in her eyes made him pause; a gentle smile played
over his face as she turned away. The staff member held the door
open for her as she rolled on into the spacious interior. Nodding his
thanks, he set the cases down on the table as the young man handed
her the door keys and bade them goodbye.

'Not a bad place; fairly squared away, but they could have dusted.'

Davies ran a finger over the fireplace's mantel as he turned back
to the low-lying coffee table. He sat, simply staring at the two black
cases as the clock over the fireplace ticked away, filling the slowly
dimming silence; the only other sounds around him were the
bubbling of boiling water and the soft humming of his companion.

The dull rumble of rubber over wood made him look up, her slim raven-haired form gliding towards him as she balanced a tray on her lap, the cups clinking together gently as she pushed herself along.

Anna's lilting accent made him smile; try as he did to hide it from her, it kept melting into his features, pulling the world-weary scowl from his face. She lifted the tray from her lap as he pushed the two black boxes aside, sliding her chair closer to the low-slung settee. She swung, suspending her weight on her hands as she shifted herself onto the small sofa. She curled her body into his after adjusting her position on the soft feather-filled cushions. He brushed his fingers against hers as she snapped the locks open on the cases.

The spring-loaded hinges pushed the lid back with a heavy clunk as it hit the top of the table. They both held a mild almost sarcastic grin as they gazed upon the black plastic crate's contents. The muted grey coveralls gazed up at them, the minute network of squares covering its rip-stop surface. She lifted the suit from its resting place, the heavy slash-proof fabric grating against her fingertips as she let it drape over her lap.

'Before you ask, babe, it is the same suit we wear, minus the impact resistant plates and reinforced joints; also the integrated water bladder in the back is missing, and if you look at the cuffs or neck, they aren't sealed from fluids.'

It fell from her grip, crumpling into her lap as she reached into box once more. The heavy square block sat in her palm as she tested its weight, her hand bobbing in the air slightly as she looked at it. The loosely woven loop of cord batting against the back of her hand, the steel clasp cool against the pinched skin of her wrist.

'G.P.S personal alarm, not too dissimilar to the Breitling watch developed for pilots, although it's not a one-use system and can send out a directional wall of disorienting sound by pressing the rubberised stud on the side there.'

Setting the alarm on the table next to the case, she reached in once more, lifting her hand out and setting aside the elasticated cloth mask and heavy-duty latex gloves that were in a small press-lock bag. She pulled free the inch-thick book that sat in the base of the box, its heavy binding and card cover stencilled with the words *Emergency Preparedness Manual*. She laughed at the moniker, its white lettering staring at her as she flipped through it.

'At least they paid attention to my reports, although they skimmed over a few of the symptoms, including the degree of violence they can display.'

He nodded as he watched her set everything back into the case, folding the coveralls neatly and precisely as the fabric hissed over her skin as she leant forwards. She set the folded bundle into its squat container. Turning to face him, she shrugged, her slim shoulder slipping through the neckline of the light-green, silk blouse she wore.

'Well, I can't say it's particularly impressive and it's less than I would have hoped they would send out, but it's something. I just hope it makes people aware of the seriousness of the calamity we are facing.

'It's only going to get worse from here on out; more and more cases are leaking out of China and Africa. Even the US has started to report cases of boats breaking through the interdiction cordon in place.'

A quizzical look passed over her face as she snapped the locks back into place, the lid popping into place with a soft thump. 'John, why do you stay with me?'

His face held a mixture of shock and questioning surprise. He slumped back into the sofa, running a hand over his shaven head, the stubble of his once black locks grating against his palm.

A soft sardonic chuckle flitted from his lips as she watched him intently.

'You're asking me this now, Anna? We have been together for just under a year and you're asking me that now?'

She held his stare, her gaze steady as he watched her face for any sign of a clue that she was joking. His heart dropped when none appeared.

'You're serious, aren't you? You can't understand why I have stayed with you.'

Again, she stayed mute, watching his face as he spoke. A sharp shard of pain lanced through his eyes, her heart blanching as she watched it ricochet through him, carving out chunks of his soul, but as much as it hurt, she had to know.

'It's simple; I love you, wheelchair and all. I couldn't care less about sex. It's not why I fell in love with you and it's not why I am here now.'

She never wavered as she watched his face, her hands trembling slightly as she held them clenched in her lap.

'I stayed with you because you... well... honestly you are unlike any other woman I have ever met. I look at you and I see the strongest person I have ever known. Yes, I have faced down all that humanity can conjure up—from religious zealots, despot, and crazed psychopaths and right through to plague-Infected civilians trying to chew my heart out of my arse. But, I look at you and know that if I were like you, bound to a set of wheels for the rest of my life, I couldn't do it; I would not be able to reconcile with it. That is what has kept me here. You give me the strength to face the day and carry on doing what I do, Anna.'

She didn't say a word; mute and unflinching, she reached out and clasped the back of his head, pulling him to her. She kissed him. It was heavy, laden with a longing she could barely contain, softly brushing her tongue over his slowly parting lips as he began to respond.

Pulling away, she looked into his eyes, her breathing heavy, his

107

dark green eyes boring into her as she smiled softly.

'I love you too.'

Hainault Forest Country Park
Hainault, Essex

Solomon held the lead in his hand as he watched Angel's slightly limping form bound over the rutted ground, the grass catching at her fur as she chased after the neon-pink ball he had just thrown.

A memory tickled at him as he watched her leap over the deep groove carved into the soft, loamy soil. Sweat trickled down his neck as he stood there, the hot light of the midday sun making his brow crinkle under the battered baseball cap he wore. He cuffed the sweat away from his eyes as he held out his hand, her muzzle pushing against his palm as she dropped the saliva-dampened ball.

Heaving it over arm, he watched it soar through the air, the sun's glare blinding him slightly as he lost sight of it and Angel as she took off in pursuit. His mind swirled slightly as he watched her return, the limp slightly more pronounced as she drew closer. Dropping onto his backside, Kingsley pulled out a collapsible bowl and a bottle of water. He let the clear liquid fall from the neck, landing with a shimmering splash in the bottom of Angel's bowl.

His hand ruffled the fur on her neck as she drank, his mind drifting back to the hot, dry dust-laden road where she had truly lived up to her name.

Northern Afghanistan
Route Irish

Kingsley stood, his hand holding the short leather-bound rope that tethered him to Angel; she sat patiently waiting for her command as Kingsley scanned the road ahead. The heavy pockmarks in the road standing prominent, the scorched remains of old vehicles and pieces of kit marking their hideous nature.

Kneeling, he ruffled the back of her neck, her ears flopping gently against his hand as he unclipped the shorter lead from around her neck. His SA80 hung by his side as Jenkins stood, watching the area around them.

'Go on, girl, seek.'

Her head dropped to the floor as the heavy-gauge webbing lead trailed along behind, its gently flopping length kicking up small clouds of dry, brown dust as she diligently sought out the IED.

A soft snuffling huff echoed from the still heat-laden air as she stopped. Her ears perked up as she pointed at the ground, its featureless surface showing little of interest, and yet there she stayed, her tail rigid as she stared with her nose and muzzle only millimetres from the cracked and barren soil.

'Good girl. Who's my girl, then? Show me.'

Slowly and with infinitesimal care, he traced Angel's path as she lay down on her stomach, paws forwards. She turned her head with a soft low growl, calling Kingsley on.

'Jenkins, call it in.'

Without looking back at his squad mate, Kingsley knelt, his hand softly ruffling the back of Angel's neck.

'Good girl; who's my good girl... such a good girl. Come on girl, let's move, slowly.'

Angel slowly pushed herself to her feet. She stepped backwards to Kingsley's feet, her paws padding through her own footprints as she edged away from her find. A small red flag fluttered in the breeze. Leaning down, Kingsley gently pressed the metal rod into the dirt just in front of Angel as she stood up.

Easing back, Kingsley and Angel edged away from the fluttering red triangle. The hairs on the back of Kingsley's neck rose as a muffled beeping filled the air. He turned, his eyes meeting Jenkins' as the ground erupted besides them. Angel yelped; she was thrown sideways, her body thumping into the road, kicking up a cloud of powdered dust and stones while Jenkins dove behind the skeleton of an old Russian truck.

Kingsley lay, his body limp. Blood leaked steadily from his nose and left ear and the torn skin along the left side of his face was caked with grit and dirt.

Jenkins screamed into his radio as Angel stirred and rolled unsteadily to her feet. Her front left leg pulled tight to her breast as she limped towards Kingsley's motionless form.

Her nose nudged at his shoulder, a keening whine leaving her as she licked at his bloody cheek. She gently nipped at his cheek, urging him to respond. Clamping her teeth around the shoulder strap of his vest, she began to pull. A deep growl of urgency left her as she dragged Kingsley across the dust-laden road.

A smeared trail of blood marked her path as she pulled and tugged at Kingsley's unconscious form. Scrub brush plucked and scraped at her haunches as she backed towards the far side of the road; her vest shifted as she twisted her body, her leg still pulled tight as blood matted her glossy, straw-coloured coat.

The stencilled halo on her side was streaked with dust and blood as she flopped to the ground, her muzzle resting in the crook of Kingsley's neck.

****

Kingsley toyed with the small pockmarks on the side of his face as he called out to Angel, the fading memory making his jaw ache.

'Come on, girl; let's go home.'

Angel's answering bark made him grin as she trotted back to his side, the twisted streak of discoloured fur marring her leg. He lovingly tousled the fur on the top of her head as she licked at his hand, her tail thumping the floor. He knelt and clipped the lead onto her harness, the halo stencilled on its side, streaked a russet brown.

She leapt with the agility of a dog half her age, her claws digging into the seat of Kingsley's Land Rover. She pawed slightly at the blanket covering the front passenger seat before settling in, her head resting on her front paws. Kingsley once more ran a hand lovingly over her head as he settled into his seat and made the hour-long journey home.

London, South Kensington

Hawk stared into his pint glass as the music throbbed around him, the table tacky to the touch as he clasped the glass in both hands, his weight braced on both forearms.

He gazed at the bubbling amber liquid, his mind lost in a vacuum of self-loathing and pain. Sitting back in his chair, he lifted the glass to his lips and drank. Rivulets of the ice-cold liquid ran down either side of his chin, soaking into the skin-tight cotton t-shirt he wore.

Slamming the empty glass onto the table, he motioned. The glass disappeared as a slim waif of a woman lifted it onto the tray balanced on her hand. Turning, he looked at her; her chestnut brown hair spilled out around her face, seemingly in a bid to escape the loosely woven, woollen hat perched on her head.

Her hazel eyes questioned him as he sat staring at her. Her slim form wrapped in a form-fitting band t-shirt and jeans that left very little to the imagination. His gaze lingered on her as she cocked one hip to the side with a sigh.

'What?'

Her Scottish lilt drew his gaze upwards, over her sparingly endowed chest to the eyes that held little in the way of interest in him or his leering gaze.

Turning with a slightly disgusted snort, he replied. His tone was curt and left little in the way of compromise as he leant on the table again, his eyes lost in his own mind.

'Same again and keep them coming.'

'Drinking to forget?'

He snorted as he watched her move off, her question lingering in his mind as he turned back to the table again, speaking softly to himself.

'Something like that.'

The drinks flowed across his table, their cold, slightly bitter forms drowning the images that threatened to flood his mind. The girl never did bother taking the empty glasses back after their first encounter, and John never paid it any heed as he drained his ninth glass, setting it with a slight waver amongst the ever-growing pile in front of him.

Watching with a detached interest, the barman nudged her, nodding his head in Stabbler's direction. A smirk crossed her features as she pulled a fresh pint and made the short journey to his table.

'Had enough yet, or can you still remember your own name?'

She set the glass in front of him and folded her arms across her chest, a look of scorn and mild pity dancing in her eyes as he cast his gaze towards her.

'No, yes, and I told you to keep them coming.'

Draining the glass in front of her, he let it drop to the table top, its echoing clatter making her jump slightly as it clanged against the others cluttering the now lager slick surface.

'Pig.'

Turning, she walked back to the bar. Her muttered comment flirted with Stabbler's hearing as he turned back to his pit of sorrow and self-loathing. His soul sank as the wall-mounted digital jukebox began to play, its slim plastic form shuffling through its files in a bid to sink Stabbler even deeper into the pit he was vainly trying to claw his way free of. He turned and glared at the box on the wall. The need to sling one of his empty vessels of loathing at it to silence its soul-wrenching wails was almost too much to bear.

His hand closed around the glass until it creaked in his hand, its strained protestations falling short of his ears. The low whine of constricting glass rose the more he squeezed. With an almost audible cry of relief, it was plucked from his grip as the girl returned and set it onto the tray she carried. Her eyes bore into his, her uncaring gaze making his soul wilt all the more.

'Boss says you're cut off; he wants you to pay up and move on, and you're making the other customers uneasy.'

Hawk glanced around him, the cautious stares of those about him only just registering; a snort of derision left him as he tossed seven fifty-pound notes on the table.

'Hey, that is way too much.'

Hawk turned, lifting the last glass from the table, testing its weight in his hand. 'It's towards the repairs.'

Her eyes narrowed as she watched him. A question bubbling in her mind. Before she could stop herself, she heard the words tripping from her lips. 'What repairs?'

With a degree of force that would have made an English fast bowler proud, he heaved the glass at the Jukebox and watched as the screen shattered. Turning, he grabbed his coat from the back of his chair and walked calmly to the door. The bouncer there moved to block his exit, his burly frame almost filling the doorway. Hawk smirked, stepped sideways, and delivered a heavy boot to the side of the man's knee.

The crunch of cartilage made the girl almost drop the tray as she watched the doorman crumble, his hands wrapped around his shattered knee as he screamed.

The other doorman watched as his mate fell, his high-pitched almost girlish screams filling his ears. With clawed hands stretching forwards, he lunged at Hawk. Stabbler ducked, his mind slowly closing in on itself as the alcohol began to seep through him, slowly erasing any trace of the soldier he once was.

A vicious downwards punch sent the bouncer face first into the stained and pitted planks of the floor. Lifting his foot, Hawk sent the toe of his boot into the side of the man's head. One of the patrons, acting on the alcohol-fuelled courage flowing through him, flew at Hawk. A guttural roar left his mouth as he spun, sending his boot into the patron's face. Teeth and blood splattered the wall as the man dropped to the floor, his mouth a mass of shattered teeth and crushed gums.

'Come on, you bunch of cunts. Who wants it? Huh? Come on; fucking do it.'

A flash of blue filled the pub as cars squealed to a halt outside. Two officers piled in through the door as Hawk continued to scream obscenities. He dropped low, his hand flying forward as he drove his hand into the solar plexus of the closest police officer. A metallic clicking was his only warning as the gasping officer's partner drew her baton and sent it screaming through the air towards Hawk's legs. Turning his hip, he felt the blow glance down his leg, a shock of white flared in his mind as the pain lanced through him.

Snapping his hand down, he grasped the end of the baton and pulled; the female constable staggered forwards as she was wrenched over her own feet. He followed round, driving a punch into her exposed back, sending her into the planked floor as she crumpled, hitting it with a thud.

Her eyes widened as she hit the floor. Rolling onto her back, she dragged the Taser from its holster and in one movement, aimed and fired, sending the barbs singing into Hawk's stomach. As the Taser clicked, he went rigid, dropping to the floor with a heavy *thunk* as his body convulsed.

11
Southwest London

The phone echoed through the room, its warbling ringing filling the small, fifth-floor flat. His hair sat in a dishevelled mess atop his head as he padded towards the wall-mounted phone. Lifting the phone receiver from its cradle, he spoke briskly, his words short and sharp as he felt the cool plastic meet he his sleep-heated skin.

'Colinson, speak.'

A muted curse left him as he listened to the caller, the voice monotone and bored as it drifted through his ear, chasing away any vestige of sleep's lulling haze.

A deep almost mournful sigh left him as he replied cutting off the speaker. 'Very well, I will be down to collect him at once. Please see to it he is left shackled. Thank you.'

Slamming the handset back onto the cradle, he cursed once more and walked back to his bedroom. Dragging a plain shirt from the rail in his cupboard, he turned and dropped to the bed, fishing in his bedside cabinet for a pair of socks. The door to his flat clicked shut as Colinson shrugged his shoulder, settling the lightweight jacket he wore into a more comfortable position. Then with a shake of his head, he turned and hurriedly descended the staircase.

****

Colinson's car slid to a stop outside. The two RMP officers were already waiting outside as he stepped towards them, both men saluting as he walked past. He didn't bother returning the formality as he strode up to the duty officer and slapped his identity card on the Formica top.

She glanced up from the screen and nodded, already fully aware of who he was. She pressed the button next to her keyboard and let him through, the reinforced steel door jumping slightly as its magnetic lock disengaged.

The two RMP officers followed closely on his heels, the cries of the people trapped behind the heavy doors of the cells around him echoed down the hallway. The discordant, garbled cries of one man made him smirk as the man pounded on his cell door, his voice so slurred it was hard to distinguish any cogent words from his diatribe as he ranted and raved.

A pool of urine seeped across the floor as an officer forced open a cell door. The man inside sent a steaming trail of yellow piss over the officer's booted feet as he waved his semi-engorged member at the young constable.

His drunken cackling rolled over the three men as they marched onwards; the cadre of police encircled Hawk's cell as they approached.

The clang of steel-on-steel echoed back at them as the officers opened the cell door for the two Royal Military Police officers. Their boots thumped against the floor as they pulled Hawk to his feet, the dark stain on the front of his trousers expanding slightly as he lost control over himself.

'You have fucked up royally this time, Stabbler. Christ knows what Baker will say when he hears of this; he vouched for you, said you were on the wagon—and this is how you repay him!'

Blearily, he looked up, a line of drool glistening as he stared at Colinson. A smirk covered his features, a dim flicker of intelligence glowing inside his alcohol-addled mind.

'Hello there, sir. Awe shit, sir, they made me piss myself. Bloody piggies made me piss all over myself, sir.'

His words tumbled out in a saliva-drenched blurt as he tried to salute, the handcuffs on his wrists making the movement even more clumsy than it already was. As he jerked his arms, one limp hand slapped him in the face making him stare at it in confusion.

'Get this piece of shit out of here; I will deal with him when we get back to base.'

Hawk's head dipped as he passed out again. With their arms secured through his, the two RMPs dragged him from the cell and down the hall, his feet squeaking slightly on the floor.

'I hope your officers are both fine.'

The station chief nodded. 'Nothing but bruises and wounded pride. Constable Renley was quick on the draw with him, otherwise things could have been a touch different. So, what happens with him now?'

Colinson sighed as he watched the slowly disappearing form of the two officers as they towed Hawks between them.

'We get him back, get him sober, and go from there; no point administering punishment if he is too damned pissed to remember it.' The station chief snorted slightly. 'Well, good luck, Captain. Sorry we couldn't meet under better circumstances.'

Colinson nodded as he shook hands with the man. Then turning on his heels, he marched quickly after the three men.

Broadhead Barracks

'He fucking did what?' Baker's rage fell in a torrent as it spilled forth, the walls of his mind crumbling under the weight.

'Left one of the doormen in hospital; the other was knocked cold and revived on site by the paramedics. The two responding officers managed to take him down. He did do some damage before they dropped him; one was left with bruised ribs and the other a split chin from him slamming her into the floor; although, she did manage to get off a shot from her Taser, so I guess it wasn't a total whitewash.'

Baker clutched at the arms of the chair he dropped into, his body sagging as he stared back at Colinson. Thoughts danced in his head as he ran through the problems Hawk and his giant can of worms had created.

'So, what's this going to cost us?'

His singular uttered sentence caught Colinson off guard, the words setting his mind whirling as he ran through the possible implications. He was silent for several seconds as he let his mind sift through the cost of keeping the situation in house and out of the public eye.

'Not a vast amount; I would need a few hours to run the numbers, but it shouldn't put too much of a dent in our slush fund.'

Baker nodded as he leant forwards, his elbows propped on his thighs as he racked his brains for a suitable punishment detail. A small glimmer of light echoed in his eyes as he settled on a near perfect solution.

'We need to set this as a burnout option, but we cannot lose Stabbler; he is too much of an effective operative. We've lost a lot of sway recently with the Americans because of Stabbler's and Richards' defection and the rapidly disintegrating communications network there. Do we still have that shipment coming in from the ROF?'

Colinson shifted his feet from the top of his desk, the screen of his computer wobbling slightly as his desk juddered; tapping at his keyboard, he brought up the shipment manifests for the next three weeks.

'Yep, Royal Ordnance due in... tomorrow, as it happens. Four trucks loaded with small calibre munitions and replacement plates for our third generation ballistics armour, and it looks like the prototype wing-packs from the Japanese have also made it in before the border lockdown; that should make the R.R.T boys happy. Hang on a second.'

Derek looked up, his grin faltering as he saw the concerned look on Colinson's face.

'What's wrong?'

Colinson looked up, his face a mixed mask of questioning worry and curiosity.

'The wing-pack shipment—it's for fifty prototype suits. The R.R.T only has, at best, half a dozen men.'

Baker nodded, watching Colinson's face as it slowly sank in.

'Why wasn't I told?'

Baker smirked, his eyes dancing with mirth as he began to speak.

'Oh, I'm sorry; did you not earlier this week request I make all data transfers and requests through secure email and not hard copy packets? Check your inbox.'

Colinson once more tapped at his keyboard, opening the internal mail client and pulling out the private folder marked for internal orders and transfers. His eyes danced as the names and combat data on the sixty potential recruits scrolled up the screen.

Nodding, he printed out the pages and set them in a pile in the centre of his desk.

'Well, my face is red; when do they get here?'

Baker smirked again as he stood and pushed the chair flush to the wall again.

'In about ten minutes, and the wing-packs came in early. Woodwrow has been toying with those for the last three days or so; the guy's nuttier than I am. I wouldn't go near one of those things, let alone ride it. Also, bud, before I get going, check for a communication CCed via me from Davies; it's about the G36c and the Diemaco.'

Colinson nodded as he watched Derek turn and move to the door. David's eyes tracked Baker as he stopped in the doorway.

Baker nodded as David turned his gaze back to the pages in front of him, shifting them in his hands as he scanned them line by line.

'Well, I've got a detail to prepare and a bollocking to dish out. Check out that email; it's a good notion on John's part and well worth looking into. Catch you later, mate.'

Colinson waved a hand as he studied the dossiers in more detail, only looking up when he heard the door click shut.

****

Baker watched as Woodwrow stood in front of the sixty recruits, their formations looser than he would have liked and their clothes a mix of issued kit and civilian dress, which made him wince at the indecisive nature it showed in some of the men.

His eyes scanned the motley assortment of soldiers; the trepidation and eager energy flowed off them as they stood in the pale, watery sunlight that was forcing its way through the heavy layer of clouds. Baker looked up as a shadow passed over him, the thick nebulous body of water vapour and ice passed across the thin ball of yellow water that had replaced the sun.

Shaking his head, he pushed his beret back into position, stood, and moved off towards his vehicle, the throaty puttering of its engine drifting across the open expanse of the parade ground.

Hunching low, Derek ducked as he pulled the door open, the heat kicking him full in the face as he stared at his wife curled in the passenger seat, her bare feet resting either side of the heater.

She glanced up as the cold spring wind nipped at her bare toes, whipping away the heat almost as soon as Derek touched the door handle. She turned, a smile ghosting her features as she stared up at his shadowed form as he slid into the driver's seat.

'Maria okay?'

Janet's smile deepened as she glanced into the back seat; their daughter was safely ensconced in her baby seat, a small bubble of snot forming over one nostril, its shimmering green film expanding and contracting in time with her breathing. She shifted slightly, the dreams in her head making her fidget, arms and legs batting at unseen foes as she slumbered. Turning into the side of the seat, Maria gently licked her lips, her small, pink tongue tracing over her mouth as she sniffed, the small bubble popping silently.

Janet chuckled softly as she watched her daughter. Reaching back, she gently wiped the small trail of goo from her top lip, the baby wipe cold to the touch as it slipped over her daughter's skin.

'Yeah, she's fine; fighting the good fight in there, probably against a big pink bunny and walking marshmallows, but she seems to be holding her own.'

Derek grinned as he pictured the scene.

'That's my girl; speaking of my girls, how's my favourite one doing?'

Janet smiled as she traced his jaw with her fingers, a peal of laughter dancing in her eyes.

'I just told you that, didn't I?'

Derek smiled slightly as he put the car into gear and began to make his way to the front gates.

'Very funny, but seriously, how are you feeling?'

Janet sighed as she leant against the cold glass of her window, the heat from the car making them fog slightly. She idly traced her finger through the condensed vapour as she thought of a reply.

'Tired, worn out, and well, stretched thin like too little paint on a very large canvas. There hasn't been any let up with the hospitals; those damned units being installed into them aren't helping things and the number of Infected being admitted is climbing. They had to cut my maternity leave short, as you well know, and I just can't keep the pace up. Maria, god bless her… she took a lot out of me when I brought her into this world. Wouldn't change it for anything, but she did one hell of a number on me. I haven't felt this tired since my days in pre-med; we need a babysitter or even a live-in nanny. I can't keep dragging her into the line of fire every time I leave the house. I am petrified that something will happen to her when my back is turned.

'But... that's not what truly scares me, not with the hospital, anyway.

'It's getting harder and harder to spot the early cases; they bare such a resemblance to people with a very heavy bout of flu that, unless they're a fast carrier and shoot through the stages to three or four in a matter of hours, we can't tell.

'Only thing that confirms it is blood work, and that takes hours, if not days sometimes, to come back. We're so damned short staffed and overworked, that some of the technicians and haematologists are pulling double or even triple shifts just to beat the backlogs. I just don't know what to do, we need help, and we need it fast.'

Derek sat silent as Janet's words sank in. The strain in her voice and the pale circles of fatigue under her eyes made her look a lot older than her twenty-nine years. Sparing a glance at the gate staff, he slipped out onto the roadway and headed towards home, a singular sentence finding its way from his mind to his lips as he flipped the indicator and merged into the traffic.

'I'll see what I can do; I promise.'

His words, although heartfelt and strong, ultimately went unnoticed as he glanced in Janet's direction and saw her sleeping form curled against her seatbelt.

****

Colinson stared at the slightly flickering screen of his computer, Davies' private correspondence sitting in stark black and white on the screen.

Derek, David, I have been going over a few of the reports from the other teams as well as previous reports from before I was on board, and while the G36c is a good weapon, it makes no sense to have it circulation alongside the Diemaco. Now, Woodwrow and the RRT have had nothing but positive feedback on the system and I feel it would be a better solution to retire our frontline rifle in favour of the Diemaco.

It makes us a far more flexible unit on the ground if we are all singing from the same hymn sheet. You'll find a few reports attached to this. Let me know what you think and if it's an implementable option. Also, on another note, I have heard from Anna about some unusual occurrences with the nightshift in the labs. I don't know whether she has raised the issue with either of you. I am checking into it myself but thought it best to raise it with both of you, as well.

Colinson leant back in his chair as he let the message sink in before lifting the phone from his desk. He leant forwards once more, hit the speed dial key, and listened to it ring.

12
June Third
Broadhead Barracks
Drop training

'Right, kiddies, you want in?'

A chorus of nods and spoken affirmations drifted on the crisp afternoon air. Woodwrow shivered slightly; he sorely missed the four days of brief sun and heat. As much as he enjoyed the jumps in France and Italy, the weather was less than hospitable when soaring through the air in excess of one hundred miles per hour, wearing only a lightweight suit.

'Who here has experience with wing-suits?'

A hawk-faced, sandy-haired soldier raised his hand, catching Kevin's attention. 'What's your name, kid? I got the list of candidates but no photos.'

The candidate shuffled slightly as he looked at Woodwrow, slightly embarrassed for being put on the spot so suddenly. 'Wayans, sir.'

Woodwrow grinned as he looked at the recruit, his swathe of curled facial hair splitting in two as he spoke.

'Right, sunshine. First off, I ain't a sir. I ain't anything but one of you. We drop together, we fight together, and we either go home together, or we die trying. So call me Kev or Woody, but not sir; that goes for the rest of you, as well. Rules are different for Captain Colinson and Lieutenant Baker; they run the show and we kill what we are told to kill. Anyway, I am getting ahead of myself here. You've got experience in the suits—good. You seen one of these before?'

127

Kevin reached down and pulled away the heavy, green canvas tarp that lay at his feet, revealing the prototype wing-pack. The recruit's eyes boggled as they stared at the slim, lightweight frame on the floor.

The pack's slightly glossed, black surface shimmered, even in the muted light that filtered its way through the clouds. The sculpted edges slid back across the body of the rig, the quick release parachute centred in the middle of the compartment.

The wings slid free as Woodwrow picked up the unit, the main spine folding outwards and clicking into place as he adjusted the harness to his body. Grasping the controls in his hands, he pushed the two small buttons mounted to the ends of the control sticks and fully deployed the wings. With a heavy clunk, they swung free, the carbon fibre panels slipping into place.

'This is a variation on the Gryphon wing developed by ESU, the German aeronautics firm. The Japanese took the design and created this platform for their fast deployment teams. It folds down and, unlike the other models, has no solid or liquid fuel rockets; this allows the user to carry in more kit and for a more compact collapsible design; however, that does limit flight time by a large amount. If you get into shit and have to eject the rig, hit these two clips and the button in the middle of your harness. A small CO_2 canister will fire it away from you and instantly deploy your parachute. We call it the Jesus handle.'

One of the recruits looked puzzled by the statement. His expression made Woodwrow smile all the wider.

'If you are wondering why, and it looks like he is,' Kevin nodded in the recruit's direction. 'We call it that, because if it don't fire, you may want to pray. If the canister fails to eject your wing, then the chute won't have enough pull to right the wing's drag and your weight. And, well, concrete and the human body tend to not make very good bedfellows.'

Several of the gathered group chuckled, while others stared at the unit in front of them with a dose of sceptical fear that was more than would be considered healthy. Ignoring their bubbling fear and laughter, Woodwrow pushed onwards.

'Right, now, you saw me deploy the wings once I had this set up properly. If you hit the same controls to retract the wings during flight, you will simultaneously retract the platform and fire your parachute, which is fully detachable from the airframe; so, once you are within three to four feet of the deck, cut the chute and roll. We drop in on the move and come up firing.'

Woodwrow glanced over the heads of the gathered recruits to the slowly approaching aircraft as its drone reached his ears. A smile spread across his features as he watched the men tense up slightly at the heavy roar of the quad-engine aircraft spreading over them.

'Okay, kiddies, who is up for a bit of on-the-job training?'

The team filed into the C130, the wing packs weighing heavy on their backs, despite it being lighter than anything else they had ever had to carry. The thick strapping pulled and pinched as they moved. Woodwrow grinned as he watched them moving with a caution born from an unfamiliar circumstance; out of the corner of his eye, he caught a flash of black as one of the recruits sent his drop partner flying into the bulkhead as the wings of his pack deployed.

Stepping towards them, he grinned. 'At least we know they work.'

Leaning forwards, he held out a hand, the gloved fingers of the man on the floor curling round his wrist. 'You okay there, mate?'

The recruit nodded as he allowed Woodwrow to pull him to his feet; he tossed a slightly perturbed glare at his friend and rubbed the ache in his hip, the dull throb making him wince slightly as he pushed his equipment back into a more stable position.

The engines throbbed as the plane began to pick up speed. The plane's vibrations pulsed through them all as it thundered along the runway.

Woodwrow's eyes glittered with excitement as he felt the plane lift, his leg juddering as he drummed his heel off the floor.

'And here comes the fun part.'

Colinson watched the plane leave the runway, his mind drifting as he watched it drag its pregnant bulk higher into the sky, the pale washed-out light of the midday sun glinting off its matte grey skin. The scent of hot sake, richly spiced Sashimi and Chirashizushi made his mouth water slightly as his mind sent him spinning into a memory so closely held to his heart that it made him ache to visit it just once more; to gain a chance at revisiting the faces of those past and present and those he wished were not gone at all.

Stepping back to his desk, he lifted a photo frame from the top. He smiled as he stared at the collection of faces that gazed up at him from the glass-shielded photograph. His eyes travelled over the smiling, happy group of people, the coffee-tinged skin of the woman in his arms as he rested his chin on her shoulder, the smile on her face and the sparkle of her eyes as she cupped the side of his face with her hand, as she grasped the waist of another man; his face a mask of happiness as he stared at the camera.

Sighing, Colinson set the picture down as the memories of those two laughing, vibrant faces washed over him; he leant back in his chair, the frame squeaking under him as he put his feet up on the desktop. The soft metallic click of his lighter filled the room as he pulled a cigarette from the pack in his breast pocket. Setting the cigarette to his lips, he dragged his thumb over the jagged, knurled wheel of his lighter as he watched the lighter burst into flame as the sparks danced over the petrol-soaked wick.

Colinson drew deeply on the tar-laden smoke as he let the memories flow over him, images dancing in his mind as he closed his eyes. He sent a wavering ring of smoke slowly floating up to the ceiling, its swirling ring of grey fog carrying with it the smiling face and loving eyes of the one woman he knew would always own his heart.

13
Japan
April 19, 2011

Silence reigned supreme as the team sat waiting for the light to hit green. Glancing at his men, Masahiro smiled, the dark faceplates of their helmets masking their expressions. He watched them intently; his men were ready, their backs rigid, shoulders squared. As the light in his head-up display blinked to green, the team rose to their feet as one and turned to face the opening cargo hatch.

The rotor blades thundered overhead as they made their way forwards, filling the space around them with a swirling vortex of wind. Ishikawa Masahiro glanced over at the man besides him, his form clad in a swathe of matte-black armour; then he nodded. Without a word, they leapt forwards, casting themselves out into the waiting arms of the void as lights and noise danced around them.

The neon kiss of Tokyo's night sky bathed their plummeting forms. With a flick of his thumbs, the wings unfurled from his back, sending him rocketing silently through the sky towards the waiting throng below.

His eyes danced over the cascading information as it danced around the inside of his helmet. The one-way mirror finished glass shielded his face from anyone and anything. Its surface was marred by scars and scuffs, no longer the pristine black mirror it once was. With a flick of his chin, he nudged at the pressure sensor, opening up a channel to the others around him. His clipped words rang in their ears as he watched four of them peel away and descend lower.

The building ahead of them loomed, a tall monolith of glass and steel. Masahiro raised his right arm as he listened to the soft whirring of the weapon mounted to his forearm. The dancing red dot traced a trail of light over the window as a glowing arc of white-hot metal burst forth, shattering the eight-foot tall glass panel, its glittering shards dropping to the ground below in a cascade of shimmering glass.

He spun his body backwards as the wings collapsed, folding away as the parachute burst forth; the crimson cloud of cloth billowed out and he felt his feet kiss the window's ledge. With a single touch, he sent the parachute drifting off into the night sky. As he surged forwards, four more black-clad phantoms dropped from the glittering ink-washed sky. They moved through the room, surging over it like a tide of locust, the torn and twisted bodies of office workers and janitorial staff littering the floor, cast aside like furniture in a hurricane.

Smooth, quick motions sent the others with him through the two connecting doors as he moved towards the hallway. His H.U.D sent a glowing shimmer over his face as he watched the blueprints of the building roll past his eyes. The ten moving dots of his team blinked slowly as they moved through the floor. A thump and mumbled curse made him turn; the wet slither of a razor through silk drew him forth as an Infected tumbled to the floor, its head rolling past his feet. Nodding at his teammate, Masahiro moved on, the weight of his weapon a comfort as he read the ammunition count in the bottom right hand corner of his display.

****

Colinson watched the screen in front of him as the men moved with a precision he had only ever seen in the most highly choreographed of ballets. As if they were made of water, they flowed over the Infected, their black forms tumbling and rolling as the blades in their hands shimmered. The matte-black blades sliced through bone and flesh as if they were butter. Colinson's eyes widened further as he watched, amazed at the sheer overwhelming speed of their assault.

'I cannot believe this. It... it makes the Infected look like they're standing still; this is incredible, Matsumoto Sensei. Who taught them?'

The man turned, his trim form belying the power it held as he looked up from the screen in front of him. A glitter of pride danced

133

in his eyes as he chuckled slightly, his eyes darting back to the screen, scanning the glowing lines of script as they rolled down the screen.

'Please, Captain, dispense with the formalities. We invited you here, not for any preening or gloating. We are genuinely looking to aid you and your men; and call me Masao. Matsumoto Sensei is far too formal for you. How long have we known one another?'

Colinson smiled as he let out a short sigh of relief. 'A very long time. You and my father served together on the joint task force in the eighties.'

Masao laughed, his deep-throated chuckle drawing curious glances from the staff around them, only to be quelled with a withering look from him a moment later. 'You don't have to tell me that, David; I remember it well. Your father was a good man and a dear friend. I miss him.'

Colinson turned away in a vain attempt to hide the welling tears in his eyes as he tried in vain not to dredge up the memories of his father.

Masao felt a twinge of regret as he watched Colinson turn away. Setting his hand on David's shoulder, he spoke. 'I didn't mean to cause you any pain, but you shouldn't let it cloud your head; we have important work to do here.'

Colinson pushed the memories aside as he turned back to face his father's lifelong friend. 'So, what's that kit they're using? I've seen something similar before, but... this... the armour looks like something from a Batman film.'

He trailed off, hoping Masao would take the bait. He didn't have to wait long; Masao sensed the prying taunt and ceded, letting the man before him have his little try at subterfuge.

'Have you heard of the wing-suit or wing pack?'

He watched as Colinson nodded and smiled slightly then continued. 'The Germans are working on a system for their men, and to be fair, any other Special Forces units that wish to try it out. They have become very accommodating in recent years. It is a step up from a parachute and a lot more effective at tactical deployment from a high altitude.

'We took the same idea and adapted it to suit our needs. You have seen how it is used; it allows us to deploy our teams quickly, quietly, and virtually undetected. With the Infected becoming a very real problem for my people, and the fact that we are usually fighting for a floor or foothold at a time, it allows us to gain access quickly and with a higher effectiveness than storming floor by floor or dropping in through the roof, as Masahiro so skilfully demonstrated. We combined the system with a ballistics combat suit based on prototype armour developed for our tier-one soldiers.'

Colinson's reaction was exactly what Masao had expected—a mix of admiration and envy that danced hand in hand with a hunger to appropriate it for his own uses. Stoking the flames, he pushed on.

'It is a completely self-sustaining and sealed suit; the armour itself can withstand assault from any edged or blunt weapon and dissipates the force through an impact gel layer beneath the plates themselves. Although, obviously, this only negates the smallest portion of the impact—enough to turn a killing blow into one that would wind or stagger the affected person.

'The suit also has a self-contained oxygen filtration system and re-breather; the filters of which are fixed into the rear of the helmet. Along with all that comes a communications suite and radar and tracking centre. All of this is integrated into the helmet and controlled through a group of pressure sensors during flight and a wrist-mounted touch interface when groundside.

'The weapons themselves are fairly basic, light armaments for faster movement. Each soldier is equipped with a forearm-mounted machine pistol, the magazine based on an old Russian system, with the muzzle located just behind the wrist. The trigger is two stage with a pressure bar mounted inside the glove that acts as the safety. There is a button housed on the outside of the index finger for either full-auto or single-shot fire, depending on how long you hold down the button… not fool proof but adequate.'

Colinson's head swam as he took the information in. It was too far-fetched to be real, yet he was seeing it in use in a full-fledged operation. Shaking his head, he laughed softly.

'I don't know what to say; you're rolling this off so calmly, yet your equipment—the armour, weapons, coms systems—it's years ahead of anything we have.'

Masao studied the man; the slump of his shoulders belied his true shame at the situation of his men. 'David, follow me. Takashi, take charge for a moment.'

The young officer nodded before bowing to his commander and taking a seat at the control centre.

'I know what you are thinking, and to an extent it's true; you are not as well equipped as my men... but... I know for a fact we would not stand a chance against what your men have and are facing. We are quick killers, suited to lightning strikes. I fear for my home, David. I truly do. If we cannot eradicate this plague from our shores, we will not survive. We are too clustered, too confined, and with our numbers of homeless and transient souls, it would spread through us like a wildfire.'

Colinson looked at the man beside him, his eyes betraying his thoughts as he looked at his father's oldest friend. Turning, he leant against the railings on the rooftop, the open helicopter behind them silent. The hum of the city below was a symphony of babbling voices and music as the city carried on, oblivious to the war being waged in its name all around them.

'How many of you are there?'

Masao dragged a hand through his hair as he let out a deep,

drawn-out breath. 'Less than fifty; we numbered more, but... as I said, we're not a unit built for attrition.'

Colinson waited silently, listening to the buzz of the people below before Masao continued. 'Higashiyamato high school. It's in one of the cities in the western area of Tokyo. I think you went there once with Akemi.'

Colinson smiled, his eyes glinting slightly as he brought the memory forward. 'I remember.'

Masao smiled slightly as he watched the flashing neon lights below. 'I thought you might. She misses you.'

Colinson's head dipped slightly as he listened to the words and just what they meant. 'Has she said anything? Asked anything? Did you tell her anything? Anything at all?'

He waited for Masao to reply as they both listened to the hum of the hive below them, the listing traffic, and its constant droning.

'No.'

Colinson's heart dropped as the word settled in, leaving the silence as a wall between them. After several seconds of stifling, almost choking silence, Masao spoke. 'Anyway, it was there. This virus... or plague... whatever you call it, had ripped through the school like a tornado. It spread out from the canteen; the children there never stood a chance. And in the end, neither did we; they cornered the team in the gymnasium. Butchered them like cattle. They put up a good fight and went with their honour intact, but I would much rather have the men by my side than their damned honour plaques.'

****

Masahiro looked around him, the floor and walls stained a livid red. With a sharp flick of his left hand, he sent a jagged line of crimson arcing across the wall. The blade in his hand glimmered with the blood of the dead at his feet. He slid the blade into the sheath between his shoulder blades and slowly moved forwards. His eyes dropped to the counter again. The softly glowing fifty made him smile; he had changed magazines at some point and not even realised he had done it.

Tapping at his wrist, he opened a channel to his team and quickly spoke as he scanned the hallway. 'Move up. Clear through to the stairwell.'

Like a pack of malevolent daemons, the men melted from the darkness, skating over the corpses beneath their feet with nary a step lain wrong. Masahiro glanced at the small cluster of images at the top of his helmet's screen, their slightly bouncing countenance showing the vital signs and placement of each member of his unit. Rolling his neck, he felt the pull of the muscles and the dull clunk as he shook loose a deep-seated knot. The tension rippled as it loosened. With a soft snort of repressed energy, Masahiro pulled the blade from its sheath and slowly but surely made his way upwards.

Konan, Minato-ku, Tokyo.

Colinson stepped from the train, the warm, salt-laced air hitting him as he glanced up and down the open platform. With quick, practised steps, he moved through the bustling crowd, ignoring the curious stares of the children and mothers as he eased his six-foot frame by them. He watched as a child stared at him, his mother dragging him down the steps by the hand as he craned his neck to stare at the passing giant.

Colinson smiled and poked his tongue out at the boy, making him giggle, a grin blooming on the boy's face as he was yanked further into the press of bodies. Elbows jabbed and thumped into his hips and ribs as he manoeuvred through the crowd; schoolgirls giggled and children babbled as they gazed at him or his uniform. His ears burned from their curious, twittering questions and the mindless mumblings of businessmen as it all, once again, filled his senses as the people moved around him.

Moving through the terminal, he paused; the scent of freshly ground coffee filled his nostrils. He stepped forwards, the scent hooking him by the nose as he almost drifted through the people around him, past the doors of the busy Starbucks shop, and to the counter before he fully realised where he was going.

He glanced across the road, the faces of the crowd blurring into one as he sipped at the rich blend of coffee and vanilla in his hand. The sharp bite of the liqueur shot made his taste buds sing as he stepped across the road and moved off towards her apartment.

His feet skimmed across the roadway. The corner of his eye twitched as a teen on a bike came shooting towards the crossing; he jumped back, cursing at the driver in fluent Japanese, the curses tripping off his tongue as naturally as if he was speaking English. As he turned the corner and moved towards her apartment, he felt a shiver creep through his spine as he spied the awning of her building and the shining glass windows that shimmered in the morning sun.

The dregs of his coffee made him wince as the bitter grounds soaked into his tongue. Dumping the spent cup into a bin, he clutched the second in his other hand as he brushed his thumb over the Kanji of her name.

The familiar sights and scents of the area made his mind hum with a sense of longing he hadn't felt in a very long time. Turning, he gazed at the shops that lined the street behind her building. The line of hole-in-the-wall bistro restaurants selling homemade cuisine that would make your mind twist with the flavours that burst forth as you bit into the indescribable food portioned out to you in the foil-lined trays. Turning away from the road, he continued down the street, his eyes set on his final destination.

He paused in front of the glass doors to the tower, his hand hovering over the button for a few seconds before he pushed down. The clipped, softly nasal tones of the desk clerk flowed from the small speaker. In near perfect Japanese, Colinson replied, eliciting a surprised reply from the clerk as he buzzed him through into the building. Smiling at the aged clerk, he half bowed and thanked the man for his compliment, drawing a wizened smile and another compliment on Colinson's inflection and accent from the man as he moved to the elevator and selected the right floor.

He stood for several moments staring at her door, the solid slab of metal and wood making him more than a little nervous. His forehead beaded with sweat, the heated droplets seeping through his hair, soaking into the band of his beret. Colinson set the still warm cup of coffee on the floor as he pulled his beret from his head and ran a hand through his now slightly damp hair. Bending down, he lifted the cup from the floor as he reset his felt cap on his head. Straightening, he rapped his knuckles on the door, listening to the echo of the hallway beyond the door.

His breath froze in his throat as she opened the door, her form silhouetted by the light streaming in through the floor-to-ceiling windows. She looked at him, her eyes as wide and scared as a deer stuck in headlights. She stared at him, her mouth opening and closing as she struggled to find the words to say. Colinson kept his

140

gaze level as she slowly gathered her sense.

'Akemi, I...'

The sound of flesh on flesh echoed through the hall as she slapped him, her eyes blooming with an anger that was seldom ever seen in her.

He shook with the blow, the sting working its way through his jaw as his left eye began to water from the heat in his cheek. Again, the echoing slap of her hand rang through the hall as she struck him once more as tears welled in her eyes.

'No call, no letter, no sign of you ever even being alive... I waited and waited, even as the week turned into a month, the month into a year. I waited... ten God damned years. I waited, David... for you!'

He stared at her as the heat flowed through his face, his hand quivering slightly as the heat from the coffee flowed through his palm. He watched the tears swell and move as they rolled down across her eyelids, tracking their way down her cheeks and curling along her jaw before finally falling to dash themselves on the collar of her night robe.

She pulled the neck closed, hiding her small, apple-like breasts from his view, the puffed pink flannelette robe a sharp contrast to her mocha-coloured skin.

'Akemi... I...'

He stopped; the pain and hurt in her eyes was like a spear through his soul as he struggled with himself.

'I... I'm s...'

She screamed, her voice shrill as she gave voice to her pain and rage that dwelt with her. Her face glowed with anger as she stepped into the hallway, backing him to the wall, her bare feet slapping gently at the un-carpeted floor.

'Don't you dare say you're sorry... nothing... nothing can make this any better than you have made it… nothing. Did you just think you could turn up and say, "Hi, Akemi. How you been? I am sorry that I hadn't called, but you know how things go…" No—it just doesn't work like that!'

He stared at her, his eyes impassive, no sign of aggression or anger as she continued to scream at him. Her fists pounding at his chest as she railed and poured forth a decade's worth of guilt and grief. As her fists rained down, she shook and thrashed, the sash around her waist slowly beginning to slip the more she slammed her petite fists against his trimmed form.

'Akemi, stop.'

She continued to pound and beat anything she could reach, driving her hands into him as the hurt and pain flowed out of her in waves, flowing from her in a tirade of tear-laced screams.

The coffee fell from his grip as he grabbed her arms, pinning them to her sides as bellowed at her to stop. 'Stop. Just stop.'

She stared up at him and he pulled her closer to him as the doors on either side of them opened, curious faces peering out at them as he held her close to him. The coffee seeped into the floor as it slowly crept towards her uncovered feet.

His gaze fell to the glowering image of the stick-thin form of a man as he edged out of his doorway staring at David. A stream of jabbering Japanese flowed down the hall at him as David's face turned to stone. He looked at the man as he ventured into the hall and turned to confront David, his eyes locking with Colinson's as he clutched the head of his cane. Without breaking eye contact, Colinson said nothing as he dropped his hands, tied the sash firmly around Akemi's waist, and gently pushed her towards her apartment door.

'Sir, please, do not interfere in matters that do not concern you; all

142

you will do is end up getting yourself hurt. Miss Matsumoto and I have been apart a very long time. She is in no danger; believe me, if she were, I would be the first in its path. So please, sir, leave us to work this out in our own way.'

The man still held his stern stare as he nodded and bowed slightly, his back popping loudly as he righted himself and shuffled back into his apartment.

Akemi watched him as she stepped backwards away from him, the edges of her robe clasped in her hands as she pulled them tight around her.

She watched as he bowed low and spoke. She took in the dip of his shoulders and the tone of his voice as he spoke to the elderly man two doors down from her own. He had changed, and she could see it. The cocky, arrogant youth who had won her heart over a decade ago was no longer there.

She turned and left him standing there amongst the puddle of cold coffee. He watched as she left him; righting himself, he stared at the open doorway, unsure of whether or not to move after her. He dug his nails into his palms and stepped forwards. He reached the doorway, willing himself to move, but he could not bring himself to step through. He stood, mute and immobile as he waited, waiting for her—not for her forgiveness but just for her permission.

He stood for over an hour, the breeze tracking over his uniformed body as he waited, her door thumping gently against the wall as he felt the silence push down around him.

Akemi watched his reflection in the windows as he stood and waited. Leaning against the wall, she slowly slid to the floor, her legs pulled tight to her as she tried to curl into herself. Her head rested against the wall as she continued to watch the man in the window.

'David...'

She watched as his head rose as he stared into the hallway.

'Come in.'

David moved; his steps weighed heavily as he stepped into the hallway. His footsteps echoed round him as he moved deeper into Akemi's home. She watched as he grew and moved through the panes of the windows. Pushing herself from the floor, she pulled the dressing gown tight to her body as he rounded the corner. She nodded at the settee against the wall then stepped into her bedroom and closed the door.

His fingers drummed out the rhythm of his heart as he waited, a cold sweat running down the back of his neck, the cold beads soaking their way through the collar of his shirt as he sat. The dark, charcoal-grey beret sat folded in two in his grip, his fingertips tracing the tight stitching of the leather banding as he cast his eyes around the spacious apartment.

He stared at the pictures hanging on the wall, the two slim bands of black silk that bordered the top corners of the only picture of him in the entire room. His throat constricted as he felt his heart stop in his chest. *She really had thought I was dead.*

He stood, his legs wavering slightly as he wandered over to the ceiling-high bookcase. The rows of books were sorted by size and author, filling the shelves so completely that not even the grains dust that clogged the tops of the pages could fit between them.

He traced his finger over the covers; authors from days gone rubbed shoulders with the classics, as others sat proud in their hard-card cases, aloof and alone.

His eyes tracked their way along the cases as he let his fingers dance along the spines, his mind awash with memories of them curled together alone on the sofa or by the hearth in his small cabin nestled in the middle of the Yorkshire dales. A wane smile crept over his features as he centred the image in his mind, his fingers leaving a gleaming trail of clean plastic and paper behind as he moved away from the bookcase. His near silent footsteps made the room quiver with a thirst for sound as he neared the desk, pushing her chair back into place. A soft chiming sounded as it moved, the bells striking in time with the ticking of Akemi's desk side clock.

Colinson closed his eyes and stood, mute and immobile in the centre of the room. He drank in the silence as he let the rhythmic click of the second hand drown his mind, its echoing clack growing in pitch and volume as he focused on that one constant noise.

He paused, his hand hovering over a sheet of polished glass, its crystal-clear surface staring back at him as his own eyes seared his soul. He brushed his fingers over the cold pane as he gazed at the two steel disks lain so lovingly on the claret pillow within.

'I found those...' She paused as he turned, pushing herself from the wall where she leant watching him. 'I searched for days for some clue, some inkling that the man I loved was even real.'

She smiled wistfully to herself as she slowly edged closer to Colinson, the sheer, grey leggings clinging to her so completely, he fought to keep his body in check.

'You were so completely gone, that I began to doubt you ever existed and to think that you had been little more than some fanciful dream of a sheltered child living in her father's shadow.'

His gaze travelled up her slim, petite form, trailing over the plain cream jumper draped over her. The swell of her meagre chest pressed against the loosely hanging fabric as she curled her arms around herself, pulling the over-large garment tighter to her frame.

'I found them caught beneath the boards of the floor; it took me an hour and a half to pry them free with my fingertips and the tweezers in my vanity case. My fingers were so bruised and raw that they had begun to bleed by the time I pulled that last steel ball link from between those two planks and finally held the proof in my hands, the proof that you...'

145

She let her hand glide over his cheek slowly, her fingers dancing over his skin as he felt her nails tug at the bristled briar that had begun to claim his chin and jaw.

'Truly had existed, that the man who owned my heart was not some phantom from a dream, but a real flesh-and-blood man.'

She leant her head against his chest, listening to his heart as it thumped, the echoing drum of his life's blood filling her head as she curled her fingers into his jacket. Her lip quivered as she let her mind slow to a crawl. Colinson's fingers crept through her silk-like hair, the long flowing strands gliding over his fingers as he slipped his arms around her, encircling her shoulders as he drank in her warmth.

'Why did you leave? You broke my heart.'

Colinson's heart seized in his chest as she stared into his eyes, her slim doe-like orbs boring into him as she looked on, pleading for any answer.

'I... had no choice. I had to keep you safe, free from whatever followed me. I cannot and will not tell you what I did and what made me leave; but I did it for you, to keep you safe and secure. I have done a lot in my life that has scarred me so deeply I will never be free of the pain.'

He pushed her gently away from him, his hands rising up to cup her cheeks as he brushed away a stray strand of hair with his thumb.

'Leaving you here alone was the single most difficult thing I have ever had to do, but if it meant keeping you safe, I would do it all over again—even if it meant never being able to do this even once more until the day I died.'

Leaning down, he pressed his lips to hers, the soft embracing kiss lingering on their lips as he pulled her tightly to his chest.

****

The outdoor restaurant bubbled with conversation. The sizzle of oil, the scent of burning fat and roasting meat wafted on the air as they made their way to two vacant stools. The joy-tinged call of the vendor as they sat made them both smile; lifting the menu from the slim-line tray in front of him, Colinson flipped it open. The vertical columns of script slipped from the page as his eyes scrolled over it, easily reading the menu. With a soft nudge of his elbow, he drew her attention, her soft, brown, almond-shaped eyes peering into his. As he showed her the choices, a coy almost girlish smile teased at her face as she saw what he had picked. A soft, red tinge painted her skin as he smiled and called over to the vendor.

'I cannot believe you remembered.'

Colinson grinned as he pulled the skewered king prawn from the bamboo with his teeth.

'I remembered your coffee, didn't I?'

Akemi smiled as she toyed with the skewer, letting the fried shellfish soak in the soy sauce for a few moments before biting off a small piece.

'Yes, you did, but you also dropped it and let it soak into the mat outside my front door, so for all I know you could have got it completely wrong. Although, this does make up for it somewhat.'

She slipped the rest of the prawn into her mouth, slowly pulling it from the slim stick of bamboo, her eyes locking with Colinson's as she finally pulled it free. A small blush tinged his cheeks as he watched her. Coughing into his balled fist, he turned back to his plate and continued eating, her soft, throaty chuckle meeting his ears as an unbidden smile teased at his lips.

Colinson smiled slightly as he stubbornly tore his gaze away from hers. As he motioned to the proprietor, the man hobbled forwards, his face beaming with a miss-matched patchwork of true enthusiasm and fake joy.

147

With a movement smoothed by years of practice, the man cleared their plates and utensils from the counter and slipped the bill between them.

Colinson quickly scanned the slip of paper and leafed through a small fold of notes in his pocket before pulling out a selection of the coloured notes and leaving them on the small, black plate. With a nod and a smile to the man, he gently eased Akemi from her seat, guiding her down towards the train station.

A shocked call echoed down the road as the wizened old cook counted the money David had left behind.

'Did it again, didn't you?'

David smiled as he let his fingers dance over Akemi's side, making her squirm as she tried desperately not to laugh. She glanced up at him as they stopped at the crossing and watched as the lights glowed and the traffic pulled to a stop.

'Come on; I'll show you how much I remember.'

****

David's eyes opened as he sat up in his chair, a contented smile glazing over his face. Pushing up from his chair, he slowly walked over to his office window, the sky just turning a deep purple as he watched the sun sink ever lower.

Flicking the ash from the end of his cigarette, he turned and dropped the still smouldering stick of tobacco into his ashtray and moved towards the door.

14

June 3rd 4:45pm
Broadhead Training Grounds
The Village

The air snapped at their clothing as they shot towards the floor, the packs on their backs weighing heavy as they gripped the controls tightly. The glow of the altimeter flicked over their eyes as they flew like the spear of Achilles, slicing through the dying rays of the day.

Woodwrow grinned like a maniac as he shot past the recruits; his wailing cry of exultation echoed through their ears as he rolled, whipping through the air before snapping the wings open. His body went ridged while he soared over the patchwork quilt of fields and farms. He watched his shadow glide over the rising bumps of hills and hedges; its black form slid across the landscape like the shadow of death as he looked upon the world below.

Banking left, he watched the blinking dots of the sixty trainees in his wake as they turned with him, their silent mass descending upon their target like the winged legions of Heaven. The muffled thump of expanding parachutes rolled past him as he pressed down on the ends of the wing controls. He snapped back against his own weight, his shoulders yowling at him as the harness went taut.

Woodwrow let his body go limp as he was suddenly jerked to a semi-stop, his mind whirling ever so slightly as his velocity dropped to all but zero. He reached up his hands, hitting the quick-release clips, which dropped him with a bone-shaking jar as he hit the floor four feet below.

His hands snapped down as he brought his weapon up to join in the chorus of the staccato pops of automatic weapons. His mind lurched as a dull crunch echoed behind him; all the while, the training group advanced, firing at the dummy targets.

'Fuck it; cease fire, cease fire. Make safe and form up.'

Cutting to a new channel, Woodwrow snapped off an emergency call to the medical team in the helicopter, the three-man team landing next to him only seconds later. Woodwrow watched, his mind clamouring for an explanation, as he looked at the crumpled and bloody form on the floor. Stepping forwards he watched the lead medic rise to his feet and shake his head as he caught Kevin's eye. Cursing under his breath, he nodded and turned back to the training team.

'Exercise is scrubbed; board the helicopter and head back to base. I will follow on shortly. You're all confined to barracks until we get this settled.'

Woodwrow's fingers traced a sweat-laden path through his shorn hair. The crumpled and twisted form twitched and spasmed as its mind tried in vain to move the shattered remains of the body it had once sought shelter in.

Kneeling, he let his eyes trace through the blood-matted clothing, torn and twisted flesh, and the shattered remains of the now useless wing pack. Pushing to his feet, he glanced quickly at the medical team.

'Pack him up and get him to cold storage. Just make sure to preserve his rig as is. I want that dropped off at the armoury; I need to take a look at this myself before Push Pin gets his greasy mitts all over it.'

The three men nodded as they laid a matte-green tarpaulin over the body and prepared to ship what remained of the soldier home.

Baker Residence
Northeast London

Baker sat staring at the television, his fists clenched in silent rage as he watched the images play out in front of him. With a heavy curse, he hurled his half-full drink at the wall, watching as it sprayed across the heavy flocked wallpaper. The reporter, her eyes wide as she looked at the reports in her hands, composed herself before she turned back to camera and continued with her report.

'The explosion in the Canary Wharf today claimed the lives of seventeen people and wounded seventy-six others; authorities were quick to respond to the scene and managed to gain control of the situation quickly. No one has claimed responsibility for the bombing at this time.'

Janet jumped when the can spun past her head as she stepped through the doorway, cold foaming beer peppering her as she looked at her husband.

'Derek?'

His nostrils flared as he pushed himself to his feet, his eyes awash with a violent anger as he looked upon the slightly nervous face of his wife.

'Sorry darling; this has pissed me off. I just don't get this country anymore. With all that's going on, people still think it's a good time to blow the hell out of a building full of office workers. With all that has happened in the world, you would think that they'd put aside their petty ideals and beliefs that their Imams and clerics denounce with as much fervour as those fanatics that they are working to stop. Sometimes I really wonder if these people are worth protecting anymore.'

He gently pushed past Janet and pulled open the basement door.

'I am going to work this loose; call me if you need me.'

With those words echoing off the walls around him, he disappeared, the blackness swallowing him whole. Janet stood quietly watching the darkness as the sound of flesh on canvas floated up from the yawning maw before her. Shaking her head gently, she moved into the front room and switched off the television before turning and heading back into the kitchen.

Janet stopped, lifting Maria from her playpen, smiling as her daughter tugged and pulled as Janet lifted her sweater up and away, freeing her breast; the sudden hit of cold air on her still overly sensitive nipple made her jump slightly. A shock of fear rippled through her as her grip loosened, Maria's panicked squeak rushing through the fog of her flushed and embarrassed mind as she slipped from her mother's grasp.

'Oh shit.'

Maria giggled as Janet bent down and scooped her daughter from her half-grasp, which had kept the baby from breaking free of her mother's arms. 'That was close, huh, darling?'

Maria batted the flats of her hands against Janet's cheeks as she raised her daughter to her face and planted a soft kiss on her forehead. 'Okay, breakfast then time for a bath; someone is getting a little stinky.'

The splash of water filled the kitchen as Janet filled the sink a third of the way and dropped the baby bath seat into it. Maria stared at her mother's moving hands, swatting at them as she was dis-robed. Her wide, blue eyes followed each and every movement they made as the baby grow and nappy were stripped away, leaving her nude and still wriggling even as she was lowered into the lukewarm water; with a soft splash, she was slid into place. Her eyes widened as the water pooled around her and a raucous fit of giggling echoed forth as she hit the water, her hands sending a glittering spray of crystal droplets into her mother's face. She watched with avid fascination as Janet squeezed a small amount of the pale-gold baby wash into her palm and set about washing her daughter's hair.

The air filled with ringing chimes as the doorbell rang. Calling out to the shadow behind the door, Janet lifted the jug of lukewarm water, and gently rinsed the suds from Maria's head as she burbled and splashed at the water, sending crystalline droplets shimmering through the air.

Lifting her from the seat, Janet picked up the plush, heavy towel and cocooned Maria in its soft warmth as she stepped into the hallway towards the door.

The slim form that greeted her made Janet's eyebrows furrow. The lightly bronzed complexion and slim-framed glasses gave her face an almost impish appearance. The faded jeans and form-fitting long sleeved t-shirt drew her age very much into question, despite the confidence that her stance and voice lauded.

'Hello, Mrs Baker, I'm Siobhan. I assume the agency phoned you, telling you I would be here today?'

Janet relaxed slightly, although the puzzled frown still sat firmly rooted to her brow. Shifting Maria's weight onto her hip, Janet held out one water-dampened hand.

'No, they didn't, but please come in. I was just finishing Maria's bath. Take a seat in the living room while I get her dried and into her playpen.'

Broadhead Barracks
Maintenance and Engineering Block

Woodwrow stood, the glowing bulb above him casting his shadow along the floor as he stared at the blood-wet pack on the table. The harness was slick beneath his fingers as he ran his hands over the inch-wide Cordura straps. His hands danced over the reinforced wires and the heavy buckle at the centre of the rig; with a deft movement, he unsnapped the catch and set the sides of the harness down on the cold metal table.

The sound of clanking metal filled the room as Woodwrow set to work with the pneumatic screwdriver hanging from the ceiling. The cold-forged titanium screws rolled past him as he lifted the carapace housing free while the lamp strapped to his head sent a wash of stark-white light into the cavernous interior.

Wires snaked and twisted as they wove their way through the myriad of rails and pistons. A network of greased-smeared gears and springs glittered like dust-tarnished gems as he let his eyes roam through the glistening field of poly-carbon plastic and titanium.

His brow furrowed as he traced his fingers over the lead guiderail; his fingers traced through the grease as it rolled and piled over his searching digits, the viscous, black sludge staining his skin as he felt the pads of his fingers ripple over the bearings buried under the oily muck. His index fingers dropped for just a fraction of a second as his brow furrowed in confusion. The jagged and burred edges of the runner plucked at the ridges of his fingertips as he traced them over the area again and again, each time finding that one fractional dip.

His eyes widened as he let his hands walk their way through the mire, sifting through the torn flecks of plastic and metal to the twisted teeth of the slide and the buckled lead arm of rotary link. *Kid never stood a chance.*

He pulled his hand free and sat down, wiping the thick layer of grease off his fingers, the rag in his hands grating against his now overly moist skin.

His voice filled the room as he ran through his own thoughts. 'Okay, come on, Kev, what ain't you seeing? The main lead slide is torn to shit halfway along, and one of the guide bearings is missing. There are no tool marks, but anyone with a modicum of skill and machinist's training could pull that off.'

He tossed the rag onto the table as he leant back, staring up at the spot on the ceiling cast from his still glaring headlamp.

'The slider on the lead arm is torn to shit as well. The rotary link, although still working, is bent at the joint of panel A; come on, there is something you are missing. None of this should have killed him. He still had the emergency release, so why didn't he deploy it, or call for help on the way down? None of this makes any sense.'

His eyes travelled over the frame, the padded crosshatched plate staring at him as he chewed at his bottom lip. *There is something I am missing here.*

Woodwrow stood, stepped over to the rest of the recruit's equipment, and lifted the lightweight jump helmet from the table. He flipped it over in his hands before picking up a small Philips head jeweller's screwdriver.

The clatter of plastic on metal rolled through the armoury as he set the screwdriver back on the bench. His fingers snagged on the edges of the casing as he pulled the helmet-mounted black box from the recorder. The camera's lens winked at him in the light as he tossed the helmet back onto the bench, a dull *clunk* biting at his ears as he slipped the disk into the stereo behind him.

Frantic breathing filled the room as the audio files began to play as Kevin dropped once more into the small-wheeled office chair beside him. '*Shit... come on you bastard. Kev, Wayans, come on, guys; I got a major malfunction here... fuck.*'

His voice grew tense, jarring at Kevin's ears as he listened to the man's final moments. *'Someone, anyone, please fucking help. My pack's fucked. Okay, calm it, Scotty boy.'*

A soft click filled the room, almost lost beneath the sounds of Hennessey's panicked breathing and the growling of the wind as he shot towards the floor. Kevin's eyes screwed tight as he listened, the scene playing out in his mind as the sucking vortex of sound swallowed him whole.

'Oh fuck me, come on, you bastard, fire. Please come on, fucking fire.'

Woodwrow jumped as the sound cut to static, the muffled crump of his impact Hennessey's final eulogy. Kevin leant back in the chair, running his hands over his face as he ground away the stray tears that plucked at the edges of his vision. Sniffing sharply, he leant forwards and stared at the still bloody remains of Hennessey's jump pack.

'Why didn't you deploy the chute, then? Or did you... no...'

Woodwrow leapt to his feet, the sound of tearing Velcro filling the air. With a frantic jerk, he pulled the padded back plate free from its mounts, sending it sliding over the floor as he threw it aside with no more care than he would show a bag of rubbish.

'Son of a bitch.'

He stared at the gauge set next to the canister; its bright-red neon stripped needle pointed squarely at zero psi. Slamming the plate against the pack, he growled as he stalked towards the armourer's office.

The man turned with a stifled yelp as his door crashed into the wall. Woodwrow's seething form stood in the doorway, silhouetted by the glare of the pendant lights behind him. The man pushed his chair back from the desk as Woodwrow advanced through the small office.

156

'You fucking lazy bastard.'

The armourer back peddled as fast as his twisted and torn knee would allow, the wheels of his office chair squeaking slightly as they ground over the bare, dust-laden concrete floor. 'Kev, what the hell?'

Woodwrow's eyes blazed with unrepentant anger as he stared down at the man before him. 'You… Bobby, you lazy bastard. You cost one of my boys his life by skimping out on the fucking CO_2.'

Bobby looked at him, his eyes bleeding incomprehension as he stared back at the glowering tower of rage that stood before him. His eyes travelled down to the film of blood that clung to Kevin's fingers as realisation slowly began to seep in. His eyes widened slightly as he stared at Kevin's slowly clenching fists.

'Kev, seriously mate, I run those checks myself. I even consulted with David's Japanese contacts about the proper maintenance techniques. I wouldn't skimp on anything with those packs. Never. Not just because they are expensive, but you guys rely on those things to survive. Damn it, man, they're your best means of getting in and out of dodge faster than the Road Runner on caffeine.'

Bobby 'Push pin' Bone pushed himself into the corner, the wheels of his chair chattering over the concrete. He stared at the advancing monolith of rage as Woodwrow stalked closer. 'Hell, you even poached my assistant into the damned program, so why would I do something that daft with the kit when he is using it.'

Woodwrow's advance ceased as soon as the words left Bobby's mouth, his brow furrowing as he looked through the man before him. 'What's the kid's name?'

Bobby looked at Woodwrow, his mind a foggy whirl of painkillers and slowly receding fear. 'Damian. Damian Wayans.'

Kevin shook his head as he slipped some of the pieces together. Turning on his heel, he sped from the room as fast as his booted feet could carry him. His chest heaved, spurring him on as he sprinted through the drill square, crashing through a squad of marching recruits as Kingsley bellowed out the drill call, his echoing baritone ricocheting through Kevin's mind as he smashed into the double doors and slid over the tiled floor of the entryway.

Susan squeaked in fright as she dropped the papers in her hands. Woodwrow glanced over his shoulder, his eyes screaming an apology his mouth couldn't convey as he flew through the door to Colinson's office. The empty chair stared at Kevin, the bruised and burnished leather seeming to twist into a sneering pastiche of a smile. Turning, Kevin slammed the ball of his hand into the doorframe, muttering a string of words so foul the walls turned a pale blue in embarrassment.

'He's not in at the moment. I think he went over to the officer's mess for something to eat; he has been missing a lot of meals lately with the mess left over from the last two engagements.'

Woodwrow nodded and trotted out the door. 'Thanks, Sue, and sorry about that.'

She smiled slightly, her eyes betraying more than she let on as she plucked the papers from the floor. 'Don't worry about it; you're not the first and won't be the last...'

She glance up at the door, its empty frame making her flush with anger slightly as she watched the door slowly swing closed. 'Fucking bastard.'

His footfalls echoed as he continued to sprint through the hallways. Swinging left, he shoved open the doors, his feet sliding under him as he forced himself to slow to a complete halt. Woodwrow sucked in a deep, juddering breath as he marched across the small lounge area. Colinson, who sat staring at him over the rim of a teacup smiled as he watched the man approach.

Woodwrow halted, his back ramrod straight as he saluted. Colinson set the cup down, the chocolate brown liquid swirling in the white ceramic; steam whispered up in a swirl of white mist as he brushed the few stray crumbs from his shirt.

'Yes, Sergeant. What can I do for you?'

Woodwrow's chest heaved as he stood taking a moment to compose himself before replying. 'Captain, pursuant to codes of conduct, section Nine Zero Three, negligent conduct in maintenance of combat equipment and section Nine Zero Seven, negligent conduct that is a direct cause of squad mate death, I am officially charging, in absentia, recruit Zero Six One One Eight, Private Damian Wayans, with the negligent homicide of recruit Nine Five Four Two Seven, Corporal Scott Hennessey.'

Colinson sighed as he lifted the teacup from the table and took a long, slow sip. He let his mind float, flickering through the pages of his mind as he pulled the file up; setting the cup back on the table, he pushed his chair away and stood, tugging slightly at the bottom of his uniform shirt as he nodded to Woodwrow to lead the way.

The door to the barracks swung inwards, the chatter dying like the rays of the setting sun as Woodwrow and Colinson entered the room.

Colinson's eyes scanned about him, his lifeless gaze landing on Wayans as he sat on the edge of his bed. Smooth plastic-coated cards glimmered in his hand. The cold, white light of the halogen tube lights shifted down his face as he chucked a cluster of matchsticks onto the growing pile in the middle of his footlocker.

'Walker, Hartlet, secure this man.'

The two soldiers opposite Wayans dropped their cards without question. Rising to their feet, they ensnared Wayans' arms and pulled him to his. The man's eyes were wide with confusion and anger as he tried to wrest his arms from their vice-like grips.

'Private Damian Wayans, you are being charged with the negligent homicide of squad member Scott Hennessey. Walker, Hartlet, get this piece of shit out of here and tell Sergeant Cocklin he has my compliments and can do with this man as he sees fit. But please ask him to be gentle; we don't want RMP and SIB asking too many embarrassing questions.'

Both men nodded as they dragged the thrashing form of Private Wayans through the barracks. A heavy, muffled *thump* echoed from behind Colinson and Woodwrow. Both men turned to see Wayans lifting himself from the floor as another soldier slowly stepped away, his left hand already turning an angry shade of red. Hartlet smiled at Colinson as he curled his hand into the neckline of Wayans' shirt.

'He slipped, sir; must have hit the doorframe.'

Hartlet slipped his foot in front of Wayans' ankle and shoved, his head bouncing off the doorframe with a stomach-churning crunch as the man's nose buckled under the impact.

'Oh look, he did it again. Wayans, you really must be more careful.' Colinson nodded as he watched the men drag the groaning human-shaped sack of potatoes out the barracks.

'That's what I saw. He most certainly tripped but do make sure he doesn't do it anymore on the way to the guardhouse, lads. Once is enough.'

****

Baker stood in the doorway to the base's gaol, his eyes searching as he studied the two men perched on the single cots as they balefully gazed back at him from behind the inch thick bars of their cells.

The dark green paint flaking off the aged steel rods, its chipped and dented layers baring out the years and tales of the countless men who had, for one reason or another, graced the four-person block with their presence.

'What have I got to do to get out of here?'

The thick Bostonian accent filled the room as Baker's gaze wandered over to the weary and weatherworn face staring up at him.

160

Baker let his eyes settle on the battered and worn figure that sat hunched over on the edge of the cot, his elbows pressing into his knees, the stained and grime-coated jeans clinging to his bare elbows as he shifted.

'I have something lined up; you may want a shower though. You have...'

Baker glanced at his watch, the hands clicking silently to themselves as he watched the second hand slide over the face of the dial. 'Twenty minutes. Then report to Staff Sergeant Bone at the armoury.'

Hawk stood and saluted as he waited for the guard to unlock the door. The heavy bundle of keys rattled against the steel bars of the door as the stone-faced soldier pulled the key free and jerked the door open. The guard stepped away, holding the door open, his eyes passively watching as Hawk quickly trotted past him and Baker heading out of the door.

****

Hawk marched into the armoury, the shoes of his dress uniform clicking as he moved along the corridor. The starched collar of his dress coat pushed his head up as he strode through the double doors, the heavy thump rolling through the hallway as they swung shut behind him.

Hawk stopped as he caught sight of Bobby, a deep sense of unease rolling through his stomach as he rapped his gloved hand against the window. The gold-banded, white peaked cap clung to his shaven scalp, sweat rolling down his temples as he watched Bone walk briskly to the door, his gait stiff and unyielding as he forced his left knee to bend against the mass of scar tissue that clung to the back of the twisted joint.

'Reporting for disciplinary detail, sir.'

Bobby cast a scrutinising eye over the man before him, his gaze

161

shifting from the shimmering leather of his shoes to the sparking glow of the brass buttons and polished buckle of his dress jacket.

'Well, lad, kudos on the polish and pomp, but...'

Bone trailed off as he turned back into the room and walked through towards the loading dock; his hand reached out as they both walked through the rear door. Hawk lifted his hand, shading his eyes as the sun pounded down upon him. Bobby smirked as he pulled the radio from his hip.

'Bring 'em through, boys.'

A heavy growl echoed through the air as Hawk swallowed sharply. Heavy beads of sweat slithered down his neck as he watched the three ten-ton trucks back into the semi-enclosed dock.

The radio in Bones' hand squelched as he watched the trucks slowly reverse into place. Lifting the radio to his ear, Bobby grinned as he listened, the heavy static-blitzed message tickling at his ear like a worm on hook.

'My advice, mate, lose the cap, jacket, and gloves. Oh, and lift with your legs.'

Bones sent a sharp reply back, watching as the brake lights flared in the heat haze as it shimmered through the pall of exhaust smoke that slithered across the tarmac below.

'Okay, I want it all unpacked, stacked, and sorted; the manifest is on the wall behind me and the part numbers are on the crate lids. You have three hours. If it ain't done by then, you're on double duty in the maintenance pool, and those fucks have seventeen hundred weapons to strip, clean, and certify before Thursday.'

Hawks' face fell as he watched the rear gate drop with a mediocre clang as the passenger crewman let it slip from his grip. With a chuckle and shouted cursive to the driver, he scrambled like a monkey into the truck bed and rolled up the canvas flap that kept the cargo concealed from the public view.

The boxes and crates filled the bed, the neatly lashed rows rising to the canvas ceiling. The dull glow of diffused sunlight made Hawk squint as he tried to peer through to the back of the truck's cab.

'You, mate, have one hell of a task. But that's what you get for going loco on a piss up. Good luck to you—oh, and one other thing, mate. See if Push Pin has a spare set of coveralls or boots; your number twos there will get buggered otherwise; but your call, mate.'

With that, the soldier smiled and wandered away, whistling to himself. With a sigh of self-effacing anger, Hawk turned on his heel and strode back into the storeroom. He stripped himself down to his undershirt with a wave of care and reverence. The corded weaves of muscle showed up stark and clear on his lean frame as he set the carefully folded clothing onto a chair in the corner of the room, his gloves folded flat atop his peaked cap, riding high in the centre of his meticulously folded jacket.

Stepping back, he turned again, his movements precise and faultless as he moved towards the now silent trucks.

****

His muscles burned as he pulled, the crate sinking into the solid, carbon-sculpted flesh of his abdomen as he lifted it clear of the stack. The heavy steel casing ground against his sleeveless flesh, causing red welts to push out of his arms as he curled his hands tighter into the handles.

His legs quivered as he walked, his feet little more than lead blocks hanging from his ankles as he reached the end of the truck bed. Gritting his teeth, he hopped forwards, his knees screaming as he hit the floor; his back cracked as he doubled over the harsh, folded edge of the box digging deep into the tops of his thighs.

His breath came in short, heavy gasps as he levered himself upright. Staggering forwards, Hawk slid the box onto the shelf, the handles clacking against the steel casing as he turned, his feet sliding on the grit-laden floor as he made his way back to the loading dock.

The sun scorched his shoulders as he dragged the next box from the bed of the second truck. Lifting a hand to his forehead, he left the box half perched on the rear bumper as he cuffed away the layer of hot sweat from his brow. Flicking his wrist, he sent the drop sailing on to the scorched tarmac before turning, crate in hand, and trudging back towards the storeroom and the blessed coolness of its shadowed interior.

15

They stood at attention, watching in silence as the cadre of military police dragged Wayans through the drill square, his eyes manic as he cursed and kicked. The men blinked hard as a shower of grit and dirt sprayed their faces, not a single eye twitching to follow as the screaming form of their former teammate and comrade was dragged away. The dull clunk of closing doors rolled over them as one of the military policemen slammed them shut, even as Wayans screamed through the impact-resistant partition at the stoic forms of his former squad mates.

Woodwrow stood next to Baker and Colinson, both men flanking him as he watched the van pull away, taking with it the sour taste of shame and the bitter note of failure. 'Court martial, I am guessing.'

Colinson nodded as they watched the van slip from the gate and turn away, Wayans' screams muffled and dying as the vehicle dragged him further and further from their sight.

'Why'd he do it?'

Colinson's eyes settled on Woodwrow as he let the words sink into the man's mind. Woodwrow shrugged, the gesture all to lackadaisical for the situation and made Colinson's anger peak slightly as he stared at the soldier in front of him.

'Hennessey was gay, motive enough for someone like Wayans. We did a full check on his internet history. Some of the message boards and chat rooms he frequented make Abu Hamza seem like Amnesty International; the guy was a class-one homophobe and unfortunately for Scott, he knew how to fuck up the kit enough so that it worked once and then collapsed on the proper deployment.

'I'll give credit where it's due; it's actually quite clever and I wouldn't have caught it if he hadn't dumped the CO_2 as well as all the mechanical tampering.

'Me and some of the other boys will be parcelling up his kit, the stuff that hasn't been taken as evidence, anyway. Maybe something more physically damming will turn up then. Small comfort it will be to Hennessey's family and his partner. The bloke was sobbing when I told him about Scott. I hate doing that—telling their kin and loved ones makes me feel like such a louse and in need of an extra shower.

'Shame, though. Scott was a good kid. Knew him of old... bit of loudmouth and could hold his booze as well as anyone, but solid as concrete under fire.'

Baker flicked his gaze from one to the other as the conversation trailed off. Coughing into his fist, he glanced to Colinson before speaking. 'Dave, which of us is going to send this through?'

Colinson's brow rose an inch as he pondered the question, his mind turning slowly as he sifted through the threads of his indecision. 'Well, I am the arresting officer and officially in command of the unit as a whole, but if you want to step in when the time comes, feel free.'

Baker nodded; snapping his gaze over to Woodwrow, he jerked his head and began to walk back towards the armoury as Kevin fell instep beside him.

'We need you to head to Brize Norton. We have a specialist advisor coming in from the US.'

Woodwrow stumbled as he coughed into his balled fist, trying to hide the fact that he had almost choked in surprise. 'Hang on... all flights have been grounded in and out of, not only here, but the US as well. He would have been either shot down on the way in or shot as he stepped down off the plane.'

Baker smiled as he carried on walking towards the squat, low-hanging brick building that was slowly growing all the larger. 'Benefit of having an influential boss; and I don't mean Colinson, not that he is my boss anyway.'

Woodwrow smirked as he turned, resting his back against the cold brickwork of the wall as he slowly let himself slide towards the floor. A packet of Benson and Hedges appeared in his hand as he dragged a cheap disposable lighter from his pocket.

'So who is this expert, then, and what makes him so damned valuable to us, that old Liz sees fit to have him or her brought in through the quarantine?'

Baker smiled as he caught the scent of burning tobacco, the dull glow of ash tickling the corner of his eye as Woodwrow lit the overly long cigarette, the blue-tinged smoke boiling away from him as he spoke.

'He is an EMT specialising in medical care in hostile environments. In other words, he is coming over here to advise the NHS paramedics on how to best prepare for casualties in Infected areas, which with the state of things, is just about everywhere.'

Kevin smiled as Baker finished speaking, a pall of pale blue-grey smoke hanging in front of him as he stared at the floor, his face a mask of indifferent humour. 'So why you sending me? Send one of the bootstraps to go pick him up.'

Baker chuckled as he pushed himself to his feet and turned, looking down at Woodwrow's crouched form. 'Like I said, it's Brize Norton. The triad of the north-west has become a pit of random infections lately, so the whole place is on high alert for anything and everything. We can't go in mob-handed, so the S.A.Us are out of the question and the Crabfats have their hands full just keeping the local civvies safe and their base secured. You will be going in, in kit with full load out and a bounce bag for our new guest. He was an Army Ranger before becoming an EMT, so he can handle himself. Just make sure both of you get out in one piece and the whets are on me.'

Woodwrow sighed softly to himself as he ground the glowing stump of the cigarette out against the ground with his foot before slipping the dead filter into the breast pocket of his jacket. Pushing himself upright, he studiously dusted himself down before sparing a parting glance at Baker. 'When does he get in?'

'Two forty tomorrow morning, so you have time to shower, change, and get your kit prepared before you leave.'

Nodding, Kevin tucked his hands into his pockets and walked off towards the R.R.T barrack block. 'This fucker better be worth the hassle. If I end up buying a piece of it protecting his sorry arse, I am going to come collecting, Baker.'

****

The rain lashed the windows as he waited, the slow rocking of the Land Rover doing nothing to abate the surge of boredom that overthrew him as the winds curled over the flat expanse of the runway. Their buffeting eddies brushed over the vehicle like water over stone as the gentle rocking of the car began to lull him into a fugue of weary sleep.

His mind wandered as he sat there, watching the rhythmic thumping glide of the wiper blades as they skated across the windscreen in a vain attempt to slap away the deluge of water.

'Great day to be a duck… or from Atlantis,' he muttered to himself. As he straightened up his eyes, he caught sight of the plane as it dropped towards the runway. 'This fucker better be worth the trouble.'

Sliding the car into gear, Woodwrow pulled to the side of the apron as the C130 slowly rolled to a stop. Kevin climbed out of the car and reached across to the passenger side, lifting his Diemaco L.M.G from the foot well and put his arm through the sling drop. The heavy, coarse fibres plucked at his fingers as he set it over his head and shrugged through it until it settled into place over his neck and shoulder. With a flat-palmed slap, he made sure the magazine was seated before sending a round into the chamber and setting it to safe. He let it hang from the sling as he pulled his helmet and HUD plate from the passenger seat.

Woodwrow shivered slightly as he set the cold lump of metal and plastic onto his head, the weight pressing down on him like a comforting blanket. He snapped the chinstrap into place and pulled his HUD plate into position; the sheet of clear, micro-meshed Plexiglas dropped into place with a dull click.

Reaching up onto his shoulder, he pulled the coiled wire from the pouch on the back of his shoulder and set the connector into the socket with a soft click. A grin slithered over his face as the screen bloomed into life, the dull, blue glow shimmering over his face as he watched it flicker and dance.

Woodwrow dropped his fingers to his left forearm and tapped at the touchscreen console. The lightweight piece of plastic glowed as he called up the preloaded file of the man he was here to meet.

'So this is what Mr Expert looks like. Norman, huh? Well, let's hope he ain't as boring as his name sounds.'

A soft snort of derision left him as he stared at the image before him; the soft-featured, bespectacled face that stared back at him was wholly unremarkable. From the close-shorn hair that perched atop his head like the fuzz on a peach to the weather-lined face that bore its age with pride, the look of self-assured and time-tested skill bled from the man's eyes.

Kevin's eyebrows rose slightly as he scanned through the man's operational history and was surprised more so at his age than the seventeen-page long list of declassified operations. 'So, he's only pushing forty; could have fooled me.'

He muttered to himself as he trudged towards the now silent aircraft, his feet kicking through the layer of water that sat atop the runway like an inch-thick sheet of glass.

The tail of the plane folded open, the heavy whine of straining gears echoed through the air as the bottom hit the floor with an almost gentle thump. Soft ripples rolled out from the ramp as the silhouette of a man made its way down as others scurried in the half-

169

light behind him.

The six-foot tall silhouette strode down the ramp. His hazel eyes seemed to glow with an innate curiosity as he turned up the collar on his weather-beaten leather pilot's jacket, the lamb's wool lining tickling the unshaven edges of his jaw.

The stubble-laden chin dropped low as he hunched his shoulders against the deluge nature had cast upon him. Woodwrow watched as he made his way towards him; the scuffed and beaten jacket glimmered in the rain as the man slowly advanced. The embroidered patch on his left breast was stained and worn, the once gleaming white cotton dulled with age and stained by the passing years. Its two-inch high lettering slowly shifted into focus as he closed the gap further. The letters 'EMT' stood muted but proud under the circular stars-and-stripes patch sewn on just below the line of the collar.

Stopping just feet short from Kevin, he looked up; a roguish grin toyed with the corners of his lips as he stuck out his hand. The rough, calloused palm grated against the palm of Woodwrow's ballistic gloves as he clasped the man's hand in his own.

'Name's Meredith. Norman Meredith. Pleased to meet ya.'

Woodwrow nodded towards the Land Rover. 'Yeah, same. Kevin Woodwrow, commander of Broadhead RRT. We shouldn't stick around too long; the decontamination team's due in any minute and they ain't too kind to whomever they find on the strip when it comes to cleaning the import kit.'

Meredith nodded as he strolled towards the vehicle. The rain dripped off the rim of his baseball cap as he reached for the handle of the door and pulled, listening to the dull clunk of the lock as it relinquished its hold and the door swung open.

'You know what you have gotten yourself into with this?'

He nodded as they clambered into the waiting vehicle, a grin tugging at his features as he settled into the seat. He glanced around him, his sense of place slightly skewed as he stared at the steering wheel on the right hand side of the car.

'Never gonna get used to that.'

Woodwrow chuckled as he set the key in the ignition and started the car. 'That's what you get for driving on the wrong side of the road, backwards ass Yank.'

Meredith snorted, a smirk playing across his face as he tugged his cap over his eyes. 'You asked if I was ready for this?'

Woodwrow didn't spare him a glance as he slowly guided the vehicle onto the roadway, rapidly cycling through the gears as he picked up speed. 'Yeah, I did. Why?'

Meredith could all but contain his mirth as it twisted his lips, causing Woodwrow more than a little discomfort as he watched the stranger out the corner of his eye.

'Well... to be honest, buddy, I am pretty unflappable ever since my mom turned around and told me she was a full-fledged dominatrix at sixty. Then the next day, I wander out of my room to find her, a young girl—no more than twenty—and a kid the same age, who, no lie, could have been my son come wandering out of the bedroom door in front of me. I mean, in that situation, with me in my underpants and them in several states of undress, what can you do but say good morning and walk right on by? The look on that kid's face, though, was priceless. At least he'd had fun, if the grin on the girl's face was anything to go by.'

****

Meredith stood before the heads of every ambulance service in the nation, their faces bleeding scepticism and scorn as he slipped the cap from his head and ran his fingers over his close-cropped hair.

'Right, first off, sorry for looking like a drowned rat, but I have literally only just gotten here and can already tell your weather doesn't like me.'

A few half-hearted chuckles and scornful tittering filtered through the room. With unabashed, self-imposed superiority, they watched as he shrugged his jacket from his shoulders. The heavy, water-saturated leather dropped with a soft thump onto the back of a chair as Norman leant against the edge of the table and stared at the captive audience.

'Okay, who knows why I am actually here? Anyone?'

No one uttered a word as they sat mutely watching him, their eyes drilling into him as he stood there waiting.

'You're telling me that not a single one of you has any clue as to why I am here. Well, shit. Why don't you all just fuck off, find a gun, and put it to your heads, because you sure as hell won't survive what's coming if you ain't even bothered to figure out why they dragged me a few thousand miles from my bed to stand here and talk to you bunch of ungrateful dicks.'

They sat stunned for a few moments; then the slow murmur of malcontent blew through the room like a spring breeze as they all slowly began to find their voice.

Norman ground his teeth together as he watched their looks of consternation and mild anger flourish into being. Closing his eyes, he drew in a slow, beleaguered breath and stepped forwards a few paces.

'Look.' His voice echoed over them as he forced himself to rise above the tumult of babbling indecision. 'My country is all but extinct because we were too ill prepared for what awaited us on the other side of the wall. These Infected will show no more mercy for you than a Nazi would a Jew. I have watched men and women go to the aid of a crying child only to be torn apart by those they had sworn an oath to protect. If you listen, here, now, today, I will give you the information and skills that will teach you how to survive a world where our common values of family and duty hold as much credence as a paper raincoat.

'But by all means, continue to whine and snivel; then walk out that door. Just let me tell you that, if you do, it will be the last thing you ever think of doing. When you do walk out, you may as well go home and cut your own throat because it's a better choice than going out there.'

He jabbed a pointed finger towards the window as he stared at the audience before him. Their looks of rapt awe and fear made him want to smile as he remembered the last time anyone had looked at him like that—their faces locked into a glazed mask of childlike astonishment as they stared at the stocky American in front of them.

'We offered the same advice and help to the Chinese. And, well, you saw what happened to them.'

A look of arrogant scorn swam over the features of one man as he sat in the front row, his arms folded over his narrow chest, as his foot impatiently tapped at the open air as he rested his left leg on his knee.

'I don't see the need for such vehement discourse; this is all a bit of a muchness; thus far, we have had nothing much in the way of problems—a couple of localised problems and that one in Central Middlesex Hospital.

'There is little chance of us going the way of your own nation. Besides, I fail to see why you feel such a personal stake in this. They're not your families.'

Norman's hackles rose as he looked down at the hook-nosed man in front of him; the arrogant smirk that slipped over his face made Norman's teeth shiver with anger as he balled his fists, the bitten, chipped edges of his nails digging into his palms as he squeezed his hands as tight as he physically could.

'Okay, kid—and I use the term "kid" because you quite clearly are not a man—you want to know what my stake in this is? Well, let me tell you a little tale.'

Norman stepped forwards, dragging a chair with him and planted it no more than six feet from the man before sitting in it and leaning forwards so his elbows rested on his thighs.

'This was back in, 2006. I was out on a run. My team had been on call for about eight hours and I had another four before my shift ended. Anyway, my cell starts to ring. I glanced down at the display—now I ain't saying this to be overly dramatic, but my heart literally went cold in my chest as I looked at my wife's face flashing at me from the screen; so I press accept, my buddy was driving so I had no problem answering the call.

'Kay, my wife, is going frantic, literally screaming at me as I hear things crashing, and her breathing as she's begging me to come home. Now, there is fuck all I can do; I am on the other side of the county on call, and my wife is going hysterical on the end of the line.

'So after a few crazy seconds I ask her what's happening. She tells me that Julia, my fourteen-year-old daughter, has gone crazy. All these red lesions round her mouth and eyes and keeps pounding on the door trying to get at her. All this has happened after she went to help the mail carrier who collapsed on our front lawn after dropping off the mail.

'Seems she was putting him in the recovery position, and he got a bit grabby and scratched her or something; well, I didn't need to be a rocket scientist to work out what had happened to the light of my life and what was about to happen to the one woman whom made my life worth continuing.

'Anyway, I got home four hours later to find my wife in the bath tub, my daughter with her head buried in what was left of her mother's torso.

'Ever had to beat your own child to death with a MAG light, son?'

The man shook his head as Norman pushed himself to his feet and stepped back, his shoulders slumping slightly as he forced the memories back down into the pit of his mind.

'Well, let's hope you never have to.

'So, anyone else want to know what is at stake here, or have you all heard enough?'

No one said a word; Norman nodded and pulled a flash drive from his pocket as he stepped towards the laptop at the front of the room and plugged it in.

16
June 18th
London
The Russian Bar

Andrey stared at the shot glass in front of him; the small two-inch tall mini tumbler glimmered in the flickering lights. The thumping music made the clear, flavourless liquid dance in the glass as drunk girls in tight dresses gyrated for over-indulgent men, who plied them with alcohol and drugs in a bid to wet their over engorged selves on the tender flesh that the women seemed to hold in such low regard.

His shoulder jerked forwards as one ample-breasted girl stumbled, hair tumbling and face twisted into a shimmering mirror of ecstasy and avarice as she leant over his arm. She let her over-abundant cleavage spill forth as she cooed at his ear, her long slender fingers tracing his jawline as he pushed her away from him.

'Stupid slut, fuck off; go fuck one of those drunken roid monkeys you love so much.'

She stumbled and tripped as she fell onto her overly plump rump, landing with an indignant squeal as Andrey lifted the glass to his lips and sent the liquid sailing down his gullet, to land in a blossoming ball of glowing fire in his stomach.

'Proshchay staryy drug,' he muttered as he slammed the glass onto the marble counter with a heavy clack. Andrey pushed himself to his feet and left the pounding music and gyrating, lust-filled bodies behind him as he went in search of something to drown the memories that filled his world-weary mind.

****

The door *thunked* into place as Andrey flicked the white porcelain switch on the wall, waiting the fraction of a second it took for his lights to slowly blossom into being. A deep, agitated sigh rolled its way up from his stomach as he shrugged his suit jacket from his

176

shoulders and set it onto the stand by his door as he walked into the empty shell of his home.

He traced his fingers over the cold melamine of the countertop. As he let his hand curl round the handle of his refrigerator, the door opened with a soft rush of air and the clink of glass on glass as bottles of milk waged war on the Heinz ketchup next to them.

Staring into the glaringly white box, he grumbled in irritation as his eyes fell on the half-block of cheese and two eggs that occupied the otherwise empty fridge. Slamming the door shut, he pulled the freezer section open and retrieved his bottle of Snow Leopard vodka he had hidden inside three empty cartons of Häagen-Dazs ice cream.

He plucked a tumbler from the draining board and walked, his gait sullen and empty, to his leather armchair and dropped into it, letting his weight bounce off the frame as he felt the leather cushions envelope him completely.

The cap twisted in his fingers as he pulled it from the bottle, the thin, steel cap landing with a dull *clink* as he let it drop to the glass side table next to his chair. With a non-existent level of care, he upended the bottle and let the crystal-clear liquid flow free, splashing into the bottom of his glass like water from a tap.

The transparent vessel sat in his hand as he stared into it, as if willing it to somehow show him a world where all those he held dear were still, by some twist of fate, alive—or at least what passed for life in whatever universe they were in. The vodka burned its way down his throat as he drank, his breath seizing in his lungs as he swallowed the rolling ball of alcohol.

With a grunt of depressed satisfaction, he slammed the tumbler back onto the table next to his chair as he sat in the vacant silence that surrounded him. Closing his eyes, he sank into the vacuous, whirling hollow of his mind.

October 2012
Moscow
Frunzenskaya Embankment 20-22

'Why me? Why put me in charge of them?'

The general stared at Andrey Gervasii as he sat behind his desk, the starched, green uniform hugging his age-worn frame.

'They trust you; that mission in Ulan-ude, that was a death sentence if ever there was one, but you came out of it. You can pay a soldier to carry a gun, you can pay him to charge a hill, you can pay them to lay down their life and take on anything in front of them. But you cannot pay him to believe. When you went up against the Infected in Novosibirsk, we had no reason to believe you would walk out of there alive, but you did; your men were right there beside you, and you walked them out.

'They didn't care that there was a possibility of none of them making it home. They stayed, standing shoulder to shoulder beside you. And why? Because they believed in you, believed that you would do all you could to lead them out alive, and you did.'

Andrey rocked back on his heels and stared at the man who sat in front of him, unable to think of a single word of reply as he let the words roll over him.

'That may be... but there is only so much fight in a person, and to be honest, sir, I can't do it anymore; there is only so much death you can take before...'

The general sighed as he stared at Andrey, a weight settling in his stomach as stared at his friend.

'...before your friend picks you up, cleans you off, hands you your gun, and tells you to kick their arse back to whatever pit they crawled out of. You are the best damned soldier I have ever met,

178

Andrey, bar none.'

The general stood up and stepped around his desk as he set his hand on Gervasii's shoulder, his thickset digits tightening on Andrey's whip-thin frame.

'Andrey, we have stood side by side, faced it all, and won. There is a saying told to me by a friend. "May you be in heaven a half an hour before the Devil knows you're dead." If we go... no... when we go and we both end up there, find me and we can crack a bottle. We are in this together. Never forget that.'

Gervasii sighed again, his shoulders dropping as he dropped his gaze to the floor, unable to stare his lifelong friend in the face.

'I am sorry, Fadei. I can't do it anymore; that's all there is to it. I am sorry, but I'm done.'

Andrey stepped out from his lifelong friend's grip as he pulled the Directorate patch from his uniform and set it down on Fadei's desk. Turning, he strode from the door and onwards down the hall, his booted feet clicking on the floor as he slowly shrank into the distance.

Pushing his door shut, Fadei turned and made his way back to his desk, a lone tear running down his face as he picked up the badge and slid it into his desk drawer. The medical report stared back at him, his name printed across the top; its red Cyrillic lettering mocked him as he let his eyes travel down its faded, white countenance to the small band of numbers nestled next to the words that had so chilled him three months before. Estimated life expectancy.

****

Andrey's mind emptied back into his body as he opened his eyes to the dimly lit haze of night as it fell through his windows like a wall of water. Pushing himself to his feet, he stepped towards the window, a fresh glass of water-coloured vodka clutched in his hand as he leant against the frame and stared out into the traffic-choked street below.

'I am sorry, my brother; sorry you were alone when the reaper came to claim you. I hope you find solace in the embrace of the Lord. I know I cannot until I make amends to those whom I owe my life. Save a spot at the bar for me; I will be joining you soon.'

Leaning his head to the glass, he clutched the small gold cross in his hand and kissed his closed fist as he muttered one last goodbye.

'Skoroy brata.'

July 7th 2013
Buckingham Palace

Baker stood silent and immobile with Colinson, backs ramrod straight, eyes forwards as they waited. The gilt hallways and framed paintings stared down at them as they waited to be called forth. The two stewards at the doors barely made eye contact as they turned as one and reached for the handles. The doors swung open with an echoing clunk as the two men pulled the gargantuan slabs of gilded oak open and stepped aside as the two officers were called forth.

Their feet echoed off the marble floor, reverberating over the pair as they reached the second set of doors. The clack of heels and a bowed head left them standing as the door was opened and they were ushered into a small, brightly lit study; the warmth and homeliness left them both slightly wrong-footed as they watched the small stoop-shouldered figure at the desk. A corgi perked up at the entrance of the two men as they waited just beyond the doorway. Its ears pricked and eyes watchful as a small growl left its throat.

A tap of one flat-soled shoe quieted the discord from the animal as she turned to face her two guests; the envelope sat on her desk sealed with a monogrammed wax stamp. The furrowed wax drew Baker's eye as he stood motionless in the doorway.

'Enter, gentlemen; you're here at my behest and no one else's. Please, in these confines, I do not stand on formality; make yourselves comfortable. We have much to discuss.'

Baker stood, his back rigid and eyes forwards as he watched Colinson from the corner of his eye. David pulled a small Shaker-styled chair from besides the desk and began to sit, oblivious to Baker's immobility. Glancing up, he caught Derek's eye as he stared forwards, his eyes fixed on the small rosebud lost in midst of the swirling floral pattern that adorned the wall before him. A small chill ran through him as he realised just what he had done.

A smile teased at her lips as she watched Colinson freeze, his bent form mere inches from the plump cushion beneath him. Her eyes settled on Baker as she smoothed out the wrinkles in her mauve dress, the wash of perfectly styled hair framing her features as she gazed evenly at both men.

'Be seated, gentlemen.'

Derek sat, smoothly unbuttoning the bottom button of his jacket as he did so. The chair beneath him creaked slightly as he settled into the aged seat, its timeworn joints stretching even under his slim frame. He coughed slightly, clearing his throat as he took a second to arrange his thoughts.

'Ma'am, we need to discuss the current situation and what we are putting in place in terms of evacuation contingencies.'

Her eyes wavered for the briefest of moments as she stared at Derek and Colinson's slightly bashful form, the tinge of embarrassment still plain on his features.

'Well, gentlemen, what are we to do? This nation is in a state of crisis and we are spread too thin to do much of anything about it. Couple that with the fact we have people within our own ranks striving to kill one another for the sake of their sexual preference, well, I fail to see how Broadhead is able to accomplish what my great grandmother set out to do all those years ago when this vile affliction first reared its head.'

Derek's eyes widened as his commander and chief spoke. The look of amusement that danced in her eyes spoke volumes as Baker fought to wipe the look of utter astonishment from his features.

'Yes, I do know what you were told about Broadhead's origins, and for a brief period, that was its purpose: the elimination of dissidents and those who threatened the crown's rule, but it has and always will be the subjugation and elimination of the plague that is now ravaging the free world. My great grandmother only carried on the orders lain down by ancestors so far back that the house Saxe-

Coburg and Gotha, or Windsor as it is now known, was but a distant dream of people yet to be born.

'Castles and fortifications, for one thing, were not always the bastion of the wealthy and places to ride out the ravages of war. Although they did start out that way, they became havens for the healthy—rich and poor alike—during times of infestation, when the Infected, or whatever they were called at time, appeared. Lords, ladies, paupers, and peasants would flee to these great stone monoliths and pray in subjugated comfort for the passing of this vile affliction.

'I know, gentlemen, that I will not stand by and watch all that the people of this country and my own family have fought, died, and bled to build crumble to dust. While there is breath in my body, I will defend all this nation stands for, and I hope I can count on you to do the same.'

Both men stayed mute as the door opened and a porter entered bearing a tray of porcelain cups and saucers. With astute silence, he set them down on the desktop and poured a measure of milk into the cup before adding the steaming brown liquid. The swirling mist of steam boiled over the lip of the cup as he set cup and saucer on the small table at the Queen's right.

Baker held up a hand at the questioning glance from the porter as he silently motioned with the teapot. Colinson nodded as he turned his attention to the Queen.

'Ma'am, I can assure you that all here and at Broadhead will gladly lay down all to defend home and country, but if we're being completely candid, it will not be for something trivial.'

An eyebrow rose as she lifted the cup to her lips and sipped at the steaming brew within, the soft blue floral pattern complimenting everything around it. Baker smiled to himself as he listened to Colinson's words slowly drift into silence as he waited for her reply.

The soft clink of cup on saucer lapped at the edges of their minds as the wait extended forwards, dragging on for a few moments as she dabbed her lips with a small cotton napkin.

'I should certainly hope not, captain. It is rather hard having to handpick the command staff for the unit, although I must say you are doing extremely well after losing Captain Pottergate and Captain Grissom in such a short time period. I know five years is not what one would call *short* but in the scheme of things, it's fairly brief. But with what you have accomplished since you both took charge of the unit, well, I am glad to see my trust was well placed when I partnered you with each other.'

Baker tensed slightly as the memories tried to beat their way to the surface of his mind; driving them away, he coughed slightly into his fist and shifted his weight before once more tuning in to what was being said.

'The situation, as Parliament and the rest of government present it, is not one that really engenders itself to being conducive to actually being alive for any given amount of time; although, as I understand it, your head of research has been rather helpful in understanding the vectors of transmission and the rate of infection, but has not presented a way of counteracting the affects in any real form. Have I got that right?'

Baker nodded as he shifted his gaze about the room, the fine scent of perfume pinching the air as he sniffed softly. The tender fragrance teased his nostrils as he drew in a slow, even breath through his nose. A small smile glimmered for a moment as he let it settle in him.

He chuckled softly to himself as images danced through his mind, unbidden scenes that made him want to leap from the chair and whist away the two people he would give anything to have with him at the moment.

'Do you find something amusing, Lieutenant?'

Baker flushed red slightly as sat up slightly straighter.

184

'No, ma'am. Just scent memory rearing its ugly head at a rather inopportune time.'

Her eyebrow arched sharply as she continued to gaze at Derek. Lifting the cup from the table at her elbow once more, she sipped gently as she regimented her thoughts.

'Very well, gentlemen, shall we dispense with the obligatory dance and get down to brass tacks? Tell me, just how bad is the situation and can we find any way to survive moderately intact?'

Derek and Colinson cast a glance in each other's direction before in near unison replying, 'It's bad; and no, ma'am, there isn't.'

She nodded, rose to her feet, and smoothed her skirt as she watched both men snap to attention, their postures perfect as they waited for her next move. Turning with a poise born of years of practice, she waved her hand gently. Her voice, although weathered and tired, still possessed the power and authority of youth.

'Be seated, gentlemen; I know this usually entails pomp and circumstance, but given the situation and the gravitas of it all, we can dispense with it for now.'

She withdrew from a drawer in her desk three sealed envelopes, and turning back to Derek and David, held them out. Each was sealed with a red circle of wax, the thick disc emblazoned with the raised imprint of the Queen's royal seal. As their hands closed over them, she continued to speak.

'Within these envelopes you will find your new ranks and insignias, as well as a set to be given to a man of your choosing for the rank of Lieutenant, along with all documentation countersigned by myself and Lieutenant General Bradshaw. It seemed only fitting, given the rise in strength and manpower within Broadhead in the last eight months.

'Also, over the coming months, I will be transferring some of my

185

duties to Harry. I realise that it may be a little galling to be answering to a younger officer, but with the pressing issues within Parliament and my need to converse between you and them, I feel it is best that he shoulders some of the responsibilities of office now.

'He will be arriving at the barracks tomorrow for an outlining of current operations and a small meet and greet with your and the unit heads. I trust you will act accordingly.'

Both men nodded as they watched Elizabeth rise to her feet, both men following suit smoothly.

'So, gentlemen, if that is all, I bid you good day.'

Baker and Colinson both nodded before bowing and turning to the door as a footman held it open, ushering them from her majesty's presence.

****

The sound of tearing paper and crumbling wax filled the air as both men tore open the envelops. Baker stared at the gold and red velvet crown in his palm, the shoulder title pins weighing heavy against his skin as he stared at them.

'I didn't see that coming,' he muttered to himself as he pocketed the pins and pulled out the rank slide. The soft piece of material grated against his calloused fingers as he ran his thumb over the embroidered crown in the centre.

Baker looked at Colinson, a grin playing over his features as he turned; his grinned slipped from his face as he took in Colinson's shock-addled face as he stared at the four pins that lay clustered in his palm. The two crowns that nestled against the shimmering gold stars glinted in the dewy sunlight.

'I... I have just been made a lieutenant colonel; I'm a freaking lieutenant colonel, Derek.'

Baker smiled as he curled his hand over the two Major's pins in his hand. He slowly slipped the envelope and rank slide into his trouser pocket. 'Congrats, mate; couldn't have gone to a more deserving man.'

17

July Twenty-second
China City Restaurant
Leicester Square, Central London

The steady flow of lager filled them all as, one after another, the bottles filled the tables around them. The scent of fried pork and beef filled their nostrils as another petite, beaming waitress set the still sizzling tray in front of them. Davies laughed as Kingsley shoved him towards the microphone, a look of utter concentration on his face as he blearily jabbed his finger at the laptop there and kicked out at Davies' backside.

'Go on; give us a show, Mr Tough Nut SAS Commando.'

Davies grinned as he stepped towards the laptop and cued up a song. His eyes glittered as he stared at the track he had selected, the glowing letters shinning in his eyes as he scrolled through the list to a group he knew all too well. Clicking on Poets of the Fall, he stepped away from the laptop and over to the microphone stand as "Carnival of Rust" shimmered into being.

The fluid strains of acoustic guitar and mixed strings flowed from the speakers. The room fell silent as Davies began to gently sing, his hands cupping the microphone as he let his voice slip from him in a gentle lilting cadence that left them speechless.

His eyes lit on Anna's stunned face as he let himself free fall into the music. His voice rose and fell in a rhythmic dance of song and soul as he lifted the microphone from the stand and stepped to the edge of the small stage and let loose all he had within.

'Did you know he could do that?'

Her eyes soaked into Derek's as Janet sat perched on his lap, a slim glass clutched delicately in her fingers as she leant against his chest.

'I had no clue. He just keeps chucking out one surprise after another; although, I have to say, he can really pull one out the bag at a moment's notice.'

His hand rested, curled over her hip as he watched Davies step down from the miniature stage and lean forwards, brushing his lips against Anna's. Glancing up, he caught eyes with Janet and Baker as they both sat staring in his direction. Derek grinned, raising the bottle in his hand as Janet lightly clapped, both laughing slightly as they watched the blush creep up his neck.

'So there is a soft side to the hard man, after all. Hell, from all the mystique you lot have kicked up, we were beginning to think they just squirted you out of packet and added water. Either that or you were all factory vended and issued along with uniforms in batches of eight.'

Davies grinned at Baker as he sat down once more, the playful jibe sliding off him like water from a duck; he shivered slightly as Anna's fingers curled with his. A small bolt of electricity slid through him as he felt her thumb trace small circles over the back of his wrist. Grinning again, he reached across the table for his drink, taking a deep pull from the bottle before replying.

'Well, I could say the same to you but, then again, you are Welsh so you are more at home in a flock of walking cardigans than anywhere else so...'

His eyes glittered with mirth as Baker laughed, almost dropping the bottle in his hand. Janet chuckled as she traced her fingers over the back of Derek's neck. Brushing her lips against his ear, she whispered quickly before getting up. Nodding, Baker looked her in the eyes as she stood.

'Let me know how she is, okay? If we need to bolt, we can do.'

Janet smiled as she nodded, plucking her mobile phone from her handbag as she slipped between the tables heading towards the door.

189

Janet listened to the thrumming ringing as she held the phone to her ear, the ambient heat of it warming her skin while she waited for an answer. After a few seconds of tense waiting, she heard the soft muffled clicking that slipped away as a soft, lilting voice followed quickly on its heels.

'Hello, Baker residence; Siobhan speaking.'

Janet smiled as she spoke, her voice slightly muffled by her smile and the six mojitos she had drunk in very quick succession, the alcohol making her head spin slightly as she leant against the wall.

'Hey, Sib. How's my girl doing?'

A soft chuckle echoed in her ear as she listened intently. The soft shuffling and giggling in the background made Janet smile as she waited.

'She is doing fine, Mrs Baker. A little squirmy; she was dozing off as you phoned, but she hasn't been the slightest bit of trouble. Here, say hello.'

The echo of crackling plastic and a soft pattering echoed in Janet's ear as she began to coo into her phone. A broad smile lit up her features as she listened to the burble of baby talk and soft patting of miniature hands on the phone's receiver.

'See? All safe and sound. Go on, enjoy your night; I will be here to watch over her until you get back, so have no worries about time or being late. I have it all under control.'

Janet couldn't keep the grin off her face as she said thank you and hit the end call button after Siobhan had hung up. Turning on her heel, she strode back into the restaurant.

A loud call echoed over her as she stepped into the foyer, a frown furrowing her brow as she turned and glanced behind her. The simple-minded mound of flesh ambled towards her, a grin plastered

190

over its adroit face like badly finished wallpaper. Weeping acne clustered over his face, the yellow-headed, puss-filled lumps hanging off his skin like a collection of melted Christmas chocolates.

'Can I help you?'

His grin widened to a sickening layer of syrup that clung to a face so stomach churning that Janet felt the vacuous mix of bile and mucus flow up her gullet, scalding her throat and tongue with a muted paste of acid and half-chewed food.

Looking up, Baker caught sight of the angel he called a wife and the six-foot tower of slime that had her backed against the doors. He watched with a widening gaze of consternation as he cocked his head to one side, a questioning look dancing through his eyes as he watched her push against the glass, the panic in her body seeping through the air and into Baker's already rage-infused heart.

Davies flicked his eyes from Baker to the scene at the door, the trembling muscles in Baker's jaw making his eyebrows rise as he let his eyes drift back to the doorway and the clutch of men slowly encircling Janet's slim form as she pulled tighter and tighter to the glass.

'Okay, fuck that noise.'

Baker pushed himself to his feet and started for the door, his fists clenched tightly into bunched balls of seething anger.

Pushing himself upright, Davies hurried after Derek, his feet skimming over the hardwood floor as he scrambled to catch up.

Reaching the door, Baker yanked it open, catching Janet as she stumbled backwards into him. Spinning her into his arms, Derek moved in front of his wife. The grinning slob's face twisted into a picture of drunken annoyance as he watched his quarry disappear in a swirl of cloth and trembling muscle.

'Oi, back off, yo; that bitch is mine.'

191

He gesticulated wildly as Davies arrived beside Derek. The motley collection of drunken morons snickered and giggled like children as the two men moved side by side through the doorway.

'Really?'

The snickering group of drunken children chorused a slurred and spittle-soaked affirmation of confirmation, their heads bobbing like spastic pigeons as they stared with half-focused eyes.

'Everything okay at home? Maria behaving?'

Janet didn't bother replying as she backed into the restaurant, her phone still clutched tightly in her hands.

'Right, I am going to give you one chance and one chance only to leave now. That "bitch" you lay claim to is my wife and no man's property; so like I say, you have one chance, right now to leave and nothing will come of this.'

The spot-laden, head idiot marched to within an inch of Derek, their faces, so close he could feel the hot mist of sickly sweet breath as it landed across his skin. Baker fought the need to heave under the stench that assailed him, its thick, cloying aroma filling his mouth and nose with a layer of heavy moist air that threatened to choke the very air from his lungs as he stared at the thing in front of him.

'S'at 'ight? Well, she seemed all too 'appy to be 'ere talking to us.'

Baker railed against himself as he somehow kept his face completely neutral, the sight of the walking pestilence before him making his stomach dance. 'That is a far cry from what I saw and as I said, she is my wife and this is your chance to walk away without any repercussions or recompense, so please. Leave.'

His face contorted into a dribbling mask of indignant rage that mingled with alcohol-induced impudence as he puffed himself out like a cold-chapped robin.

'And what if me and my boys decided we didn't want to? What if we decided we want to come in and stay for a while, maybe help ourselves to that nice food there?'

Baker sighed as he looked down at his hands; they hung, relaxed and ready at his sides. Davies shifted his feet slightly, his hands cupped and loose just at the level of hips.

'You really going to force this? You can still walk away. In fact, I am begging you to walk away; just walk away and nothing more will come of this.'

The figure before him sneered his lips, curling into a semblance of what his pickled mind told him was scornful. The lopsided look did nothing to assuage the sheer lack of physical appeal that his features held.

Glancing behind him, Davies spied Janet wildly pointing towards the doors as Kingsley looked up at him and Derek, a look of non-concern plastered over his face as he spied the slowly closing circlet of drunken idiots.

Sighing, Baker glanced once more at his hands as they snapped closed, tightening into a fist so tight his skin groaned like canvas being stretched over an awning.

'Okay, then.'

Baker twisted, driving his fist deep into the man's kidney as his knee crashed into his solar plexus. The man's eyes widened as he dropped his breath, disappearing in a violent explosion of air and mucus.

Davies spun with a grunting growl as he drove his leg forwards, sending another drunken lout the floor in a flailing tangle of arms and legs. His body folded around Davies' driving foot as it collided with his chest. They moved in a shimmering dance of wet slapping impacts as flesh met flesh with each violent thrust. With each crushing blow, another fell until all that remained of the once menacing clutch of alcohol-fuelled erections was a whimpering mass of groaning flesh and bloodied teeth.

Crouching, Baker lifted the whimpering collection of flesh that had been the cause of it all by the shoulder and said in a soft almost gentle voice.

'Now is that going to be the last time you hit on another man's wife and are you going to, from now on, leave when you are asked?'

Baker watched as he nodded; then with a gentle pat on the man's shoulder, he rose to his feet.

'Good.'

Stepping over him, Baker headed towards the door as Davies pulled his slightly rumpled shirt back into place and followed suit, a soft smile gracing his lips.

'Derek, does that count as PT for tomorrow?'

Baker snorted as he pushed the door open and made his way back to his table. 'Not if Colinson has anything to say about it.'

'Oi Dave, John wants to know if that little spat counts as PT for tomorrow.'

David looked up as Akemi cast a glance over her shoulder in their direction, a puzzled scowl weaving her brow together. Leaning in, she whispered in his ear.

'It means physical training,' he replied in a quick burst of Japanese.

He then turned, leaning across the back of his chair to look at Davies' slow approach. 'Only if you broke a sweat; did you?'

Tugging at his shirt, John searched for any sign of perspiration.

194

Finding none, he sighed and shook his head.

'Then no. I want you on the field in PT kit at zero five thirty.'

Nodding, Davies picked up his pint and set it to his lips, taking a long, lingering pull from the amber-coloured liquid. 'Fine, I'll be there. We going through full drills or just a shakedown session?'

Colinson smiled as he pulled Akemi tighter to him, settling himself into the chair further before replying.

'Full drills so bring your pads.'

Davies smirked and dropped into his seat, slipping his fingers through Anna's once more.

Derek looked at Janet as she stood slightly shaken by the bar, a slim, olive-skinned waitress at her shoulder. The woman quickly looked up as Derek approached, a small glimmer of concern in her eyes that all but vanished the instant he appeared.

Before Baker could utter a word, Janet spoke. The glass of water in her hands rippled slightly as she stared up at his face, the grim set to her eyes speaking volumes.

'Teach me!'

Baker looked at her slightly askance, his eyes widening imperceptibly as he gazed down at her.

'Huh? Sorry, darling, teach you what?'

Janet pointed with her chin towards the door as she set the glass on the counter and stood, turning towards the loud bubble of noise and energy that was their friends.

'To fight like you do. I am sick to death of playing the damsel to your bloody white knight. Do you know how embarrassed that makes me? Every time something happens that I can't immediately control, you leap in. I am not useless, Derek!'

Baker rubbed the back of his neck as she continued to speak, drawing several curious glances from, not only their friends, but the other people around them.

'If you won't do it, I am sure John, David, or Solomon would be more than happy.'

A heavy-throated retort rolled over the heads of every one there as Kingsley shouted across, his reply drawing several chuckles from those around them, including Derek.

'No we bloody wouldn't. You would probably try and poison us in our sleep; then again, you do work for the NHS, so we would probably be dead by the afternoon.'

Her withering gaze silenced any formal reply he could have mustered as she turned back to her husband and stared at him. Her arms were crossed over her chest and her jaw set as she slowly let one eyebrow rise, her emerald green eyes boring into him, waiting for that final moment when she knew that chink would open and his defences fall at her feet.

'Fine, but when you're in the ring, you're just another recruit. If we're doing this, we're doing it right. Not some pansy-arsed, half-hearted go at it.'

Both her eyebrows rose as she lined up another salvo ready to tear into him, but as she stared into the twin blue discs that held her gaze, she could see he was deadly serious. She saw just how scared it made him to admit that he was beginning to become a first-line defender and not the stalwart fortress he had always been to those he loved and cherished.

'Okay.' Was her only reply as she snaked past his reaching hands and slid into his waiting grasp. She slid her arms round his neck and drew him to her, her lips locking over his in a deep impassioned kiss that left Baker reeling and a little embarrassed as a cacophony of

196

wolf whistles and laughing taunts echoed up from around them.

Glancing around him, Kingsley suddenly felt very alone as he looked at the others either calling or clutching their spouses as their inhibitions fell away in the flood of food and alcohol. A heavy lump settled in his chest as he hung his head. The well of sadness and loneliness that suddenly rose around him made him all too aware of his own station and mortality.

He jumped slightly as a small hand tapped at his shoulder. A slither of white paper clutched between slender caramel-coloured fingers danced in his vision. Turning, his eyes travelled over the slim figure holding it, her almond-shaped eyes glittering as she smiled shyly. Kingsley slipped the paper from her fingers and into his pocket.

A grin spread over his features as he watched her slip back through the door, a coy smile fluttering through the air as she cast a glance back over her shoulder and finally dropped from view. Hopping to his feet, Kingsley slapped the tabletop, drawing all eyes to him as he raised his drink into the air.

'To Lieutenant John Davies, Major Derek Baker, and Lieutenant Colonel David Colinson, I want to say…' Kingsley paused as he watched the expectant gazes hang on his words. 'Thank Christ it wasn't me.'

A wave of laughter rolled through them as Kingsley grinned, his left hand patting the air as he motioned for quiet once more.

'But in all seriousness, I couldn't think of two men I would rather serve under than Derek and David. Both have shown time and again the lengths they will go to keep not only their families and country, but also their men safe from anything that would come their way; I, for one, am honoured to be able to call them not just my commanders but also my friends. Love you guys. No matter where you are, how deep the problem, call and I am there.'

London NW1
Actual location Unknown

Fury and madness swirled in equal measure in his glazed eyes as he stared at the photo in his hands. The smiling face was smeared in camouflage paint and dirty, running like fire through his mind.

The slim aquiline features of the man to his left made his heart heave. The path he trod in the name of vengeance left him with nothing. Cold and alone, there he sat; a soiled canvass camp bed his only comfort as he felt dampness and mould seep into his lungs. The hacking cough that spilled out sent crimson droplets over the glossed paper in his grip. Tears pricked at his eyes as footsteps pulled his attention to the door behind him.

'Sir, the men are ready; you give the word, and we'll proceed. Our man inside has already set the worm into their system, but ...'

The operative trailed off as Ridgmont's gaze turned to him.

'What?'

The operative shifted nervously as he adjusted his grip on his weapon. 'He went off script and has been snatched on murder charges. However, his breach into the mainframe has yielded valuable intelligence.'

Ridgmont sneered as he rose to his feet, his slight form standing in stark contrast to the armour-clad soldier before him.

'No matter; we will proceed as planned. Have Trojan continue to monitor the package. When a window presents itself, they are to acquire the target; until then, we will proceed as planned with the operation.'

The operative saluted and turned on his heel, striding from the room as Ridgmont pulled a disposable phone from his pocket.

Pressing down on the one key, he watched as the screen lit up and auto dialled the preprogramed number.

'Move on the secondary target. Location is Lovell Buckinghamshire. You have your orders.'

A heavy beep filled the air as Ridgmont ended the call. He turned the phone in his hand and tore the back free. With a smooth, practised motion, he drew the battery and sim card from the housing before tossing the sim and handset into a lit brazier in the corner of the room.

****

The screen sent a shifting glow across his features as he tapped and prodded at the keyboard. The list of names danced over his skin as he clicked on one after another.

The secure phone on the desk next to the matte-black hard drive pinged as, one after another, payments were made and each man was bought. A vicious grin curled over Ridgmont's lips; he watched the screen fade as he pulled the hard drive from the port and slipped it into the heavy padded pocket as he stood.

His lungs burned; phlegm, blood, and searing bile rose through his throat as his chest heaved. Reaching into his trouser pocket, he pulled out a stained and bloodied handkerchief, his vision swimming as his body shook and he began to cough. Thick wads of clotted blood and phlegm coated the cloth in his hand as he sank to his knees, the room around him echoing with the sounds of a dying man.

The sound of rustling paper echoed the scurry squeak of the rats in the walls as Ridgmont pulled a photo from his breast pocket. The aged and worn piece of photographic paper was creased and foxed at the edges. Greasy thumbprints mottled its surface as he stared into the camouflage, paint-smeared face of his son.

'I'll make it right. I'll make it right. I promise you, I'll make it right.'

August Fourth
Greater Manchester
Northwest England

His breathing came in ragged gasps; the air, cold and fresh, stung his lungs as he drew it in. The frozen haze of his bitter breath misted in front of him as he listened to the pounding of his feet, their offset beat echoing his heart as he ploughed on through the rising gloom of a new day.

He listened to the scraping sound of trainers over gravel as the hand he clutched so tightly in his dropped, almost dragging him down with it.

'Liz, c'mon; we have to go. We can't stop.'

He pulled at her arm as she tried to force herself to rise, her knees scraped and raw from the nights she spent earning enough to keep death from their door began to slowly weep, their crimson tears sliding through the torn laddered tights that clung to her unwashed skin.

Her dirty, matted, and frayed hair hung low over her eyes as she stared up at him. Her face was lined with a layer of grime that sheared her tender years from her, leaving her an embittered shell of a girl. His eyes gazed at her, dispassionate anger warring with his need to protect as he hauled her upright, the size-four trainers that covered her worn and blistered feet, scraping through the grit-filled mud as he pulled her into a staggering run.

'What happened this time?'

She bit her lip, sucking the dirty flap of skin and flesh into her mouth as she sucked at the scabbed cut, the coppery taste of her own blood filling her mouth as she tore the scab free. Spitting the wad of blood and sputum to the ground, she shrugged. Her frail form was swamped in the muck-tarnished hoody that hung from her like a limp dishcloth. She stumbled once more, her feet tangling in the flapping laces that danced about her ankles.

'Damn it, Liz, how many times have I told you to tie those damn things? Fucking c'mere.'

She shrank back from his ire-filled glare as he pulled her towards him, the look of fear mingling with a swirling mix of shock and utter resignation. She curled her arms into the hoody, pulling it tight to her small body; the bones of her shoulders poked free of the neckline as she bunched it under her chin.

Robbie sighed as he stared at her starved and malnourished form, a sharp spike of guilt and self-loathing driving through his heart as he looked at her.

'I'm sorry; I didn't mean to shout.'

He knelt in front of her, quickly tying the loose strands of her laces into tight bows before once more standing and taking her hand.

'C'mon the place ain't far and I think we have lost Toni's boys; I don't want them anywhere near you anymore.'

He pulled her forwards, her feet slapping the ground as they once more began to run. Echoed shouts of anger made him turn as Liz froze in place, her body trembling as she began to cry, her crystal tears leaving growing lines of pain in her dirt smeared skin.

Leaning down he pushed the matted curtain of hair from Liz's face. A grim shimmer of certainty danced in his eyes as he looked at her; the dull curtain of self-loathing and dead innocence hung like a veil across her mind as he looked into the two once glittering orbs of blue crystal.

'Run straight down here, go left after the metal sign post; you'll see a dumpster with a big red circle sprayed on it. Behind that is a window; climb in there and stay as quiet as you can. I'll come and get you. Go as fast as you can, Liz, and don't look back.'

She nodded, turning as she did so, and ran as fast as her slim legs could carry her, the tears shimmering in a glittering line of dancing diamonds along her face.

Robbie's hand slipped into the folds of his torn and mould-stained jacket. His fingers curled around the masking tape-covered handle within, a shiver of apprehension slithering through him as he listened to the shouts and pounding feet as they closed in.

He watched with a deep, gnawing need to flee as they closed the distance, their heaving chests and sweat-soaked brows creased with rage as they slowed to a crawl, advancing inch by nerve-rending inch towards him.

Robbie began to shake, the trembling of his muscles filling him completely as he bounced slightly on the balls of his feet, his hand flexing around the handle that he clutched so tightly. His thoughts bunched into a jumbled mess as he watched them slowly begin to encircle him, their towering forms seeming to blot out the rising sun as he slowly began to back away. His palm was slick with sweat as he closed it tight around the handle of the serrated kitchen knife as he pulled it free.

'Well, lookie here, lads. Little Robbie's all tooled up. W'at you g'nna do, Rob? Stick me with that shank, yeah?'

The knife hung easily in his hand as he settled the weight into his palm. The tape gripped his skin with an assuring pull as he shifted his feet, crouching slightly, his eyes flickering from one man to the next as he continued to back away.
'Where d'you tink you're goin' boy? We got business wit' that piece o' cunt o' yours. She ga'e my boy ere some nasty bites. Y'know, you shud teach 'er to mind her manners, man; won' get much repeat customers, she keep biting people like tha'.'

Toni grabbed at his crotch, waggling his genitals at Robbie as he stepped closer. Robbie tensed, crouching lower as the crew around him laughed. Stopping eight feet from him, Toni laughed as he released his hold on his semi-engorged phallus.

'So, you g'nna give 'er up, or wot?'

Robbie shimmered as Toni's eyes widened. The man's sneering face locked in a rictus image of surprise and shock as he felt the cold kiss of the serrated steel as it slid up through his solar plexus and deep into his chest. Robbie twisted the blade hard as he pushed it deeper, his hand curling into the back of Toni's Lacoste sports coat, drawing him deeper onto its cold, biting edge.

Blood splattered the floor, staining Robbie's jeans as he pushed the stunned form from him. Toni hit the floor with a thump, gasping like a goldfish in its bowl, his lips smacking together in a pantomime gasp. Their sound fluttered up amongst the stunned group, hanging on the air like wet rags on a washing line as their wet slapping echoed like steak on a chopping board.

Robbie turned, his eye glinting with an undisguised malice to the next in line and lunged. They scattered, their pride gone with the wind when Toni finally hit the floor. With a feral growl, Robbie turned and knelt, his knees soaking up the morning dew from the dirt below as he stared at the still gasping man beneath him.

'Now they know, Toni. Now they know. Unfortunately for you, it was too little...' He set the blade against Toni's skin and with a vicious sawing yank, severed his throat. 'Too late.'

Robbie didn't let up until he felt the jagged teeth of the knife grate against Toni's spine, the spray of crimson life dancing across his skin as he finally pulled the knife free. With a callous smirk, he wiped it clean on Toni's coat. The rapidly expanding pool of blood made Robbie skip back as he slipped the knife back into the cardboard sleeve duct taped to the inside of his jacket.

****

Robbie slid through the window to a peel of frightened squealing and scurrying limbs. He dropped with a soft thump to the floor,

203

reaching up and pulling the panel of wood and cardboard boxes back into place. He smiled at the improvised camouflage, the spent tubes of stolen glue lying in a heap beside his feet, their heavy scent clinging to the air as he turned and fished in his pocket for the small pencil light and its one remaining battery.

The small shaft of dull-yellow light flickered around the room as Robbie searched for any sign of his baby sister. The ovoid puddle of urine-coloured luminescence skated over the floor as he made his way into the darkness. His voice low and throaty, he called out for the one person who he would die to protect. He knew people said it is easier to die in defence of another than it is to kill, as you can only die once. Either way, he didn't care what happened to him or the Tonis of the world. His only concern was making sure his sister—the one dull, almost faded candle in his dark and dismal existence—remained alive and burning. He would kill or die; all he wanted was to be sure of that one simple thing.

'Liz, it's me. It's Robbie.'

A soft rustling filtered through the dark, sliding over his ears as he stopped and listened, trying in vain to pinpoint just where it had come from.

'Prove it.' The voice was soft, barely a whisper, but full of life that he longed for her to keep for as long as she was able.

'Remember when you were three and we went swimming with Mum at Pembray Beach? You bugged me all day to go look at the rock pools and you fell in, disappearing completely, and that man fished you out by your leg.'

The shuffling echoed past him again as he smiled at the memory.

'Yeah, what about it?'

'Well, remember what you said to the man when he asked if you were okay?'

The shuffling rustle of cloth on concrete grew closer as he strained his ears, trying in earnest to pick out its direction.

'Yeah, and what did I supposedly say then?'

The stern self-assured tone caught him off guard slightly as he heard her stop.

'That you had drunk all the swimmings.'

A set of slim arms ensnared his waist, sending him sprawling to the floor; all five stone of her slammed into his back as she threw herself at him.

'I was scared you wouldn't come back. Toni and his crew were so nasty to me. They... they... did things I didn't want them to... things to my bottom that I didn't like. It hurt a lot.'

Robbie gently eased the arms from his waist and pushed himself into a sitting position against the cool concrete wall. Tentatively, he reached out, pulling her into his lap where she curled against him. She pulled her legs tight against herself as she rested her head against his chest.

'I didn't want to, but they made me. I said no. Said you wouldn't like them doing it, but they laughed at me and put their things in me, in my bottom. Please don't let them do it anymore. The other things I don't mind. It's yucky, but it doesn't hurt. Please don't let them, Robbie, please.'

He pulled her close, her thin, bony, almost skeletal frame pressing into his chest as he settled his chin against the top of her head, tears stinging his eyes.

'No one is going to do that to you again ever; I promise. Try to go to sleep now, Liz. We can see if there is any food left here later on, okay?'

She nodded, her hair catching in the zip of his jacket as she squirmed against him to get comfortable. The tears fell in earnest from him as he stifled a sob, knowing full well that he had just lied to the only family he had left—a lie that would haunt him until the day he died.

Letting his head thump back against the wall, he closed his eyes and tried to think of how they were going to survive the next twenty-four hours.

The rain dripped from them as they plodded past the throngs of shoppers, their jostling busy forms flitting past like bees in search of a flower. Their eyes darting and uncaring as they averted their gazes from the two filth-covered forms that threaded their way through the crowd.

Robbie's hands danced as he bumped to and fro, a purse here and wallet there, always dropping back to his sides and pack on Liz's back. The mould-covered drawstring bag hung from her like a bull's scrotum, its pendulous weight banging against her backside, its rhythmic thump nudging at the corners of her mind and the pain she had endured only a day earlier. A soft tug drew Liz to the right and the pair disappeared into the mouth of an alley, its litter-strewn length a haven nestled between a Kofte kebab house and a Betfair betting shop; the smells of fried meat and the sickly sweet scent of alcohol made their stomachs lurch as they sank deeper into the grime-laden stretch of derelict ground.

Robbie pulled the bag from her back as he sank to the floor beside an over flowing dumpster. The squeal of rats rose up to meet him as he let his weight settle against the pale green metal. With a jerk of his head, he called Liz to sit down, his eyes watching her slightly limping gait as she squatted on her heels beside him.

'How much?'

The quizzical call grated at his nerves as he tugged the neck of the bag open and fished inside. His hand returned, the leather wallet clutched inside, nestled between his digits like a money-choked clam. 'I don't know yet; I haven't even looked inside this one, let alone the others.'

Liz bowed her head, sniffling slightly as he peeled back the layer of leather to expose the plastic and paper innards that held their lives captive. With an ease and well-honed dexterity born of a lifetime of scrimping and surviving on his own wits, Robbie filtered the money and plastic into two separate piles, the towering stack of notes held down by a lump of brick while the cards lay silent and immobile in their glistening piles of wealth-infused plastic.

'Okay, so we have enough cash to get some food and drink for the next... Robbie did a quick mental leap as he tabbed through exactly what they could buy with enough shelf life to survive not being refrigerated. 'Week and a half, if we go easy and slow with it; no pigging out like last time. I know you like canned peaches, but you ate all five tins in two days and what happened?'

Liz blushed slightly as she remembered exactly what had happened for the next three days afterwards. 'I know; I'm sorry.'

Robbie smiled as he checked the rest of the slots in the last wallet they had. 'Don't be; you need the vitamins. Just don't do it again.'

A small slip of paper dropped into his palm, the four hastily scratched-out digits in its centre made his eyes widen with surprise as he stared at them.

'Thank Christ for idiots. Liz, stuff the money into the bag while I drop the cards down that drain there; we have to find a cash machine quick.'

She scrambled furiously to do as she was asked while Robbie disposed of the evidence of their misdeeds.

They slid to a halt amidst a flurry of clothes and flailing limbs, and with the urgency of a father on a forgotten birthday jammed the card into the reader in front of them. Then, with infinite care, Robbie tapped in the four-digit number.

207

Robbie's eyes slid closed as he silently prayed to a God he no longer cared for or believed in that the pin code still worked. He was wrenched out of his pious ministrations by an excited girlish squeal; dragging his gaze downwards, he stared at the shimmering blue screen and the carefully laid out numbers.

Quickly skimming through the balance, Robbie checked exactly what he could withdraw, milking the account for as much as he could before his window of opportunity snapped closed forever. With a static *whirr*, the notes slid into his hands, the crisp, clean ten and twenty-pound notes filling his heart as he stared at the ever-increasing pile.

Standing on her toes, Liz whispered in his ear the one question she had been wanting to ask again ever since he had found the pin code. Closing his fist around the wad of notes Robbie pulled Liz away from the machine, abandoning the card as they made a hasty retreat from public view and the cameras that stalked the streets.

'Okay, we have nearly a thousand pounds here and three hundred in the bag. So all in all, we have a little under twelve hundred pounds.'

He could feel the mounting glee in his younger sibling as he spoke. Cutting off her joy-filled squeals before they could happen, he continued to speak. 'We're not going stupid with food. We are getting some new clothes first; nothing fancy, but tough and comfortable, then we get food and head back to the hole, okay?'

Liz nodded, slightly subdued from the semi-scolding as she kicked at an empty can by her foot.

'Right, turn around; I want to hide this lot before we get caught with it out in the open.'

Tugging the bag closed, he reached forwards, squeezed Liz's shoulder gently, and turned her to face him again. 'We are also getting you a haircut and some soap so we can at least have a cold wash with some bottled water.'

He watched his sister's face light up as his words sank in and couldn't help but laugh as she flung her arms round his waist and hugged him as tight as she could manage.

'Come on let's get going.' Pulling her from him, he took her hand and slowly moved into the flow of people disappearing into the faceless mass as easily as a drop of water into a river.

18
August Eighth
Broadhead Barracks

'Right, okay, yes; I understand the urgency, but I am afraid we can offer little in the way of assistance at the moment. We're stretched thin on the ground as it is dealing with our own problem here. Yes, I do appreciate the impact the Infected are having there. Yes, I do pay attention to the international news, but as I said, without a way to suddenly ease the burden here, we cannot commit men to aiding your own forces. They're just going to have to subsist without our intervention; I am sorry, but that is all there is to it. Good day to you, too, sir.'

The phone clanged with the muffled chime of a bell as he dropped the receiver back into the cradle. Dragging his beret from his head, Colinson ran a hand over his sweat-dampened hair, a deep sigh of anger and agitation rising from him as he listened to the high-pitched chiming of his phone as it began to ring once more.

'Oh, for fuck sakes.' Lifting the receiver to his ear, he spoke, his voice politely neutral as he listened to the pleading female voice that barraged him with plaintive calls for aid.

Colinson leant his head against his folded arms as he slumped over his desk. The phone was finally silent for the first time since six thirty that morning; his eyes drooped as he lay with his head nestled in the crook of his elbow.

The sounds of the morning's waking denizens filled his office. The chirping of birds mingled with the distant drone of long-haul traffic as it passed them by, shielded by the five miles of fields and hedge-lined roads that wound their way to the base's gates.

The door to his office slowly slid open, drawing his attention for a moment. Looking up through strained and bleary eyes, he stared at the willowy figure in the doorway. The petite, trim curves were tantalisingly familiar to his senses, and yet he could not place the

210

form that was slowly swimming into focus.

She slipped across the floor with the slow grace of a lazy jungle cat, covering the distance in a slow walk that begged to be watched with unscrupulous candour. His eyes travelled over the curves of her hips to the supple wave of her stomach and chest, drinking in every line and every subtle imperfection as if it were the last thing he would ever see.

Reaching out with a slender arm, she let the folder drop from her grasp, the inch-thick file falling to the desk with a crack akin to a rifle shot. The echoing report jolted him to his senses, his eyes dragged into focus by a wave of shock and adrenalin so sharp and sudden he felt as if he had been cleaved in two. Staring upwards, his eyes connected with Susan's, her gaze quizzical and almost concerned as she stared down at her boss.

'You okay, sir?'

Colinson ground the balls of his hands against his eyes as he chased away the thought dogging him before trying in vain to reply. 'Yes, fine, thank you Staff Sergeant. I'm going to take a personal hour. Could you see to it I am not disturbed? After the morning I've had, I want to try and stave off the migraine I can feel marching its way up my spine as long as possible.'

Susan nodded as she turned and crisply marched from the room. With a pain-tinged groan, Colinson unfurled the blinds and let them drop into place. The echoing clatter made him wince as the blind finally clattered against the windowsill, coming to a rest in a rippling sheet of slatted steel. David pinched at his temples as he slumped backwards onto the small settee in the corner of the room, the padded faux-leather seat cushioning his fall as he hit, air rushing out from under him in a high-pitched whoosh that left a childlike shimmer of a giggle in his stomach.

With a shrug, he slipped his jumper over his head, letting the merino wool and polyester pullover fall to the floor in a crumpled heap. With a smooth, quick movement, he slipped his fingers through the top three buttons of his shirt, letting it sag open. The cold air in the room tickled his sparsely haired chest as he swung his feet up, his clothes twisting slightly under his weight as he fought to find a more comfortable position. Finally settling on his side, Colinson shifted his shoulder, resting his head on his folded arm and slowly slipped into a fitful sleep.

****

Sweat fell like rain as they moved, their forms twisting, spinning like dervishes as they clashed and danced. Hands and feet a blur of impacted movements; a dull grunt echoed as fist connected with jaw, the sound of a body hitting the hard, compacted dirt filling the air.

'Keep your guard up; do you expect anyone or anything to be as lenient as I am?'

Derek stepped forwards as he spoke, his hand outstretched to help Janet up from the floor. With anger shimmering in her eyes, she slapped the proffered hand away. Pushing herself to her feet, she launched herself forwards, her balled fists scything through the air towards Derek's face.

Ducking past the miniature wrecking ball, he caught the flying fist, levered Janet's arm up, and twisted against her elbow as his body moved, dragging her still moving form across his hip; with a muffled yelp of surprise, she sailed over his head to land in a dust-obscured bundle of arms and legs five feet away.

'Don't rush your opponent blindly; are you fucking stupid? All you do is leave yourself open for exactly what I just did or worse. I could have had a knife, a gun or anything else in my hands and it would have opened you like a fish from muff to jaw.'

Janet stayed mute as she levered herself back onto her feet, her eyes aflame as she dropped low and slowly began to circle Derek. Her eyes flitted from his hands to his feet, watching for the slightest shift in his posture, a subtle swaying of his weight to another position—anything that would give her some indication of what could be coming.

Derek swept forwards, his feet shifting in an instant as he watched Janet's eyes move back to his hands. Shifting through her rising arms like sand through a sieve, he struck, his elbow rising and connecting with the base of Janet's chin as he hooked his leg between hers. She tumbled backwards, her weight and balance lost in the deluge as she collapsed over his leg.

Derek's hands snapped downwards, his right hand curling into the collar of her shirt as he raised his left and sent it sailing towards her throat. Janet's eyes snapped shut as she saw the hand descend, her mind racing as she waited for the impact that would inevitably end her existence; but there was nothing, just the cold air humming over their heated sweat-drenched bodies. She listened to the sounds of birds and the muted popping carried on the wind from the ranges beyond the borders of the base's interior.

Slowly, her eyes opened, stung by the glare of the noon sun as it hung high in the cloudless sky. Shifting her gaze, she let her eyes settle onto Derek's as he stared at her, his breathing even and steady as his fist sat mere inches from her exposed throat.

'Never watch their hands.' His only reply to her questioning gaze. Letting his body relax, he stood, pulling Janet none to gently upright as he did. His eyes were impassive and unmoved by the dishevelled and slightly scuffed woman before him.

'We will pick this up next week. I cleared it with the hospital administrator. Kevin will fill in for you. Women's showers are over there. He jerked his head in the direction of the barrack block as he turned his back on her.

'Clean yourself up and I'll meet you at the car in an hour.'

Without another word, he left. His form quickly vanished to nothing as he strode away, leaving a slightly bewildered and none-too-pleased woman in his wake. Janet retrieved her coat from where it lay on the grass outside the ring. She winced as a sharp spike of

213

heat lanced up from the base of her back. Grimacing, she pressed her balled fist into the bunched and over-tightened muscle, righted herself with a slow, deep breath, and made her way towards the barracks.

****

The ride was silent; the only sounds filling the car were the incessant drone of the engine and the sound of the road beneath the wheels. Neither of them spoke as they began to wind through the slowly darkening streets as they chased the dwindling daylight.

The hum of twilight insects filled their ears as they stepped from the car, her gait slow and uneven as she limped from the bruises on her hip. Watching her move like a half-crippled leper made Derek's heart drown in its own tears, but part of him knew, even relished the thought of being able to count on her to protect their daughter if anything should ever befall him.

Silence reigned supreme as they stepped inside the house; its dark sanctum was a cool, inviting well, a safe hidden harbour from the oppressive heat of the day that seemed to linger on the air, even as the day slipped into night and the sun once more dropped from view, chased away by the snapping dogs of the moon's onward advance.

Swallowing his pride, Derek cleared his throat, drawing Janet's attention away from the advancing silhouette that slowly approached from the darkness. Looking past her, he caught eyes with Siobhan as she stopped short of them, a small smile plucking at her lips as she pushed her glasses back into place.

'Sib, could you go check on Maria, please, and give us a couple of minutes?'

A small frown crinkled her brow for a moment, but any retort or reply fell away as she took note of the situation for what it was. Nodding, she quietly scampered up the stairway and vanished from sight. Baker turned and looked at Janet, his face a mixture of emotion as he stared at the set of emerald orbs.

'About earlier, I...'

He stopped, unable to think of anything beyond those three words, his mind a swirling mess of conflicted emotions and temperamental self-loathing.

'Well, I don't honestly know what to say. I mean, I could say something but whether or not that is the right thing to say remains to be seen.

'I could end up saying the wrong thing and just make things worse… or I could say the right thing at the wrong time and that would be just as bad as saying the wrong thing, which is just as wrong as saying nothing, and saying nothing doesn't seem like a good thing, as saying nothing means I don't care. But I do care, and I don't want to seem like I don't care by saying the wrong thing and saying the wrong thing is worse than saying nothing, and yet everything I say except the right thing would be just as bad as saying nothing or the wrong thing. Does that make sense?'

Janet stood staring at her husband as he babbled like a confused teenage girl, his hands roving through the air, flitting about like errant birds as he stared at the floor, unable to make even the simplest of eye contact.

A loud crack echoed through the corridor, a stark silence filling the void it left behind. Derek felt the heat spread through the side of his face as he went rigid, unable to fully process exactly what had just happened in the second it took for Janet's hand to connect with the side of face. A stinging welt of sour red spread through his cheek as he slowly felt himself gather the scattered pieces of his fragmented mind.

A deep, coppery tang filled his mouth, the hot scent of burnt pennies filling his nose as he touched the inside of his cheek, his fingers coming away stained with the taint of his own blood. Nodding, Derek slumped back, coming to rest on the bottom of the staircase. The wide, open, bottom step rose up to meet his descending form.

'I needed that, thanks. Never thought I would be thanking someone for slapping me in the face.'

A soft snort left him as he finally glanced up at his wife, her palm glowing red, a look of pain and anger slipping across her features as she rubbed her thumb over her palm.

'Derek, honestly, what can we say to one another about today? You did what I wanted you to do and I got what I asked for. You told me exactly what was coming and how it would play out. There is honestly nothing to say that would in any way change what has happened. Besides, I know you; you would have kicked ten bales of shit out of anyone else who had tried to teach me half of what you did, regardless of whether or not you knew about it. I love you, Derek, but there are times when we need to set aside feelings and just get on with it, and this.

She pointed to the rising welt on the base of her chin and the swath of abraded skin that ran down her shoulder and across her side like a sadistic watercolour. A slowly purpling haze of blood flooded her shoulder and side; the pale sickly stains of bruised flesh were beginning to rise to the surface.

'It's all part and parcel of it; nothing can be avoided if I am going to learn what I need to. I can't play nursemaid to the injured and sick while you go out hunting the depraved and the wicked, then expect you to come running at the drop a hat to rescue me when things don't go how I want them to. Life doesn't work like that.'

Derek sat mute as Janet stepped forwards and leant against the banister, her arms pulled tight around her as she looked down at the man who, through it all, was still the same bumbling boy she had met at nineteen when he had stumbled into the accident and emergency room of King George's hospital where she was working as an intern.

'Sorry for babbling like that.'

Janet smiled as she stroked the back of his head. Nudging his shoulder with her hip, she made him move and slid down beside him, her arm sliding through his as she leant her head on his shoulder. 'Not the first time I have seen that, is it? Or had you forgotten your bungled pickup lines as I sewed you back together?'

Derek smiled as he slipped his arm around her waist and pulled her closer to him, placing a gentle kiss on the top of her head. 'You know, I had almost forgotten about that—the babbled pickup line, I mean; not the stitched back together bit. Still, it was nice work, although if I remember correctly, it was probably because that trainee nurse's uniform kept billowing open at the neckline and you were wearing nothing but a bra underneath it.'

Janet grinned as she remembered the scene, a small giggle leaving her as she pictured the look on Derek's face as she had leant forwards.

'So, you did notice that. I was wondering at the time if you had hit your head, you were babbling so much. Nice to know it wasn't the concussion drawing your attention away from your mouth.'

Baker touched the small, ridged scar on his chest, the slim, three-inch-long line of puckered flesh a twisted reminder of just how lucky he had been that day. Easing away from Janet, he stood, his hand gently caressing his wife's cheek as he moved away from her.

'I am going to relieve Siobhan of her duties and grab a shower; I'll see you upstairs.'

Janet nodded as she watched him make his way upstairs, her body aching with the tension and stiffness in her muscles. A small wince shivered through her as she rolled her neck, listening to the soft clicking of partially displaced cartilage. Setting her hands against the side of her chin, she began to slowly apply pressure as she forced herself to push back against them.

A soft crunch echoed up through her ears as everything, all at once, jumped back into place. Rolling her shoulders as she shook out the last vestiges of pain, she stood and followed the now vanished form that she called her husband. Her footsteps filled with the tentative poise of a five year old as she fought against the quivering fatigue that plagued her over-taxed muscles. Her feet moaned with every step she took. Stifling a groan, Janet pushed on, mumbling to herself. A deep undercurrent of annoyed weariness plucked at her as she moved.

'If this is how he feels every damned day, no wonder he is such a grumpy shit in the mornings.'

****

The smell of burnt cordite and gunpowder filled their nose as orange bursts of light flashed across their eyes. The pale-yellow glasses did little to dilute the already spots-inducing glare from each pull of the trigger. The target in front of him jumped and bucked as he sent the searing hot lumps of copper and lead slamming into it, the sneering head splitting open like a rotten melon as the magazine slowly began to run empty.

The rhythmic thump of the pistol in his hands began to fill him, his mind dragging forth everything he fought to suppress. Images danced in his head… of Sarah and the look on her face as she fled from his arms. The look in her eyes saying more than screaming, tear-filled rage ever could.

Hawk knew she blamed him for Remy's death, and in some small way, he agreed with her. He'd had all the chance in the world to latch onto the drag hoop of his best friend's vest and pull him free.

John bit down hard on the inside of his cheek as he snapped a fresh magazine from the pouch on his belt and slid it into the well in one clean motion. Three rounds had left the muzzle before the empty printed piece of steel had a chance to hit the floor. The acidic taste of his own blood filled his mouth as his teeth slowly pierced the tender flesh of his cheek.

With a heavy, meat-laden *thunk,* he smashed his fist into the button on the side of the range stand and listened to the mechanical whirring over his head as the target slowly made its way towards him.

The mass of pulped paper that had once been the target's head and heart hung from the frame like wet wool, the singed edges coiling thin vaporous trails of smoke towards the ceiling as Stabbler ripped it from the frame and tossed it away behind him. Pulling another from the slot in the wall beside him, he tacked it to the metal stand and hit the button once more, watching as it was dragged, flapping and snapping away from him.

The target stopped with an echoing clang as it hit the end of the rail. His pistol rose with a speed born of practice and a need to live longer than his enemy. The sights danced into his line of vision, lining up almost instantly as he squeezed the trigger once more, sending the round crashing through the paper in a hail of red-hot lead.

19

August Eighteenth
U.S. Army Medical Research Institute of Infectious
Diseases
Fort Detrick, Maryland
USA

The radio hissed and crackled as the airwaves filled with a rippling sea of white noise. He watched the needle as it danced to the ever-looping bounce of the wavering signals. Carl's teeth ground together as he glared at the still non-functioning satellite link, its blank-faced monitor staring back at him with an all too human-looking grin as the light bent across the LCD monitor.

'Fucking useless pieces of shit.' He smashed his fist against the top of the HAM radio, its casing echoing lightly as he watched it bend inwards. The needles jumped wildly as the table shook beneath it.

Carl watched the needle jump once more, the broken hiss of static dying away as a smooth Welsh-laced voice rolled from the speaker, its deep gravel-dashed tones crackling through the haze of crackling backwash.

'Colony, this is Monarch, you there?'

Carl snatched the handset from the table, his thumb driving the button deep into the side of the microphone as he spoke.

'Yeah, we're here!'

His voice quivered, a slithering worm of fear riding through all he said. Carl looked at the microphone in his hand as his nerves began to tremble, the heavy cloak of fear and self-doubt falling over him, driving the air from his lungs as he listened intently to the calm, self-assured voice rolling through the radio.

'How many you got? What's your status?'

Carl felt his stomach boil as he ran through it all—the deaths, the countless wall of slathering, carnivorous flesh that dogged their every step.

'Not good, Derek. Not good at all. We lost two million in the first break, seven million in the next. New York, Chicago, Manhattan, anywhere with high-rises and dense populations, they... they just vanished. Whole islands and cities just going dark in minutes. We blasted bridges, dropped skyscrapers into the streets; it was nine eleven in stereo... none of it worked. They rolled over everything we tried to set up, just brushing us aside like paper.

'We're scattered to the four corners here, regrouping is all but impossible. I made contact with two units of SEALs, a half battalion of Rangers out of Fort Lewis, and the Third Battalion out of Fort Benning in Columbus. They weathered well, pulled everything they could in from the outlying areas, and sealed up tighter than a Dutch whore's buttocks, so we've some decent manpower in those areas, but fuel's in such short supply that we can't get them to where we need them without suffering ridiculous losses.

'We are getting mismatched reports coming in from other holdouts; but... it's not good. Losses are heavy, suicides are worse; we lost three units last week. One of the boys cracked when his little sister got Infected and went for him and the others in the room. He... he choked her to death, Derek; he couldn't bring himself to shoot her so he strangled her with the straps of her dungarees. It was brutal. Then he turned the gun on those around him and eventually himself; it was over before we could even dream of doing anything to stop him.

'Supplies are rarer than rocking horse shit. At AMRIID, where I am, we have about a month or two of water with extreme rationing. Food is dwindling, as we can't spare water for the gardens, and the vehicles are running on fumes. We've no way to restock what we use up. Anyone we send out to recover dead drops and ammo dumps, they just either abandon the ops or just vanish. One thing is certain

221

though, if something doesn't change soon, we're finished.'

The silence hung heavy in the room. Carl watched the dials dance and jump as the signal slithered through the aerial antenna, his heart beating out a slow, dull rhythm as the orange glow bathed his gaunt and weary form in cold light.

'Hang tight; I'll have the boys from Brize run a drop over to you. If we can get some of the aerial tankers into position, we should be able to drop enough munitions and food on or around your location to allow you to re-supply and re-arm… at least enough to give you a fighting chance at getting to those Rangers and the other outposts. What's JSOC's or SOCOM's situation?'

Carl chewed at the inside of his cheek, small lumps of dead flesh peeling away as his teeth pinched and pulled at the tender lining. Wincing slightly as his canines dug deep into the meat of his face, he drew in a deep slightly shaky breath and replied.

'Honestly, I don't know. They grouped tight in on their key locations, pulling their families in with them, as well as all the top-tier government members and went silent. We don't know if they're even alive and kicking. We get rumours from time to time but, other than that, it's just one big black hole—nothing in, nothing out. Our only link to any form of government here has been the Special Activities Division; they blow through about once a month, sometimes twice. We were blessed a while back; they had a full complement of their tactical boys in their sealed armoured suits, that look like a cross between a wetsuit and motorcycle armour, and carrying those bracketed Lexan shields.

'Thing that got me most, though, was that they were all armed with those Gladius machetes and the Kel-Tec bullpup rifles. They must have carried at least three thousand rounds per man, all in magazines on their chest and legs; it was nuts. They just rolled up in heavy trucks—at least fifty of 'em—then these guys all piled out, formed into pairs and just started pushing forwards, the men with the shields firing out of ports mounted into the side and the ones behind them taking out any that slipped past.'

Carl paused, his hands shaking as he desperately searched for something else to say, trying in vain to keep his one connection to home and his old life alive as long as possible.

'And... uh...'

His mind faltered, his words sliding into a lump in his throat so thick he found it all but impossible to breathe. He swallowed in a vain attempt to clear the mental obstruction as he felt the tears begin to prick at the edges of his eyes.

Cuffing them away, he shook slightly with fright as Derek spoke. 'Carl, you need to check yourself; have you been sleeping?'

Carl sighed as he felt himself sag against the chair, its solid steel back biting into his skin as his weight pulled him against its unyielding surface. His tongue skimmed against the dry, flaking, split skin of his lips. The searing yelps of his mind slipped through him as he found the paper-thin slits of tender, living flesh that cowered beneath the layers of dead skin.

'Not really, I... when I... it's...'

His mumbled and stumbling reply made Baker sigh, his deep baritone making the speaker in the radio tremble and buzz as the feedback looped through the microphone clutched in Carl's hand.

'Yeah... I get it. Listen, find a room, closet, cupboard... anything I don't give a shit if you have to crawl into an air vent or sleep in the toilet u-bend, but no matter what, you have to sleep. I know what you are like, Carl. Get some sleep. I will radio back in two days. If you haven't had at least five hours sleep in that time, then I will come over there personally and knock you the fuck out.

'I may owe you my life but I am damned if you are going to throw yours away by killing yourself through fatigue. Are we clear?'

Carl bit his bottom lip hard as his chin trembled slightly; hanging his head, he pushed down on the talk button, his voice quavering slightly as he replied, 'As crystal, sir.'

He sighed as he struggled to control himself, the trembling in his core worming its way through him as stared at the microphone in his hand. The sounds behind him grew louder as muted gunfire echoed through the corridors behind him.

'Derek, can I ask you a favour? Can you find my ex and my son? Tell them… tell them I am sorry for all that happened and how it ended. And tell my boy that no matter what he chooses, what path he walks, or who he falls in love with, that his dad will always be proud of him.'

He could almost hear the frown that crossed Derek's brow as his words filtered down the line.

'Yeah, but Carl you can tell him yourself. You are going to make it home; I know you.'

Carl's barked reply cut through Derek's words like a knife through butter as he sent the chair clattering to the floor. 'Not this time, Cherry. They're knocking at the door and I am the only one home to answer. I have ten minutes at best—not a lot of time to say what needs to be said. I know that... so... I guess this is goodbye. I'll see you at the bar with a cold one waiting. Catch ya later, mate.'

The sounds that echoed around him filled his senses, their pulsing beat drumming in his ears as he pushed himself towards the door, the microphone springing from his hand as the cord stretched and snapped it free from his loosening grip. With a clatter of wood against plastic, the black, sweat-slicked block crashed across the tabletop like a stone across the waves, its skittering form colliding with the radio as Baker's voice boomed from the speakers.

All sound died away as he watched their cadaverous forms move beyond the door, the chattering hoard scraping at the glass as the window began to bow and crack, the heavy steel mesh bulging and bending as they began to claw their way towards him. Carl watched as the door rattled in its frame, their undeniable lust for sustenance drawing them in as a flood of oil-black blood began to slowly edge its way over the floor towards him.

Carl levelled his weapon, his aim set squarely on the door and the slowly splintering pane of meshed glass. With a slow, slightly nervous breath, he curled his finger over the trigger and waited.

****

Derek stared at the radio as it hissed and crackled, his fist closing ever tighter around the microphone as the static cackled and burped; the rolling cloud of empty electrical hissing filled his mind as he stared at the matte-green box in front of him.

The vortex of hissing sound that enveloped him sent a chill so deep that it kissed the very centre of his soul. A deep well of loneliness and regret began to pour into him as images spilled through his mind; images of men caked in mud and dust as they trudged through fields so laden with water and overgrown grass that it was more jungle than farmland. Pictures of sun-baked faces laughing as they dug into the steaming bags of re-heated mush doused in chilli sauce, dancing mosaics of jumbled memories filtered past his eyes as the silence drenched him completely.

Baker sank back, the chair creaking beneath him, as he watched the dials jump and waver. Memories still danced in his eyes as he stared at the dull orange glow that seeped from the eyes of the box in front of him. Without uttering a word, he reached forwards and flicked the small chrome switch, the heavy thump of the speaker reverberating around him as the speaker was silent once more.

Rising to his feet, Baker turned; the weight that rode on his shoulders pressed all the heavier as the slowly creeping realisation sank into him, the singular thought that he was the last man left from a team established almost fifteen years before floating amidst the jumbled detritus of his mind; one that he had never thought he would ever face and now with the dying whine of the radio hanging in the air like the mocking laughter of the insane, that thought, that one insignificant line of thinking was all that remained of [1]Kilo Three Four.

---

1   Carl's final story and fate revealed in
    DESIGNATED DECLASSIFIED: The Kinkade file

Broadhead Barracks
NCO quarters

'Corporal Stabbler, this conversation's not over with; return to your seat immediately.' Hawk ignored the anger-licked call as he pushed the doors aside and marched down the corridor, his rage-fuelled charge echoing around him as his heels clacked against the flooring.

A uniformed Marine stepped into his path, hand hanging by his holstered sidearm as Hawk advanced towards the entrance foyer. 'Boy, unless you want to be sucking dinner through a tube, you will get out of my way.' The young Marine bristled as he stared at the still advancing Stabbler and the charging officer behind him, the man's breathless cries echoing past Hawk as he continued to advance. 'Do not let that man leave. Do you hear me, Marine? Do not let that man through that door.'

The echoing crack of a pistol rolled through the hallway as Hawk stumbled, his hand rising slowly to his chest as he fell. A rolling ball of cold slowly seeped through him. Staring at his blood-slicked palm, his eyes caught the shifting spots of red as he sluggishly raised his head.

Staring upwards, Hawk tumbled forwards, his knees smashing into the floor as his strength faded like ink through water.

He stared with a detached fascination as his hands reached out, the image of the soldier fading to nothing as a slim figure clad in red slowly made her way towards him. The whimpering plea of a dying man slipped from his lips as he stared at the cold, blue eyes before him. 'Please, I... I tried... I tried to…'

His eyes followed her every move as she knelt before him and gently caressed his cheek, her fingers warm against his cold, pallid skin. Leaning forwards, her hair brushed his face as she whispered into his ear. 'You left him. Like you left me… both of us.'

Sarah pulled away from him, her hands growing cold as Hawk looked up into the ripped and distorted face before him. The eyes glowed with hatred as its hands slipped up to either side of his face. The foul, putrid scent of death and rotting flesh filled his nose as its mouth opened a full-throated scream, leaving its shattered lips.

'You left us to die!'

Hawk sat upright, his skin running, alive with sweat as he stared about him, his chest heaving as he fought to ride the wave of panic and fear that had crashed over him. Tossing aside the soaked bed sheet, he swung his feet out and onto the cold floor. The thin stiff pile of the carpet scraped at the soles of his feet as he leant over, a rippling pool of nausea rising up from the pit of his stomach as he held his head in hands, trying in vain to stop the bubbling mire of acid and bile as it teased the back of his throat.

With shaking hands, he reached out to the small tumbler on his nightstand, lifting the condensation-slicked glass from the pot cupboard next to him. The cold droplets slid over the tumbler and down his knuckles as he opened the small drawer with his free hand. The rattling of pills in a bottle filled the air as he lifted the white pot free. With a practised movement born of months of repetition, he sent the lid curling from the bottle to land with an almost inaudible *thud* at his feet as he shook three pills from the bottle, letting them land in his open mouth.

The bitter taste of chalk and chemicals filled his mouth as he crushed the tablets to a white paste with his teeth. Lifting the glass, he sent the foaming paste of medication swirling down his throat as he drained the glass in one smooth pull.

The tumbler clacked with a diamond-like ring as he dropped it back onto the top of the pot cupboard as his mind screamed from inside the prison of his skull; dropping his head into his hands, Hawk fought back the overwhelming urge to scream as her face danced past his closed eyes. Her voice echoed through him as he stared at the lines in his palms. The unbidden memory playing like a movie across his scarred skin.

'Tell me, what do you want from this? If this all ends tomorrow, what happens then?' Hawk smirked as he held her in his arms, the smell of her hair filling him as she leant back against him.

'I don't know… marriage, children… a life.'

The lines in his hands danced as tears swirled in his eyes. Closing his eyes, he fell back into the memories as warm, swirling pearls fell, his tears crashing against his skin where they burst like stars in the night.

Her face twisted in a feral scream as she stared at him, his dirt-stained face reflected back in her eyes as he stood there with Remy's tags clutched in his fist. Her hands beat against his chest as she screamed and railed, his words falling dead in the air as his head snapped sideways, a shimmering red stain spreading across his face.

'Why you? Why aren't you dead? Why him?'

Hawk stood mute as he tasted blood on his tongue. Her seething, rage-soaked body only feet away as he set the tags on the table beside him.

'He made me leave; if we could swap places, I would.'

His soft words floated on the air as she spun and stared into his eyes. Her shrill scream sliced through to his heart, cutting his so deeply, he had no idea if it would ever truly heal.

'*He's still dead.*'

Hawk's mind cracked as he screamed back, his rage giving way to all he held inside as he slowly began to crumble.

'*He sent me back, for you!*'

Sarah sneered, her eyes brimming with un-shed anger-laced tears as she stared straight into his face. 'All he sent me was the constant reminder of all that I don't have. Some consolation.'

Hawk ground the balls of his hands into his eyes as he dropped back into himself with a sickening thump. Lancing shafts of light carved their way through the gloom as the blinds began to glow; the birth of a new day filled the room as Hawk pushed himself to his feet, which wavered beneath him as he slowly made his way to the bathroom.

Stepping into the watery sunlight, Hawk squinted as he stared about him. His uniform hung from his frame like a wet potato sack as he moved with all the purpose and drive of a narcoleptic sheep dog.

The stifling warmth of the air soaked into his lungs as he drew in a breath that weighed on his chest like a block of lead. Pushing open the door to the mess hall, he stepped forwards, weaving and bobbing through the tables as he moved towards the bubbling silver urn at the far end of the hall.

Steam boiled over the edge of the cup in his hand as he pushed the lever down, sending the boiling hot liquid sailing into the bottom. The tar-black fluid was like the blood of Hades as he lifted it to his lips, the sharp bitterness filling his senses as it scorched a path from tongue to stomach. The caffeine slithered through his veins, igniting his mind like a flare as he sent the scalding liquid falling down into the depths of his gullet.

He stared at his reflection; the dark shadows lined his eyes, drawing his gaze as he watched his face twist and bend in the curved metal mirror in front of him. Setting the cup down on the steel countertop at his elbow, Hawk turned and strode back through the hall, his footsteps echoing off the walls around him.

20
August Twenty-sixth
Lillingston
Lovell
Buckinghamshire

Rufus Shaw swung his feet down onto the carpeted floor of his bedroom, the strong scent of body odour filling his nostrils as he sat at the edge of his mattress and stretched; the heavy tension reverberated through his spine and neck, tickling the bottom of his skull. Slipping his feet into the backless lamb's wool-lined slippers, he padded into his kitchen, scratching at the crease of his backside through his pinstriped boxers, the tightly woven cotton catching at the curled hairs clinging to his buttocks.

With a half-stifled yawn, Rufus yanked the wall-mounted cupboard open, the faux pine door covering tickling his skin as he stood staring at the four solitary mugs pushed into the corner of the shelf. Hooking his finger through the handle, he dragged one towards him as he plucked a small premixed sachet of coffee from the jar on his countertop. The sound of the packet slapping against his skin echoed through the kitchen as he set the cup down and tore the sachet open with his teeth as he jabbed his finger down on the button for the chrome steel kettle.

The kettle bubbled and hummed as the water slowly began to boil. He paddled into the small, cluttered living room, stepped over to the IPod dock next to his television, and scrolled to his workout playlist. Tapping the centre button, he opened the list and scrolled down to the first song and hit play. The room filled with the heavy strains of 'Hero' by Skillet as he stepped back towards his kitchen, rolling his shoulders and neck as he moved.

The hot water streamed from the spout as he poured it into the cup, watching the granules of coffee and powdered milk swirl and dissolve under the deluge of boiling liquid. Taking a tentative sip, he moved into the living room once more and set the cup down on the floor as he dropped into the waiting seat of his weight bench and lifted the barbell from the rack.

****

His chest was heavy, sweat running off his brow as his feet
pounded against the tarmac. Traffic flashed past him in a spray of
grit and a tumbling pall of exhaust fumes, the cloying stench filling
his lung as he drew in another sharp breath.

The ache in his shoulders made him smile as he carried on
forwards. Turning left, he followed the road as it left the paved and
covered roads of civilisation, falling into the trodden and water-laden
pathways through the patchwork blanket around him.

Shaw's feet aquaplaned on the thick, cloying mire of mud and
fermented cow shit that filled the gateway in front of him. His arms
flailed and spun as he fought to keep his footing. The swinging body
ahead of him, battered by the breeze, sent the branches swaying, a
dull creak echoing out from the rope around its neck as the
deadweight pulled it back and forth like a metronome.

The glimmering bead-like eyes of the crows on its shoulders
swivelled to him as they sunk their beaks deeper into the disgorged
sockets of the dead man's eyes. A soft glinting of shifting silver
caught his eye as he stared at the round steel disk nailed to the man's
forehead.

Dropping his hand to his hip, Shaw jabbed his thumb sharply
down on the three and waited for the autodial to kick in. Lifting his
phone to his ear, Shaw listened to the buzzing ringing as it slithered
through his mind, sifting his brain like a sieve as the sound buzzed
around inside his skull.

'Please confirm identification.' Shaw sighed as he spoke, his voice
slightly breathless as he drew his breathing back to normal. 'Sierra,
Alpha, Three, Four, Three.'

'Thank you, patching you through to Lt Colonel Colinson now.'

Shaw listened to the deep rumbling tones as the line shifted and bounced from one point to another until it was cut like a knife through silk by the crisp tone of Colinson's voice.

'What is it, Shaw?'

'Tenth man down, sir.'

Shaw had to pull his phone from his ear as a wall of cursive-filled noise boiled from it. Setting the phone once more against his ear, Shaw listened as Colinson spoke with an agitated sigh lacing his voice. 'Where?

****

'Damn it; it's Eccleston. He was on leave for two weeks. His son turned three last week and he wasn't supposed to be back until Monday.'

Running his hand through his hair Colinson stared up at the rope that still ensnared the branch twelve feet above their heads. Colinson stared at the sodden soil beneath his feet, the deep-rutted tracks marking the passage of many a vehicle. Kneeling, he traced his fingers through the water-filled indents, his long slender digits dancing over the ridges and dips as his brow furrowed. The offset marks made his eyes widen slightly as he felt a noticeable dip in the pattern that slowly reared its malignant head every three feet.

'Shaw, can you get onto Westing and Lincruster? I want a full inventory of the Motorpool and a check on our fuel reserves. This doesn't feel like an outside job. Someone had to have access to our records to know when we would be out and vulnerable. I just hope nothing else was siphoned off. Well, there is fuck all we can do standing here; let's get out of the way so the SOCO boys can get the job done.'

They turned and trudged back through the gateway, careful to not disturb the area any more than they already had.

Colinson stood in front of the assembled clerical staff, the motley collection of civilian and military as they waited for him to speak.

'We are going back to basics. Our systems have been compromised; someone, be they one person or group has gained access to our systems and this has compromised the safety of not only our operations but also our team members and their families.

'So I want the systems scrubbed, all data on them synced to hard drives then pulled from the system, and anything left on them wiped clean. I do not want anything left—not one word file, data packet, or jpeg left on any system connected to our severs.

'From now on, we are hard data only. Paper files will be held in the vault under twenty-four hour guard and only removed by an authorised clerk. That goes for all invoices, inventories, deployment rosters, flight manifests—even the amount of ink in our printers. Am I understood?'

They nodded with annoyance and mild anger simmering beneath a layer of stoic perseverance as they turned and moved off to their desks and offices to begin the purge.

Over the next three hours, the hum of a thousand computers fell into a silence so filling that it smothered everything it touched. Colinson's ears rang, a high-pitched keening squeal reverberating through his skull as he stood in the now tomb-like room. The corpses of a hundred steel towers standing sentry over the desolate remains of the now eviscerated hard drives.

The heavy scent of static-filled ozone and recycled air invaded his lungs as he drew a deep breath. The room once so alive with the flickering of LED lights and the hushed hum of cooling fans was now little more than a tomb for the ill-gotten gains of evil men.

Stepping from the room, he paused momentarily at the keypad by the door. Sliding his fingers over the heavy chromed siding, he searched, poised for any sign of deviation or variance in the otherwise flawless block of machined aluminium. He felt a sharp tugging at the pads of his finger as they slipped over the curled and damaged edge. The split seam of brushed metal bit into the tip of his finger, a fine line of scarlet slipping through the ridges of his fingertip as he pulled his hand away.

'Hmm, thought as much; sloppy, whomever it was.' Lifting his finger to his lips, Colinson gently sucked the blood from its tip. With care-filled ease, he tapped in a code and set the room to automatic cleanse, watching as the casings filling the room began to smoke and bubble, the heavy acid eating through the remains of everything in the room.

The echoing clatter of retreating feet filled the small anterior room as Colinson moved towards the stairs and up into the bitter August sun.

****

Derek stared at the disc in his hand, the twisted hole in the top a testament to the arrogant and callous disregard with which the man was treated even after death. Baker sighed as he dropped the dog tag onto the desk in front of him, an overwhelming sense of fatigue and anger boiling through him as he watched the shimmering dance of the metal tag as it slowly settled against the veneered desktop.

He stared at his reflection as it danced in the light playing off the steel circle; the shifting wave of letters and numbers seized his eyes, slithering into his mind like water as he gazed upon them.

'It's a message, ain't it?'

Baker nodded as Shaw stepped partially into the room, stopping just inside the doorway, his hands clenched inside the pockets of his jeans. The light streamed around him, casting an incandescent, almost ethereal halo of white about Shaw making Derek's eyes water slightly as he stared at the man.

235

His footsteps shattered the silence as Shaw made his way forwards, the rough threadbare carpet doing nothing to mute his passage as he reached the desk and stopped. Rufus' eyes lingered on the dog tag as Baker shifted and turned to face the window. Shaw reached forwards, plucking the tag from where it sat on the desk.

'So, whose is this, anyway? Name's been carved out of it. It's a naval number; other than that, it's not one I recognise.'

Rufus stared at Baker, watching as Derek's shoulders slumped forwards and his head fell into his waiting hands. His reply was muffled, the words nothing more than a jumbled hiss of baritone noise as he spoke. Shaw frowned intensely as his ears strained to pick out the words. 'It's my tag number; it's a part of my old set of tags. Only one person I know could have gotten his mitts on them and that bastard has been dogging my footsteps for well over twelve years.'

Shaw nodded as he twisted the piece of steel through his fingers. 'So, you're saying that Ridgmont's picking off my boys because of you?'

Shaw watched as Baker spun his chair away from the window and looked directly at Shaw. 'How do you know about him?'

Rufus smirked, the sarcastic sneer twisting his lips as he flicked the steel disk at Derek. 'Every squaddie here knows about that mother fucker and his band of scum. Division fucking Twelve; bunch of sadistic bastards.'

Derek picked the steel disk from off his desk, turning it through his fingers as he dipped into the wells in his mind, his gaze never leaving the battered and dented piece of steel that slid over his palm.

Anger blossomed within him, glowing like a ball of flame as it swelled; the searing sphere of boiling rage flowed from his deepest depths, sweeping aside all reason as he slammed his hand against the desk. Pain lanced through him, blood seeping through his fingers, pooling around his hand in a crimson print. The thick, gelatinous mess sealing his hand to the desk as the burred edge of the steel disk sliced deep into the palm of his hand.

Lifting his hand away, he stared at the glinting lump of metal as it ran alive with his blood. Derek gritted his teeth as he teased the two-millimetre-thick piece of steel from his palm, letting it fall to the desktop with a dull *thunk*. With an agitated grunt, Derek pulled open one of his desk drawers, took out a wad of tissues, and stuffed them into the rent in his palm.

Pushing himself to his feet, Baker stepped past Shaw, heading for the door as the wad of snow-white tissue slowly bloomed red.

21
August Thirtieth
Askham,
Nottinghamshire

Tony sat at his kitchen table, the cheap melamine surface cold against his age-worn skin. Lifting the cup to his lips, he drank the warm sugarless tea. With a deep, heavy sigh, he set the cup on his plate and pushed himself up from the chair. Carrying his plate to the sink, he set it in the bowl before lifting the blue dishcloth from where it was draped over the tap and wiped up the crumbs of his breakfast.

Staring out the window, he watched the morning sun flirt with the slowly paling sky as sparrows and bullfinches flitted from branch to bush in his garden. The water poured over his hand, chilling him to the bone as he rinsed out his cup. The dishcloth pulled at the skin of his knuckles as he scrubbed out the cup; he set it onto the draining board before beginning the tasks of the day.

Stepping from the kitchen door, the sun bathed him in its warm glow as the new day slowly began to awaken; the cool, crisp breeze blowing in from the fields around him filled him with a vigour he had thought long lost to the youth he once held. As he stretched, his back clicked and popped, then he settled onto the back step and slipped the dark-green Wellington boots onto his feet. He walked across the rutted and damp ground towards the paddock and the small stable and stall next to it.

The morning's dew clung to his boots, making the green rubberised fabric shimmer in the sunlight. Setting the bucket under the outside tap, he set the ice-cold water crashing into it, relishing the sound of the torrent as it collided with the hollow plastic tub. Tony approached the gate to the paddock, the bucket of feed and pail of water held loosely in each hand as he shunted the latch up with his elbow and pushed the gate open with his hip.

Reaching the stable, he called out before entering the slightly gloomy interior. 'Hey, old girl, how are you this morning?'

A heavy whinny greeted him as he stepped through the door. The heady scent of warm straw and hay filled his nostrils as he made his way towards the only stall in the building. A large chestnut-coloured nose peered out from the stable door as he approached.

A set of large brown eyes watched him approach; the clopping of hooves and a shaking head greeted him as he raised his hand and patted the side of her face.

'Hello, old girl, hungry today?' A heavy snort made him smile as she pushed against his hand, urging him to empty the bucket into the trough on the door.

'Patience, Llamrei, we will go for a run when I get back.' He pressed his head to the side of her nose, feeling her push back as he stroked her neck. 'There's a good girl.'

Turning, Tony headed back towards the house; his pace quickened as he neared the back door, the sharp ache in his knee and hip drawing him as he kicked off his Wellington boots and sat down at the kitchen table. Lifting his hand, he flicked open the cabinet by the door; the rows of pills and boxes of bandages and plasters stood in a regimented line.

His eyes strolled along the neatly typed lettering that clogged the labels, dosages and chemical names makings his eyes lose focus momentarily. He then plucked a small white bottle from its post and snapped off its top.

The bitter bite of chalk and powdered codeine filled Tony's mouth as he let the tablets sit on his tongue, their slowly dissolving plates of white pain relief doing little to alleviate the searing ache that descended from his hip to his knee. The twisted scar tissue that made up his outer thigh pulled and bunched as he hobbled towards to the kitchen sink.

A wave of melancholy rolled over him as the cold water crashed into the glass in his fist, a deep-seated ache that bloomed out from his heart, drawing tears to his eyes. Downing the last of the frigid liquid, he strode as best as his leg would allow into the hallway and snatched the phone from its cradle. He lifted the black Bakelite receiver to his ear, his chest rising and falling rapidly as he drew in a deep, heavy breath before dialling. The heady rush of painkillers flooded his mind as he listened to the lilting voice that filled his ear.

'Hello, Baker residence.'

Her voice echoed through the line as he began to reply, his eyes widening as a shimmering female voice filled his mind.

'Tony, how are you?' His head whirled as he fought to find a name for the voice, his memory falling at the first hurdle as her voice continued to ring through his mind.

'Tony, you there? It's Janet, your daughter-in-law.'

Her gentle nagging drew him out of the vortex that had formed in his skull. 'Janet, sweetheart. Yes, I'm sorry… the old war wound is playing up and I am currently golfing with Pavarotti, or so my pain killers would lead me to believe; how's my favourite daughter-in-law?'

He heard the musical tinkle of Janet's laughter as he leant against the wall in the hall, his broad shoulder pushing against the smooth plaster as he felt the receiver grate against his chin.

The salt-and-pepper hair that plagued his temples and scalp belied his age. A smile teased at the corners of his eyes, the skin crinkling like dried leather as he glanced at the pictures in the hallway. At sixty-five, he had the fitness and stature of a much younger man; the regimented life of a soldier and police officer had been something that followed him on into retirement, and his overtly active lifestyle made him as sprightly now as he had been thirty years earlier.

'I'm great, thank you; just on break now and thought I would give you a call to see how my favourite silver-haired soldier is, but seems you beat me to it.'

Tony laughed, his voice deep and raucous as he filled the near silent house with the sounds of his mirth. 'It always amazes me, my dear, at just how lucky my son is to have one such as you; why, if I were thirty years younger, I would give him a run for his money.'

Janet giggled, causing Tony's smile to deepen as he scratched at the stubble on his chin.

'I was considering popping down for a week, if that is fine with you and Derek. I don't have anything planned for the next few weeks aside from Llamrei's exercise and some light gardening, so, what do you say? Fancy seeing this old codger for a bit?'

There was a slight pause as he waited for a reply; he could feel the wheels turning in Janet's head as she thought through the ramifications of his visit.

'I don't see why not; Derek would be glad to see you, and Maria hasn't met her gramps yet… well, she has, but I doubt she would remember it or was even awake for it. So, yeah, come on down. When were you thinking of coming?'

Tony leant back as he stared at the ceiling, the elasticated cord of the phone pulling taut across him as he sorted through his mental calendar.

'Probably the ninth or tenth of September… gives me enough time to make sure Llamrei is taken care of while I am away and also allows me time to get my vegetable gardens covered over to avoid the crows pecking at my damned tomatoes again. Bloody things are a nuisance.'

Pushing off the wall, he turned as the mail slot on his door rattled, the collection of white and brown envelopes clattering into the white enamelled cage on the back of the door.

'Sounds perfect, Tony. I will let Derek know and get the guest room prepared. Oh, and just so you know we have a live-in helper now, as well. She helps me with Maria whilst I am working, so you behave yourself; I know what you're like. I married your son and the pair of you are as bad as one another when it comes to flirting with anything with boobs.'

Tony chortled as he clutched the phone between his ear and shoulder whilst filtering through his post.

'I suppose you're right there, my dear. I blame my father, as I don't doubt Derek blames his, but there we are. It's a Baker trait and one that we have no power over unless, of course, it allows us to land the woman of our dreams. It did so for me, and from what I understand, it did Derek as well. Just don't tell him I told you that or he would surely kill me. Anyway, my dear, I must go. I have some bills to pay and Llamrei needs her morning canter. I'll see you on the ninth.'

With laughter plaguing her voice, Janet bid Tony farewell. The conversation ended with the chiming of a bell as he dropped the handset back into its cradle and moved on into his living room.

A soft voice echoed in the back of his mind as he turned to drop his six-foot-six frame into the overstuffed sofa. Grasping with flailing arms, he stopped himself mere inches from the sofa, the bottom of his Deer Hunter coat brushing the cushion, the hem kissing it like the wing of a dove as he forced himself upright. 'Sorry, sweetheart.'

Turning, he made his way back out into the hallway, peeling the coat from his shoulders as he reached out for the handle of the under-stairs cupboard. Tony stopped cold, pain gripping him as he caught sight of a picture on the wall. Reaching out, he softly drew his fingers along the portrait's cheek, a single crystalline tear rolling down his own cheek as he stared into the shimmering blue eyes.

'You have no idea how much I miss you. You would be so proud of Derek, oh so very proud. I will see you again, my love. One day we will be together and we can go walk by the sea again.'

Kissing his fingertips, he pressed them to the smiling lips of the picture before stepping back into the living room, heading towards the coffee table covered in bills.

September Ninth
North East London

The rain fell, its cold pearls shimmering in the cold light of the moon. He listened to the drum of their relentless assault on the roof of his car as he stared at the shimmering wall of amber water sliding over the windowpane.

His eyes glowed with a sweltering pall of malevolence and violence as he watched her move behind the window, her rippling shadow dancing across his face as he stepped from the car and walked slowly to the door. The nail gun in his hand made him smile, the red reinforced plastic and steel body sitting heavy in his palm as he pulled a small metal disk from his jeans pocket. A malicious grin played over his face as he approached the gloss black door atop the four-tread staircase.

His hand rose, lifting the Fairbairn Sykes dagger and dragging it through the thick panelling in front of him, watching as he slowly carved out thick, curving lines of oak.

The compressed air canister that hung from the sling over his shoulder pulled him into the floor, its weight making the strap bite into his skin as he pressed the nail gun to the door. Aiming the head of it at the hole of the dog tag, he squeezed the trigger, sending the nail into the door at over a hundred pounds per square inch, driving the steel rod deep into the timber.

His smile deepened as he watched the woman behind the rain-lashed glass jump at the sudden noise. Flicking the tag with his finger, he sent it spinning around the anodised steel nail and ran through the water-drenched street to his car, the idling engine filling the quiet night's air with a heavy guttural throb.

His foot hovered over the accelerator like a fretful mother as he watched the woman shift and move behind the window, dragging clothing over her lithe frame and disappearing from view. A vicious grin slithered across his lips as he watched the door swing open, her silhouetted form bathed in the golden glow of the hallway light.

She jumped as the engine roared across the street, its echoing primal growl filling the air as it ate the road and sped from view, a glowing trail of oil-stained water and shimmering red-tinged rain lying in its wake. Janet turned, watching, fear and trepidation filling her as she stared at the word carved into the door and the spinning steel disk slowly clinking against the door panel.

****

Derek traced his fingers through the word gouged into his front door. The wood and paint was slashed and torn, leaving the pale scars of white oak standing stark against the black glossed door like blood on snow. Derek grunted as he wrenched the nail from the door, the rough neck hammer in his hand leaving a deep welt in the panel as he pried the three-inch long bar of steel from the centre of the door.

The heady ring of metal on concrete filtered through the early morning traffic as the nail hit the floor, bouncing down the steps of his home to the gutter at the edge of the road.

The dog tag sat in his palm nestled against the compression pad, covering his hand and the crepe bandage wrapped around it. He winced, suppressing the bitter tang of pain that lanced through his hand as the stitches stretched against his skin, tearing into his flesh as he closed his fingers over the tag, crushing it into his palm.

Shoving the door away, Derek strode into the hallway and kicked the door shut, letting the echoing slam of timber on timber roll over him as it crashed against the frame.

Janet watched as he stalked through the hallway, his bandage-covered hand so tightly clenched that blood ran from between his fingers, leaving a claret trail of glistening crumbs in his wake. She reached out tentatively, her hand stopping short of his shoulder as he paused, pivoting his head slightly as he glanced at her, anger and hatred dancing in his eyes; his eyes held such utter contempt that it crushed the man he was. Janet pulled her hand back, her fingers toying with the slim gold band on her finger as Derek looked away and carried on down the hall. His hunched form disappeared into the gloom-laden doorway leading to the basement.

His hand ached with the incessant throbbing of torn flesh as he lifted the door from its hinges and set it onto the two sawhorses. The deep gouges in the wood stared at him as he snatched the belt sander from where it sat beside his feet. High-pitched whirring seeped out into the early morning sky, the sound dulled to the point of near non-existence by the rapidly swelling din of London traffic.

Janet watched from the top step, a small holdall slung over one shoulder as she stepped down towards the pavement, the trailing red cable of the extension lead snaking down from the empty doorway behind her. Stopping short of where Derek stood, she watched as the bunched muscles in his shoulders tensed and relaxed while he worked the sander over the wood in front of him. Her eyes travelled over his worn but still chiselled body. Her brow furrowed at the heavy mottled bruising that covered his left shoulder and disappeared beneath the lines of the vest he wore.

'I'm off now, babe. I won't be back until tomorrow after twelve, unless the rota changes or I'm called in for something else; if I am, I'll text or call you.'

She waited for any form of acknowledgement, her ears straining for even the faintest of replies, but she heard nothing but the incessant drone of the cars and the heady whine of the sander.

'I love you.'

Again, nothing stirred as she watched the play of the sander and Derek's almost automaton-like movements; shoving back tears and the heavy, soul-rotting loneliness that had begun to worm its way through her, Janet turned and unlocked her car. Tossing her bag on to the back seat, she slipped into the driver's seat and locked her belt into place before glancing up into the rear view mirror, her eyes locking onto Derek. He held the still buzzing sander in his hand as he watched her, his eyes boring into hers as she stared at him from the mirror of her car. The faintest of smiles ghosted over his lips as he looked into her emerald green eyes.

With a shift of his thumb, the sander snapped to a stop, the safety button clicking into place as he let it clatter to the floor. With a pace and fluidity born of hard-won survival, Derek closed the gap between himself and Janet, dropping to his knees beside the driver's door as she sat belted into the seat of her car.

Cars screamed and drivers bellowed as the still flowing traffic passed him by mere inches. He felt the heat and grit-laden air flow over him as he pulled himself up. Leaning through the driver's side window he spoke.

'I love you too.'

Cupping her chin with his dust-coated hands, he drew her to him as close as he dared before ensnaring her lips with his, the heat and longing that burned through him tingeing her cheeks as they met. Pulling away, he smiled; the lines around his eyes deepened as he looked upon her startled form, the red hue of her cheeks making her eyes dance with a semi-bewildered joy.

He stood, grasping the top of the door with his hand. 'And don't you ever forget that.'

Janet nodded mutely, still too confused to say anything remotely coherent as she watched him move away. Her eyes lingered on him as he stepped to the middle of the pavement. Janet started the car and moved away from the curb, a coy grin playing across her features. With one last glance at her husband, Janet merged with the steady flow of early morning commuters and vanished from sight.

As Derek watched her disappear into the heaving flow of London's pulsing core, the beeper on his hip vibrated before bellowing out its shrill cry.

Sprinting up the steps, the door forgotten, Derek snatched his go bag from the under stairs cupboard, the door cracking against the plasterboard wall, before screaming out for Siobhan's attention. The young woman's startled form appeared in the kitchen doorway seconds later, bowl and spoon in hand.

'I have to go; get someone to finish that.'

Siobhan glanced from the bag, to Derek's beeper in his hand, to the look of harried, excitement-tinged fear in his eyes; a curt nod was her only reply before he sprinted back out the door, leaping to the pavement as he launched his bag through the open rear window of his Jeep.

Sighing heavily, Siobhan turned back into the kitchen, fishing Maria from the high chair. She wiped the remains of the baby food from around her mouth with her bib before plucking it from Maria's neck and setting her down in the playpen in the living room.

The throaty roar of the Jeep's engine slashed through the air as Derek pushed his way through the traffic that streamed past the door, the flashing blue light on his Jeep's roof saying more than his blaring horn and over-revving engine ever could.

Stepping back into the hallway, Siobhan squealed as she dropped her hand to the baseball bat inside the living room doorway. She watched the figure in the hallway advance; her hand stopped for a moment when she saw the easy smile and silver-tinged eyebrows overshadowing a pair of glittering blue eyes.

'Hello, love, sorry to startle you like that. Is my son home, or was that who I saw barging his way past three vans and a Skoda just now?'

Siobhan visibly relaxed and stepped fully into the hallway, her hand outstretched.

'You must be Tony. And yes, that was my rather un-illustrious employer you saw violating about seven different traffic laws; I'm afraid Janet is also out, and I have no idea when either will be back.'

Tony smiled as he set his suitcase beside the hallway table, the handle sliding down into the well in the top of the case. As he turned back to face her, Siobhan smiled, her eyes glittering with impish mirth as she watched his face take on a slightly worried cadence.

'You don't know anything about carpentry, do you?'

22
Broadhead Barracks
Central Operations Centre

Colinson watched, one eyebrow quirked slightly as Derek barrelled into the room, his sawdust-tinged skin shimmering under the strip lights above him.

'Catch you at a bad time, did we?'

Derek flipped his raised middle finger in Colinson's direction as he stepped towards the front of the room. 'What have we got?' Colinson turned back to the monitor mounted on the main wall, the glowing panels flickering as images shuffled past their eyes.

'Fucked if I know. This was an outside trigger; someone is calling, we just haven't got a clue who.'

Baker scratched at his chin, the thick briar of curled hair making his jaw ache with an irrepressible need to scratch. 'Damn it all to hell.'

Colinson cast a sidelong glance at Derek as he dragged his chipped and dirty nails across his chin, a white flaking powder drifting down the front of his already dust-laden vest.

'First off, go get changed and shaved, mate. We can finish off the thousand and one questions in a bit. Shaw and his mob are dropping in on the source of the signal now; all we are doing is playing information footsie with whoever we have out there.'

Paddington Station
Central London

The centre and right rails hummed with the flow of electricity. Cocking his head to one side, Shaw listened intently, his chocolate-brown eyes squinting as he watched the dull yellow glow slowly fill the tunnel's mouth. A high-pitched squeal and gout of warm air boiled forth as the royal blue and yellow carriage rolled to a stop, the driver's cab whipping past in a flurry of flashing windows and chattering wheels.

The driver leapt from the door, scrambling past Shaw, his eyes wide with fear and a look seen all too often on the faces of those who bore witness to the heinous crimes of others. Shaw shivered as he watched the man. The memory filled his head of men, women, and children with the exact same look in their eyes, fleeing their homes and villages as they were butchered in their thousands for simply being Muslim.

He turned, motioning to the men around him as the memory continued to dance behind his eyes. The man's clattering feet drew his gaze as he watched him flee into the arms of another squad member; the driver's scurrying body a sight he remembered all too clearly watching on the television in his mother's house as he started his homework.

He watched the footage of a mother carrying the body of her dead daughter past a UN checkpoint. The chattering, feral faces of Bosnian Serbs filled the screen as they chased the mother and daughter through it. It was at that point that he made up his mind to become a soldier—so no mother, not his or any other, had to go through what that woman on the television had.

A movement out the corner of his eye drew his attention. Snapping his weapon to his shoulder, he turned as the figure lurched from the rear of the train; soot streaked and bloody, there was no denying what was slowly clawing its way to its feet and beginning to lurch across the platform.

'Steps, Stoors, move to suppress… fire only when certain. Westing, be a babe and call this through to Colinson for me. Rest of you, three-sixty arc of containment. Nothing is getting out of here that isn't hale and hearty.'

Westing winked as she opened a channel, cupping her hand over her ear as she spoke.

'Vatican, this is Four, say again, Vatican this is Four. Infection confirmed at location. Containment of localised area implemented, please advise.'

Colinson stared at the wall monitors, the bouncing images of SAU Four's helmet-mounted cameras making him slightly nauseated. Reaching forwards, he flicked the raised switch, opening a channel through to the members already in play.

'Push inwards, we're cleared to execute.'

Westing's lilting West Country accent poured from the speakers as she replied. *'Acknowledged. ETA on One and Three?'*

Colinson snapped the switch back once more as he scanned the monitor at his elbow.

'Three ETA 34 mins, traffic is being cleared to the main street side entrance. One is six from your local, coming in on a maintenance tram.'

'Acknowledged. Four out.'

The speaker hissed and fizzed as silence engulfed the room, the bobbing images edging closer to the tunnel entrance.

'Transport Police are sealing stations along the lines connecting with Paddington, and we have scattered reports of contacts in other stations on the Central and Northern lines. We've had minor skirmishes on other lines that feed from stations yet to be closed along the Hammersmith and City line and Circle line, but containment seems to be holding.

'The SCO19 teams on the over ground paths have deployed multiple sniper units with added three-man teams on platforms and stairways. Although this has stretched them very thin on the ground, leaving little to cover other areas of the network, as a precaution I have arranged for teams eight through eleven to be dispatched to key jump points along the three rail lines in greatest danger.'

Baker nodded as Kirkland finished talking, her hands danced over the touch screen monitor as she flicked her fingers, sending the data feed through the wireless connection to the wall monitors. The images showed grainy, slightly blurred feeds of all the above ground stations manned by the Special Officers of Section 19.

The staggered flashes of silent gunfire flickered across the screen as three of the black-clad officers slowly advanced, their weapons blazing tongues of monotone light as the Infected ran, their mouths hanging in silent screams towards the three men. All the while, the cameras silently recorded it all.

****

Wheels clacked off polished rails as they found themselves drawn through the twisting hash of interconnecting tunnels. The chain link and concrete fencing around them zipped past as the driver opened the throttle completely. Distorted flashes of rifle fire glittered in the dwindling daylight all around them as they rolled through the crypt-like stations on their way to their final destination.

The harsh rattle of MP5s over lay the rough chattering of assault rifles as it echoed through the air, rippling through the heavy rumble of the diesel engine that was dragging them along in its wake. Sharp watched the stations flutter by as the tram car rocked beneath his feet; the driver's door thumped against his booted foot, the rhythmic beat sending a lulling vibration up through him as he watched the throbbing lights of men fighting for their lives flash past in a burst of light so bright his eyes watered.

The driver's monotone voice punctured his thoughts like a pin through a balloon as they neared the station. Clapping the man on the shoulder, Sharp turned to face the open side of the cart. He dragged his night vision goggles into position on his forehead as he edged closer, the toes of his boots bumping into the raised lip surrounding the decking.

Sharp's hands shook in his gloves, the armoured knuckles heavy as he fought the cold shiver of adrenaline-laced fear that wormed its way through his spine. A heavy, electric *thunk* echoed through the halls and platforms as, one by one, the breakers snapped open and blackness crept from the corners like rabid wolves, consuming light with a ferocity that left the unprepared reeling and lost as it blanketed all in its path.

Store fronts and corridors fell dark in a matter of seconds; Sharp watched the Marauder APC trundle forwards, driving the heavy steel grate down the entryway, sealing the entrance like the portcullis of a medieval castle as it came to rest millimetres of the Victorian, iron-shod buttresses that surrounded the archway.

The hot stench of diesel smoke filled his nostrils as Sharp hopped down onto the platform. The heavy thump of his boots was drowned out by the echoing clunk of the breakers as they continued to drain the light from the world.

Sharp eased his feet forwards, the dry crust of vomit crackling beneath his boots, the passing homage from some drunken foray into the swirling dervish that was Central London. A dark grin teased at his lips as he wondered if the alcohol-soaked sot had made their way out into the bustling metropolis or if they were now playing aperitif to someone far less sober.

He slowly scanned the area ahead of him, the dark swatches of blood staining the dirt-streaked, polished concrete. Deep patches of black slowly drained the colour from the world around him as it dripped with a staccato pattering from the signs overhead, hitting the floor with an echoing splat.

'Four, this is One. We have landed at the lower platform and are moving up to your location.'

Static-filled cracks filled his ears as he listened to the play of gunfire shiver through his headset, the rolling echoing noise falling over them as they moved through the tunnels, the twisting half tubes fracturing the sounds until they were little more than shattered ghosts of their former selves.

'One, Four. Multiple contacts, topside snipers report dozens of contacts at all street-level exits, Marauder APCs in place at main entrance and the taxi rank.'

'Bridgewater, Kane, left flank. Plug that fucking hole.'

'We have them contained to the platform and train car, but I don't think we are going to be able to hold them here.'

Sharp stifled a curse as he stared at the trains around him, the long stretch of dead ground between them making his skin itch as he pressed his fingers against the call key strapped to his rifle's fore grip.

'Acknowledged. Hold position until we make contact.'

Sharp flicked his hand to his right and left, sensing more than watching, his men move, their rifles up. The muted *fut* of silenced shots echoed through the cavernous station. Pigeons fluttered overhead, loose feathers and excrement dropping around them as they flew for cover, scared from their perches by the rampant violence acted out beneath them.

Sharp snatched his aim to the left, a squeeze of his trigger creating a fist-sized hole through the chest of a woman as she launched herself from a carriage door. Her hands clawed through the air as she reached out in desperation for the man before her. She hit the floor with a gut-churning crunch, her limbs twisting against her joints as she collided with the polished floor of the terminal concourse.

Light danced, casting spectral shadows across the walls of the trains around them. Sharp squinted slightly as a blast of orange light shimmered through his vision, his eyes watering. Dragging his eye back to the Leupold Prismatic Tactical Scope mounted on his rifle, he centred the dark red cross on the fourth button his target's shirt. He squeezed the trigger again, sending the hot, pointed projectile of copper-coated lead slicing through the air, shattering bone and cartilage as it cleaved the man's chest in two. Sharp watched his chest fold inwards, collapsing back on itself as everything behind it was reduced to a thick paste.

Screams of fear and pain echoed from the carriages as they pushed forwards. The Infected streamed from the trains either side of them as one passenger after another succumbed to the plague and set upon their fellow man like locust upon a farmer's field. The high-pitched wails of children made him shiver as he caught sight of a woman sinking her teeth into the nubile flesh of a girl's cheek, a crimson flood bathing her lips as she pulled. The child's flesh twisted and stretched as she writhed in the vice-like clutch of the woman atop her.

The skin snapped like over-taut elastic, the girl's head slamming into the floor of the train as the woman's jaw churned, pulping skin and flesh into a thick, creamy paste before she swallowed. The girl's movements slowed as shock and pain dulled her mind. The innate need to flee gave way to the dull numbness of shock and fear as it mingled into one all-consuming anaesthesia of the mind and soul.

Sharp grimaced as he dragged a phosphorous grenade from his vest, sending it crashing through the glass of the train's window and into the child's lap. Her dull lifeless eyes locked onto the cylinder that sat in her blue, cotton-covered lap, her dress stained a deep brown by her own blood and stool as the plague began to ravage her body.

The grenade detonated, filling the interior of the carriage with a

256

radiant light, heat rippling the air as glass cascaded over the men and the floor around them. Sharp winced as his cheek was torn by the flying squares of shatterproof glass. He watched for a second as the child slowly melted, her form vanishing as it was consumed by the rolling wall of white fire. With eyes scorched with the images of a thousand deaths, he moved, watching for anything and everything. Sharp's shadow danced and wavered as the orange cones of rifle fire flickered all around him, the glass wall of the metro shopping district shimmering with the incandescent light as men and women fought for their existence.

****

Shaw felt a quivering in his chest as the smoke and glass poured from the shattered train windows. The glittering rain of squared glass bounced past his feet as it hit the floor around him. He felt the slithering crunch of spent brass beneath his boots as he turned; the teeth-jarring squeal of metal over concrete made his teeth itch as he spun on the balls of his feet to face a new foe.

The rifle bucked and bounced against his shoulder, the comforting rhythm of his own beating heart setting the pace as he ejected a magazine and drove another into the well, slapping it home. He kicked away his would be assailant, the man's business suit torn and ragged as he slid head first into the grill covering the entranceway. A dull, gong-like ring rolled through the terminal as the sliding office worker connected with his final resting place.

Shaw shivered as he watched the man's head open like a stuck egg, his skin sloughing off his skull as it split, morphing round the tubing like a melon on the pavement. Blood and brain matter sprayed forth, the gelatinous mass covering the floor like wet rug.

'One, where the hell are you?'

He snapped his aim to the left as he squeezed the trigger, the boy's chest sending crimson pearls dancing through the light as he was lifted from his feet, skidding the last seven feet on his back. Shaw shifted to his next target; his aim centred just right of the

257

centre of its chest as he sent another short burst of hollow-tipped lead forth. A flurry of screams and shattered bodies filled the air as the encroaching wall of slathering flesh fell aside. The shallow breathing forms of SAU Two stood there, the heavy shadow of a dying day at their backs as they slowly carved a path to Shaw's feet.

The knot of soldiers bloomed outwards, tongues of orange dancing in the gloom as they pushed on, driving the Infected against the walls of the mammoth ticket hall. The scent of overcooked burgers filled the air as Sharp passed the Burger King kiosk. The half-gutted remains of one luckless till worker lay spread eagled over the counter top as another bubbled and hissed, her head and shoulders buried in the roiling pool of bubbling cooking oil. The skin on her upper arms already starting to crisp and split as she was slowly cooked from the outside in.

'Four, push through down onto the Bakerloo line. We are heading into the main concourse.'

A sharp double click entered his ear as Shaw responded. Nothing more needed saying as both teams split and began the slow, painstaking task of cleaning the virus from the face of this small patch of earth.

'One, Four, Vatican, Directive E6, full containment, scrub the site.'

Sharp clicked twice on the button mounted onto the fore grip of his rifle and carried on forwards. A ball of ice formed in the pit of Sharp's stomach as he listened to Shaw; the man's clipped response sent a blast of cold-laced fear up his spine as he felt the nudging taunt of long repressed memories begin to fight their way up from the cage in the bowels of his mind.

'Confirmed, executing now.'

Sharp listened as Shaw sent a rapid burst into whatever was before him as the connection finally clicked shut.

Glass ground against the polished concrete beneath his feet, the crystal-like squares covering the floor in a glittering blanket.

His eye watched the bouncing red cross of his scope as he pushed deeper into the shopping court. The blood-smeared floor told him all he needed to know as he passed the overflowing conveyor belt for the sushi restaurant. With a wave of his hand, he listened to the crunch of passing feet as Roberts and Hooper slipped away, moving towards the upper level, their footfalls growing weaker as they moved further from the collective embrace of the squad.

'Move and execute, nothing to be left standing.'

With that, Sharp set off at a fast walk, his feet finding their way through the mire of broken glass and detritus that filled the floor like a poorly stitched blanket. Sharp winced as the muscles in his neck quivered, sending pin-like barbs of pain through his skull. As he turned left, his feet slid through the melted remnants of an ice cream as he set his sights on the woman heading towards him.

Her eyes were wide with fear as she slipped into a staggering run that, at any other time, would have made him laugh, but nothing stirred, no quirk of an eyebrow, no hitch of a lip as he listened to her cries for help and slowly squeezed the trigger. The red cross etched into his scope's lens jumped slightly as the bullets closed the distance to nothing, her chest opening in a spray of bone and glimmering ruby-coloured orbs. Her body hit the floor with an echoing thump as screams filled the air, the howling cries of Infected returning their call.

Clutching at the call button on the front of his weapon's fore-grip, Sharp opened a channel to the rest of the team.

'Push through and cleanse. E6 authorised.'

****

Sharp stared at Shaw as the man strode by, his arms folded across his stomach, cradling his rifle in his arms. A cold shiver danced up his neck, the man's body was so calm and relaxed that it made Sharp intensely nervous. He had executed more than one E6 in the three years of being in Broadhead, but Sharp could see it in how Shaw walked that, for his first E6, he was far too calm.

23

The Baker residence
North East London

Tony stepped back, staring with a mingled sense of pride at the smooth, black gloss of the door. Siobhan stepped out holding two steaming cups of coffee in her hands. As she held out the red and black mug, she smiled, her bespectacled face reflecting in the glistening paintwork.

'Not bad, Mr Baker. Not bad at all.'

Tony turned, a smile teasing his lips as he raised the smooth, semi-sweet liquid to his lips and drank. 'It's not my best work, but it's a damned sight better job than my boy could have done, that's for sure. His painting skills were not the best, putting it politely.'

Siobhan smiled round the mug as she breathed in the earthy aroma. Her glasses misting slightly around the bottom of the lenses as she tipped the mug, savouring the smooth and slightly tart flavour of the percolated coffee as it slid over her tongue.

Wrinkling her nose slightly as she caught the taste of slightly burnt beans, Siobhan turned, her trainers squeaking slightly on the flooring as she moved into the living room. Her gaze travelled over the sleeping form cocooned in the pale-blue baby grow and smiled as Maria stirred, her legs kicking as she swatted the air with her partially curled fists. Her seven-month-old form twitched as she slowly began to relax and drift deeper into sleep.

Dropping into the comforting embrace of the plush sofa cushions, she flipped open the book in front of her as she leant forwards, setting her mug on the slate coaster. The soft clack of pottery on stone flirted with her ears as she settled back into the overstuffed sofa cushions.

Heavy footsteps echoed behind her as Tony entered the room, in search of a place to set his empty mug, the dark swirling mass of congealed coffee dregs pooling in the bottom. With a sigh, Tony twisted the tap; the corded muscles of his arm flexed against his battered skin, the tattoo on his forearm dancing slightly as his leathery hide shifted over sinew and muscle.

'This is not how I imagined this starting. Oh well, once a father always a father.'

Setting the mug upside down on the drainer, he turned and moved towards his suitcase at the foot of the stairs, his footsteps thumping on the carpet-less treads as he made his ponderous journey to the guest room.

Tony perched on the edge of the double bed, his hands and shoulders throbbing from the vibration of the sander he'd held mere minutes earlier.

A dull buzzing filtered out from his coat pocket as it slipped from the top of his suitcase. The battered and scratched Motorola flip phone tumbled to the floor. He stared at it; it was a gift nearly a decade ago from Derek and Janet. The SBS cap badge etched onto the back of the casing was pitted and dirty from years of use, and yet, despite Derek and Janet's insistence, he had never had the heart to replace it.

Scooping the phone from the floor, Tony flipped it open, the dull light of the screen sending a shadow over his hand. The soft click of the buttons filled the dead air as he listened to the dull hum of the traffic outside.

Messages from Derek and Janet flickered past his eyes, both saying the same thing—mild apologies and assurances of spending some decent time with him whilst he was there. Janet, he knew, could be passably reliable in living up to the fair-weather promise; but Derek, Tony smirked, he knew the only way his son would ever be able to live up to that promise was if he was discharged or dead and neither option was likely anytime soon. A cold ball settled into his stomach as Tony closed his eyes.

At least, I hope neither of those happen anytime soon… honestly think that would break me right now.

Tony snapped the phone shut, tossing it onto the bed as he fished his wallet from his pocket and pulled the dulled and yellowed photo from behind the swathe of notes.

Staring down at the face of his wife as she held his new-born son, he felt the salt sting of tears.

'Right now, Derek, that really would break me; stay safe, son.'[1]

---

1   Tony's story continues in DESIGNATED DECLASSIFIED: One Last Hurrah.

Broadhead Barracks

Derek watched as the two Marauders rumbled through the gates, the bored expression on the drivers' face making him wince mentally. The lead man saluted lazily as he slipped the truck past him and turned left, heading to the maintenance sheds.

Sharp hopped out the back of the last truck as the gates closed with a dull, lifeless *thunk*. He stood in front of Baker, his face a drawn mask of self-loathing and regret that mingled in a sordid copulation with the layers of cold, indifferent determination and the driving need to get the job done, no matter the cost.

'Sir, I need to inform you of actions that have come to my attention and I believe they are of urgent address. Corporal Shaw has given me cause for concern in his self-conduct and mental stability.'

Baker stared at Sharp as the man stood there, his skin swathed in a layer of grim and stale sweat as patches of gore pooled in the folds of his suit.

'My office, twenty minutes.'

Sharp nodded crisply and then moved with a speed that belied his fatigue, towards the barracks and blessed warmth of a shower. Derek watched him go as the in-house decontamination team moved to sanitise the area, the coverall-cloaked men moving like hypnotised bees in search of that one elusive flower.

Turning, he headed back into the burgeoning presence of the T.O.C. with a nagging itch tickling at the base of his skull. He stopped, spun on his heel, and followed on after Sharp, heading towards the barracks. Nudging the door with his shoulder as he fished in his pocket for his mobile, Derek scanned the room. His eyes settled on Damien, who sat hunched over the toe of one boot, the black-stained cloth in his hand pulled tight over two fingers as he bulled his boots to a mirror shine.

'Colins, you got a minute?' He watched the man nod and set his boot aside, the black-stained cloth falling into the boot neck as he stood.

'S'up?'

Derek jerked his head towards the door and turned, Damien following closely behind him. The door closed with an echoing thump, a dozen set of eyes watching them depart.

'You still got contacts in Poole? I would call in some old favours, but most of my contacts are either in country, dead, or inactive for one reason or another.'

Damien's brow furrowed as he watched Derek fidget idly as he pulled a beaten and battered packet of cigarettes from his pocket and slipped one between his lips, before cupping his hand over the end and lighting it.

Derek drew in a deep, glowing lungful of nicotine-infused smoke, the heady rush of endorphins flooding his mind as he sated the itch.

'Yeah, I can get on a line to Brewer and Harris and see who is still kicking about.'

Colins scratched at his itching backside as he watched Baker, a sense of intrigued unease shivering its way up his spine. 'Come on, Cherry, out with it.'

Baker sighed as he blew the tar-soaked smoke from his nose and tapped at the white paper hide of the cigarette, watching as the ash spun and sparked on its way to the floor.

'I need a favour, mate, a serious one; it's off the books and on personal time.'

Damien shrugged as he leant back against the barracks wall, his breath fogging slightly in the chilled air.

'So, what do you need?'

Derek sighed, his eyes dark as he twisted the cigarette, peeling it apart and setting the shredded remnants in his pocket.

'A watcher team. You know my history with Ridgmont; you were with Durden's mob at the same time as I was, kicking about with selection. Anyway, he is getting close, mate… real fucking close. I found my other tag nailed to my bloody front door and his son's tag number carved beneath it.

Twelve is in his fucking pocket, and they won't think twice about putting a bullet in my wife and kid, let alone Sib. Poor kid hasn't got a fucking clue what's going on.

It's volunteer only. I want them to have complete deniability in place if it goes south. I don't know what they will expect, but I can pull the files on the guys in Twelve. Colinson kept tabs on the ones who signed up to that pay-by-the-bullet outfit. So at the very least, they'll know who to look for.'

Colins stayed silent for a moment, gathering his thoughts as Baker shifted his weight from foot to foot, his impatience mounting.

'Wait here a sec.'

Damien vanished through the barracks door, the heavy plastic and steel door crashing against the frame as it left his hand.

****

Roberts looked up, his brow furrowing as Colins met his gaze; with a sideways nod of his head, Colins turned and exited the room, closely followed by Roberts. Their silent exchange and rapid departure was followed by a myriad of confused and intrigued gazes as the door once more slammed closed.

****

The silence was deafening as Baker stood there watching the two men walk towards him, their footsteps slow and even as Colins gesticulated slowly, his movements measured and fluid.

'Damien tells me we have a bit of an issue… something about rabid dogs and a bunch of scurrying black rats.'

Baker smirked slightly as he pulled another cigarette free and held the packet out to the two men in front of him. A flurry of waved hands and shaking heads greeted his offer; nodding, Baker slipped the packet back into his hip pocket, his steel Zippo appearing a fraction of a second later.

Breathing out the hot, grey pall of tobacco smoke, Baker nodded before speaking.

'Yeah, something like that. Know any good exterminators?'

Roberts grinned darkly.

'A few. Shall I give them a call?'

Broadhead Barracks
Baker's office
Debrief

Sharp dropped into the only vacant chair in the room as Baker shoved a cup of black coffee into his hand. The room sat silent as Derek moved back to his chair, the jumbled stacks of paperwork framing him as his face danced in shadows from the glow of his computer monitor.

'So... you were saying something about Shaw?'

Sharp nodded as he held the cup in his hand, the heat from the coffee leaching into his skin making his palm itch slightly as it burned away layers of dead and calloused skin.

'I think he's got some wires loose or at least crossed; that E6 was fucking brutal. Next time, send in the Swarmers or something. I never want to have to slot a six year old again. Shit, her eyes are going to give me fucking nightmares.

'He was just so damned calm about it. One mother tried to run with her kid, boy must have been two or three, old enough to know things were bad, but not why.

'Anyway, he just turns, lines up on the middle of her back, just below her shoulder blades, and lets rip. Drops her like a sack of rotten spuds then strolls over and puts a round in her head and in the kid's like he was killing off rats or even ants.'

Sharp paused, lifting the steaming mug of black liquid to his lips before taking a none too tentative sip, his mind too wrapped up in its own musings to even acknowledge the scalding liquid that rolled down his throat.

Baker watched as Sharp set the cup back on the armrest, the corners of the man's mouth glowing a dull red from the heat, waiting with infinite patience for him to continue.

'By the end of it, it was hard to tell the civvies from the tangos, especially how most of them ended up in a jumbled heap after Shaw herded half of them into the middle of the Go Sushi foyer and set about them with the Gimpy.

'He's a class-one nut bar; I swear it, off his fucking trolley. At the end, he didn't even bat an eyelid. He just wombled out and hopped into the Marauder like he was off to fucking Tesco.'

Derek sipped from the cup in his hand as he leant back in his office chair and stared at the small patch of black mould just above his office door. A jumble of contradicting thoughts danced through his mind as he sifted through it all in search of a solution.

'Do you think he's fit for duty?'

Baker cast a glance at Sharp as the man pushed himself to his feet and strode across the five-foot gap to the quietly bubbling coffee maker.

'I've seen blokes like him before; they always get the work done, but no one trusts them. To be honest, Derek, the guy belongs in a padded cell at the bottom of the fucking ocean, and if he was back in Sterling he wouldn't even be rated for range duty.'

Baker winced at the none too subtle remark. No one in the SAS or any Special Forces unit wanted to be bumped down to range duty; it was a career death sentence.

'That bad?'

Sharp nodded as he dropped back into the chair, cup in hand.

'Yeah, that bad.'

Derek sighed, not wanting to see the writing on the wall for what it was. Reaching into his desk drawer, he pulled out a single A4 sheet of paper, its off-white colour making it clear to all exactly what

269

it was for.

'Okay, I need you to countersign this. He will never see it and it will go straight to the TRiM team, probably have one of Colinson's lot do the eval. Do you know who it is in Shaw's squad?'

Sharp shrugged, making a non-committal noise as he picked up the sheet of paper.

'Although, goss has it that it might be Carla. Wouldn't mind having a chat with her sometime. Nice arse on her even if she is a chopper jockey.'

Baker smirked slightly as he watched Sharp turn to leave.

'Keep your hands to yourself, Staff Sergeant; I don't need a harassment case as well as this crap.'

Sharp chuckled slightly as he pushed the door open. Despite the laughter he left in his wake, Derek could see in the way he walked and the slump of his shoulders that this situation was weighing on him heavily.

Turning back to the paperwork at hand, Baker sighed as he inked the date and coding stamp and pressed it into the box in the left-hand corner before scrawling his signature and setting it aside. Derek's mind was a fog of images and harried thoughts, the seething mass making his head spin as he tried in vain to pluck a single polished answer from the jumbled mass of chaff and coal scrapings that now choked his brain.

Sharp leant against the wall, watching as Westing pushed the barbell away from her chest. Her cheeks, flushed from the exertion, glistened under the harsh glare of the strip lights in the ceiling. Sharp's eyes travelled over her body, taking in the sight of the soaked sports bra clinging to her modest frame like a second skin. She let the barbell drop with a heavy clang onto the T-shaped mounts above her head. With a guttural grunt, Carla heaved herself upwards, a film of glimmering sweat clinging to the bench as twisting spectres of steam rose from her heat-soaked body.

'So, you gonna stand there and perve on me all afternoon or you gonna hand me a towel and tell me what the hell you want, Dick?'

Sharp smiled contritely as he stepped into the room, the paper in his hand flapping as he moved.

'Well, I had considered it, but then I wasn't sure if your golden nuggets would poke my eye out if I moved too quickly.'

His Scottish brogue sliced his words in half as he spoke. Westing's eyes glittered with mirth as she cupped her breasts, jiggling them slightly as she spoke, her words laced with laughter.

'Oh aye, these are damned deadly in the wrong hands, watch yourself, soldier.'

Sharp smirked as he lifted his eyes from her modest cleavage, his grey-green orbs landing on Carla's for a second before he stepped towards her, his body relaxed and loose as he set the A4 page in front of her and nodded towards it.

'Gonna need you to liaise with Baker and Colinson on this. I've got some "concerns" about Shaw; it's to do with the Paddington op. Don't know what it is, but he was too calm, too collected, and too damned casual. Need you to go scooping and see what's what.'

Westing nodded as she looked over the page in her hand. Sighing, she plucked her towel from the floor and ran it over her neck and hair.

'No problem. Gimme three days to get a time set up. I am due to work on setting up the six new support crews coming; RAF has been kind enough to send us over some of Harry's mates, benefits of having Lizzie as a boss I suppose; but this...

She waved the page in the air as she spoke.

'Shouldn't be a problem. We don't need section fours running around the shop. In country or not, it's a weak link we don't bloody need. Now go on, fuck off; I need to get this set finished and showered before those flying penises get here. RAF boys are hornier than you bunch of swinging dicks.'

Sharp barked with laughter as he moved back towards the door, the sound of the weights clinking off one another filling the room as Carla's soft grunts of exertion flirted with Richard's ears.

****

Shaw sat staring out across the expanse of grass and copses of trees that bordered the ever-expanding base. He glanced at the pistol in his hand, the .38 calibre weapon glinting dully in the evening sun. He sighed as he set it on the bench beside him and clasped his hands together, staring at the glowing yellow ball just above the horizon. Images bounced in his head, pleading calls and the tears of men and women as they begged him for their lives.

The smouldering, hate-filled stare of an aged man as he knelt on the floor tearing back the sleeve of his shirt as he brandished the tattooed numbers that crawled up the inside of his forearm, the muttered Hebrew curse floating through the air as he spat at the toes of Shaw's boots.

The blinding flare of his weapon's muzzle as he squeezed the trigger silencing the pleas in a wave of chattering brass and hot lead.

'Is that thing really going help anything?'

Carla stopped four feet from the side of the bench, the revolver between Shaw and her as she cocked her head to one side, shoulders relaxed and hands hanging loosely at her sides as she waited for him to reply.

'Probably not, but it would certainly clear my head of the horror show bouncing round in there at the moment.'

Carla did all she could not to smile at the dark humour, as much as it gnawed at her. Motioning at the empty space on the bench, Westing spoke, her voice soft with an almost musical note to it.

'You know you missed our appointment. I was sat waiting in the naffi for over an hour.'

She watched mutely as Shaw shrugged, his demeanour cold and uncaring as Carla stepped closer to him, a question leaving her lips as her trainer-covered feet sent gravel chips skittering away.

'Mind if I take a pew?'

Shaw shrugged once more, pulling the revolver closer to his hip. She sat, the steel slats of the bench cold against her denim-covered rump. Carla wiggled slightly as she sat, tugging at the inner seam of her jeans as it began to grate against her skin.

She felt, more than saw, Shaw's lingering sidelong gaze as she plucked and pulled at her jeans.

'They're worried, you know.'

Westing's head snapped to the side, her eyes locking onto Shaw as he spoke, suddenly unsure of herself as she sat in the isolated corner of the base.

'Who are?'

Her voice kept its soft lyrical cadence as she fought with herself and her sudden involuntary need to flee. Digging her fingers into the

273

meat of her thigh, Carla focused on the sudden burst of pain as she slowly rearranged her thoughts, letting Shaw's sudden statement sink in.

'Everyone… you, Baker, Colinson. All of them, really. I know Sharp made a formal statement about me. About Paddington and what I did.'

Carla shifted slightly closer to him, her fingers scatting over the cold metal beneath her, her clipped nails digging into the weather-worn paint that coated the anodized steel.

'And what makes you think they're so worried, Rufus?'

He cast a baleful look in Carla's direction as he leant forwards, his elbows resting against his knees.

'The fact that right at this very moment, I am scared shitless of myself. How ironic is that? I am... scared... of myself.'

Carla sat and watched his face for a moment, studying the play of emotions that flowed like water across his features, the haunted shimmer of self-doubt and fear that glowed in his eyes, mingled with the encompassing pall of anger.

'And why do you think that makes people worried about you?'

His eyes darkened as he stared at his hands, his hands reflexively opening and closing as he leant forwards trying in vain not to cry.

'Because it makes me the weak link, that point in the chain that will eventually crack under the strain and do something stupid. I thought I could hide it behind a veneer of indifference and calm self-assurance, but I can't.

'I can't get that girl's eyes out my mind, the look of pain and shock spreading through her as I pulled the trigger. She was supposed to be able to look to a soldier for help; instead, I betrayed her and the hundred others in there.

274

'If I am the weak link, then how can I lead my tea? How can I get them in and out of country safe and intact? I *can't* is the answer to that.'

His voice cracked as he turned to look at Westing, her pale, watery, blue eyes filled with sympathy and a heavy, comforting dose of familiarity.

A small smile ghosted over her lips as she set a hand on his shoulder, her right slipping across her lap to the revolver that sat between them. Her fingers carefully and quietly lifted the weapon, its weight settling into her fingers as she let it glide slowly over the thick layer of paint. Leaning forwards slowly, the weapon slithered past her denim-clad buttocks, falling deftly into her right hand as she pushed the drum free and emptied the rounds from the chambers; their soft semi-metallic clink flirted with her ears as they hit the floor, rolling into the leaf-clogged gutter below.

'Rufus, you have a track record longer than my old nineties ponytail, all of it flawless and irrefutably perfect. A weak link is something you are not.' She let her hand rest against his forearm, her fingers soft and teasing as she carried on talking. 'The only people I have met with more force majeure than you are Derek, Davies, and the old guard.'

Rufus glanced down at her hand as it softly kneaded his upper forearm, his face a blank mask as he turned to stare out at the open fields and horizon as the sun slowly made its descent.

'That's a crock of horse dollop, and you know it. *Force majeure?* What did you do, swallow a fucking dictionary?'

Westing ignored the pointed comment and continued the subtle guidance.

'May well have; fuck knows what they shove in the mash in the mess hall. Half of it tastes like burnt rat shit, anyway.'

Shaw snorted derisively, his shoulders loosening slightly as his mood began to shift. Sensing a break in his armour, Carla softly squeezed his arm as she spoke, shifting her weight, slowly drawing his slightly off balance.

'Come on, let's get you back to the sack rack; you look tired as hell.'

With a gentle tug, Carla drew Rufus to his feet as she stood up, leading him with soft words and a sympathetic smile to the Land-rover thirty yards away, the now empty pistol safely tucked into the pocket of her jacket.

24
October 21st
Broadhead barracks
Biological studies division
Laboratory one

Anastasia stared into the lens of the microscope; the sample swimming through the slide made her skin crawl. She watched as the cells collapsed in on themselves, folding as their bodies twisted. The tentacle-like protrusions latched onto one of the last surviving normal red cells, drawing it into its oval embrace, the waving black tendrils piercing its walls as they broke free and slithered their way towards its fragile core.

Anna lifted her gaze away and let her eyes linger on the stack of reports and manila folders. The laundry list of cases made her soul ache, the litany of Infected team members weighing heavily on her as she lifted the top folder.

Her eyes brimming slightly as she took in the name and all that followed it. Rawlings, James, post-death fluid analysis showing no sign of Infection, although white cell and adrenalin levels were far above the normal. She sighed as she set the folder to the side. A smiling photo of Rawlings slipped from the pages, landing with a soft hushed swish on the top of the desk.

With a harsh grimace, Anna slipped the photo from the top and it pushed between the leaves of paper as she dragged another folder from the stack.

Anastasia listened to the wheezing, rasping cough of the man who now claimed residence in the observation cell at the far end of the laboratory, the whirring oxygen filters in the ceiling adding a hideous cadence to the noises that filled the room.

Leaning back in her chair, Anna sighed as she pressed her open palms into the middle of her back, feeling her spine pop and ripple as she stretched.

With a deep groan, she pinched the bridge of her nose, massaging the tender slip of skin between thumb and forefinger as she stared at the glass and chrome-panelled ceiling. Shifting herself into a more comfortable position, she grasped the cold, chrome steel rims of her chair's wheels and swung herself into the aisle.

The tread hummed over the tiles as she pushed herself closer to the rasping form behind the clear reinforced wall. His hunched and weary visage perched on the edge of the wall-mounted cot.

'How are we feeling today, Joshua?'

As he lifted his head to stare at her, his eyes glowed with a menacing light, which filtered through the very core. Anna felt her stomach lurch as she watched his skin waver and pulsate as the bulbous swellings heaved and peeled open.

The viscous sludge slid over his skin as Joshua slowly pushed himself to his feet. A grin wormed its way across his features as he leant his arms against the wall, sore-cratered nose scant millimetres from its powder-blasted surface.

'Why, if it isn't the Doctor.'

His voice was smooth as silk; the undercurrent of bubbling mucus that coated his lungs lent a slightly snake-like rasp as he spoke.

'To answer your little query, I feel fine. Never better, in fact; are you here for more...'

He paused as he lifted his middle and index finger to one of the weeping sores, coating them with the bilious excretion. He ran his thumb over it, feeling the thick gelatinous muck slid across his battered fingertips.

Joshua's gaze never left Anna's as he lifted his fingers to his lips, his tongue languidly rolling free as he flicked it across his fingers.

Sliding the ooze-laden digits into his mouth, his grin broadened as he watched the fleeting spectre of utter disgust dance behind Anna's eyes. Pulling his fingers free, Joshua continued speaking.

'Blood samples, hmm?'

His smile faltered as he watched the woman before him; with a nod of her head, she motioned for Joshua to slide his arm through the hole. Anastasia callously pushed his sleeve up past his elbow as he watched her, his skin wrinkling as he rested his forehead against the cold plastic wall. Anna moved forwards, her movements precise, almost mechanical as she slipped the heavy elasticated band from her pocket and looped it round his arm.

Her eyes tracked the flowing river of veins that bulged against his sallow skin. Anna's gloved fingers pressed into his cold flesh. The hollow tube was cold against his pliant skin as she aligned it with her chosen target.

'You'll feel a sharp pinch.'

Anna's words rang hollow and meaningless as she pushed the needle through and into the waiting vessel below.

The slick, steel tube pierced his flesh as she moved it slowly, searching for the wayward vein. Blood flowed into the vial as Anna pushed it over the rubber tip. Joshua watched with bored detachment as the smooth metal twisted in his flesh, his arm twitching involuntarily as Anna brushed the needle against the bundled fibres of his muscle.

A hollow clink made both of them flinch, a deep sigh rolling up from Anastasia's chest as she lifted the broken syringe to the level of her eye.

'Sorry about that; I'll have to get it out.'

Joshua smiled as he pulled his arm from her grip, the cold grip of the Lexan sliding over his skin as he set his thumb and index finger either side of the pin-sized hole. Squeezing the punctured flesh with a soft muffled grunt, a glint of pleasure glittered in his eyes as he watched the hollow tube slowly push itself free of his flesh.

'I must say, it has become rather malodorous in here. Is there, perchance, a way for me to maybe take a sojourn from this well of a human sideshow and maybe take a walk? After all, it has been over three weeks since I stopped soiling myself.'

Anastasia didn't know what to say; the spectacle and the man that stood before her were so far removed from what he had been that it was like talking to a completely new person. His head dropped to the side as Anna moved away from the Lexan wall, a cruel and vindictive smile twisting his features.

Joshua paced towards the centre of the room, his soft-soled, slip on shoes whispering against the floor as he moved; his back was ramrod straight as he shuffled to the cot once more, perching on its edge as he waited for the tray to appear.

'So that's a no to the walk then?'

His humour-laced words made Anna shiver. Her ears burning and her skin tingled with the cold press of fear as he continued to call out across the vacuous expanse of the room.

'Please, dear heart, do consider it. I am most dreadfully bored in here. You never know, you may get to like me once I am out of here. I know I am getting excited at the notion of knowing you, more... intimately.'

****

Her pen rasped over the pre-typed page on the desk in front of her, the dull glow of her desktop lamp casting a halo of yellowed light over the form. Glancing to her left, she paused as her eyes lingered on the photograph at the corner of her desk. A winsome smile teased at her lips as she felt herself begin to drift on the subtle ebb of an unbidden memory.

280

A low, hushed creak made her start as he door swung open, the shadowed form filling her doorway, sending a shiver through her very soul. The dull, soulless eyes that locked on her own filled her with a fear so primal that if she could have, she would have run in fear of her life.

The soft almost ivory coloured lips curled into a smile so filled with malice that it would have made the devil cringe in fear. With near silent steps, it advanced with eyes glittering and smile slipping into a grin as the soft glow of the desk slide lamp shone off the polished steel of the chef's knife clutched in the shade's grip. Her violet eyes widened as she watched it rise, a soft laughter-tinged voice filling her ears as it descended.

'Finally, dear heart, we have our time alone.'

Anna jerked awake, her eyes streaming as papers fluttered around her head, the echoing clang of her desk lamp colliding with the unyielding surface below making her jump. A cold jet of fear-laced adrenaline coursed through her as the light bulb burst with a sudden snap.

A heavy hand clasped her shoulder, eliciting a shriek of surprise and fright from the already shaken biochemist.

'Hey, what's that all about?'

Anna tentatively turned her gaze, alighting on Davies' grinning form, the inch-long thatch of black briar coating his chin giving his features a slightly haze-ridden form in her watery gaze. Pushing her glasses away from the bridge of her nose, Anna rubbed at her eyes, the cool rivers of her tears sliding over her fingers as she sniffed sharply before turning her gaze back to John once more.

'Just a very bad and very vivid dream. That is all; it was nothing to worry about.'

She smiled as she took his hand in hers, turned it over, and planted a soft kiss in his palm before resting her head against his forearm. He stepped around her, perching on the edge of her desk, his hand cupping her chin as his eyes searched her face. His dark-green orbs scanned her visage for any sign of deception or hidden meaning, his brow furrowing as he caught the repressed glimmer of whatever was plaguing her mind. Davies shifted his weight to the right as he brushed against the empty plastic photo frame, a dull clack rising from behind his left hip as it tumbled down the back of the desk.

'Right... if you say so.'

Davies kept his eyes locked on her for a moment longer before hoping back to his feet and grabbing the back of Anna's chair. With a sudden jerk, he pulled her away from the desk and pushed her out into the hallway.

'Day shift can take over; you, my lovely, are going outside. I cannot remember the last time I saw you outside of that sterile cube you call a laboratory.'

A wane smile teased at Anna's lips as she felt the burgeoning worry and fear begin to slowly melt away. The vibrant energy and lust for life that poured from the man who now had hold of the back of her chair filled her with a simmering hope that the future she saw in the lenses of her microscope, the red smear of wanton decay and chaos, would remain just that—a smear of dead blood on a sliver of glass.

But try as she might, Anna couldn't shake the devil from her shoulder any more than she could stop the whispering voice in her ear, a voice that carried with it the seeds of doubt and prophecies of death and wanton destruction.

Joshua watched as Anna and John slid past the window, Davies' silent laughter making Joshua smile as he once more gazed at the slip of photographic paper in his hands and the raven-haired woman who stared up at him with a set of iridescent violet eyes.

Colinson stared at the plans laid out before him, his eyes narrowing as he studied the white and blue image.

'Okay, I can see its merits, but how would we feasibly deploy this in the field? It can't be trailered in; it would totally defeat the purpose. That only leaves an air-drop, but to have this on a parachute would be a disaster waiting to happen.'

The three technicians glanced between themselves before their gazes drifted over to Rook as he leant against the table's edge next to David.

'Way I see it is we have an excess of Chinooks out there; we retrofit the belly hatches with the clamping configuration these boys cooked up and carry it in that way. They are carried in the chinny, it hovers at, say, twenty-five above the deck, and then the guy inside hits the go switch and—boom, instant fire base.'

Colinson nodded as he stared at the plans, scenarios already forming in his head. The implications of what he was looking at were extremely pleasing, if it could be done with minimal risk to the crews manning them.

'Okay, have three working platforms ready for me in two weeks then we will do some dry drops into the village with Simunitions. You reckon on a drop ceiling of twenty-five feet?'

Colinson glanced at Rook as the technicians nodded emphatically, the operator merely shrugging in acknowledgement.

'Okay then, we will start at thirty-five and see if it takes it. If not, drop it by five feet on the next run. How much ammunition do you expect to be toting in the hoppers?'

Rook again shrugged, his nonchalance grating at Colinson's nerves slightly.

'I'd estimate around two hundred, maybe two hundred and fifty thousand rounds. That gives us a healthy margin on the ground. That's not counting, of course, the munitions for the riflemen or the backups for the chair gunners. If you are counting them, then I'd wager in at three hundred and fifty thousand. That's my best guestimate.'

Colinson winced as he ran the figures through his head. Sighing, he nodded, drumming his fingers against the table as he subconsciously chewed at his lip.

'Okay, if you think we can make it work and the chinnys can take the load, you have my GA. Just don't make me regret this.'

Turning away from the quartet that flanked him, Colinson began to leave as a small tentative voice called him back.

'Uh, Colonel, there is one more matter; the package from our operative in the United States...' The technician coughed into his fist. 'It is still waiting in the armoury stores. We as yet haven't had permission to pull it from isolated storage.'

Colinson pinched the bridge of his nose in exasperation. Sighing slightly, he stared at the trio of white-coated men and women.

'You waited this long to ask me? Dear god, I am dumbstruck that you lot are actually able to get anything done. Go pull it from I.S and bring it through to room D. We can sort it out there.'

The two techs disappeared out the door before Colinson had even finished speaking. They appeared moments later, followed by an entourage of slightly red-faced techs, the heavy cases clutched in their hands still sealed with black and yellow hazard tape around the centre seam and locks.

284

A soft hissing filled the room as the tape split, Colinson watching with wry amusement as the locks were eagerly snapped open by the waiting men and women around him.

He watched them bunch together like children around a Christmas tree, each jostling for a new position from which to better see their waiting prize. A collective grunt of annoyance spread through them as one of them lifted an empty box magazine from the crate, its square form falling to the table with a clatter as he tossed it aside.

'Check the next one; we have got to have something of use in these damned things.'

Crate after crate fell open to the gathered throng, exposing more and more of the boxed receptacles of copper-laced death, until in one of the final ten crates, gold was struck. The exultant yelp of one of the women drew many a curious glance as she slowly raised above her head the source of her glee.

Packed in protective foam and surrounded by dozens of dehumidifier pouches sat twenty Keltec RFB carbines. As the other crates fell open to the elements for the first time in four years, their oiled and greased forms made more than one member giggle with unrepressed glee as they were, one by one, lifted from the crates.

'These are a work of art. The eighteen-inch, chrome-lined barrel, short-stroke gas piston and semi-automatic fire make this a rifleman's wet dream. Coming in with a 7.62 mm NATO round, this thing will stop just about anything in its tracks.

'Only drawback we have is the FAL magazines, which although "drop free" and thus do not need to be tilted in, only hold twenty rounds.

'But I think if we can adapt the magazine heads on the Beta C magazines we have in stores then these should theoretically be able to carry up to one hundred rounds a piece.'

A fluttering of paper filled the room as the woman plucked one of the manuals from a mesh pocket in the lid, reading aloud as she scanned the pages.

'The muzzle is threaded 5/8x24 TPI and comes equipped with an A2-style Flash hider...'

She tapped the muzzle with her index finger as she continued to babble.

'Longer barrel lengths of 24", 26" and 32" will be available in the future...' A snort left her and, under her breath, she muttered, 'Not likely.'

'It says here that all controls are fully ambidextrous and the reciprocating operating handle can be switched to either side. There is some other typical blathering about the trigger mechanism. That's just publicity tosh, but it looks like the safety disconnects the trigger and blocks the hammer action, so we will want to let the boys in the field know that if they need to strip it in country, other than that a Mil-Spec picatinny rail is attached rigidly to the barrel. No surprises there; on top of that, it says—and I quote—"No open sights are provided, allowing the user to select from the very best new optics and sight systems available." Isn't that nice of them? But it does come with a plethora of other gubbins that may prove very useful.'

She stopped reading and dropped the pamphlet back into the box as she cocked the rifle and let it dry fire, repeating the process for all of the twenty weapons in the crate at her feet.

Colinson stepped forwards, plucking the glossed pages from where they lay discarded in the top of the box, his eyebrows rising as he scanned the last small paragraph the tech hadn't paraphrased.

'Okay, so a four-sided Picatinny fore-end, bipod mounts, a removable bayonet lug for use with NATO style bayonets, including their own Folding Bayonet, not bad.' Turning from the paper in his hands, Colinson called Rook over to him and spoke, gesturing to the rifles on the table. 'Think these could be used in your drop boxes?'

Rook scanned the weapons his lips tightening as he thought it through.

'Well, Keltec is a bloody good armourer. Their shit doesn't cop out under pressure; more than one unit in my old division used them in place of the type 0 carbine I carried, so I should think so. Plus, the shrunken dimensions will make carrying them down easier on the guys hitting dirt. As long as we can get the issue with the mags sorted, I don't see any problem with them. Obviously need to send a few rounds down the spout before we dish 'em out; no one is perfect a hundred percent of the time.'

Colinson smiled as he walked past Rook, his parting words making the man groan slightly as the he left the room, the door closing with an echoing clunk. 'See to it then. This is your baby; you clean its mess.'

Token sat with his back to the window, hunched and contorted over his workbench. The magnifying lenses over his eyes made him look like an amorphous hybrid of man and insect as he peered through them. The curved glass bringing the small drone in his hands into sharp focus as the scent of hot solder filled his nostrils.

Sweat glistened over his shaven head. The dark brown of his scalp almost glowed as heat radiated from him, sending trails of misty vapour into the crisp air around him.

'How they looking Ibrahim?'

Kweku's thick accented voice was little more than a mumbled whisper as Colinson approached the workbench.

'They are shaping up nicely, sir; although, I am not able to fit as much explosive in them as I would like to. The casings have made it a very pleasing challenge.'

Colinson stopped as he reached Token's shoulder. He watched the soldier's hands moved with a self-assured confidence, the intricate wiring and circuitry making David's eyes blur as he strained to follow its passage through the minuscule drone.

'If you want to test one out, I have at least a hundred done and some more with another drone operator. The explosives won't detonate unless you command them to.'

Colinson shook his head as he stepped away and moved back towards the door. 'No need, Kweku; I trust in your abilities. You should have come forwards sooner with your technical skills. We could have used these a while ago.'

Token sighed as he set the soldering iron back into its stand and carefully laid the drone down on the rawhide mat. 'I know, sir, and for that I apologise, but for me, it is a source of shame and pride. My father, he was not very accepting of my choice to become a soldier and even less so of my skills with electronics. He wanted me to follow after him—become a paediatrician—and for a while it is what I did. But, well, when I signed up to the medical corps, he was ashamed and has not spoken to me since...'

Colinson nodded as he let the door slip from his grip, the pain on the young man's face making him pause. A small sigh slid through him. Colinson moved back towards the bench, pulling a wheeled office chair with him.

'Go on; when was the last time you spoke to your father?'

Token stifled the tears that glittered behind his eyes as leant forwards, his elbows braced against his knees, a pain-racked draw of breath filling him as he started to speak.

'Not for a very long time, sir; not for a very, very long time.'

Baker residence
North East London

The cold, blue glow bathed his features as he watched the frenzied picture on the screen before him. His thumbs drifted this way and that as he guided the MPUAV through the smog-laden air over London, its sole target weaving in and out of the throng of people below.

'Package approaching door, say again, package is approaching door. Zero sightings.'

Static buzzed in his ear as he heard the radio squelch coming in from his compatriots at street level.

'Watcher One, pulling drone for recharge and damage check. T.T.O.R fifteen minutes.'

Another squelch of static filled his ear as he guided the quadro-copter back to his rooftop nest, letting it land with a soft whistling whine on the foam-padded case to his right. He snapped the charger into place and watched the digital counter slowly begin to climb into the green.

****

'Watcher Two, Tango sighted, west of my position, red building, third floor, second window from right. Confirm.'

His earbud buzzed as he stared down the scope of his rifle, the cross hairs sitting tight on his target's chest as he waited for confirmation. He watched as the barrel rose above the lip of the window. His gaze flicked down to the four-inch monitor to his left, the high-resolution image of the front of Derek and Janet's home drawing his attention as the door swung open.

289

'Belay confirmation, Tango has eyes on package, weapon in play.'

He squeezed the trigger, the rifle bumping into his shoulder as he absorbed the recoil; he watched the figure in the window jolt as the bullet tore through their chest, dragging bone and tissue with it.

'Tango is down, need to confirm, but shot was good.'

A figure appeared in his sights a minute later, hand waving over their head, fingers splayed apart. Pressing the rubberised pad on the stock of his rifle, he sent a reply. A heavy, aged voice filled his ear a second later as the figure slipped away from the window.

****

'Drone in play and tracking; Watcher Three, do you have eyes on?'

The line danced with the hiss of white noise and static as Watcher One waited for a reply, the muffled sounds of his own breathing filling his ears as he watched the screen flicker slightly.

The infrared beacon hanging from the strap of Janet's shoulder bag blinked and blipped as she wove through the throng of people cluttering the pavement around her.

'Six, swing drone four to task, drone two moving to sector six, Watcher Three is not responding.'

The carbon fibre blades sliced the air as the drone banked sharply to port and swung out over the traffic-choked road and headed in the direction of the silent watcher.

Ridgmont watched as the drone drifted silently across the rooftops. The radio controller next to him softly beeped as it cycled through myriad of frequencies that blanketed the air around him. A widening grin spread over his features like wet mud over a stone as a soft beep filled the air.

The controller sat, cold and heavy in his hands as he let his gaze drop to the screen; his thumbs danced over the twin joysticks as the drone swung backward towards One. The auto loader clunked as it dragged a shell into the shotgun's chamber, the barrel rising into place as the drone swung level with One's position.

'What the fuck is going on here?' One smashed his fist into the side of the controller as the screen shifted, his moving form filling his vision as One turned to stare at the hovering drone. 'Oh, bollocks.'

The blast echoed across the milling throng below, making them squeal with fright as the drone jolted slightly with the recoil of the twelve-gauge round detonating.

The hot lead pellets tore into One's bomber-jacketed form. The clacking bolt lent a lilting rhythmic cadence to the chugging thump as, one after another, the smoking black casings fell to the rooftop below.

****

Janet's head swivelled at the sudden sound as the man twenty feet behind launched himself forwards, pinning her to the floor. The air left her lungs in a rush, the heavy smell of sweat and cigarettes filled her nose as she struggled to draw a breath.

'Stay close.'

The man's hand curled into her coat as she was hauled to her feet, a matte-black pistol appearing next to her face as she was pulled back towards her front door.

'Keep your head down and move it.'

Janet stumbled, struggling to keep her feet beneath her as he pushed her up the steps and into her home. Janet jerked her shoulder from his grip as she stumbled forwards. 'Get the fuck off me. Who the fucking hell do you think you are?'

He spun to face Janet as the door slammed shut. Striding forwards, he shoved her deeper into the house. 'I'm Sergeant Thomas Martin, Special Boat Service. Stay down, stay quiet, and you'll stay alive.'

The sound of footsteps filled the air as Martin spun, his aim snapping to the top of the staircase as his eyes slid along the cold polymer slide as the sights aligned.

Siobhan stared at him, eyes wide with fear as she clutched Maria to her shoulder. 'I ... I ... I heard gunshots; what's going on?'

Martin snagged Janet's sleeve and hauled her upstairs, pushing her into Siobhan as he herded both of them towards the back of the house. Maria began to whine as the noise and confusion soaked into her tiny form.

'Shut her up and get in there.'

He pushed the trio towards the empty box room at the far end of the corridor. Spinning on the balls of his feet, Martin sped down the corridor to the staircase. With a grunt of exertion, he vaulted the stairs, leaping to the floor below as the front door began to swing open.

****

The echoing crack of a nine-millimetre pistol filled the hallway as a hooded form slipped past the gloss black door. The scent of burnt cloth and blood filled the air as Martin slid into the heavy oak panelling of the door.

Wet gurgling greeted his ears as he pushed himself to his feet. A heavy twinge of pain skittered across the base of his back as he levered himself upright. He stared at the man as blood soaked his chest, the ragged hole in his neck oozing as he stared through water-hazed eyes at Thomas' advancing form.

'Dying is never pretty, is it? But fuck me, mate, you are ugly. Division Twelve is really scraping the bottom of the proverbial barrel if you are what they're dishing out.'

He lifted aside the unzipped hoodie and began emptying out the dead operative's pockets. Martin pulled his hand from the inner pocket of the hoodie, his knuckles slick with blood, and flipped open the dead man's wallet. The MOD identification card stared up at him from the clear plastic panel, a dour, pockmarked face glaring back at him.

'Traitorous cunt.'

Curling his hand into the corpse's collar, he dragged it away from the door. He cast a glance at the slack, ashen features, a shiver of disgust snaking its way up his spine as he crossed the threshold and dumped the slowly cooling body beside the sink.

Pressing his fingers to the call pad on his throat mike, Martin opened a channel. *'This is Three, package is locked down, Tango eliminated, anyone eyes on, I need an update.'*

The earphone bead in his ear hissed with a storm of white noise as he watched shadows dance past the kitchen window, their fluttering forms flirting with his eyes as he quietly moved towards the back door. The sound of booted feet on wooden planks rose through the tumult of panicked cries, lending a muted accompaniment to the drumbeat of death that pushed its way into his head.

'Well, isn't this just dandy? Three mags full of nine-mil hollow points, a deck full of psychopaths in high-end body armour with classified weaponry, and nothing but a doctor, a nursemaid, and a bloody baby as back up… oh, and a dead radio.'

His words echoed in the silent hallway as he made his way towards the stairs, hoping in vain to manufacture some kind of bottleneck. Once more, his fingers found the pad on his throat, the soft rubber-covered button clicking slightly as he pushed.

293

'This is Three, to all watchers, package is under threat, I repeat package is under threat, anyone in vicinity respond.'

****

Baker stared at the police tape covering the railings that bordered the carved stone steps. The flashing lights cast dancing spectres across the granite-hewn walls of his home. He watched with anger and fear-tinged eyes as, one after another, black sack-filled stretchers were wheeled forth. Their clacking wheels sent spears of ice into his heart as they made their way to the waiting ambulances.

The Sco19 officers that flanked the tape-lined steps moved to block him, their black gloved hands rising to clasp his shoulders.

'Touch me and I will rip your throats out with my teeth. Fucking move.'

The two men glared back at him from beneath their Kevlar helmets, their towering forms squaring up to him as a voice split the air around them.

'Bridge, Drapper, bloody move. You idiots wouldn't last thirty seconds against him. Don't you recognise the name on his damned jacket?'

Both men blanched as their eyes dropped to the patch on Derek's jacket, the embroidered red arrowhead inlaid with the queen's crown, his name in block white lettering beneath it.

Both men shrank visibly as they stepped aside heads nodding in the direction of the still open doorway.

'Baker.'

Derek paused and turned to glance at the Sco19 commander. 'She's fine. Shaken, but fine.'

Derek nodded as he brushed past the two officers and made his way up the steps to his front door. Baker's mind whirled as he stepped through the doorway. The coppery smell of blood filled his nostrils, the claret spattering standing clear against the cream walls of the staircase, photos lay discarded, the shattered glass stained crimson at the edges.

Derek knelt, picking the glass from the frame, his fingers tingling as he felt spear-like shards slide into his skin, droplets of claret liquid seeping through the pads of his fingers.

He stared at the picture his father holding his daughter with his wife standing next to the loving duo, a beaming smile on her face; although, what Derek now looked at was the charred hole where his wife's face had once been. Setting the shattered picture at the foot of the stairs, he stood, brushing the crystalline shards from his knees and stepped towards the chaos that was once his living room.

Siobhan sat, curled next to Janet, Maria held between them as the young woman sobbed into his wife's shoulder, her mouse brown hair draped over Janet's back as she shook with the violent exhalations of her own fear-drenched outpouring.

Derek's eyes cast their gaze around the room. The two paramedics, who knelt around the only person he didn't recognise glanced his direction as they began to pack their bags. Discarded latex gloves and empty packets quickly stuffed into a thin polythene bag before they made their way from the room, their dark-green uniforms a stark contrast to the pale skin of the topless man they had stood next to.

Baker made his way to the edge of the sofa, his hand settling on Janet's shoulder as he squeezed it gently, her head leaning into his hip. Eyebrows furrowed, Derek spoke, his voice measured and monotone despite the current of fear that pierced the baritone cadence that filled the room.

'Name and rank.'

The man looked up, a sharp snarl of pain skating across his face as he moved too quickly, the stitches in his shoulder tugging at the tender skin that walled the cavern carved through his shoulder. 'Martin, Sergeant, three-three-four-one-eight-nine-two-three.'

Baker nodded as he gently tapped Janet's shoulder before moving away, his eyes never leaving Martin's even gaze.

'Thank you.'

Thomas smirked, wincing as he did so, his hand reflexively moving to rub at the bandages covering his shoulder before he stopped short and set his hands in his lap once more.

'Don't be. "By any means" doesn't just cover ops, Major; you know that. We look after our own. You know you're still the poster boy at Poole. Hell, you're what every sneaky beaky, and sprog wants to be when they grow up.

'I should know, I was one of 'em, but that's old news. This was just something we do—once a Marine, always a Marine.'
As he said this, Martin waved a hand around him, the dagger tattoo on his arm catching Derek's eye as he took in the devastation. The pockmarked walls and red-tinged carpets showing all too clear what he meant. 'Now, if you don't mind, I think, if my eyes aren't deceiving me, there is a bottle of Glendronach in that cabinet.'

Baker smirked as he moved towards the cabinet, plucking one of the surviving tumblers from the carpet before lifting the bottle free and carefully pulling the cork from its neck.

Handing the glass to Martin, Derek turned his arm. The ink scarred into his skin drawing Martin's gaze as Baker cast a glance towards Janet. Martin smiled slightly as he nodded, Derek's silent acknowledgment saying more than anything else ever could.

'Not a scratch on them. I made sure of that. Got a couple'a more notches on my belt and a few new stories, but hell, it's nothing new. They're still clearing the bodies from the second floor and, I'm ashamed to say, the lil'un will need a new cot. But that's a damned sight better than you needing a new daughter; I'd have slotted myself if that happened.'

Derek glanced at Martin once more, his words soft and choked as he set the bottle next to Thomas' leg. 'Keep it, least I can do.'

Turning away from the man who sat before him, Derek stepped forwards and knelt before his wife, his shoulders bobbing slightly as he kissed Maria's forehead.

Thomas watched for a moment, before forcing himself upright and moving towards the door. Janet's hand slipped out and clasped his wrist, her lips meeting the top of his hand before her soft voice filled his ears. 'Thank you.'

Thomas smiled as gently pulled his hand from her grip, his eyes holding her gaze with an even stare, his reply gentle, hiding the pain that lanced through his beaten form. 'Any time.'

His footfalls echoed through the corridor as he disappeared from sight and made his way out onto the street.

December 6th
Australia

Kingsley sat in the cold confines of the Hercules C130J, the heavy drone of the engines lulling him into a soft doze as Angel rested at his feet. The orders and request had come as a surprise to all but Colinson, with Solomon's presence requested by Brigadier McDaniel himself. With a yawn, Kingsley leant forwards, rubbing the gritty granules from his eyes before lifting the folder from the seat next to him and flipping it open.

He felt the heat leave his feet as Angel stretched and hopped up onto the seat next to him; Kingsley's fingers ruffled her ears as he flicked through the pages of the file, soaking in the details like a sponge in a glass.

'Looks like it's all kicking off down the yellow brick road, girl. You ready to give them a hand?'

His only reply was a soft, velvety tongue licking his palm and a short yap of acknowledgement, before Angel settled down, her head resting on his thigh.

'Yeah, I thought so too.'

His fingers gently danced through her straw-coloured fur as sleep once again claimed him.

****

The wheels squealed as they touched the scorching tarmac, Kingsley's head bouncing against the rapidly heating skin of the aircraft.

'Son of a...'

Kingsley rubbed at the back of his head as he sat upright, the heat in the plane rapidly climbing as it coasted along the runway.

298

The side hatch popped open as Kingsley stood, his back popping and clicking as he stretched his frame. He jolted slightly as Angel tugged at the lead tied to his belt. A small tug of pride slipped through him as he watched her immediately back up and sit at his heel, her head bowed, realising she had done the wrong thing.

His free hand ruffled her ears as he plucked his holdall from the floor and stuffed the discarded file into it. Solomon glanced up as Angel growled, the sun-tinged face that peered in through the doorway drawing his attention.

'George?'

The face broke into a wide grin as its owner stepped up into the aircraft. 'Solomon, god dam, Kingsley, how the bloody hell are ya?'

Kingsley smiled warmly as Angel continued to growl deep in her throat. 'I am good, George, bloody good.'

George stepped forwards, his hand rising. Angel leapt forwards dragging Solomon with her as she did so, her teeth bared and a heavy yet slightly high-pitched bark rising from her.

George jumped back several feet as Kingsley yanked Angel back to his side, a anger-tinged command leaving him as he glared at her. With a whimper of submission, Angel lay down next his feet before rolling onto her back, completely submissive.

Stepping forwards again, George crouched as he cocked his head to the side, looking at the straw gold Spaniel as he patted the deck lightly. With a nod from Solomon, Angel cautiously approached him, her ears head low and gait anxious as she slowly inched closer to him.

'You don't remember me do you, girly?'

Angel's head cocked to the side slightly as she tentatively sniffed at George's outstretched hand, her form relaxing with each passing second. A grin spread across his features as her tail began to wag slightly, the subtle coils of recognition at a familiar scent weaving their way through her tired and slightly ruffled form.

'Well, looks like you're wrong there, Porgey. It just took her a minute. Looks like they still use your mother's name, Artino.'

Pushing himself to his feet, his hand tousling the fur on the top of Angle's head as he straightened, George nodded his head towards the baked and sun scorched world outside the aircraft.

'Come on, mate, we've got to get moving. The official welcoming committee is over in the terminal building, but suffice it to say, welcome to Swartz Barracks, or as it is also known, Oakey AAC.'

With a soft tug at Angel's lead, Solomon followed George to the open door and out into the rolling waves of heat that shimmered across the black expanse of ground that surrounded the plane.

'So, what's the situation? Briefing was sparse, to say the least.'

Artino scratched the back of his neck as Angel softly panted at Kingsley's heel.

'I'll, uh, let the big wigs fill you in, mate … it's not looking too good, and well, you need to get the full picture, not the barrack chatter.'

Kingsley nodded as they reached the rear entrance of a stark-white building, the heat shimmering across the wall as he reached for the handle.

George reached past him, barging Solomon away from the door. 'Not trying to be a prick, mate, but with the highs we're hitting this summer, you don't wanna touch these handles without a glove on.'

The door swung outward, the sudden rush of artificially cooled air hitting them all like a sledgehammer as Angel whimpered slightly. George motioned Kingsley through the doorway, the click of Angel's clawed feet filling the air as several sets of eyes turned to greet them.

'Ah, Solomon, good of you to join us. Tell me, how good are you with tunnels?'

Kingsley blanched as visions of the cramped and stinking sewers danced through his head, a muttered curse filtering from him as he sighed.[2]

---

2   Continued in Designated: DECLASSIFIED: Yellow Brick Road.

25
January 8ᵗʰ 2014

Baker's mind stirred, awash with the myriad of thoughts plaguing him as he trudged across the parade square, his feet crunching against the grit-laden surface as he continued making his way to the small Jeep he kept parked behind the main training grounds.

He was ferreting through the mass of pockets that seemed to increase every time he looked for his cars keys, his fingers brushing over the age-worn denim of his jeans as he patted himself down, his attention lost in its own world when the sirens began to wail, their long, drawn out keening, freezing everyone to the bone.

His keys forgotten, Baker turned, sprinting across the parade square like a frightened rabbit. He dropped his hand to his hip, yanking his mobile phone from the plastic clip holster, punching in the number from memory as he ran.

'Come on, answer. Damn it, Janet, answer the phone.'

Despite the situation, he couldn't help but smile as his mind pulled forth the image of Tim Curry sashaying through a crowd to the strains of "I am a sweet transvestite."

His mind whirled as his phone suddenly died, the signal blinking to nothing as he stared at the screen. Baker's feet pounded at the concrete beneath him as he continued to run, barrelling into the door leading to the operations centre.

The room was a hive of confusion as analysts and technicians scrambled for some sign as to what was taking place. The babble rose and fell as Baker strode across the room, covering the distance in less time than it took to blink. Kirkland pushed her chair from his path as Derek snatched a secondary headset from the desktop and keyed into the wide-band circuit, overriding everything as he pushed call.

302

'This is Charlie One Charlie calling all call signs, we have mobilization order I.C.O.4. Recall all units and ready for immediate deployment, Charlie One Charlie out'.

****

Joshua watched with mounting amusement as the white-coated forms outside his cell scurried like mice in a maze. Flurries of movement punctuated by foul-mouthed rantings filtered through the plastic wall of his cage.

A soft chuckle left his throat as he nonchalantly rose to his feet. The slim bar of hollow steel in his hand gently teased the disk away from the hole in the outer wall as he watched the last of his would-be captors depart. The strobe-like red emergency lights lent a slightly club land look to the utter chaos of the room that he now surveyed.

With a grunt of exertion, Joshua contorted his body, driving his arm through the hole until his shoulder kissed the inner lip; he winced as his ear was twisted against the cold sheet of Lexan. Walking his feet up the wall beside him, Joshua blindly slithered his fingers across the stippled surface of the concrete pillar until his fingertips caressed the cold aluminium of the keypad's fascia.

His eyes slipped closed as he listened to the soft beeping of the keys as he hummed the tune he had come to know better than his mother's nursery rhymes. His face twisted into a maniacal grin as a hiss of compressed air greeted his diligent patience. Pulling his arm free, Joshua rolled clear of the wall as the door slid aside, its edge scything across the hole where his arm had been moments before.

'Ah, the sweet smell of freedom.'

His nostrils flared as he breathed in the heady scent of sweat and disinfectant. Rubbing his hands together, he hopped down from the single step that ran the length of his former home and quietly strolled towards the open exit. An energetic whistle left him as he slipped into the hallway, his hand snatching at a white lab coat dangling

303

from the hooks by the door.

'Well, dear heart, shall we see what we can see?' His muttered thought floated on silence as he walked out into the crisp, cold air, his lips curled in a grin at the thoughts of the events to come.

The entirety of Broadhead stood in parade formation, the drill square a mass of bodies so closely packed that it was hard to see the dirty, grey concrete beneath them. The tension was palpable, a seething undercurrent of adrenalin and fear that mingled into a thick miasma of sweat-soaked energy.

Derek let his eyes ghost across them, the heavy drone of the two C130Js climbing into the sky filled the air as they whisked away the entire R.R.T unit, their targets already waiting for them.

Clenching his jaw, Derek swallowed his mounting fear and spoke.

'Right boys and girls, this is crunch time. I won't hold us up with useless pep talks. Just get in, do your job, and get home again is all I ask.

'We are strictly tasked with rescue and evacuation of civilians, government members, and the Royal Family. Team One with me, we are tasked with the Royals and the Prime Minister. Team Two, you and Teams Four through Eight are tasked with evacuation, security, and civilian safety. The rest of you are dropping in with Rook and Hawk in the pods. Make me proud and make it home.'

Davies stuck his hand up, feeling slightly foolish at the child like gesture. 'Boss, what about Team Three?'

Baker stopped mid-turn, glancing back at Davies with a soft look of regret in his eyes. 'Never made it home from London.'

With that, Baker turned, followed by the rest of his team to the waiting helicopter.

Davies and the rest of Team Two hit the floor running, dispersing from the landing zone and immediately getting to work. Their weapons chattered as they took aim at the swarming mass of savage, blood-crazed civilians. Shadows danced and bodies fell as the Infected dropped, a wave of fire pouring forth, sweeping all aside like a tsunami of boiling lead.

With a curt wave of a hand they began to spread out, their job just beginning. Davies' eyes scanned for any sign of movement. The likelihood of a survivor—human or Infected—among the stagnant carpet of corpses was remote, but it had to be done.

Single shots began to fill the air as the still living were sent on their way, their souls slipping forth to whatever awaited them once they were wrested from their mortal coil.

John's brow furrowed as a human voice reached his ears over the staccato sounds of far-flung gunfire and the fear-soaked screams of the panicked and dying. The tiny echoing call of a fear-pricked voice rolled over the rooftops to their ears, its plaintive call doing little to stem the tide of migrant refugees that scurried like rats in a maze from the horde that nipped at their heels.

'This is an emergency announcement. Please, remain in your homes and places of business. When it is safe to do so, please proceed to an emergency evacuation point.'

The caller paused for a moment before beginning his panic-laced soliloquy once more. The voice echoed off the buildings, rolling over everything before it snapped closed, a guttural pain-lashed cry driving into everyone with the force of a nail gun. Panicked shouts and the soul-withering sounds of a man's final seconds filled the streets, the roads echoing with tin-laced sound of gunfire as the last throw of the dice was cast.

'Guess some one didn't like the DJ,' Reiley remarked, a morbid, dark look crossing his eyes as he spoke.

Baxter chuckled then snapped back to reality as he brought his rifle up and dropped another Infected, the spray rounds shattering its fragile countenance as it dropped a pool of steaming fluid pooling beneath it.

Davies glanced around him, his eyes strained and tired; the lines at their edges deepened as he watched for any hint of movement, the flecked premature lines of grey streaking his temples, stark and transparent like lighting flashing through the midnight sky.

'Okay, lads, cut the chatter—double time it. We've got to find that downed patrol. Get their evac location and get it re-secured until help arrives; fuck knows who else is going to bloody do it.'

Davies glanced at the screen mounted on his forearm, his brow creasing as he stared at the grime-covered monitor.

'Ping point puts the patrol at three blocks over. We can cut through that department store there and then slip through Debenhams. That should bring us roughly a block and a half away from where the patrol was last recorded.'

They nodded and took off at a fast trot, rifles raised to their shoulders.

The Diemaco rifle felt comforting in Davies' hands as he scanned the streets. He swallowed hard, fighting to keep his rising tide of unease in check. The burgeoning need to get home to the one person who made his life worth living, sinking an ever-deeper hold on his heart.

The men around him moved with an efficiency born of hard-won practice as they took up covering positions and waited for the others to move past before carrying on forwards. The sounds of their passage through the car-choked streets filled the world around them, as the symphony of fear continued to rain down.

Baxter and Hamilton dropped to a knee, their bodies pressed loosely to the crumpled remains of a BMW. The soft hiss of its punctured radiator drowning their thoughts as they knelt, facing opposite directions, their eyes missing nothing as they scanned the world around them.

'Fuck me!' Hamilton's eyes widened as a wall of shifting black filled the road ahead of him. 'Contact right.'

His words echoed off the buildings as he began to fire. Hamilton shook as his weapon chattered, the screaming form ahead of him tumbling, her ragged blood-smeared form crumpling into a heap as 5.56 mm rounds carved bodies to pieces.

Baxter spun, weapon tight and unwavering as he squeezed the trigger. Bodies fell, gore soaking the road. The advancing mob trampling the dead into dust as they surged forwards, passing through the street like water.

Davies and Clarkenwell leapt forwards as Baxter and Hamilton opened fire, their hands closing over the drag hoop between each man's shoulders, hauling them to their feet.

'Forget it, too many.'

Glancing back as he hauled Baxter to his feet, Davies veritably screamed at the men around him. 'Triple time it, fucking move.'

****

Davies' shoulder rammed into the doors, his mind awash with a maelstrom of conflicting thoughts as he barged the doors aside, not caring what was waiting in the darkened interior.

The shop lay empty, its cavernous interior as silent and dead as a tomb. The eight team members scrambled as fists hammered on the doors behind them. The sounds echoed, filling the shop as they sprinted through rows of shelves, their contents scattered over the floor. The stinging scent of coffee mingling with pickle brine filled their noses as Davies stumbled.

His booted foot shattered a jar of peanut butter, its pulpy mass clinging to the sole of his boot as his foot slid, arms pin wheeling as he began to topple backwards. Jones caught John's arm, hauling him along beside him.

'Cheers.'

Jones nodded as they ran, the sound of shattering glass and twisting metal filling the air as the doors gave in and the horde of screaming bodies descended.

They tore into the shop, smashing aside the shelving as if it were paper. Turning and backpedalling, Jones fired three sporadic bursts. Bodies tumbled, vanishing beneath produce and feet as they began to gain on Davies and the others. Glancing backwards, Clarkenwell blanched as he watched a boy of no more than ten crushed as he toppled head first over a stand of magazines, his still snarling face vanishing in an instant.

The team surged forwards, tearing through the aisles, uncaring of what lay ahead. Whatever it was, it was preferable to what was behind them.

****

Team One landed in the parade grounds of Buckingham Palace, a deep sense of dread filling them all as they surveyed the area. The once pristine grounds lay choked with the bodies of the dead, their blood-soaked forms covered in a mire of their own fluids and excrement.

Derek snorted, flies buzzing at his face as he tugged at the chinstrap of his helmet. 'Fan out, check for anything alive.'

Baker felt his heart heave as he cast his gaze over the bullet-riddled corpse of a woman, the lifeless form of a baby perched on her back.

Derek's eyes wandered over the scorched holes in the back of the seat rest, a cold ball of anguish unfurling in his stomach as he stared at the still smouldering circles of burnt plastic and material.

Tearing his gaze from the tableau in front of him, he cast his eyes upon the bloodied and torn corpses still clutching their rifles, their dead eyes staring back at him.

'Don't look too encouraging, does it, boss?' Sharp's muttered question fluttered on the still air as he turned to look at Baker, his booted foot pushing the corpse of one solider over onto its side as he made his way up the steps.

Baker shouldered his rifle without answering and made his way through the doors of the palace, their battered and gilded forms hanging askew as they gently bobbed on the wind.

****

Light danced in pools of white as their barrel-mounted torches cut swathes through the darkened gloom of the hallway. The interior sat dark and silent, enveloping all that dived into its vacuous abyss, the glowing rays of the sun shut from sight by the reinforced steel plates that covered the windows and doors.

Baker knelt at the foot of the stairs, his gloved hand reaching out and pulling the body of a maid over onto her front, her pallid face locked in a snarling grin of lustful pleasure. Sinuous strands of flesh caught between her opalescent teeth and glossed nails. Letting her shirt fall from his grip, he cast his eye over the uniformed soldier beneath her.

The look of uncomprehending pain and shock in the man's eyes told Baker all he needed to know. With quick motions to his right and left, he sent Mariani, Collins, and Roberts peeling off to begin the fraught task of clearing and searching the rooms around them.

'Judging by the disarray here, they were caught halfway through the lock down.'

Hooper looked at Baker, his eyes questioning. 'How d'ya figure that one, chief?'

Baker nodded to the floor and the two bodies at his feet.

'His eyes say it all; they were locking down the palace and couldn't get everyone screened in time, the girl here shows as much.

They can't have been Infected more than an hour. The whites of her eyes are virtually clear; if she had been further along, they would be swimming with distended capillaries, but look.'

He knelt, his hand curling into the woman's hair to turn her face towards Hooper.

'Nothing. Crystal clear. Her only problem aside from being Infected is that she's dead, otherwise she looks fine. Probably what got her through the screening in the first place.'

His hand opened and the woman's head fell back to the marble staircase with a dull crunch.

'I would say, at a guess, that they fell back to the living quarters here. I would have; they had the room fitted out as a panic room in case the house was breached six years ago.'

Pressing his fingers to his throat, he called the other three men back to him. 'Alpha two fall back and rendezvous on wing entrance D. We can discount other survivors; you won't find anything down here, at least.'

A dry double-click was heard through Baker's ear bead.

****

Howls and guttural screams filled the air as they fled into the darkness. The screaming wall of hatred and hunger that snapped at their heels left any semblance of military practice impotent. Taunting calls and yells of teasing malice filtered through the air like bloated flies.

An Infected threw itself forwards, her bloodied and beaten form crashing through the rack of women's lingerie that stood between them and satiating the gnawing craving for sustenance that ate at its stomach. Jaws snapping, strings of dripping gore hung from her crimson-tinted teeth. Her hands flailed; chipped polish and split nails tore the air, clawing at them all, passing Reiley's nose and missing

311

his soft, sweat-stained flesh by mere millimetres.

'Jesus Christ!'

He snapped his rifle up and fired six rounds from the hip, striking the crazed psychopath in the throat, chest, shoulder, and head. The rest carried on, their footfalls filling their senses as the gap slowly widened between them and the slathering wall of hunger at their heels.

The twisting aisles, bodies, and debris sent dozens sprawling and still they charged onwards. Davies and those around him threw anything they could in their path. Jars burst and cartons split as they hit the floor and were crushed into oblivion like the Infected that fell around them.

Bursting out the doors, Davies gasped as cold winter air bit at his skin. His knees collided with uncaring concrete beneath them as he spun, dragging his rifle to his shoulder. A burst of orange death echoed into the dull, listless morning as Clarkenwell jumped upwards, his fingers closing over the bottom lip of the roll shutter.

Not bothering with any thought of self-concern, he dropped, his weight sending the clattering mass of metal down to the floor. Reiley scrambled, dragging a zip tie from his belt and threading it through the lock before yanking it closed.

Their breathing rasped in their ears as they listened to the indignant cries of those behind their rippled steel salvation, the team stopped for a few seconds, their movements harsh and unsteady, their weapons held at the ready as they listened to the howls of anger and pain just beyond the chipped, blue painted shutter.

'Come on, lads, not too far. We have to hold that evacuation point; you all know what's at stake if we don't.'

The rest nodded as they sucked slowly warming water from the three-litre bladders on their backs; with a nod to the men around him, Davies moved off, his feet pounding at the black tarmac as he slipped into a mile-eating jog. One by one, they took off moving in a staggered file in the direction of the evac patrol's last known position.

****

They passed through the shattered double doors of Debenhams with little trouble, their forms hunched and eyes scanning the store's hanging cavernous hulk. Lights sparked in ink-black cold as they listened to everything and nothing. With infinite care, they entered the department store. Glancing about them, Jones cautiously moved towards a clothing rack, his weapon tight to his shoulder as he scanned the floor, his eyes taking in the discarded hangers and torn clothes that lay strewn about the mangled and torn remains of a dead civilian.

'Who the fuck loots Levi's jeans and hoodies in an outbreak? What a bunch of mugs. Some people seriously need their fucking priorities checked.'

His muttered question hung limp in the dead air as he stepped away from the tortured montage and followed the slowly diminishing forms of his squad mates.

****

The sight that greeted them as they reached the patrol's position made the bile rise to their gullets. The heavy thumping chug of the idling engine lent a steady rhythmic drone to their overly cautious approach. Several Infected littered the area, their bodies riddled with bullets, heads peeled open like over ripe melons, organs and brain matter coating the roadway like a wet paste.

Reaching forwards, Jones slowly wrapped his gloved fingers around the handle of the door, its thick form clinging to the non-slip palm of his ballistics glove. With a quick reflexive jerk, he opened the door to the Jeep.

A muffled grunt escaped him as he stepped backwards, the blood-

313

smeared window squeaking in protest as the shifting mutilated corpse of a Marine Commando tumbled out. His eye, vacant in its socket, stared balefully up at him, the untold agony seeping out as the dull, dead orb pleaded for someone to end the pain. Stark white patches of shimmering, wet bone peered through the man's rent and torn flesh.

Jones dragged the corpse from the driver's seat, whispering an apology as he felt the weight shift in his grip. Jones and Reiley both swallowed sharply as the Marine's wounds finally became clear; ragged and torn flesh was the only thing that remained of half the man's face and the entirety of the front of his neck. Teeth marks were clearly visible on the chipped bones of his exposed eye socket.

Reiley retched deeper, the smell of fresh excrement and the stagnant content of the man's stomach seeping into his throat. Stepping forward, he none to softly dragged the body away from the vehicle.

'Poor bastard. You deserved better, brother.' His muttered words filled the air as he knelt and dragged the dead Marine's tags from around his neck.

'Davies, remember that one in Bristol? You know, the one that almost bit Hamilton's nose off.'

Davies chuckled. 'Yeah, Rory, how the hell did that one get you? It had no eyes—or nose, now that I think about it.'

Hamilton unconsciously rubbed at his nose, his mind willing him to check it was still there.

'Shut up.' Was his only reply to the stilted laughter echoing his way.

'Clarkenwell, jump in there and dig out their route map. See where the pickup point was.'

The rest of the men fell into a defensive posture. Baxter and

Hamilton moved towards the front of the vehicle, their weapons scanning the area around them. Reiley and Jones covered the rear using the vehicle-mounted, general-purpose machine gun and the heavy machine gun mounted on the passenger side and on the top of the vehicle.

Stepping back into dying rays of the sun, his uniform stained with gore from the four dead soldiers they had unceremoniously dragged from the vehicle, Clarkenwell handed Davies the route map.

'Great, just bloody great.'

The others looked at him curiously. Sighing, he climbed into the back of the vehicle as Clarkenwell climbed into the driver's side. 'The pickup is Trafalgar Square. I hope you boys have life insurance, you're going to need it.'

Pressing a gloved finger into his ear, he cocked his head to one side, leaning further into the cramped interior of the vehicle in a vain attempt at blocking out the growing wall of noise that was driving closer to their position. 'Luck seems to be with us, ladies. We've drone obs coming in and helios in bound; best not keep 'em waiting, hey boys?'

****

Baker and the rest of his squad approached the royal living quarters, their footsteps pattering quietly against the plush carpet beneath their feet. The walls around them, once lined with lush papers and silks, now drew them down a corridor streaked with gore and the powdered remains of bullet holes. The stench of death and battle deepened the closer they got to the gilded oak door.

Uniformed bodies of men and women lay alongside the punctured remains of Infected, the thick pile beneath the soles of their boots oozed blood and excrement. Steaming coils of the stagnant, repugnant odour wormed its way through their nostrils, burning down into their lungs as the glittering taint of burnished brass teased their eyes. The mingled scent of potpourri and lemon-scented table polish tickled at the backs of their throats as they passed by shattered doors and splintered tables.

Stepping over the body of another Grenadier Guardsman, they reached the door to the Queen's bedchamber. Fisher stepped to the side of the door as the others stacked up around him.

'Boss, what was the Royal family doing here, anyway? I thought Windsor was the Royals' home.'

Baker shook his head. 'You're an English man and a Royalist fan boy—you tell me what the date is today.'

Fisher thought for a second. 'January eighth… oh, yeah, she was opening a new Barnardo's halfway house in Epping. Weird though, she only just opened the new headquarters in Barkingside last December.'

Baker smiled sarcastically, his nodding driving home the fact that Fisher was more than a little obsessed. Mariani cast a sidelong glance at his teammate as his hand flexed around the front pistol grip of his weapon. His mind slipping momentarily as he slipped in a slightly barbed jibe at his lifelong friend's expense.

'Bloody fan boys do my nut in. The fan girls aren't too bad, though; although some of them… well, paper bags still have some uses I suppose.'

Baker stared at all of them, his eyes burning with anger, the men around him paling slightly under his gaze. Immediately, the levity that had plagued them vanished like the cold mists of morning, as hands tightened and bodies tensed. The once jovial mocking replaced by the focused tension that had been bubbling just below the surface.

Leaning forwards, Fisher turned the handle on the door slowly, his mouth dry as he felt the lock begin to give. Sam was yanked forwards, the door sailing open as he plunged headfirst into the room, his body pin wheeling over itself as a wickedly curved blade descended towards his throat.

His startled cry echoed through the corridor as the rest of the team charged in with weapons raised. Anger-filled cries and bellowed challenges filled the air as Sam stared up from where he lay prostrate on his back, coming face-to-muzzle with the rifle of a Gurkha Rifleman.

Baker put his hands out to the sides, holding his Diemaco by the fore grip. 'Stand down, boys; we're the good guys.'

The Guardsmen didn't budge, rifles trained on the men in front of them. 'That's enough gentlemen; they obviously are not the enemy.'

Baker stepped forwards and removed his gas mask. 'Ma'am.'

Baker snapped a clean cut salute, his stance faltering as the Queen smiled and nodded, her reply sending him off kilter as he slowly lowered his hand.

'Mr Baker, what took you so bloody long?'

Recovering quickly, he smiled, unable to hide the mild spear of pride that wormed its way through him as he stared at the proud and stern, yet diminutive woman.

'We're here to take you to the evacuation site and get you out of the Infected zone. My team and I will escort you and any surviving members of your family and household to the waiting helicopter, but I must press you, we need to move now!'

She simply nodded as the dozen remaining Gurkha Guards formed up around her, their stances wary; the shock that slithered below the surface held in check by the almost fanatical loyalty to the woman who claimed the crown.

Then under the watchful eyes of Baker's team and the unflinching gaze of the Guardsmen, they made their way to the helicopter outside the palace.

'Major, please tell me, what happened to Captain Pottergate?'

Baker was slightly shocked at the question. Turning, he looked at the head of the Royal family. 'Ma'am I assumed you had been told.'

The Queen smiled at him. 'I am aware of his death and where it transpired. I simply wished to know the circumstances under which the captain met his end. Some things are left out of the reports I receive, although I am at a loss as to know why.'

Baker sighed deeply.

'Believe me, ma'am, it is a good thing they were. Needless to say, the captain lost his life in Russia, but take it from me, your Majesty, you do not want to know how. It was hard enough to see and is not something I would wish to remember, and if you grant me pardon, I have a job to do.'

'I understand.'

With that, the helicopter lifted into the air, the battering storm of air and grit making him squint as he watched it slip away into the haze-ridden sky, towards what Baker hoped was safety.

Team Two ground to a halt grit and glass sprayed in all directions as the vehicle slid through the rubbish-choked gutter. Dragging the steering wheel hard to the left, Clarkenwell swung the unruly beast of steel and canvas into the entryway to the square as he drove the accelerator into the reinforced floor, sending it bolting forwards. Sand bagged emplacements and concrete barriers snaked their way behind them past the fountain as a barrier was dropped into place, the heavy whine of the forklift worming through the air as the barrier descended to the floor.

The slabs of concrete stretched along the roadway, snaking through the thoroughfares and roadways, carving their path like a plough through snow. Davies followed their passage with his eye as it wound past the front of the National Gallery to the two roads past Canada House, effectively turning the area into one giant human corral.

John shook his head as he surveyed the area, the central hub around the base of steps in front of the National Gallery, the concrete K-rails topped by rising spires of chain link fencings, the rolls of razor-edged wire woven through its links and slithering along the floor like roots from a tree. Davies glanced at the men at his sides and could see that, like him, they had to grudgingly admit that for its flaws, it did the job of cutting the other side off from the square.

Trucks and vehicles littered the area, their cold and idle hulks abutting the fence line as the team glanced around them, eyes darting to and fro, as they drank in the details. Max's eyes narrowed as he watched the thirty military personnel scurry from point to point like mice in a maze, as shield-bearing, armed police encircled the outer perimeter of the square.

Reiley shook his head slightly as he took in the utter disarray that filtered past them. 'No order… they're just milling around; this is fucking stupid.'

Reiley gesticulated wildly in disgust as John nodded and motioned with his free hand. 'Reiley, Baxter, take the east side and get them formed up and into defensive positions.

'Hamilton, Jones, take the western side. Me and Clarkenwell will take the northern edge. You know the score here, boys; let's make sure at least some of the civvies make it out.'

They all moved forwards, the men splintering off as three men approached them, two Police officers and the third a corporal with the Royal Marines.

'Who are you, and where's the reconnaissance team?' barked the corporal as he stared at Davies' back.

John didn't turn to look at him as he unloaded some of the gear stowed in the vehicle. John's eyes flicked to the driver's side mirror as the bristle-chinned soldier advanced; the heavy *thunk* of reinforced plastic filled the air as Davies pulled the black crates from the cargo deck of the Land Rover. With as much bluster as he could manage, the frightened and struggling corporal all but screamed at Davies, his voice cracking slightly as he fought against his fear and sudden need to flee.

'I asked you a question, soldier; where the fuck is my reconnaissance team?'

Davies whirled around, his six-foot-four frame towering over the fraught NCO as he glared at the man before him, the vestiges of fear and fatigue still clear in the pinched lines around his eyes and mouth.

'It's *lieutenant* not "soldier" and your reconnaissance team is *fucking dead*! Now what dull bastard sent them out with a loud hailer?'

Davies glared at the corporal in front of him, his anger mounting as he watched the man step back a pace. 'Report, corporal, just who the fuck is in charge of this cock up on wheels?'

The Marine looked stunned, and paled visibly as he stepped back several paces, his hands quivering as he reflexively opened and closed his mouth, struggling to find the words for the thoughts dancing in his head.

The two police officers flanking him looked at one another, exchanging a very knowing and unsympathetic look as they stepped forwards and held out their hands.

'Sergeants Mackleroy and Drapper SCO19 at your service.'

Davies nodded, the rage and violence he had shown a second ago gone from his visage as he cradled his assault rifle. 'Okay, not to be funny, but I don't really think we are going to be alive long enough to bother with learning names; appreciate it but just forget it. What've you got fire power wise?'

He studied their features, his eyes probing every minute twitch for any sign that his previous statement had rattled their stoic visages.

John's eyebrows rose as both men shrugged. Only the young Marine looked put out by the thought. Drapper was the first to speak up, Davies' eyes darting to him.

'We knew it was the likely outcome when we took this position, so it doesn't matter either way. The guy in charge was Staff Sergeant something-or-other with the R.M.C and was forcibly assigned to this evacuation point.

'He went off on a foot patrol ninety minutes ago and never came back, so he's either dead or fucked off somewhere.'

Davies nodded as Drapper continued, motioning for the three men to follow him as he moved towards the main hub at the foot of the gallery's steps.

'Me and Mack have both lost our families. We were stationed in Mile End and were right in the path of the initial break. We have nothing left to give but our lives, so if it comes to that...' Drapper shrugged, his eyes shadowed by anger and guilt in equal measure as he fingered the mobile phone in his left trouser pocket, 'so be it.'

Mackleroy gave his friend a very concerned look. 'I worry about you sometimes.'

Davies smirked at the little exchange between the two men, his eyes missing nothing as he deftly sidestepped the burgeoning wall of hatred and sorrow that both men wore like a cloak. Soft clicking punctuated the air as John slipped his coded PDA from its holster on his forearm and handed it to the communications officer.

'Practice that, did you?'

Drapper just shrugged again as he motioned for Davies to follow him. Moving over to the back of a transport truck, he opened several security crates. 'Mp5s, Sa80s, and L115A3 long rifles, with enough ammunition to see us through World War Three.'

Davies cast a worried eye over the stacked boxes, numbers cycling through his mind as he tallied it all together. 'Right, well, that's not going to be enough, but one thing they drill into you is to make do with what you've got.'

Davies turned and moved back to the billowing canvas tent that sat fat and square in front of the white granite building. He stepped around a collapsible table and pulled his knife from the sheath on his chest, using it as a pointer.

'I want your best shooters at these positions.'

He pointed out six different locations throughout Trafalgar Square; Drapper and Mackleroy nodded as they called in their men and pointed out each position. Watching as the stern-faced officers each nodded in turn and took off at a lopping run towards the buildings around them, Davies couldn't help but feel a faint sliver of hope bloom within him, despite the overbearing finality of their situation. Looking to the Marine, John nodded, drawing the man's attention and jerked his head in the direction of the vehicles.

'We need the heavy shooters set up at every intersection and junction to give us as much opposing firepower as possible. You and

I both know these barriers aren't going to hold forever, but, we can drag them out as much as possible by carving those bastards a new hole with the fifties and Gimpies on the Land Rovers.'

Tapping the map again, he motioned with his knife to the corresponding places about them. 'I want claymores and anti-personnel mines every twenty feet in concentric circles, starting four hundred feet in front of the vehicles then pulling inwards to a central cordon around the main barricade, the last line pulled in tight in front of the bags; that will give us a last-ditched breather.

'Remember to string them at head and chest height, where possible, in a slight downward gradient. We know that what we're facing were once civvies and the like, but now, they're just another tango, so it's kill shots only. You know what the A box is, right?'

The corporal nodded his head as he started to tremble slightly. Davies sighed as he watched the police commanders shake their heads.

'If you draw a capital A from the top of my head with my shoulders and collar bone as the line in the middle with the sides of it passing through my shoulders and down my arms, that is your A box. Any shot in there is a guaranteed kill shot; you will ether drop them instantly or hydrostatic shock will liquefy their organs and do it for you.

'So A box only. Okay, we need to conserve the ammunition; if your gunners start laying suppressive, pull'em out and get a fresh shooter in. We're looking for body count, not force suppression. The Infected will not stop for the man next to them and they definitely will not give two shits if you blow the git in front of them to pieces. A couple may stop and pull the carcass apart, but the rest will keep coming. At no point are we to let up. If the barrel overheats or the gun jams, get rifles in there in its place and another man in to clear it and make ready. At no point are we to stop firing.'

The corporal looked scared out of his mind. His face was beginning to turn ashen, and if Davies left it any longer, he could easily see him losing the command element. John could not, and would not, let that happen. For a soldier of rank to lose face in front of his men in such a manner would destroy any and all respect they had for him. In a situation like the one they faced, he needed the full support of the men under his command if anyone was to make it out alive.

Taking him to one side, Davies put a comforting hand on his shoulder, his gloved fingers closing slightly as he drew the man's eyes to his own.

'Listen, bravery is being the only one who knows you're scared, and right now I can see you got it in spades. Trust me when I say this; we're all scared out our bloody minds right now, every last one of us, but we have a job to do. If we get only one civilian out of here, we have done our job; that one person could mean the difference between us winning this thing or going out like a candle in a storm. It doesn't mean we won't be scared shitless as we do it as long as it gets done.

'Then after that, what's there to lose? You signed up for the service knowing that dying was part of the deal. We all know it; we pledged to serve the crown and all it encompasses. That means every man, woman, and child, no matter who they are.

'The only difference here is you can choose how you go out. Do you get what I mean, mate?'

The corporal nodded, looking calmer, the colour slowly returning to his face, but both of them knew he was just as petrified as before.

'Good. Now go on, get going and brief your boys. You're a corporal for a reason.'

The trooper seemed to swell inside his uniform and took off at a flat sprint to his unit on the far side of the square.

'Baxter, Hamilton, head over to the boys on the landys and fill 'em in, but make it quick; I've got a feeling we ain't got long.'

****

A nervous tension settled over the men, the stench of pulsating static souring the air. John watched the sky darken, casting the world in a monotone grey as clouds enveloped the sun. Davies winced as his back shivered with pin-like lances of pain as he hefted the last sandbag into place and took position.

The world around him erupted into a torrent of terrified screams, the mingled voices of men, women, and children flowed together like sand through his fingers as a flood of survivors drenched the square.

Davies stabbed his hand in the direction of three running police officers as he all but screamed at them over the tumult of noise that raged about him.

'Keep them away from the pad otherwise the birds won't be able to land.'

His words vanished as the world around them was crushed into silence as the sky split apart. A white, arcing bolt of lightning snapped to the ground, lighting up the thoroughfare.

'Oh, dear mother of god,' Davies heard one of the police officers mutter as he watched the light bounce off the windows, illuminating the roadway like stadium arc lamps.

They stood, still and motionless as the heavens pounded down upon them, the floor beneath them alive with swirling vortex of detritus and offal spilling from their bodies. A lone figure stood before the pack, its eyes glittering in the light cast off by the raging maelstrom above.

Raising his gore-soaked hand, sallow cracked skin stretching over the extended digits, he began to scream. Battered trainers pounded the rain and blood drenched streets as he cast his red-tainted hands forth, the charge of the Infected swallowing him whole as they slowly answered his call.

Davies swallowed, glad no one could hear his heart pounding in his chest as he watched them descend. Their guttural cries of lust-filled hunger soaking into them all.

John's mind swirled as a passage rose to the forefront, its words swimming free as one of his father's favourite poems burned its way through him, the words echoing in his head as he watched the Infected edge closer to the outer cordon.

Half a league, half a league, half a league onward, all in the valley of Death rode the six hundred. 'Forward, the Light Brigade! Charge for the guns!' he said: Into the valley of Death rode the six hundred.

The Tennyson quote slipping softly from his lips as he lifted the detonator and squeezed. Bodies vanished in a flash of glittering ball bearings and shrapnel and still they ran. In a hail of blood, bone, and searing metal, they ran. Circle by tightening circle, they closed upon the defenders of Trafalgar Square, the advance never slowing as a noose of their creation closed around the defenders' throats.

The chattering guns of the men manning the vehicles filled the air as the undulating wall of bodies drank in the hailstorm of copper and lead and yet still they ran. To a man, the defenders knew with certainty that they were on the upswing of death's scythe and the reaper stood, waiting for his call.

Davies looked about him, a smile tugging at his lips as he saw that despite the cold grip of death's hand tightly enclosing around them, not a single man or woman flinched from their post.

The impact was ungodly as the ravenous charge collided with wall of shields, the dull crack of steel and wood on bone and flesh filling the air as the officers began their slow walk backwards. Fists soaked in gore and brain matter rose and fell as the Infected paid in full for every centimetre claimed.

As the last officer cleared the barricade, Davies yelled, his face set in a feral snarl as he screamed out his final command.

'Pin 'em to the fucking wall.'

Baker stared at the PDA on his forearm as he scanned the scrolling data feed. A rising tickle of fear wormed its way along his spine as he drank in the luminous green lettering that skated over the scratched and grazed screen.

Roberts pulled his hand away from the side of his head as he approached Baker, a tinge of urgent panic coating his voice as he spoke. 'Boss, Team Two has reached evac point Delta. Civilians and other personnel have made safe entrance to the site, but it's under heavy assault from the Infected. Davies has said he's done what he can to shore up some sort of defence there but wants to know the ETA on the evac choppers.'

Baker sighed in resignation, a sense of inevitability boiling within him as he spoke. 'Get on to Lincruster and the air wing. Tell her to get three Chinooks in there on the double. If they give you any grief, tell them I'll fucking shoot them myself if they don't get airborne with the next six minutes.'

Roberts nodded and radioed through to the air wing. Hefting his rifle, Baker looked at the others.

'Right, now what.' Baker stood for a moment as he tracked back through the data feed for anything of use, his eyes widening slightly as he stared at the flashing report heading.

'Roberts!'

Dean spun on his heels as he looked round at Baker, giving him the thumbs up as he finished off the radio message. 'Yeah, boss?'

Stepping closer to Baker, he looked at him enquiringly.

'Get a chopper to our location now!'

Baker scratched at his stubble-coated jaw, the itch of new growth grating at his already frayed nerves. 'Right, ladies, listen up; we've got a slingshot mission to do. We head from here to Number 10 and

328

see if the Prime Minister is still on site. Downing Street was locked down just before the Palace but has since gone dark; no one on the ground can get to it.

'From there we head to the Square and pick up anyone left—if there is anyone left. We make it quick and clean on the ground and get in and out. Our boys are waiting for us and are sitting in a world of hurt, so if the PM is a wash, then we bug out and move on; I don't want anything to hold us up.'

The six men in front of him nodded as Roberts called in the helicopter. The Bell 212 landed with a spray of dust and broken glass, and within forty seconds of its skids kissing the war-torn tarmac, they were making their way to Downing Street, Baker's sense of trepidation and unease growing the closer they got.

Baker shifted from his seat, half stepping from the open door of the helicopter, his foot resting on the diamond printed steel of landing skid; with a nod of his head, Baker watched as a dozen small drones floated from the doorway of the hovering helicopter before zipping towards the open gloss black door, its copper numbers dulled with the clotted and drying blood of the dead officer who lay in a crumpled heap over the concrete steps.

Derek leapt from the helicopter as it stopped three feet from the body-strewn roadway. The thumping of feet rising around him as the helicopter rose into the smoke-laden sky, sending a shaft of heated air collapsing down upon them like a mountain of snow. Fisher knelt, grit, glass, and shattered brickwork grinding against the hardened plastic plates covering his knee and shin as he stared into nothing.

The images from the tiny quadro-copters shimmered across the head-up display (HUD) in front of his eyes, the world about him bathed in a cool, blue light as he dropped to a knee next to Derek.

The hardshell pack on his back pressed down on him as it slowly rolled itself shut, the soft whine of its electric motor barely breaking the slowly enveloping silence.

'Find anything?'

Fisher shook his head. 'Nothing but bodies. Before you ask, the drones have mapped out the building and the bodies are marked.' Fisher tapped at the touch screen pad on his arm, a soft beep echoing in his ear bead as he finished. 'Map should be on your HUD now.'

Baker nodded as he scanned the image quickly before sending it to the top left corner of his visor. 'Right, floor by floor. The drones aren't infallible; I want this place cleared top to bottom.'

They nodded, moving forwards, their feet carrying them up the small set of steps to the open doorway. Turning to the left, Roberts stepped forwards, his booted foot rising as he kicked the door through. Spinning to the right, he moved out of the way of the door as the rest entered, rifles raised. A unanimous, call of 'clear' bounced through the open mic they all wore round their throat as Derek took point.

Room after room, floor after floor, they moved as one, their voices echoing in the still air around them as they came to the final door.

Its solitary form sitting in its frame, hanging like a gangrenous wound, Baker's breathing rasped in his ears as his feet carried him over the threshold.

Derek silently cursed as he stared at the desk, the dull glow of daylight slanting through the dust-laden air, its cold white beam encircling the desk as the rest of the team slipped through the door.

Collins was the first to shatter the silence that had swallowed them all, his solitary words echoing their thoughts as he shook his head.

'Damn it.'

The Prime Minister lay still, his skin sallow and waxen as he hung, bent backwards over his desk. His slowly clotting blood dripped in a steady, rhythmic beat from the gaping hole in his throat. The white shimmer of cartilage and bone glittered in the sunlight, wet flesh framing his torn oesophagus.

The black uniform on the creature atop him saying more than any of them needed to know. Baker stepped forwards and pulled the body off the corpse of the Prime Minister. A dull thump echoed as it hit the floor, its head clanking slightly as the long swan-handled letter opener that hung from its eye socket struck the oak floorboards.

Baker's hands danced through the Prime Minister's pockets, searching for the small plastic-coated sheaf of card. Its cold countenance settling into his gloved palm as he pulled it from the pocket of the man's stained suit trousers.

'Okay, let's get out of here. No point hanging around; we have what we needed here and he certainly ain't going anywhere in a hurry.'

Sharpe chuckled darkly as he pulled a phosphorous grenade from his hip pouch and tossed it onto the desk, thick black smoke billowing moments later as the bodies began to burn.

'Last man out.'

Sharpe's words echoed through the slowly burning building as he stepped through the front door and into the frigid winter air.

26
Trafalgar Square

Screams and wails filled the air as the petrified civilians cowered behind the barricades, their huddled forms clustered behind the slowly dwindling line of men and women.

Davies stared as they fell around him, the chatter of gunfire and screams of fear fading from his ears as another magazine slipped empty into the pouch on his stomach.

He dragged a full magazine free as bloodstained hands clawed at him, a hailstorm of boiling lead and copper driving it back as its falling form was crushed beneath the ranks of onrushing Infected.

His weapon bucked against his shoulder as the bolt shot home, sending another spear of anger into its boiling breach. The heat haze of red-hot steel shimmered around the muzzle, distorting his vision as he squeezed the trigger.

Hundreds lay dead at the edge of the barricade, their torn and twisted forms spattered with the gore of a hundred more as they continued to throw themselves against the beleaguered defenders.

'Contact left,' Baxter screamed as the vehicle beneath him rocked, its groaning form teetering on its springs as hands and feet clawed for purchase on its metal skin.

He twisted to and fro, dragging the thumping weapon in his hands across the soft yielding backs of the people he had once sworn to protect. Even as they fell, a dozen more drove forwards, their feet crushing their still clawing forms into the gore-smeared roadway as hot, twirling cylinders of brass rained down upon their heads.

****

Joshua smiled as he stood on the rooftop watching the scene

below him, a glimmer of red-tinged teeth showing as he watched Davies teeter forwards, clasping hands, and snatching fingers pulling him across the top of the barricade.

His eyes widened as he saw John's feet leave the floor. A snarl of rage left his lips as he watched a black-clad figure draw him away, tongues of fire leaping from the weapon in his hand as he pulled Davies upright.

The photograph in Joshua's hand crinkled slightly as he shook with anger at the sight below. The undulating horde of his kin beginning to wane in its efforts as the withering hailstorm battered their assault.

'They are more resilient than I gave them credit for. Being locked in that box for so long must have dulled my mind more than I thought it had.'

A soft hand stroked the back of Joshua's neck as he cast his gaze to the farthest reaches of his little playing field. 'Come now, my boy. You think that their probing and tests did little more than give them your blood type? I thought I had taught you better.'

A smirk coated Joshua's face as he glanced at the man next to him, scorn dancing in the back of his eyes as he turned back to the scene below them. 'I know, father, I know, but still the mindless glut of flesh below doesn't seem to be giving them the trouble I thought it would.'

The hand patted his shoulder as its owner stepped away from Joshua, their footsteps receding as Joshua continued to stare down from his perch.

'We shall see, my child; we shall see. The day is young yet.'

****

Raking his weapon back and forth, Baxter lay down belt after belt of shimmering copper-coated death. The heat washed over him as he

333

clipped a fresh box into place as the Marine at his left turned his aim, carving apart the Infected that had rushed into the sudden void. Gritting his teeth, Baxter felt his fingers char and blister as they came into contact with red-hot metal of the rapidly overheating weapon.

'Where the fuck are all these coming from?'

David didn't answer as he feathered the trigger, eking out as much time as he could before the final box ran dry. Chancing a glance to his left he blanched slightly as he watched one of the three Marines left with him get torn from the vehicle's roof, his flailing form vanishing beneath the writhing mass of flesh that was rising with every passing second.

Right up until the time he died, he would forever hear that young man's screams and cries for help as the Infected descended upon him, their throbbing mass tearing him asunder. David's only comforting thought was found in the fact that he knew it wouldn't be for very long.

'Contact, Contact.'

The panicked scream lost amidst the tumult of noise and the heavy full-throated roar of the .50 heavy machine gun from the far right as the young Marine corporal obliterated all that stood in his path.

The gargantuan weapon thudded as glittering tubes sparkled in the noonday sun, their thick, searing-hot forms clattering over the bloodstained skin of the vehicle as he pounded round after round into the wall of flesh beneath him.

The thick spears of copper and lead cleaved limb from body as they passed through all in their path like a nail through silk, obliterating body and mind in a salvo so rampant that would make the grim reaper pale with fear.

Davies gasped as he squeezed his trigger, his feet sliding over the still warm brass beneath his feet as the hand of his saviour finally released him.

'Thanks.'

John let the magazine fall free as the last casing spun free from the ejector, spinning with a soft clink to land amongst the ever-growing pile.

'Mag change, cover me!'

The Sco19 officer stepped up MP5 chattering away as he fired into the encroaching wall of Infected, their fevered minds seizing on the dwindling opening. Stepping back into the fray, Davies fired; shadows danced as his muzzle flared, pin pricks of light dancing in their eyes as the flare lit the faces of those around them.

'I'm Davies, what about you?'

'Thought you told the others there was no point in taking names?'

Davies laughed, his voice strained and raw as he choked out a reply. 'Cheeky git. Yeah, I said that, but I thought I might want to know the name of the bloke who's just saved my arse—I'm polite like that.'

All through the impromptu conversation, neither man once stopped firing, their throats raw with the taste of cordite and the taint of burnt gunpowder as they yelled to make themselves heard over the song of their rifles.

'Bridge, Richard Bridge, if you must know. I was a rifleman in the Royal Anglians before I joined the Met; pleasure to meet you.'

Despite himself, John couldn't help but grin, the world around him shifting into deeper focus as he felt his burden shift slightly, the man at his side soaking up the pressure that had mere seconds before threatened to eat him whole.

'I asked your name, not your life story.'

Bridge smiled, the motion easy and natural as he continued to fire, the metallic clack of a dry bolt rising to his ears. *'Cover me; mag change!'*

Bridge dropped to one knee, fishing a magazine from his webbing as he did so.

For three solid hours, they kept it up—civilians stepping forwards, swallowing their fear as they scooped up magazines by the armload, scurrying like thieves in the night as they ferried them to three police constables who, throughout it all, had been doing naught but reloading the discarded magazines.

Head bowed and eyes fraught with fear, he ran. The child's feet skimmed over brass and stone as he clutched a canvas satchel to his chest, the polymer and steel boxes within jumping and clanking as he slid to a stop next to Reiley and Jones.

'Thanks, kid!'

The young boy beamed at them, his smile soaked in terror as he turned to run back, his trainer-covered feet sliding over the tarnished brass beneath him. Reiley glanced at the boy as he finally edged away, the child moving no more than three feet before a muffled cry of pain and anger erupted from behind them, a glittering incandescent spray of blood bathing them both as Reiley turned, his eyes widening and heart screaming as he watched Jones vanish over the sandbag barricade.

Jones' rifle spewed fire as he raked it from side to side. Kicking, thrashing, elbows crushing nose and eye alike as he sank his boot into the face of one, the butt of his rifle descending into the soft and pliant throat of another. Chris fought, his body twisting, rifling chattering as darkness closed around him, shadowed hands pulling at him, even as the sky above vanished beneath the black pall of death.

Reiley screamed, his throat raw and split, the coppery taste of his own blood coating his tongue as his feet carried him forwards without any conscious thought. His eyes wide with anguish and terror, his weapon bucking in his hands, finger curled tight on the trigger as he unleashed a full auto spray into the seething bodies that enveloped his friend.

Spires of blood and flesh rose into the air as the rounds tore into the rippling sea of flesh that blanketed the still bellowing soldier.

Jones' torn and bloodstained face appeared over the twisting mire of bodies, his black gloved hand reaching forwards as he clawed his way towards the barricade. Throwing himself forwards, Max's fingers brushed against the leather-coated palm of his friend and partner. Jones grimaced, blood coursing down his chin as his fist closed on Max's and for a fleeting second, they connected.

'Hold ... on ... don't you ... dare let go.'

Tears rolled down Reiley's cheeks as he watched Jones' hand slip as his feet slid from under him. Chris, in that one second of hope, smiled, his hand sliding free from the black leather glove clasped in Reiley's fist.

'No ...' Max whispered as the chipped and gore-soaked nails of a woman passed by his face, their ripped and shattered edges gliding past his eyes by millimetres as he threw himself backwards, his feet sliding over the carpet of smoking casings that littered the floor.

Pushing himself backwards, his feet thudding over the paving stones, Reiley could do nothing more than watch as the Infected began to force their way over the barricade. Torn hands and bloody feet rose over the concrete and sandbags as their eyes fixed on the squirming form before them.

Max rolled to his right as he brought his rifle up, finger curling over the trigger as the Infected closest to him erupted, its chest disappearing in a fountain of bone, chips, and blood, he snapped his head to the left as his rifle bucked against his shoulder.

With a face filled with surprised fear, the boy stood, chest heaving as he clutched a shotgun in his hands. The smoking barrel nestled sixteen inches from the side of Max's head as he rolled over his shoulder, coming to his feet. The child stood, the thick rubber pad of the buttplate pressed into the meat of his hip, the rhythmic thumping blast filling the air as the boy pumped shell after shell into the now semi-retreating horde, heavy shot decimating all it hit.

Stuffing his pain and fear into a ball in the pit of his stomach, Reiley ejected his now empty magazine as he cast a strained compliment at the boy. 'Nice one, kid; saved my arse there.'

The boy smiled again as he clumsily forced the speed loader into the breach and pushed the thin column of shells through the chrome-plated slot.

'How'd you know how to do that?'

The kid pointed to the three police officers in the ammo store. 'They showed me.'

Nodding he continued shooting. 'Remind me to thank them when this is done.'

A sharp pang of guilt lanced through him as the child nodded, his soft, slightly squeaky voice flirting with Reiley's ears as he brought the weapon up again.

****

As the night wore on, sporadic calls began to filter out as more and more men ran empty, their ammunition drying like water on a hot stone as their plaintive cries were answered by the desperate calls of frantic fear from the officers as they scrambled in vain for anything that hadn't already been expended.

Davies dropped his rifle to the floor screaming 'sidearm' at almost the same time as Bridge, both men firing in single controlled shots one after another as they began to slowly pull back. Davies jabbed at his throat mike, pain lancing through his throat and hand as his desperation blended with anger.

'Where the fuck are my transports?'

Static burst through his ears as Lincruster's silk-like voice seeped into his ears.

'Team Two, this is Delta control, E.T.A three minutes on the Helios; hang in there, we're coming for you.'

Her calm voice soothed Davies' nerves as he listened to the clicking tap of fingers on keyboards and the heavy whine of rotor blades floating through the air.

'About bloody time too, love; we are bingo on ammo and down to pistol and knives. Hurry the hell up. We have almost five hundred people here; we cannot wait much longer.'

The line crackled again as her honeyed words once more bathed his shattered nerves in a comforting salve.

'I know, John; we're on our way. Sit tight.'

Tossing his now empty pistol at an onrushing Infected, Davies drew his knife, the matte-black blade sitting comfortingly in his hand as he hunkered low and braced for what was to come.

'What a fucking day.'

****

Clarkenwell and Hamilton glanced at one another as they drew their reserves, the sharp rasp of automatic fire drawing Clarkenwell's gaze as Hamilton aimed the P90 into the swollen wall of Infected, a dark smile rolling across his features as he dragged the Browning from its holster on his thigh.

'We ain't walking out of this one, are we, dude?'

Hamilton shook his head. 'Nope.'

Clarkenwell shrugged. 'Oh well... today's as good as any!'

His reply dripped in resigned finality as he kicked out, his booted foot sending an Infected woman sprawling as she flailed, her yowling form landing in a crumpled heap on the other side of the barrier as Hamilton silenced her forever.

****

Baxter looked around him; smoking barrels hung silent and limp as he hauled himself from the gunner's pit atop the land rover. He was alone now; the two Marines left with him were long dead. Their screams echoed in his head. As he leapt, hands scraped at his legs as he crashed onto the roof of a Marauder, his feet scrapping at the back door of the vehicle as he dragged his weary form towards the waiting machine gun.

The air was bitter with stagnant tang of gunpowder and smoke. A heavy, laboured sigh left him as he dragged a dead Marine from the seat, a thick rebar spear lodged in the Marine's throat.

He'd already been bitten three times, the little finger missing from his left hand and the thick pulsing wounds in his right calf sending snaking bolts of pain through him; he knew it was only a matter of time before he succumbed. The pain in the back of his skull made his vision blur and twist as he dropped into the seat, feeding a new belt into the weapon as he swung it to aim. The sights danced as he struggled to focus, but until his body gave in and he finally was overrun by the virus, he was going to do his utmost to stop the Infected and he had over five hundred reasons to do so.

With a heavy pain-filled grunt, Baxter racked the bolt and fired, the blinding thunder of the weapon filling his ears.

****

Davies cast his eyes about him. He knew the defence was failing; point Delta was all but done for. He listened to the screams and cries of pain as, one after another, men fell to the horde pressing down upon them. Wiping sweat from his eyes, John stabbed forwards, his blade slicing deep into the soft flesh of an Infected's neck.

Knives, fists, feet all rose and fell like cleavers in a butcher's shop as they hacked the Infected apart, blood and flesh peeling away like paper soaking them all to the core.

As the sun dropped, its glowing yellow form losing the battle to darkness, the air began to tremble, its cold and bitter form broken by the rhythmic thump of the twin rotors of a dozen CH-47 Chinooks. Their hatches lowered as gunners began to fire, the mounted mini guns cutting swathes through the tide of Infected.

The first one landed in a swirl of air and dust, suited forms leaping free as men and women jumped from the side doors of the gargantuan airlift platforms, their weapons up and firing before their boots touched the ground.

'Corridor now, haul what you got, get them to the choppers.'

Davies' hoarse cry drowned the night as he turned and ushered the people to the safety of the waiting helicopters. As he turned, a blood-soaked set of teeth clamped down on his shoulder driving deep into his suit-covered flesh.

'Son of a ...'

Anger and sorrow filled him as he drove his blade down through the top of the Infected's head.

'Well, I'm screwed!'

Heat filled his shoulder as he looked to Bridge for a reply, but all he saw was a pair of booted feet being dragged away into the writhing amalgamation of flesh around them.

'*God damn it*!'

John turned once more to see Reiley, battered and bleeding sprinting towards him, carrying a ten-year-old boy. Blood-covered welts covered Reiley's neck and side, the thick gouges oozing crimson as he charged through the snatching hands and snapping teeth, sheer fanatical determination blazing in his eyes as he ran.

Stumbling, he threw the boy at Davies as he turned and went down on his back, pistol firing even as he was enveloped by the slathering beasts around him.

Shaking and scared, the boy clutched on to Davies' vest as he stared at the deep dents in the thick straps covering John's shoulder.

'Come on, kid off with ye. The rescue's here.'

He lowered the boy to the floor and shoved him away as gloved hands wrapped themselves through the boy's shirt. Davies nodded at the armoured woman as he kicked back an Infected, its scarlet-covered fingers snatching at the child.

Hamilton and Clarkenwell moved simultaneously, weapons blazing as they sprinted to the helicopters.

'Boss, the flank's gone; we couldn't hold it any longer, we lost—shit—we lost near everyone.'

Davies nodded; his eyes glowed with rage and regret. 'Get your arses on that chopper now. Go on, both of you; I want an escort with these people. Go.'

The two men looked at one another. 'But—' The question left them almost simultaneously.

Cutting their arguments off at the head, Davies yanked down his collar to reveal the red-tinged flesh covering his neck and collarbone.

Hamilton opened his mouth to speak, his words dying on his lips as Davies glared at him. One the two men moved the helicopter teams, cutting a path to them as they followed on after the receding column of refugees.

Limping and weary, Baxter made it to Davies' side, his eyes shining with fever-tinged rage as he drove a fist into the face of a snarling teenage girl, her teeth collapsing over the armoured knuckled of his glove.

Davies cast an eye over him as he hacked and slashed, his shoulder screaming in pain as the flesh throbbed. A fist drove into the side of head, his eyes bursting with white shimmering light as he blacked out for a hint of a second. Staggering, he fell hard into the thick lip of a concrete barrier, his eyes widening in pain as he felt a rib crack.

'Fucking bastard.'

His blade flared up as he lifted the Infected from its feet, red blood-crazed eyes rolling upwards, blood fountaining from its lips as Davies kicked him away.

Back-to-back, the men stood, blades raised as the horde closed in. Hands and teeth grabbed at them as they hacked and slashed, buying the last few moments for the helicopters to take off.

Baxter's leg gave out as he was slammed into from the left. Tumbling, he caught John's eye and winked. Glancing at Baxter's outstretched hand, he saw the pins from David's last few grenades hanging from a bootlace. He threw himself sideways as they detonated, blasting shrapnel and body parts in all directions.

Winded and dazed, Davies struggled to his feet and turned once more to see a Bell 212 touch down behind him. Staggering to it, he threw himself into the cargo bay as the helicopter began to rise once more.

'Anyone else left, John?' Baker shouted down at Davies as the roar of the wind drowned out anything else.

Davies shook his head as he dragged the side door closed. John forced himself into a sitting position, wincing as he sucked in a breath that tasted of glass and blood.

'Civvies got out, but we got chewed to pieces, Cherry. I sent Clarkenwell and Hamilton off as escort with the survivors. Everyone else is… well…'

He dragged down his collar and showed Baker the livid red flesh of his neck, Derek's brow furrowed as he stared at the darkening bruise in the centre of his collarbone.

'Everyone else is what?'

Davies stared at him, his eyes narrowing as he stared at the confusion in Bakers eyes. 'Infected, you dick. Can't you see it?'

Baker nodded, his eyes lightening as he set a hand on Davies' shoulder, squeezing tightly. 'Yeah, I can. I can see a damned lucky son of a bitch and a bruise that'll last a week.'

Derek keyed in the camera feed from the small high-resolution camera on the side of his helmet and held out his arm as he pulled the camera carefully from the mount. John stared at the dust-and-grit-covered screen as a wall of tear-filled relief flooded through him. The livid purpling bruise was slowly darkening as he stared at the flickering image on Derek's arm.

Baker smiled as Davies choked back a sob, his relief and heartache fighting for control as he slumped against the door of the helicopter.

'Oh, thank Christ. Dear sweet Jesus, thank you!'

The others around him smiled as they watched Davies lean his head against his knees, shoulders shaking as fatigue and sorrow crashed free.

Turning back to face the others, Derek snapped the camera back into place, a sad smile playing across his lips as the chopper dropped into a clean silence. No one moved. No one said a word, even as the deathly quiet was broken by John's softened sobs.

Closing his eyes, Baker sighed and let his mind slip slightly before he took in a slow steadying breath and looked at the others, cinching the strap under his chin tighter he spoke. 'Well, boys, we've got a job to do.'

Then men nodded, settled determination in the faces of them all.

'Woodrow and the rest of the R.R.T are still out there as well as the other teams; we are not losing any more, you hear me?'

The men nodded again. A small smile emanated from Baker as his ear bead chirped, sending a ripple down his spine and making his skin crawl at the familiar four-beat burst of sound that sparked a lifetime of bad dreams. The voice that crawled down his ear made bile rise to his gullet as it oozed over him.

'Hello, Derek, so glad you could enjoy the fruits of my labour. Your wife is enjoying my hospitality as we speak, as is your daughter. Lovely girl, by the way... so ripe, so sweet; does she know life's tender affections? She is, after all, only a budding rose.'

Baker's eyes flared as he listened to the cold, sickening tones tickle at his mind, his jaw spasming as he clenched his teeth.

'And the earliest blooms do smell so sweet. Shall I let them know you're coming or am I going to be keeping them company tonight?'

Baker's eyes glowed as he stared ahead of him. 'You touch them, and I swear, by all that is holy and pure in this world, I will kill you. If you run, I will find you. I will hunt you down and visit upon you tenfold all that you've done to them.'

He heard the smirk slip across Ridgmont's lips as he waited for a reply. 'I look forward to it. Ta ta. Oh you probably want to know where we are. Well, we're where life began and the world ended.'

27
St Mary's Hospital
Paddington

Six hours earlier.

Janet cuffed the sweat from her forehead as she pushed the door open to the operating theatre. Kevin Newcroft turned and nodded to her. The fluctuating beep of the heart monitor filled her senses as she made her way towards the table. She lifted the head of the patient and turned it, checking to make sure that this one wasn't Infected.

'You know, Maria was born here.'

Kevin chuckled softly as he held the unconscious patient on his side. 'Making small talk while we condemn people to death, nice.'

The guard at the door looked on, impassive, detached. Sighing, she looked at Kevin who nodded in agreement, then resigned herself to what was coming next as she motioned to the guard.

He stepped forwards, hard-soled boots thumping against the pristine white tiles; the small drain set in the floor was stained a deep russet red, the tiles around it clotted with thickening dried blood and flecks of skin.

Small fragments of greying dried bone were stuck in amongst the rivers of dead brain tissue; like icebergs in an ocean, they sat locked and unmoving. The guard looked down at the man, his darkened grey eyes locking with those below him. The lifeless brown orbs gazing up at him accusingly as if the man knew what was awaiting him, the soft snap of the pop stud echoed around the room as the officer began to draw his pistol.

The muffled padded rasp slowly rose to a roar as he pulled the Glock 26 from its holster and levelled the nine-millimetre pistol to the man's forehead, his finger curling tighter as he squeezed the trigger.

The heavy muffled pop made Kevin flinch as the weapon's silencer drank in the sound of the gunshot.

Stooping into a crouch, he bent and plucked the rapidly cooling brass casing from the floor and dropped it into a bin beside the bench as an orderly wheeled the trolley away.

'I am sorry you have to do this.' Janet didn't know what else to say to the man, he was quiet, efficient and effective; the Sco19 officer just nodded and resumed his station snapping the catch closed on his sidearm.

Screams erupted in the corridor, drawing their attention. All eyes fell to the door as a bloody, mangled corpse was thrown in through them, sending the plastic-coated slabs of fireproofed wood into the tiled wall. The body slid to a stop at Janet's feet as its owner followed in its wake.

The screaming blood-drenched ghoul stood in the doorway, its eyes wide, filled with the primal lust only a truly shattered mind can conjure. Its gaze flickered left and right, the tangled strings of sinew and flesh that hung from its glistening maw swayed in the onrushing air as it gasped and wheezed. With a feral glare, its gaze travelled from person to person, seemingly evaluating each one in turn.

The Sco19 officer snapped off the catch to his holster, drawing the beast's attention.

'You take this.' He pointed at Kevin. 'Take the doctor and go. I'll deal with this.'

Janet stared, shock and fear piling high as she momentarily froze, Derek's voice filling her head as she stared at the feral form standing in the doorway.

'We have to go; we...we... have to go.'

Her gaze pivoted from Kevin to the officer and back again as her mind screamed at her to move. Kevin snatched the slim slip of plastic from the officer's hand and clamped his arms around Janet, dragging her to the door as they fled the room. Its head cocked to one side as its gaze fell upon the officer. The tight blood-drenched lips slid back, skinning away from its teeth in a vicious grin, the room blurred in a flash of movement and flailing limbs as it howled, launching itself bodily at the stoic officer.

He snapped the pistol upwards, his body dancing through the long practised motions as he quickly but gently squeezed the trigger. The round went wide as the Infected impacted with him, sending him sprawling backwards, a deep cavern of flesh opening up along the side of the man's sore-encrusted face.

With a guttural growl of anger, he lunged forwards. The bloody flesh-encrusted teeth snapped at the officer's face as he pushed it back, his forearm pressing hard against the soft brittle cartilage of the snarling creature's oesophagus.

A deep sickening crackle echoed up from the Infected's throat as its windpipe was crushed under its own weight. Flesh and cartilage folded as it raked its raw, bloodied, and torn fingers over the compressed ballistics vest of the officer's uniform. The sickening scrape of wet flesh over the thick webbing straps was heavy in the officer's ears as he brought the pistol to bear on the daemonic creature so intent on tearing the life from him.

Forcing it back with a heavy shove, he brought the iron sights of his sidearm to line as the Infected lunged once more. His gun spat hot molten death as the distance closed, the bullet tearing into the beast's head as it continued its descent. The back of the Infected man's skull exploded in a shower of shattered bone and brain matter, arcing out in a glistening spray. The blood shimmered like diamonds as the destroyed pieces of flesh pattered to the ground like wet wool.

Jaws snapping, reflex taking hold as the shattered remnants of its mind tried desperately to keep the rapidly quieting form below it from falling silent forever. The body landed with a thud on top of the officer as he turned his head, feeling the warm almost gentle patter of cascading blood and cranial fluid over his skin. With a deep grunt, he heaved the body off of himself sending it rolling into the cold steel of the table as he levered himself to his feet.

The screams of women, children, and men mingled into a pulsating wall of primal anguish and fear that settled over his mind like a cloying vapour sucking the air from him as it sought to extinguish the guttering candle that was his sanity. Snorting in disgust, he pushed himself to his feet and followed the fleeing doctor. His head thumped like a drum as he staggered into the corridor, the sounds of echoing footsteps clattering off the walls around him as he stared at the carnage that painted the hall.

The corridor was a maelstrom of death and terror as a mass of Infected flooded through the hospital, filling the hallway like a wave of churning water, sweeping up all in their path as they flowed over the weak and fearful, engulfing them whole.

Gritting his teeth, the Sco19 officer raised his sidearm and shot the six Infected nearest to him as he began to run down the corridor. Violent, rage-laced screams filled his ears as their cries cascaded through him, their ululating waves buffeting his mind as he screwed his eyes shut, willing them away.

Tears filled him as he ducked his head, raising his arm as he crashed through a set of double doors. The echoing crash drew out the already bloated and overfed malcontents that seeped from the very walls around him.

A lancing arrow of heat and pain filled the officer's lower back as his knees buckled, sending him sprawling into the corner of the nurses' station. He opened his mouth to scream, his voice choked and vapid as his chest heaved, his lungs paling under the impact as he careened off the reinforced plastic desktop. He rolled on to his back as the lights above him swirled and twisted. A deep feral chuckle filled his ears as he tried in vain to push himself upright.

'Ah, ain't that a shame; poor little piggy fell down and can't get

350

up.'

The officer's eyes dipped in and out of focus as he watched the shadowy form fill his vision. A metallic clang filled his ears as the stench of blood and wet meat soaked into his nose as it leant close to his face, the tongue lolling free, tracing its way along his cheek.

'Good thing I like fresh bacon, ain't it, piggy? Let's see if we can make this one squeal.'

A sudden bolt of cold filled his shoulder, his body tensing as he felt his flesh peel apart. Steel grated against bone, sending searing barbs rippling through him as he screamed, his voice cascading across the walls and ceiling as he thrashed against the weight on his chest.

'Good piggy. I liked that; now let's see if we can soften you up a bit.'

Feet and fists descended, battering his head and shoulders as the officer raised his arms, his shoulder screaming as the wound flexed and twisted. The flesh rolling and sloughing apart like over-cooked beef as the white splinters of chipped bone wormed their way through the sodden, weeping mass of torn fat and muscle.

Pain filled him as he felt the fists collide with the side of his head, his eyes dancing with shimmering lights as he slipped in and out consciousness, the torrent of blows slowly drawing the life from him.

'Aww is the little piggy falling asleep? Well, we can't have that, can we?'

The Infected reached forwards, peeling the officer's eyelids up away from his eyes. He stared into the dilated, unfocused eyes, their orbs twitching as his brain began to slowly shut down. The scarlet vessels crisscrossing his whites like crimson spaghetti. Reaching forwards with one blood-encrusted split nail, the Infected slowly dragged it over the slimy film coating the officer's twitching orb, pressing down into the fibrous muscles that ringed the bruised socket, feeling each strand tremble and flick as he dragged the split and chipped nail deeper pushing forwards, his digit sinking into the soft malleable flesh.

A grin split the Infected's countenance as he watched the officer's face contort and twist below him, his thrashing form bucking against the savage being's weight as he curled his finger, slowly drawing the police officer's eye from its socket.

Blood flowed over his fingers, the glistening strands of the officer's optical nerve stretching as the man continued to thrash. A liquid-filled gargle rose from him as his torturer cackled. Driving a fist into the side of his throat, the Infected watched him gasp and convulse as his head was lifted from the floor, the officer's mouth foaming as he tried in vain to give voice to the agony coursing through his skull.

'Exquisite, isn't it, piggy? Let's see if you taste as good as you look; I hope you do.'

Lowering his head, mouth opening as he pulled the eye closer to his saliva-coated lips. His tongue flicked forth tracing over the filmy cornea as he slid his teeth over it. With infinite care, he dragged his teeth over it the thick film folding over his tongue as he pulled the creamy sphere from between his lips. A wave of euphoria rolled through him as he swallowed, the silk-like disc sliding down his throat. As he dragged the eye free, the elastic snap of the officer's optical nerve made him shiver as he opened his mouth once more, letting the milk-white ball roll across his tongue as he bit down, the thick creamy vitreous gel jetting free as he chewed; he shivered as he felt it swirl, the taste of its cool water oozed down his throat.

****

Glancing back behind him, a wave of terror washed over him as he saw the deranged faces only meters behind them. Heaving and gasping for breath, they reached the door, Kevin screaming at the black-clad officer as he turned to drag it closed.

'Glad you heard me.'

The officer nodded as he breathlessly pointed to the corridor to the left. 'Down there is the in-house armoury. Get to it and grab a gun. There are emergency exit doors in the back wall of the room.

'Go and I'll hold here, one of the fucking bastards stuck me with fuck knows what before I made it in here; may as well do some good before I end up going all Hannibal Lecter.'

Kevin jogged, the officer's elbow drawing his attention for a moment as he held up the slim square of plastic the other officer had handed him minutes earlier.

A small smile flickered across the man's features as he plucked it from Kevin's grip and slipped it into a small box next to a computer. The clicking of keys filled the air as he glanced at Janet.

'You two need to get out of here; tell the others what's coming. No one is prepared for a crash like this. Those things are everywhere. I saw eight of my guys go down in seconds; they just don't stop. Before, they would freak at the sight of a gun, but now, they just keep coming. I have taken down suicide bombers and fanatical jihadists; even they, after a while, saw sense and gave up, if they didn't make you shoot them first. But these things, I haven't seen anything like it. If you don't go now, well...'

He winced, clasping his side as he plucked the card from the reader. Janet opened her mouth to protest as the officer pulled his hand away, revealing what she feared the most; the dark viscous paste that covered his hands told her all she needed to know. Any heated protestation died on her lips as she cast her eyes down, hiding the salt brine tears that welled up, their shimmering trails running down her cheeks as she spoke, her words quivering on her lips.

'Thank you.'

The officer cracked a small smile. 'No need. I'm still on the clock here, just doing my job; now go on… get going.'

Kevin set a hand on the man's shoulder, squeezing as the officer locked eyes with him and nodded the unspoken thanks and acceptance dancing between them.

'Take this.' He pushed the recoded key card into Janet's hand; the sliver of plastic felt cool against her fear-heated skin.

Kevin pulled Janet down the corridor, the card pressed tightly to her palm. Squaring his shoulders, the Sco19 officer forced himself to stand and staggered through the door, into the centre of the corridor.

Slowly, he ejected the magazine and inserted another, slapping the butt of the pistol grip once, making sure the magazine was locked tight. He slid his feet across the grit-coated tiles, the powdered film grinding against the ceramic flooring as he moved into position. Shifting his right foot backwards, he levelled the pistol, locking his arm straight. A soft, comforting voice echoed in the back of his head as he sighted down the gun.

'Remember, Jacob, always lock your arm. The Weaver stance can cause you to shake after a while. Locking up your dominant arm counteracts that—and don't forget, squeeze the trigger, never yank it and always slow your breathing.'

Locking his eyes on the first target as he slowed down his breathing, the walls of the hospital seemed to fall away as he focused on nothing else. His breathing rasped in his ears as the world stilled, the halls around him devoid of sound as everything slowed to a crawl. As his breathing levelled out, a small measure of peace fell upon him. His lips curled into a smile as he gently squeezed the trigger.

'Bullseye.'

His world blurred around him as he fired, round after round singing down the corridor, each shot landing perfectly. The corridor ceased to exist, as the walls darkened, his vision tunnelling as he

354

watched one Infected after another tumble and fall, their flailing limbs dancing like afterimages on damaged film; the impact of their broken bodies echoing through his mind like voices in a cavern, their rolling bodies skipping and bouncing across the floor.

He snapped his hand down, drawing out another magazine as he dropped target after target with near mechanical precision, the clattering metal ringing in his ears as he slid the last one home, the click of the catch drawing a small smile to his lips as he lifted the weapon back to his eye, the orange flash from the muzzle filling his vision as he finally faded to black.

****

Kevin stared at the room, dumbfounded; the sheer mass of weaponry was astounding. He idly thought that any Hollywood action film crew would have been green with envy but pushed it aside just as quickly as he listened to the ever-decreasing momentum of the Sco19 officer's shooting. He turned to Janet as she turned to the door, her eyes wide with tension and fear.

'You know, I tried to prepare for this, to make myself stronger than the simpering cow everyone always thought I was.'

Kevin opened his mouth to protest, Janet's stern ire burning them away before they ever gained flight.

'Don't even bother denying it, Kev; I know what they all thought, what you yourself thought at one point.

'I have spent my life trying to gain the praise of the men in my family, my father, brothers, and cousins. All of them were strong people, bastions to the weak and feeble, my big strong protectors; not one of them ever allowed me to show them what I knew I could do. And what did their bravery get them? Dead is what it got them, and now another man has just given his life for me, and for what? So you can drag me away to some dark, little hole in the wall to sit and wait for death?

'We never knew his name, and yet there he is sixty feet away, dying for two people he knew for all of three minutes. I am fucking sick of it. The only man who has ever looked past the tits and blonde hair is off saving every other fucker while we're trapped here. Well, at least I can prove to myself that his belief in me isn't some fervent waste of energy.'

She ran her fingers along the grips of the matte-black pistols, their chequered handles plucking at her fingertips before she curled her hand around one, pulling it from the cold, steel crevice it rested in, expertly disassembling and reassembling the gun before sliding in a magazine.

Kevin stuttered through several sentences before Janet deemed it useful to reply. 'You don't spend twelve years as a wife to a black operations soldier without learning a few useful things, Kevin; now stop blubbering and choose a weapon.'

Silence descended upon the room; Kevin turned nervously to the window in the door as he spoke. 'Janet I don't hear anything.'

She smiled at him, 'I know; nice, isn't it?'

Kevin shook his head. '*No,* I mean I don't hear *anything*, not even shooting.'

As the words left Kevin's lips, the stillness was shattered by a singular gunshot. 'Janet, we have to go, and now!'

Kevin stared out the reinforced wire meshed glass inset into the steel doors of the armoury, the light slowly disappearing behind the crushed faces of the Infected as they piled into the corridor.

Blood slowly seeped from the Sco19 officer as he lay on the cold, unforgiving floor of the hospital, his pistol still clutched in his hand, the slide locked open as a small, whispering strand of smoke curled from the open breach.

The officer had, in his final seconds, made a promise to himself, his mother, and his god that he would not end up another mindless ghoul and, with what little of himself remained, had used his final round to ensure he never would.

Kevin, his face pressed to the glass of the delivery window watched as the pooling blood haloed around their saviour's head.

'Thank you,' he quietly whispered before pushing away from the window. His eye caught the blurred passage of pictures as he turned. He stepped towards the photo-lined duty roster. There in the black and white passport-sized photo were the faces of the two Sco19 officers. Tracking his eyes down the pictures, he settled on the block script printed beneath each image.

Jeremy Martin Thomas and *Jacob Dietz*.

Reaching out, he pulled the page from the board and carefully folded it, tucking the names of their saviours into his right hip pocket before he snatched up the large disc-shaped riot shield and heavy steel baton from the locker on his right.

In five quick strides, they left the hospital and any semblance of normal life behind them forever.

James 'Jimmy' O'Hara stood at the back door to the hospital; his hands trembling as he gingerly lit one of his six remaining cigarettes. The soft paper-coated filter was a familiar comfort for him and one of the few things he found could calm his shattered nerves. Even as he took the first juddering draw from the slimline white column of tobacco, he found himself struggling to shake the images of his brush with death from his mind.

His black jaw-length hair hung low over his face as he raised the lighter to relight the half-burnt tip. His hair hung like a curtain, shielding his eyes from the sun's chilled evening glare and the encroaching, slow stalking death that was quietly encircling him.

'Fucking, god damned, mother fucking prick-arsed psycho. Try and bite me, will you? You wrinkled old bastard.'

The Infected eyed him with a suspicious hunger, wary and nervous for any clue that he was aware of their slow advance. They had seen their brothers and sisters enter the hospital moments before. The way they moved filled them with dread and fear as the Infected slipped away and into the darkened alleys surrounding the building, eagerly seeking out a less energetic meal.

Sensing nothing from the slim form now sucking eagerly at the slim white stick clutched between his lips, they moved as one, bodies loose, limbs held light as they began to close their snare.

Jimmy's skin prickled, a familiar sensation he had built over the many years of bullying and paranoid suspicion—one that made him aware of people watching him, even if no one really was.

Looking up, his eyes went wide with fright as he saw the ring of Infected that had, unbeknownst to him, slowly penned him against the side of the hospital. His head snapped left and right as he desperately searched for a way out as the noose tightened the hungry red eyes boring into him.

Backing away slowly, his mind screamed at him to go anywhere but backwards, and yet he kept on moving. A metallic clunking scrape echoed up from the floor as his foot collided with something, its hollow tone tugging at his ears. Darting his gaze downwards he clapped eyes on a piece of scaffold piping. His quick mental evaluation guessed it to be about two feet long. Closing his eyes for a second, he sent a silent prayer of thanks to whatever god was listening, praising them for creating lazy workmen.

Clutching the cut off piece of metal in his hands, he squared his shoulders and braced for the onrushing end and the pain that would fill the final moments of his life. A soft clicking caught his attention as a cold rush of air sent a shiver down his spine, closely followed by a set of hands curling themselves into his charcoal grey zip-fronted hoody, their slim, strong grip lifting him off his feet.

Slowly, James cracked open his eyes. He had always thought dying by Infected consumption would have hurt more, at least that is the impression Janet had always given him whenever she had stopped to talk with him. He also thought that heaven, or where ever the heck you ended up, would not be so cold or smell like industrial disinfectant.

The pungent fumes stung his nostrils and trickled down his throat, leaving a cloying sickly, slightly acidic taste in his mouth. Gingerly, he patted himself down; his fingers danced across the front of his t-shirt, the black cotton felt, somehow, oddly reassuring. Tracing the contours of his own form lower, he ran his hands down the sides of his legs.

The denim rasped slightly as he checked by touch alone for any bites, cuts, scrapes or tears, too afraid to do anything more. The thought of staring into the mangled, fleshless, bite-induced void that carried his death on its bloodstained wings, wasn't something he really wanted to have as a final image. A soft sigh of relief escaped him as his fingertips' search found nothing.

'Hi!'

A cheerful impish face appeared in his vision, drawing from him a less than manly scream of fright. Dragging him to his feet, she

359

propped him against the wall as the rose-tinged face before him smiled. The opalescent white teeth she bared shimmered under the stark-white hospital lighting as Jimmy stood somewhere between hysteria and sheer exhausted panic. His eyes caught on the black printed t-shirt, its cotton and vinyl print stretched to near transparency over her chest. The rhythmic rising and falling mesmerised him, her breathing pushing her ample bosom against the black silk-like fabric of her t-shirt, his eyes shifting ever so slightly as he tracked their rise and fall as she breathed softly.

It was something that didn't go unnoticed by Jimmy's unwitting saviour. An impish, playful grin spread across her features as she saw his blatant and unchecked stare. Pushing her shoulders forwards ever so slightly, she bounced on the balls of her feet, making the rise and fall of her chest ever more pronounced, the form fitting t-shirt shifting against her peach-toned skin, her ample swell showing like a golden sand beneath water as it pressed against the sheer cotton.

Her top shifted, sliding across the flat, taut, smooth skin of her stomach as she gazed at the man before her. She smiled playfully as she watched Jimmy's eyes follow every movement her ample assets made. Slowly, his eyes rose from their chosen perch as a soft lilting giggle caught his attention; a deep crimson blush stained his features as he locked gazes with her deep-blue, grey, and emerald-flecked eyes. The mirth that danced within them was infectious as he found himself soon hiding a bashful grin from her soul-penetrating gaze.

A soft, slim hand shot forth as she reached out, tucking her other hand behind her she slowly curled it around the handle of the heavy bladed carbon steel chef's knife she had tucked between her belt and waistband.

'Hi, I'm Millie.'

Jimmy's blush faded slightly as he reached out and clasped her slim hand in his. Closing his hand around hers sealed his fate as she moved. Millie moved with the finesse of a dancer as she spun around Jimmy's stunned form, her hand curling round his wrist twisting it, the bones in his hand bending as they were forced back against his side. With a grunt of anger, she drove him forwards, face first into the wall, his move opening in a rush of stale nicotine-tinged air. As his weight sank against his chest, the heavy cold blade of the chef's knife pressed tightly against the side of his neck as its diamond-etched edge began to slowly bite into his skin.

'Move and I will fillet you like a fucking fish, you got it?'

Jimmy nodded vigorously as he felt the blade ease slightly, his forehead rubbed raw against the concrete wall. He swallowed sharply as he felt the pressure on the blade increase again, his skin itching as it began to bite through his flesh as a thin rivulet of scarlet blood run across the glinting metal.

'Good; now that we have that sorted, were you scratched, cut, bit?'

Jimmy began to stutter slightly as he tried to articulate his current physical condition.

'No, no I wasn't; some crazy bastard tried to but—'

He was quickly and harshly cut off midsentence as Millie pressed the blade hard against his pale skin.

'I asked a simple question, dipstick, not for a life deposition. Shut the fuck up. Did one of them spit at you, get blood, or anything on you?'

Again, Jimmy went mute as he felt her free hand slide over his slim form.

'Fucking answer me, you dumb pussy.'

Jimmy stuttered and groaned as her hands slid over his jeans, her rampant patting drawing his mind to places he really wished it wouldn't go.

'No, nothing. You dragged me in here before they got close enough.'

Nodding, she stepped away from him, the chef's knife held in front of her clasped in both hands as she stood with her legs set shoulder width apart.

'Okay, move.'

Motioning with the knife, Millie watched as Jimmy sedately moved away from her, heading down the bright, sterile corridor. Her head snapped round as the steel door behind the pair rocked in its frame, the dull thud of flesh on metal making both of them jump. Her eyes bulged in her skull as she watched the metal begin to bow under the increasing weight against it.

'Okay, uh, we have to, um, we uh, have to…'

She began to panic, terror slowly worming up through her, smothering the false bravado she had so eagerly displayed mere moments before. Jimmy spun on the spot, something inside him seeming to click into place as he reached forward and wrapped his hand round her wrist.

'We have to bloody well go, is what we have to do; now run!'

Dragging her along behind him, he sprinted for all he was worth; pulling along the stunned and mind-numbed form of his would be captor.

'Just my fucking luck, meet the one woman in this whole damned city who seems nice, and is rather good looking to boot, and she pulls a fucking knife on me. My mum was right; I should have stayed in Cardiff.'

The words echoed inside his head as he pulled the stumbling and panicked woman through the sub-basement lift's doors and hit the button that would take them down.

'Just hope I am doing the right thing here—basements were always a bad move in the movies; then again, this isn't a movie,

although I am stuck with the one person who would always be the first to die, man I am screwed.'

He turned away from the near hysterical female next to him and stared at the aluminium sidings of the elevator as he decided on his next move.

St Marys
Maintenance Tunnels

Steam shifted, buffeting them as they moved, the shifting curtains of heated water soaking them as they listened. For what, they had no idea. Janet cocked her head to one side, her mouth open, slightly dulling the sound of her own breathing.

Kevin waited, breath baited, his throat dry and ticklish as they both stood silent and immobile. The rattle of pipes and fans echoed off the smooth concrete that surrounded them. The heavy baton in his hand sat sweat-slicked against his palm as he nervously shifted the riot shield strapped to his arm.

With a shake of her head, Janet set off down a side passage, Paul following cautiously in her wake.

****

Jimmy crept along, his caution born more of the fear at the woman he was now towing with him, than anything that was following. His feet shuffled through the darkness. Dull orange workers' lamps casting pools of staggered light ahead of them.

He could feel the heat from the woman at his back, the sound of her breathing roaring in his ears as he strained to listen for any sign of a tail or threat. The tremble of her hand gave away the underlying current of panic that was coursing through her. Jimmy squeezed her hand, watching as she swallowed tightly and plastered a look of stoic on her fear-flushed face.

'We're going to be okay.'

Millie didn't say a word as she gripped the knife in her hand all the tighter, the sound of approaching footsteps flirting with them both. Jimmy tugged at her, drawing her into the darkened maw of an open storage room. The hum of electricity through banks of fuse boxes masked the soft squeak of the door's hinges as he carefully pushed it closed.

****

Janet stepped slowly, a grease-filmed pool of water sloshing against the soles of her trainers. She crouched slightly as she approached the corner. Cupping her hands around each other, she pulled the pistol tight to her chest, narrowing her profile as she pressed her back to the wall.

Kevin watched as he followed her every move, shield and baton held ready as he trailed in her wake.

A hushed whisper flirted with their ears as Janet edged ever closer to the corner. Kevin's voice echoed softly; she turned to glare at him, her eyes glowing as she sawed her hand through air just below her chin.

Kevin nodded as Janet peered round the corner, her eye just breaking the line of the wall, a door ahead of her swinging closed as she scanned the corridor.

'Okay, stay low, stay quiet, and move to the door a quarter way down.'

Her voice was little more than a shadow of a whisper, but, to Kevin, it was as clear as a scream in the woods. They moved in a stumbling rush, Janet's footfalls pattered subtly as Kevin tried in vain to keep pace. The patter of his footfalls sent crashing echoes through the tunnels, their sound a screaming siren to anything that would listen.

Howls echoed and rampant shadows danced across the walls as lights flickered. Janet snapped her head towards the onrushing noise, her stomach curling into a ball of ice as she grabbed Kevin's shirt and dragged him around the corner, fear and an irrepressible need to survive driving her haste.

The door sat only a few feet ahead and yet she could almost feel their teeth at the back of her neck. Reaching out, she dragged the door open, throwing Kevin through it before sending it swinging closed. Her body slumped to the floor, feet braced as she listened to the stampeding herd fly past.

A muffled scream and the sound of metal on plastic drew her attention from the deluge that surged past the door.

Kevin's shield-cover arm rose as the slender form of a person she knew all too well drove a vicious looking knife down onto it. Her voice hissed as she called to Jimmy, his fear-pinched eyes snapping to her as the knife once more skittered over the hardened surface of the riot shield.

'Janet... I... I mean, Doctor Baker.'

Janet couldn't help but smile, a soft laugh escaping her as the noise at her back began to abate. She held one slim digit to her lips as Jimmy stared at her through the dully-lit gloom. Her hand slithered over the steel door, working its way to the handle, the touch of the cold chrome-plated handle shocking her slightly as she closed her hand around it.

The hinges rolled; Janet's eyes crushed shut as she silently chanted to herself. The whispered words filtering free of her lips as she pulled the door open. The shadows of former patients, friends, and co-workers, all of them twisted beyond any semblance of their former selves were slowly vanishing. Janet shifted, pulling the door shut again as she turned to the others around her.

****

Light stung their eyes as Janet and Kevin stepped from the tunnel mouth, the access ramp dropping away from them as the sounds of feet on concrete floated from behind.

'Millie, Jimmy, stick close; this isn't going to be easy, but if we're lucky, we can reach Derek and some possible semblance of safety.'

Guttural snarls filled the air as Janet spun; body dropping, arm rising, she brought the gun up. Her balance shook as she set her eyes on the shifting shadows behind them.

Millie screamed and thrashed as scarred, bloody hands closed around her. Jimmy yelled in fear and surprise. He watched her eyes widen as her feet left the floor; he slashed and hacked as the darkness closed around his momentary companion.

The sound of gunfire split the air as Janet fired. Millie convulsed as her chest shook, blood spilling over her chin as she went limp and the darkness swallowed her whole.

Jimmy spun, his eyes bulging as he stared at Janet, disbelief crawling across his features. 'You ... you shot her ... we could have ...'

He trailed off completely as Janet turned from him, her body taut, anger dripping from her as she skulked forwards. Kevin grabbed Jimmy by the front of his shirt, the scrabbling hands of Infected missing his back by millimetres as Kevin's baton crashed down, jaw and neck shattering under the impact as he threw Jimmy towards Janet.

Her hand ensnared his wrist, dragging the bedraggled maintenance technician into a loping run.

'Jimmy, you better have your fucking car keys.'

****

Smoke filled the air, rampant screams and guttural yells flowing over them as they crouched, shielded from view by the bulk of an overflowing dumpster, the dull grey plastic bulging under the weight of its stinking load.

Janet waited, her chest heaving as she watched another gaggle of cackling cannibals stream past the mouth of the alleyway. Jimmy stirred, pushing against her back, sending Janet's balance reeling as she fell forwards, her hands sinking into a mire of decomposing Chinese food and dog excrement.

With a grimace of disgust, she pushed backwards, sending him sprawling as Kevin clamped a hand over the young man's mouth. Jimmy's eyes grew wide as a look of anger and consternation plied for dominance.

'In four we're going to move; you stick to my arse, and when I get the door open, get inside as quickly as possible. There are too many of them out here for this to be small.'

Janet stared at both of them, her eyes hard as she struggled to push down the fear that filled her to the core. A soft whisper found its way from her lips to Kevin's ears as she pushed herself to her knees.

'Mummy's coming, Maria; Mummy's coming.'

28

Paddington
City of Westminster
West London
Five hours earlier

Token stared behind him, eyes bulging in fright. Looking to his right he saw a slightly red-faced Patterson keeping pace with him. A sly smile crept on to his face as he stared at his crimson faced comrade.

'You know, this is very good practice!'

Patterson looked up at Token's frightened but smiling face, his soft Ghanian accent lending a twisting lilt to his words. Huffing and breathless, Patterson forced out a reply.

'For what?'

Token grinned at him, a mischievous twinkle in his eye as Patterson frowned. 'Running away from lions… and Infected, lots and lots of Infected.'

Glancing over his shoulder, Token yelped slightly as he watched the twelve dozen psychotic cannibals stumble and sprint after them. Patterson almost choked on his own breath as he forced down laughter at his companion's words.

Token pushed Patterson aside as a screaming blood-soaked form crashed into the floor. Bone and blood showered them as both men stumbled. Token's shoulder crashed into a parked car, its alarm flaring to life, deafening them both as Patterson rolled backwards over its bonnet.

'Great it's raining fucking Infected now. What's next Daleks and Cybermen?'

Token leapt over the car, grabbing Patterson by the back of his harness, hauling him to his feet as Andre's comment filtered through the miasma of hate and fear.

'No, no Daleks, but plenty of crazies and lots and lots of pain; to think I wanted to be a doctor. I wanted to help people.'

Glancing over his shoulder once, Token all but shouted at the beasts snapping at their heels, 'I did not want to be chased by this shit!'

Token quickly made the sign of the cross on his chest as he muttered an apology before shoving Andre towards the end of the road, both men stumbling into a jagged run.

'Sorry, mother, I did not mean to curse, but it seemed like the best word at the time.'

Ahead of them, the rest of the team dropped in quick succession through an open manhole as Walters screamed at them. 'Move it, fucking move it!'

Patterson dropped into a rapid slide as he saw King jump down into the tunnel below, closely followed by Walters sliding over the edge of the hole. Patterson hit the stagnant, foul-smelling waters below, sending the putrid sea of pestilence into the air.

Token sprinted forwards, dropping through the open manhole as he snatched at the ladder. Gaining purchase, he hastily dragged the heavy iron cover over him as he fired a last cursed insult at the mass of groaning flesh-starved beasts.

'I hope you eat your mother!'

With a dull *clunk*, the cover slid into place, sealing them away in its safe but decidedly foul-smelling embrace.

****

Shaw stared down through the lenses of his binoculars. The shifting mass of Infected flesh below moved as one, a living carpet of rage and hunger; he spat over the edge, his lips skinning back from his teeth as disgust and revulsion boiled through him.

'Putrid scum.'

Stepping back from the wall, he walked over to the small trestle table in the centre of the rooftop. Setting down the binoculars, he gazed at the chart in front of him. Tracing his finger slowly over the streets and roadways, he grimaced as he lifted the grease pencil and marked out several points.

'How we looking, chief?'

Shaw looked up, catching the eye of his teammate, staying mute and shook his head; stepping away, he motioned at the map in front of him. Interlacing his fingers behind his head, he stretched, groaning slightly as he felt a rippling *pop* run up his spine.

Kane glanced at the map and smirked.

'Fucked then, yeah?'

Shaw nodded, his mouth set in a grim line as he stared at the map.

'Basically, we're hemmed in on all four sides; basement on this place is non-existent so no exit there. Stepps and Stoors laced three of the stairways with anti-personnel charges, and the door has been snap welded with micro charges.'

Shrugging, he turned back to the wall, bracing his foot on top as he leaned out.

'So we should be okay for now. Rations, if we're careful, could last a week; water though, will last half that, maybe less. If the weather holds then we shouldn't have to worry about exposure but, this is England so it could rain in the next sixty seconds, for all we know.'

Kane smirked. 'So worse than fucked then.'

Shaw laughed as he nodded. 'Basically.'

A soft rasping preceded a heavy muffled pop, the gentle tinkling of brass echoing softly on the air as Faux ejected the spent cartridge.

'Nice.'

Pepper shifted his spotting scope slightly. The rubber cushion was hot against his sweat-slicked skin. The rubber sucked against his eye as he pulled his head away and a small shiver ran through him as the cool evening air rushed into the vacant space, cooling his overheated ocular orb.

Opening his left eye, he glanced at his partner quickly. 'Seriously, that was a bloody good shot, mate'

Faux smiled around the stock of his rifle as he let the crosshair rest on the side of his next target; slowly, his finger grazed the trigger.

The rifle kicked against his shoulder. 'Bingo,' he muttered to himself as he watched the 7.62 mm projectile punch through the Infected's cranium, sliding through the woman's brain matter as it dragged it out through the other side in a conical spray.

Blanking out the sight below, Faux shifted once more as the second casing bounced to the tarmac beneath them. Round after round he rained down until the floor below was a silent carpet of dead meat.

Rolling away from the weapon, Faux pawed at his eyes, trying in vain to rub away the tense pain behind them and the images from ground below.

A strangled groan emanated from him, drawing a concerned look, from not only his spotter, but also his commanding officer and anyone else close enough to hear it.

Slowly, Pepper shifted his hand closer to his sidearm, his glove softly rasping over his ballistics vest skimming over the surface of his uniform as it inched its way closer to the butt of his pistol.

'Don't even think about it, Pots; I'm fine. I just need a break. My head is killing me and my eyes are sore as hell. I just need a kip and something to eat.'

Miles Josef Pepper nodded as he watched his friend begin to move. A small, sly grin tugged at Pepper's lips at the use of his nickname.

Pushing himself up from the floor, Faux made a direct, if not slightly unsteady, walk over to the table, grabbed a half-empty bottle of water, and began to sip slowly.

A soft, whispered cry echoed from the alley below, catching the attention of Stoors and Stepps. Both men walked closer to the wall, glancing over the precipice to the floor below.

Stepps opened his mouth to fire off some witty remark as he watched the small group backing away hurriedly from the encroaching threat of death.

The lithe blonde leader of the group raised her face to the sun, her crystalline, emerald-green eyes meeting his dark-brown orbs briefly. Any remark or cynical comment he had died in his throat as he realised just who she was. 'Fuck me!'

Stoors looked at his friend quizzically. 'What? Who the fuck is she?'

Stepps hurriedly snapped a drop line onto his harness as he swung himself on the wall and stepped backwards to the edge.

'The boss' wife.'

And with that, he was gone, the high-pitched rasping of nylon-impregnated rope cutting through the evening air as he descended towards the floor.

Stoors stood dumbfounded for all of ten seconds before he found himself running towards the edge of the roof, line in hand. In a small leaping hop, he was over the edge and running down the side of the building, the line spilling out behind him as he all but sprinted down headfirst.

****

Janet raised the Sig Sauer pistol and fired, her eyes flinching closed at the bright flash and ringing bark of the gun.

Huddled behind her were Siobhan and two of her co-workers, their children, and her eleven-month-old daughter. The whimpering cries stung her ears as she faced off against the encroaching wall of Infected. Jimmy and Kevin stood shoulder to shoulder with Janet, fear running rife through them all as they stood their ground.

Jimmy's fingers tightened in nervous apprehension as he watched the advancing wall of death. The stench emanating from them was unbearable as the wind picked up slightly, the frigid stale air around them being drawn down the miniature cavern as it passed by, dragging the thick, cloying pall of offal and excrement down upon the small group.

'Well, Mrs Baker, I have to say this has been an experience—one I would've missed if I could, but at least its lasted this long.'

Janet cast a sidelong glance at Jimmy as he tensed up, bracing for the inevitable end; the knife in his hands shook slightly as he suppressed his urge to run.

Kevin looked across at the pair of them, a small reluctant smile playing across his features. 'Fuck it,' he murmured as he pulled Jimmy towards him and kissed him.

'What the fuck, man?' Jimmy crowed as he stared at Kevin in a mixture of surprise and confused outrage. 'I've known you for six years and now you pull this shit?'

Janet looked between them with a confused smile on her face, her mind whirling with the panicked need to find safety for her and her daughter and the sheer dumbfounded confusion at Kevin's actions.

Kevin turned away from them, rolling his shoulders to loosen them up as he gazed headlong at the advancing wall of Infected. The vicious, smirking grins that twisted the faces of their would be captors sent a shiver through him as he cast a sidelong glance at Janet and Jimmy.

'You don't know until you try it, Jim, and I didn't want to go out without knowing.'

Janet's eyes, despite the situation, danced with laughter as she watched a red flush creep up Jimmy's features. All mirth died on her breath as she let her eyes drift back to the motley cluster of evil and death that slowly stalked towards them.

Her heart quivered in pain and fear as she set eyes upon the blonde-haired and brown-eyed girl that stared at her from between the legs of two women, her satin blond hair matted with gelatinous globules of blood that clung to her scalp like limpets. A smile cracked the child's face as her eyes met Janet's, her crimson stained teeth spotted with the remnants of her last meal as she licked her lips and waved. The bulbous sores around her mouth and eyes pulsed as she pushed past the two women and slowly began to creep closer.

'No, Kirsty, oh lord, no!'

Janet's eyes clouded with tears as she stared at the slowly advancing child, the gun in her hands quivering as she lined up the sights with the centre of the girl's chest.

A heavy rasping thud drew her attention. Glancing around her quickly, she all but screamed as a grey-clad body dropped from above and filled her vision completely.

A second thud, followed quickly by a metallic *clink* rolled across her senses, followed in very short order by a short, startled yell from both men.

'Ma'am, stay back and keep the rest of the civilians with you.'

Stepps and Stoors, stood an arm's length apart as they slowly raised their LMGs and squeezed the triggers. The alley erupted into a pulsating wall of noise as the light machine guns roared, bodies dancing, shredded like confetti amidst the deluge of bullets.

Janet spun, dragging Siobhan with her, shielding Maria from the cacophony that washed over them. Kevin stood watching, his eyes wide and jaw slack as he soaked in the utter and inescapable devastation. Bile rose in his throat as his eyes alighted on Kirsty. The impish waif glared at him, mouth wide, locked in a feral scream as round after round tore into her.

Ropes slapped at brickwork and concrete as other grey-swathed forms dropped into view, weapons chattering as they began to slowly push forwards.

Two men broke from the pack, running towards Janet and the others, ropes in hand. One roughly hauled Janet to her feet, forcing the rope around her chest and under her arms. A thick metallic clack sounded behind her head and the soldier snapped the carabiner clip through a quick-release link and tugged at the rope sharply.

Janet left the floor with a pain-soaked squeal as the rope bit sharply into her chest. Maria wailed in her grip as she squirmed. The twisting blanket began to slip as Janet fought to keep her daughter in her arms. Bricks and concrete shredded skin from her bare arms as Janet turned her back to the wall, desperate to keep Maria safe.

Hands curled into her shirt; rough gloved fingers snagged on her bra straps, dragging the meshed lace into her flesh as she was hauled over the edge of the roof and sent sprawling on her back.

The rope slithered under her as Pepper dragged it free, tossing the line back over the edge of the roof without a second thought as Faux hauled Janet to her feet.

'You okay?'

Janet stood, her mind spinning as she struggled to keep up with the rapidly spiralling scenario that was swirling around her.

'Ma'am, are you okay? Is the baby harmed?'

Faux reached out, his fingers brushing over Janet's hands as he went to lift Maria from her grip. She moved without hesitation, her mind dropping back on sheer instinct as she spun, her grip sending Faux to his knees as she snarled.

'Touch her and I will rip your fucking eyes out.'

Michael stared up at the glowing green eyes, feral anger dripping from her as she bent his arm back upon itself; he frantically tapped at her elbow, pain lacing his words as he fought to speak.

'Okay, okay! No touching the baby, I get it. Now give me back my arm before you fucking break it!'

Kevin crested the wall, his eyes falling on Janet and Faux as he tumbled onto the grit-strewn rooftop. Pushing himself to his feet he ran over and wrested Faux's arm from Janet's grip as he turned the wild-eyed woman to face him.

Her eyes flared as she stared at his blood-spattered form, Siobhan tumbling with a panicked grunt to the rooftop as Kevin's hand crashed across Janet's cheek.

'Snap the fuck out of it; he just helped save your hide.'

Janet's mind reeled as she felt the sting of his hand across her cheek and jaw. Pain lanced through her, flaring the world back into focus... the sound of gunfire, the smell of death rising on the crisp air, the frantic wailing of her own daughter, and the staggered sobs of the survivors who were being hauled from the jaws of death. She turned her gaze to Michael as he slowly pushed himself upright, her eyes watching as he massaged at his wrist.

'Sorry.'

Janet's words were taut and clipped as Faux batted at the air, his words shaking slightly as he rotated his fist, testing his throbbing wrist. 'Don't worry about it. Now, is she okay?' He nodded towards Maria's still screaming form as Janet began to slowly shush and rock her daughter.

'She looks okay; let me look her over.'

Faux nodded as he gestured towards the table on the far side of the roof. The hiss of rope through spools made him turn as, one by one, the rest of his comrades were hauled to safety.

****

The rippling call of the infected soaked the air, taunting calls mixing with the monotonous groans of the simpleton drones that surrounded their pack masters.

'They're like wolves.'

Shaw cast a glance over at Kevin as he sat, legs dangling over the edge of the roof, his eyes playing back and forth as he watched the undulating horde below them.

'The way they move, the fact that you can tell the smarter ones from the simpletons just by looking at them—it's like a wolf pack. An alpha male surrounded by subordinates.'

Shaw leant out, looking down at what had so captured Kevin's attention. His gaze locked onto the Alphas almost immediately, their movements fluid as they sent roving groups of Infected off in all directions.

'Faux, take position. We've got MVTs down there. Clear 'em out and we should be able to get out on foot without too much trouble.'

Faux nodded as he dropped back behind his weapon, the scope nestling in front of his eye as he began drawing out his targets. Shaw once more turned back to Kevin, his face locked in a softly hopeful glaze.

'You said you could pick out the Alphas?'

Kevin nodded at the question.

'Okay then, do it.'

Shaw turned to Pepper and motioned to the tripod-mounted scope at the end of Peppers roll mat.

'Set him up and knock 'em down. We can't stay up here and wait to die.'

Shaw flinched as his ear bead squawked, a harsh burst of static sending a ringing peal through his skull as his coms went dead.

'What the fuck was that?'

His words were cut short as the sound of rotor blades flooded their air, dust and debris peppering them all as the rooftop erupted in a deluge of wind and grit.

'Contact, high!'

Janet dragged Maria's blankets over her as black-clad bodies leapt from the hovering helicopter, the static whine of air projectile Tasers hissing as they fired. Bodies dropped, convulsing as electricity coursed through them. Shaw spun, barbed spikes striking his lower back as he began to bring his rifle to bear on the black, faceless shadows that were surrounding them.

379

Janet screamed as a black hood was dragged over her head, the static hiss of multiple shotgun fired AP Tasers mingled with sporadic gunfire as Shaw's team tried in vain stop her capture.

'Cargo retrieved, two casualties, zero fatalities.'

The words rang hollow in her head as a voice filtered through the thick bag that was slowly smothering her.

'Is the child with her?'

'Affirmative, mother and child aboard, on exfil to site alpha.'

'Very good. Make sure nothing harms her until you get here.'

'Roger that, Clipper out.'

29

Now
Kingsland Road
Dalston
London

Derek stood outside the security door, his hand hovering over the intercom button; his mind was awash with a myriad of contradicting thoughts. The helicopter had dropped him there seven minutes after the Ridgmont's radio message had silenced any and all other directives. His fist curled into a ball as he smashed it into the reinforced glass panel in front of him, the impact echoing up the cold concrete stairway behind the door.

'World be damned, no one fucks with my family.'

He jammed his thumb against the intercom button, listening to the electric hiss as a buzzer sounded somewhere deep inside the building.

Incomprehensibly slurred Russian poured out of the aluminium-fronted speaker, the voice layered in alcohol and self-pity. Baker ground his teeth together as he fought the urge to scream at the disembodied babbling that slithered from the speaker like a lobotomised snake.

'Andrey, it's me; I am calling in the debt.'

The speaker fell silent for a moment as his words sank through the Vodka-filled haze that surrounded Andrey's mind. An indignant snort greeted Baker's words before Andrey finally replied.

'Fuck do I care? World going to shit… who gives a fuck about stupid debts now, huh? Go find someone who gives a shit.'

Baker sighed as he leant his helmet-covered head against the door before pressing the speaker button once more, his words soft almost pleading as he spoke.

'Andrey, Ridgmont has my wife. He has my daughter; I need your help… please.'

A heavy rustling filled the speaker as Derek waited for an answer.

'Why didn't you say that in the first place? You Debil, the door is open. I need ten minutes then we go find this Ublyudok and cut his fucking head off.'

Derek pushed the door open as the magnetic lock clicked off, the crackling buzz of the alarm filling his ears as he stepped inside, letting the heavy steel and glass slab slip from his fingers. The dull rolling bang of the door hitting the frame filled the stairway as he trudged through the winding spire of concrete and metal towards Andrey's apartment.

****

Andrey stopped, his chest heaving only slightly as he patted the air with his open hand as he stepped backwards slowly, motioning Baker into a doorway.

'Der'mo, Demony.'

Baker's eyebrow quirked at the word as he flexed his fingers around the fore grip of his weapon. Andrey didn't once look back as he called Baker forwards, muttering an explanation.

'Zarazhennyy...'

Sighing at Baker's limited understanding of his language translated, albeit begrudgingly.

'Fucking Infected, Glupyy ublyudok.'

Baker grunted a reply as he stepped forwards, slowly edging past

382

Andrey towards the edge of the brick porch. Derek's eyes scanned the roadway as he slowly leant forwards.

A cold chill ran across the back of his neck as he stared at the throng of Infected that filled the road ahead. He watched in fascinated horror as a woman was dragged from a ground floor window, her legs snagging against the shards of glass as she was yanked across the shattered remains of the windowpane.

One Infected girl, a slim teen, her face scarred by the throbbing orbs of distended puss-filled skin, slammed a fist into the side of her head as the girl snarled at her, the woman's screams ending in a petrified yelp. Derek watched the female youth bite deeply into her own lip, blood welling up in the Infected girl's mouth before she pulled the woman to her feet, planting her bloody mouth on the lips of the thrashing woman; her tongue danced across the silken tender piece of flesh of the slowly quieting form wrapped in her arms.

The teen's hands roamed across the woman's fear-slicked skin as she deepened the blood-coated embrace, soft moans of compliance worming from the woman locked in the teen's embrace. One gore-streaked hand slid up to cup her bosom as the girl's other petite hand slipped inside the waistband of the woman's running shorts, the sheer fabric morphed over the Infected girl's hand as she dipped it lower, her fingers vanishing between the crevice of the woman's legs.

Baker tore his eyes away, his mind dancing with questions to which he had no answer as he listened to howls of the teen and her slew of drones.

'What the fuck did I just watch?'

Andrey smirked as he stared at the bewildered expression on Derek's face. In a coarse whisper, Andrey replied, his eyes darkening as he stepped deeper into the porch way, silencing himself momentarily as the woman and her teenage leader sprinted past.

'That is a whole new problem. I have seen many such as those two. A new generation controlling the last; Anastasia told me of

383

them only today. She has tried to contact you, but communications from base are not working so good at the moment. She took a chance on you coming to find me and told me of the one she had in the lab. Joshua she called him; he was first of new breed... very big Psikhopat.'

He watched Baker's eyes narrow as Andrey's words failed him; fumbling in his mind for the correct translation, he fell back on his training and simplified the problem.

'Crazy man, loony as toons, as people say.'

Baker nodded, a small smile flickering over his lips as he edged back to the corner of the wall and peered out once more, before glancing back at Andrey. The man's matte-black assault webbing stood in stark contrast to his red shirt and silver tie, the finely polished Italian leather shoes and suit trousers lending a very business-like look to the highly trained killer.

'Yeah, well, psychos are easy to find these days. All you got to do is point and shoot; you're bound to hit one at some point. Hang on, Andrey—you said *had*. What do you mean *had*?'

Shifting his grip on the silenced MP7A1 in his hands, Andrey glanced away as more Infected sprinted past, drawn by the guttural cries of the teen and her 'pack'.

'As in he is no longer there, he has split, flown out of the coop, gone bye-bye.'

Derek grimaced as he flattened against the wall; a corpulent mound of Infected flesh lopped past, its stomach folds slapping against its boxer-covered thighs as he struggled to keep pace with his rapidly vanishing compatriots.

'Fuck it. Okay. We have to move. Can you keep pace with me in those things?'

Andrey grinned as he lifted his foot from the floor, revealing the soft Vibrams sole of his shoe and the hidden mesh panels around the arches of his feet.

'I may like to look good, my friend, but I also like to stay alive; in my line of business, it is good to combine the two.'

Baker smiled humourlessly, his mind turning over the implications of all he had just learned as he crouched and watched the roadway. Lifting his hand away from the fore grip of his rifle, he silently counted down from five before sprinting from the safety of the porch way and diving into the gap between two cars, his knees grinding into the floor as he slid into the gap.

Lifting his head above the boot of the car, he looked out through the rear windscreen and side windows as several Infected looked around them, the sudden burst of hurried noise echoing off the walls around. Andrey peered out from the porch as he cautiously glanced between the Infected and Derek, his friend's hunched form pressed tightly to the rear bumper of the Mazda CX5. Baker let his rifle go, the sling tugging against him as his fingers danced and slowly signed out the basics of their next move.

They moved with a purpose, their haste tempered by overt caution as they moved down through the lines of stalled cars and gutted lorries. The still flaming wreckage of a police car pinned under the overturned carcass of a Whitbread delivery truck sent dancing shadows over the walls of the buildings around them.

Lathered foam from burst beer barrels and the sticky remnants of sugary alcopops clung to their feet as they crept to the far end of the container. The rippling crackle of drying sugar and shattered glass made both men wince as they prised their boots from the tarmac, the hissing glue-like rasp filling the air as a deathly hush consumed the world.

****

The muffled pop of weapons fire mingled with the thready screams of pain and fear as they scampered forwards. Their hunched forms searched with weapons raised and eyes pressed tight to the illuminated sights of their weapons as they scanned from window to door. Their sights danced from road to alleyway and back again.

Derek gazed at the front of the Co-operative bank, the smoking hulk of the number forty-three bus making him shiver as he stared at the charred and blackened remains of the people caught within its twisted carcass. Shaking his head, he cast his eyes around the intersection the flashing lights of a police car, dazzling him slightly as he watched it race towards them, both men jumping apart as it shot through the space between them. The manic fear-pinched face of the officer behind the wheel snatched at their eyes as he sped onwards, the car swerving wildly as he weaved through the stalled and overturned river of vehicles towards Angel station, smoke rising from the concourse below.

'Come on; we have to move. That car is going to bring the whole fucking city down on our heads.'

Andrey nodded as they slipped into a lopping trot, their weapons pressed lightly into their shoulders as they continued to watch the unfolding chaos around them.

'We make it to King's Cross St Pancras and we can hook up with SAU Three. They should be there… I hope they'll be there; I've lost enough men already.'

Andrey stayed silent as they continued to run, Derek's pace quickening as they slipped past Joseph Grimaldi Park, the small patch of green a welcome respite from the world of shattered glass and steel that enshrouded them.

****

King and Lucas sat, eyes pressed to the rubber cushions of their optics. Kings spotter's scope swung back and forth from target to target. The rampant forms and frantic movements sent a shiver through him. He softly whispered to Lucas as he watched them slowly converge on a bus, the screaming forms within rushing to the centre isle as Infected closed in.

The driver cried out in fear as he watched hazy lines spread through the windscreen of his bus, the heavy plastic bin clattering to the floor as it bounced off the thick sheet of shatterproof glass.

Lucas watched with stunned fascination as the Infected ceased their onslaught, their writhing forms parting like the Red Sea before Moses as one Infected strode forth, his bloodstained suit jacket tossed casually over one shoulder as he neared the door to the bus. A light, almost joyful skip entered his walk as he stopped in front of the doors; a smile teased his features as the Infected man lifted his hand, rapping his knuckles on the thick panes of glass set into the door before him.

The driver's eyes bulged as tears and sweat mingled with the mucus pouring from his nose, the grinning form of a man filling his vision as he neared the concertina doors of the bus. The Infected's gaze dropped to the emergency access button next to them, the yellow button glowing as the orange ring around it shone with an iridescent light.

The doors hissed open as the pneumatic hinge spun, the heavy clack of metal and plastic warping the air as, slowly, one footstep at a time, he made his way aboard.

'Well, hello, ladies and gentlemen—and children. I do hope your journey has been a comfortable one, but unfortunately, due to unforeseen congestion on the route and several large accidents, you will have to de-bus and proceed on foot. Of course, due to the current climate and present affliction afflicting many of the local residents I cannot guarantee your safety.

'Therefore, I offer you the chance to join me and my compatriots. Of course, there is one minor stipulation; well, I say *minor*, but it's actually quite substantial, and that is, that you must give yourself over to our way of being, if not...'

He trailed off leaving the ravenous gaze of the Infected just outside the glass to drive his point home.

'Need I say any more?'

He perched on the bottom step of the staircase leading to the upper deck of the bus, his suit coat still tossed over one shoulder as he reached into the breast pocket of his shirt and pulled out a slim metal case. The polished chrome tube glinted in the sunlight as he pushed the top off with his thumb, the rhythmic ring of the polished chrome steel bouncing against the filth-laden floor of the bus filled the air as he raised it to his mouth, his teeth closing over the protruding cigar as he dragged it from the tube.

The trim, pre-cut tube of tobacco and paper hung from his lips as he bent down and plucked the canister's lid from the floor before slipping the empty container back into his shirt. With a contented sigh, he fished in his trouser pocket for his lighter, the matte-black square of pressed steel filling his palm as he stared at the grinning devil printed on the face of it, the eyes staring up as he flicked it with his thumb, watching the top of Lucifer's head fold away as the lid snapped back with a metallic click.

The sharp rasp of metal over flint sliced the silence as his sore-split face was lit by the sparking flash of his lighter as he dragged his thumb on the ridged wheel.

'Oh, and just a by the by, you all have until I finish this cigar to decide. Then I will allow my compatriots in, and, well, they are all a little hungry or angry, or both; anyway, have fun deciding.'

****

Derek slipped around the corner, his form coming to rest behind the smoking wreck of a car, the shattered beast of steel and glass lying on its side. The smell of wet pork filled his nostrils as he peered around it at the group of Infected that surrounded the double-decker bus.

His throat itched, the splash of red ringing his neck sat blistered and sore beneath the pads of his throat mike. Velcro tugged at his

388

slowly chaffing flesh as the scent of his own blood mingled with the air. Derek's ears tickled as he strained to hear Andrey's near-silent approach.

'Infected?'

Derek nodded as Andrey sank to one knee.

'How many?'

A soft snort left Derek as he twisted his booted foot, scraping against the glass-strewn floor beneath him.

'Enough, but, you may want to reload.'

Andrey grinned as he slipped the half-empty magazine from the well of his weapon and set it into the drop-leg magazine pouch on his thigh, the matte-black plate of pouches cluttered with half a dozen half-full magazines.

The soft click of a fresh magazine slipping into the well made Derek smile for the briefest second as he pushed himself upwards. His thighs trembled slightly as he moved past Andrey and patted his friend on the shoulder.

Derek paused, listening once more to Andrey's near-silent movements as they both moved into the shadows of the container lorry.

30
Kings Cross St Pancras

'You see that?'

Lucas spoke, his voice soft, almost whisper quiet as he tracked the sudden flash of movement to the corner of a lorry two hundred meters from the train station's front door. The buttstock of his rifle was pulled in tight to his shoulder, the stale stench of sweat filling his nostrils as it skated down the side of his face pooling around his cheek where it sat pressed tight to the rubberised plastic.

'Yup, that wasn't an Infected; I can tell you that much.'

King shifted his weight slightly, his elbows screaming at him as the grit beneath him bit deeper into his skin. A sudden flash of light dazzled his eyes as he stared at the dark, swaying shadows. King blinked rapidly, trying to clear the dancing spots of rippling glare from his eyes as the flashing started again. Drawing back on the magnification, he counted the glittering bursts of light as Lucas panned his rifle back towards the bus.

Pressing his fingers to his throat, King opened a channel his voice soft, just above a muted whisper as he spoke, his eyes still glued to the pad of his spotting scope.

'Mike, Oscar, Zulu.'

His hoarse croaking words made Lucas' eyebrows arch as he set his sights on the hunched and sweat-stained back of an Infected. The agitated, sporadic movements made his finger itch as he stroked the trigger of his rifle, his mind aching for him to curl his finger and send the copper-jacketed hunk of lead hurtling into the twitching mass of flesh below him.

'Alpha, Romeo, Tango; Confirm receipt, over.'

A smile tugged at King's lips as he let his sights drift over the area ahead of Derek's position.

'Receipt confirmed, come on in; we'll clear the way.'

Baker's voice filled King's ears as he shifted his sights to the nearest Infected, calling him out to Lucas as the man zeroed in.

'Negative, bus, priority action. We'll cover approach from ground level; you provide sniper and aerial support. Cleared for swarm pod.'

A dry double click filled Derek's ear as a soft whine flitted through the air.

****

Token stood watching the world below him, his head lost beneath a helmet that looked like the bastard child of a motorcycle crash helmet and a fish bowl.

The shifting blue haze that bathed his face made his eyes tingle as he watched the thirty dancing images relayed to him by the circling drones below.

'We have a total of twenty-two tangos encircling the bus, and what appears to be one...' Token paused as his brow furrowed. *'He seems to be sitting down and uh ... well ... he's smoking.'*

Token's radio blipped in his ear as Derek's voice filtered through.

'SAU 3-6 repeat last transmission.'

Token, sent a drone whirling through an open window at the rear of the bus, its carbon fibre rotors noiselessly cutting through the fear-soaked air. The high-resolution camera whirred in its housing as Token zeroed in on the man in the suit. His white, blood-spattered shirt and gore-smeared trousers marked him more victim than victor to any but the most stringent observer.

The drone banked sharply as Token guided the minuscule bot through the doorway and out into the street. The shuffling, agitated, and hunger-crazed Infected barely registered its passage as it passed barely three feet above their heads. Their minds so consumed by the need for sustenance that it rendered everything around them completely inconsequential.

Guttural snarls and simpering whines mingled with the drifting blanket of death's song as they shifted impatiently at the edge of their imposed cordon. With the skill of a ballet choreographer, Token guided the buzzing swarm, their trim, minuscule forms drifting as close as he dared to take them to the salivating mass of ravenous flesh below him.

'In position, waiting to execute.'

Derek's clipped, stress-laden tone invaded their minds as his order rolled forth. A declaration so vilified that it defied all cognitive progression as the Infected below drew their final breaths.

'Execute!'

The world burst into a kaleidoscope of noise and panic as the people trapped behind the walls of steel and glass that encased them were rocked by the sudden litany of explosions. The Infected at the front of the bus leapt to his feet, the half-dead cigar slipping from his lips as he watched his brethren fall.

The drones detonated, their steel and carbon fibre shells rupturing as the packets of high explosives within burst in a solid ball of boiling fire and energy. The steel ball packed explosives sent blood and gore bursting forth, plastering the sides of the bus in a rain of skin, shattered bone, and torn flesh.

The chattering clatter of suppressed gunfire filled the echoing void as the suit-clad Infected tore from the open doors of the bus, his feet sliding through the layer of ruptured flesh and entrails that covered the road around him. A flush of warmth rolled down his

392

spine as he raised his head, crimson rain bathed his face as he watched the last remnants of his butchered cohorts descend from the heavens.

His ears rang with the bells of a thousand dead men, straining as the ghostly pale vestige of a figure emerged from the darkened shadows of the world around him, tongues of fire dancing forth as more of his brethren fell to the shadow's daemonic sword.

'SAU3-4, 3-5 you have eyes on. Confirm secure.'

The Infected listened to the words trickle forth as his ears buzzed and stung, the burning haze of his own unbidden tears filled his eyes as the shade before him began to swim into being.

He watched as the shade's hand rose to its ear and dropped mere moments later, the movements so precise, yet fluid that they seemed ingrained into its very being as its fire-belching lance of death rose, shifting in his direction.

'Down on the floor!'

He couldn't move; his hands shook and knees buckled as he watched the approaching spectre.

'I said down on the fucking floor!'

His knees buckled as the shifting swirling mass of anger and rage edged ever closer.

'Do you not hear me? I said, down on the fucking floor!'

His eyes bulged as his stomach clenched, the sudden impact from the spectre's anger-soaked lance buckling him as he slid to the floor, the legs of his suit trousers drenched in the quagmire of his kin.

Andrey crushed his foot into the back of the blood-soaked Infected, his hands sliding the thick semi-ridged bands of plastic around the man's wrists before dragging them closed, sealing the prostrate form's hands together.

'Up Svoloch!'

Andrey dragged the dazed and stunned figure to its feet as the doors to Kings Cross St Pancras crashed open. The grime-smeared and weary forms of S.A.U 3 poured free, their weapons raised and eyes scanning the area as they charged towards the stalled and blood-spattered bus. The pulsing corpses that ringed it were already beginning to fill the air with the pungent aroma of offal and excrement.

'Check it, tag it, and get it inside; not one more person is dying on our watch, do you hear me?'

An echoing chorus bounced through the air as Derek and Andrey dragged the staggering Infected form towards the train station concourse.

'Sit down, you piece of shit!'

Andrey all but threw the bound form into a vacant chair, the legs lifting from the floor as the Infected's weight crashed into the tubular chromed steel frame.
Andrey's eyes flared with a primal anger as he watched a blood chilling smirk play across the Infected's features.

'He's coming for you...'

The Infected's lilting singsong words echoed through the cavernous ticket hall. The stifled sobs and keening moans of the people around them stilled as his cackling laughter filled the air.

'He... he's gonna make you all burn... the fire of our dominion shall cleanse you all from the face of this wretched world, us and the black twelve.'

His face twisted as the pulsating sores began to split, the yellowed puss mingling with his tears and blood as he leant forwards, his mouth foaming as his voice began to climb.

'He's coming, and you will all burn...'

His eyes fell to Derek as he made his way to Andrey's side, his footsteps cutting the Infected's words apart like meat on a butcher's block.

'You, your little blonde whore, and the spawn or your rutting loins will burn; he will fall upon you like the sword of Damocles and tear your world asunder. Their screams will fill the air as you watch on in horror, drowning in their blood as it stains the earth at your feet.'

Derek's eyes bore into the Infected as he twisted against his bonds, the smell of fresh blood filling the air as the thick plastic encircling his wrists began to bite deeply into his flesh.

'Enough of this shit!'

Derek strode forwards, letting his rifle slip to his back as he dragged his blade from the sheath on his thigh, settling the weight into his palm as he dropped to a crouch, his weight resting on the balls of his feet.

'Drown in blood, huh, that's a new one.'

Derek shifted his weight slightly, gaining a more stable stance as he rested his elbows on his knees.

'Not very original though, and well, you know you haven't actually told me who is going to be doing the whole "casting my world asunder" thing, as you put it.'

The Infected leant as close as he could before Andrey stepped forwards shoving him backwards into the chair once more. Derek continued to crouch in front of the chair; the Infected's eyes widened his mouth foaming, white froth stained red as it poured down his chin.

'The one who treads in his steps, the one who sat imprisoned until the time of our coming.'

Baker's face flushed as he pushed himself upright, his foot lifting as he slammed it into the Infected's chest.

'Enough of the Biblical bullshit!'

The Infected clattered to the floor. The echoing crash of the chair beneath him riding on the back of the stomach-churning crunch that issued up from the man as his face contorted in agony. The bones of his wrists were crushed to dust under his own weight.

Baker stepped forwards, his body oozing malice and anger as he set his weight down on the Infected's stomach.

'You tell me now, just who is behind this, or I swear to you, you will be wearing your intestines as a box tie and your cock as a fucking watch!'

The Infected grinned as his eyes brimmed with unshed tears of pain and anger. Derek's matte-black blade hovered, its flat razor-edged surface clutched in his hand reflected in the martyr's gaze as it met Derek's own.

'It matters little what you do to me; the whore in the chair knows all too well what my lord is capable of. He comes for us all, and the time of his arrival is nigh; the world knows of our legions, of our passage across this vapid land.'

Baker watched as the Infected lifted himself upwards, the sound of splitting bones filling the air as he pushed himself on to Derek's blade, piercing his eyes as he screamed.

'He walks among us all, leading us to the promised lands, and his name is Joshua!'

The Infected threw his head forwards, Derek's blade sinking deep into his skull as either man could do little more than watch as the matte-black slab of carbon steel slid effortlessly through the soft pappy tissue of its eyeball, until the grating vibration of steel on bone shivered through Derek's arm. Andrey set his hand on Derek's shoulder, softly pulling him to his feet as the blade was dragged from the dead man's skull.

'Yeah, I know, Andrey; we have to move.'

Derek stood and wiped the blade on the dead man's shirt. As he did so, he turned, motioning to two of Patterson's men.

'Get this sack of psychotic shit out of here.'

Turning to Andrey, he nodded to the door. 'Let's move. I've wasted too much time here. You locked and loaded?'

Andrey nodded as they made their way towards the door, their footsteps tarnished by the bloody smeared corpse being dragged in their wake.

31
St Mary's Hospital

Derek swung round the corner, his eyes wide and bloodshot. Stress, panic, anger, and pure unadulterated rage mingled in the vacuous vortex of his eyes, its bilious slop flowing over his face in a twisting blood-tinged mask. The blade in his hand hung from his grip like a manacle as blood slithered from the powder-stained wound in his forearm, running along his arm, dripping from his fingers.

Derek snarled; dropping his shoulder, he charged forwards, teeth barred in a vicious howl of rage as his heart pounded in his chest. Images danced in his mind, the ethereal forms of all he held dear shimmering and fading, drifting on a wind of his own creation as he ploughed on, sending his battle-bruised body careening through the door.

****

Wood splintered around him, bullets arcing through the air as time slowed to a crawl. He watched, turning his head as his eyes tracked the bullet, its hot copper-coated form passing his face by millimetres.

Andrey appeared, filling his vision, the man's weapon chattering, its rapid muted cough puncturing the air as he sent a searing wall of lead and copper into all that stood, barring their way.

Baker turned his eyes back, training his gaze on the black-clad soldiers before him, his mind a cold, hard vacuum of pure incandescent rage. Rage poured from him in waves as he raised his pistol and curled his finger, feeling it tighten around the trigger as the slide bucked against his hand.

Derek watched the plumes of blood erupt from their forms as the .40 mm hollow-point rounds passed through their black-clad bodies.

Bodies fell limp to the floor as the pulped and mangled contents of their shattered bodies burst forth like a cacophony of human geysers.

The shattered splinters of bone and blood, flesh and brain matter glimmered in the flickering lights as it landed with a wet splat on the cold, uncaring ground.

His breathing huffed through his ears, heels grinding against the floor as his back connected with the wall. Derek's heart pounded out a deep bass rhythm of life and death. A life born to punish, erasing the wickedness from the face of the world with a tide of unrelenting, unforgiving death.

Andrey crashed through the door as a bellowing wall of rage and death careened through the body-strewn corridor.

'Baker... Go!'

His eyes flared as Andrey lifted the leather-handled tomahawk from the base of his vest. His final magazine sat in the well of his pistol, the MP7 long gone, discarded in the maelstrom of death and destruction left in their wake.

'I've got this.'

Andrey shoved Baker back through the doorway, grabbing the cold steel of the handle as he wrenched the door closed; the echoing crash of steel on steel momentarily dulled the pall of noise rolling from the mouth of the corridor. Andrey grunted as he twisted his wrist, sending his weight down through his shoulder, shearing the handle from the door.

Derek stared through the Plexiglas at the black remorseful gaze that met his own. Nothing had to be said as Andrey nodded, his final words ringing in Baker's ears as he turned and squared his shoulders, his joints screaming as he rolled his neck, the heavy tension singing through his muscles.

'Go save them; do not fail like me!'

Andrey stared at the pistol in his hand as they stormed into the entryway, the door behind him standing as a flush reminder of the single outcome that had fallen at his feet. Steeling himself for the onslaught, he grinned as they began to close in.

'Come and face Andrey Gervasii, the Russian grim reaper!'

Shrugging out of the empty and useless assault vest, he swept it up with his foot launching the spinning mass of webbing and pouches into the faces of the three nearest approaching men.

The balaclava-covered faces tangled in the matte-black mass of assault gear screamed as Andrey dove forth; the pistol in his hand barking as he snapped his aim to the six men behind them. Andrey rolled bullets searing as he drove his tomahawk through the air, driving it down and through the top of the man's helmet-covered head. He watched as his eyes rolled backwards, the spray of cranial fluid bathing Andrey's face as he dragged the hawk free of the man's skull.

Gervasii bellowed as he snapped his aim to the left, the pistol roaring as heat-soaked copper casings spun through the air, searing his flesh as it burnt through his cotton silk blend shirt. The smell of his charred skin filled the air as his pistol continued spewing its lethal fire. Andrey's face twisted into a psychotic grin as he screamed in rage and bloodlust; a blaze of orange filled his vision as the forehead of the man in front of him evaporated. The man's head snapped back, crushing the throat of his partner as they continued to pour into the room.

Andrey's blood-chilling bellow filled their ears; with an energy born of rage and adrenaline, he launched his now empty sidearm at one of the men as he brought down his tomahawk, burying it deep into the chest of another soldier and dove forwards, roaring like the devil itself.

****

A deep rush of cold air filled him, chilling his soul as he raised his booted foot and kicked it backwards; the door crashed open, its dark void gaping wide as a grim smile twisted Derek's lips, his feet carrying him into the arms of the unknown, his body twisting, flowing over all in its path as the images continued to play past his eyes.

He watched the Infected tumble backwards over the banister, careening towards the unforgiving arms of the earth below. They flailed and screamed at him, hands clawing, eyes wide, and teeth bared as they fell. Their bodies bounced, bones shattering like porcelain, skin tearing like silk, casting a halo of crimson water around them as they finally and permanently came to their final stop.

Rolling forwards, he came to a halt, his knees biting into the cold tiles beneath him, the hard plates of his kneepads lost long ago in the deluge of screaming flesh and teeth. Harsh blue eyes tracked across the room as he finally let himself breathe. Derek's gaze stopped as he saw the pale mirage of satin blond hair and alabaster skin. The spooling trail of golden tresses flowed out from the still form in a halo as they lay still and lifeless on the cold emotionless floor.

Derek pushed himself to his feet as the Infected leapt forwards, their hands clawing at him as he batted them aside, his body reacting on instinct as he gazed upon the prostrate silhouette. Hands and feet tore at him, streaming around him like water over stones as his hands moved in a blur.

His mind was blank, a slate of purest black as he parried even the most desperate lunge. Grasping hands and bared teeth fell aside in droves as he tore free from the talon-like fingers tearing at his clothing. Their impotent, guttural cries of hunger and rage dripping off the air like rain from the clouds.

Derek kicked out, sending the Infected before him sliding over the tiles, the muted squeak of skin on ceramic rising up as it crashed into the wall. A dull crunch echoed through his mind as he shot a fist forwards, the snarling face to his right disappearing under the weight of his Kevlar-knuckled fist.

Baker's hand snapped out, blade clutched in his grip scything through all in its path as he pushed forwards, desperation rising in his gut as he stared at the still, motionless figure.

He watched with an emotionally vacant gaze as he stared at the shimmering droplets of arcing arterial spray that hung like diamonds in the bitter frost-stung air.

He spun over the ball of his left foot as he kicked out, sending his right crashing into the head of the nearest Infected; the dull crunch of shattering bone was lost in the deluge of noise as he charged forwards.

Ridgmont's eyes never left the scene of utter devastation, a cruel almost gleeful sneer curling his lips as he stared at the man below him, his mind burning with unadulterated joy as if he was watching a swimmer fight a tide they had no hope of overcoming and yet, through it all, he waited; standing over the blonde angel at his feet, Maria struggling in his grasp as he clutched at her chin, lifting her head up tight against his hip as he pulled her from the floor by the back of her tiny cotton dress; her eyes screamed out in pain and fear as small rivulets of blood seeped out from around Ridgmont's clawing nails as they sunk deeper into the tender flesh of her cheek.

Time collapsed in on itself as he reached them, his knees buckling as Derek staggered up the steps of the raised dais in the centre of the room. Its brick-built form raising them above the tumult of flesh that clogged the floor below. Derek's mind tumbled as his senses boiled over. Sound, taste, pain, scent all rushing in like a wave of boiling water as time realigned around him.

Its uncaring weight crushed him to the floor as his breathing rasped in his ears, his mind finally registering the hot beads of his own slowly leaking blood that was rolling down the side of his face. The soft scraping of nails over tiles rattled through him as he stared at the still, warm, motionless form of his wife.

His gaze lingered on the fallen angel at the feet of the devil. A shrill cry of pain and pleading fear shattered any thought in his mind as Maria's plaintive screams filled the room.

Derek's gaze snapped upwards as he bellowed, his body moving before any conscious decision was made. Everything around him ceased to exist as he charged, his eyes fixed firmly on the two people before him, the willow-thin vortex of pain and malice that had ensnared the only sources of light in Baker's rapidly dying world.

Ridgmont dropped Maria as Baker careened into him, the human embodiment of hate slithering past Derek as his daughter dropped from view, landing with a bone-jarring thump against the cold floor beneath them. Ridgmont's hand crashed into the back of Derek's neck, sending him to the floor in a crumbling heap of flesh and bone as his mind went blank.

The room swam and danced as he pushed himself up on all fours, bile and spittle dripped from his mouth as he coughed and wheezed, spitting into the pile of fluid slowly pooling between his hands.

'Oh my, are we feeling unwell, Baker?

'My, my, my, honestly, Derek, what would Janet and Maria think if they could see you like this, cowering on all fours like a dog when your darling daughter lies there crying for you? Can't you hear her calling you?

'Can't you hear her plaintive little whine?'

His voice rose an octave as he forced himself to mimic a small girl as he knelt beside Derek's slowly stirring form.

'Wah, wah, wah, wah; god, how infuriating.'

Ridgmont pushed himself upright as he sent a boot into Derek's ribs, the force of the blow driving the air from Baker's lungs as he slid across the floor, curling into the foetal position against the railings as he struggled to breathe.

'Pathetic; you and your snivelling little cunt of a child. Why don't you just curl up and die like that vapid little slice of slut cake that you called a wife?

'Oh my, was she a beautiful piece. Why I toyed with her for hours before I called you. I was honestly toying with the notion of breaking in that little cherry that you coddled so much, but then I saw your blonde slut squirming against the bonds I had her under and well... I'm only human.'

His voice dripped with a layer of self-indulgent glee. He cupped his scrotum in his hand and gave it a loving squeeze as he lifted Janet from the floor by her hair, cupping her chin with his free hand as he stared at Baker. A bubble of malevolent joy built within him as he looked at the pleading pair of eyes that bore into his own.

'Please... no... don't.'

Janet's eyes opened slowly, her emerald-green orbs locking onto her husband's as he reached forwards, his gloved hand straining as he pushed himself onto his knees. Her voice filled his ears as she whispered through the veil of pain and anaesthesia.

'Derek?'

'Oops, time's up.'

With a glee-filled smirk, Ridgmont's hands twisted as Janet's head snapped to the side, Ridgmont's fist crashing into her temple. Her hair spun in a halo of shimmering gold, the light dancing through it as her body shuddered. Ridgmont's fingers dug deep into her flesh. Janet's eyes widened for the briefest of moments, their shimmering countenance so full of life blinking into nothing almost instantly as she dropped from Ridgmont's grasp, her limp form falling with a dull thump to the floor.

'No!'

Slowly, with shaking hands and a trembling heart, Derek

tentatively reached out. His soul screamed at his mind, the pounding, broken, centre of his being refusing to accept what years on the battlefield told him to be true. Rolling Janet's limp form into his arms, his eyes travelled across her pale visage as she hung loose in his grasp, tears stinging his eyes as her head lolled backwards into the crook of his elbow.

He brushed stray strands of her golden hair away from her face, the long sun-tinged locks clinging to her skin like moss on a stone. He watched as it tugged at her bottom lip, the once rose-coloured giver of love now a pale, blue-tinged impostor, ghosts of their once vibrant selves.

Gently he leant in and placed a soft, lasting kiss on them, her fading scent leaking into him as he let his lips linger against hers. Derek's eyes widened for the briefest of moments as he felt her breath on his lips, the slow drawing of life from a shocked and unconscious form. With infinite care, Baker lay her unconscious form back upon the cold, uncaring floor beneath them and sat on his haunches as he stared at the hidden eyes before him. Those iridescent pools of cooling green that had so filled his heart now lay shadowed and dull behind her lidded eyes.

A soft, plaintive mewling filled his ears, drawing Baker's ruined gaze away from the all-consuming pit of depth-less despair that he had teetered over only moments before. With a staggering gait of a drunken spider, Derek pulled himself towards the source of the noise.

A small, quivering hand scraped at the edge of the steps before him, its searching grasp, snaring Baker's heart as he threw himself forwards, his arms curling round the cold, quivering bundle as he pulled her to his chest.

'Maria, darling, sweetie. Come on, Daddy's here. There's a good girl.'

Her hands clutched at his collar and chin, curling herself into his chest. Derek smoothed down the tousled strands of her auburn hair, his hand slipping through the downy strands as she nestled into his warmth.

Baker's voice broke as he brushed his fingers over her peach-tinged cheek, moving the stray strands of hair back behind her ear as he stared at her. Derek stood there, his mind an empty shell as he gazed down at the last embers of the dying light that had filled his world, their soft orange glow fading to nothing, leaving him alone, lost in the dark as he sank to his knees, unable to bear the weight that now lay upon his cold and lonely form.

Leaning forwards, Derek gently eased Maria's fingers from his collar, setting her down on the tiles, his hands guiding her into her mother's arms as he leant down and gently pressed his lips to her forehead, a soft yawn of fear-soaked fatigue claiming her diminutive year-old form

The room echoed with a clattering bang. Both men turned to face the noise as Andrey crashed through the doors. The final blood-drenched black-clad form sailed away from him as he strode into the room, the jangling mass of metal in his hand his only testament to the carnage he had left in his wake.

'Vy gnilostnyy lezhal meshok s gryaz'yu, ya budu imet' svoy grebanyy golovu!'
You putrid sack of filth, I'll take your fucking head!

Baker's roaring denial ceased all movement from the rage-infused Russian as he charged towards the maniacal colonel.

'No, Andrey, please. Voz'mite moyu zhenu i doch', on moy!'
Take my wife and daughter; he is mine!

Andrey nodded as he moved past Derek, his feet near silent as he plucked the motionless forms from where they lay and, with infinite care, vanished into the darkened maw of the corridor.

Ridgmont's glee-filled gaze locked upon the blue eyes of the man before him, his glazed eyes shining with a light only curtailed by the sheer weight of his mania.

'Oh, how sweet; you have a little nursemaid to clean up your messes. Well, that is yet another life on your hands, Baker, one more tag on your bracelet.'

His giddy gloating faltered, his face paling slightly as he saw the cold light that glowed in the iridescent blue orbs that claimed his sight.

The soft, hushed rustle of webbing on leather filled the silence as Derek shed his vest. The heavy, weapon-laden rig thumping to the floor as he stepped forwards. The cold lump of his empty pistol hit the tiles with an echoing clatter as he unsnapped the holster from his thigh; the hardshell holster skittered over the tiled floor as its weight carried it away from his body.

Ridgmont began to step back, his feet sliding over the tiles, pushing him backwards as he scrambled for a way out; his eyes darted about the room, their panic-widened gaze drifting over everything as his lip quivered with poorly concealed fear.

Adrenaline pumped through his frantically beating heart as it hammered at the walls of his chest, the panicked beating filling his ears as he came to rest against the railings of the staircase behind him, and still Baker advanced, his hands relaxed and ready as he strode forwards inch by inch, closing the ever shrinking gap between them.

Baker watched the fear and sweat-laden countenance before him as a cold, irreversible calm settled over him, his eyes saying nothing as he walked on silently; lifting his hand, he cupped the back of Ridgmont's neck and closed his fingers.

They settled around the slim muscles like a steel vice, closing with a force he never knew he possessed. Then, with a flick of shoulders, he tossed the source of his anguish and rage back through the door and watched as the limp and ragged form slammed into the table in the centre.

The twisting of limbs and metal met nothing but silence as Baker turned and followed Ridgmont back into the room, the bloodied and lacerated bodies of the Infected filling the floor as Derek strode up the shallow steps.

Lifting his boot without a word, Derek sent it crashing down onto Ridgmont's chest. An explosion of saliva and mucus fountained from Ridgmont's gasping mouth as his lungs collapsed under the impact. He pulled his foot away then kicked forwards, sending the psychotic colonel, the table, and chair tumbling into the far wall. A staccato symphony arose as the conglomerate of man and furniture clattered over the floor, coming to rest in a tangled heap against the far wall.

Baker leapt forwards, his calm façade still in place as he lifted the battered man to his feet, his curled fist rising as he ploughed forwards, his right arm snapping back and forth as he pummelled Ridgmont's aquiline features in upon themselves. Blood coated his hand and knuckles, Derek's skin splitting as he crushed them against the shattered bones of Ridgmont's nose and cheeks. Rivers of blood ran from Baker's arm and fist as he released the semi-limp, mewling form from his grasp.

Lifeless blue eyes watched as Ridgmont tried to rise, thick congealed lines of mucus-infused gore dripping from his shattered face like string from a kitten's claws, the soft whimpering mewl worming its way past the twisted remnants of Ridgmont's lips as he attempted to rise. Lifting his foot, Baker kicked Ridgmont's hands away from him, watching as the man's own weight carried him face first into the floor.

Lifting his boot once again, he brought the heel crashing down upon the weak helpless fingers of Ridgmont's left hand.

He wanted to smile as the man cried out as his finger bones shattered beneath his boot. He wanted to laugh as he watched the shards of Ridgmont's shattered digits slice through the soft flesh of his hand. He wanted to roar with delight as he listened to pained and pleading cries emanating from the man beneath him.

However, he couldn't. Nothing would come forth. No notes of triumph. No sounds of delighted retribution would ever leave him. All that had been good in Baker's dwindling world had vanished with the blonde angel now lying broken and beaten in the arms of his friend. All that was left for him was vengeance—cold and emotionless justice in a world gone mad, so he raised his boot again and sent it sailing down onto Ridgmont's left knee. Again and again, he pounded the joint to dust as the man beneath him pleaded for clemency from a deaf court and its silent executioner.

His arms snapped down and dragged the beaten man to his feet, hurling him once more into the wall. A red cloying smear of Ridgmont's blood marked its passage down his face as he collapsed to the floor. Baker fell to his knees atop the trembling and quivering mess below him.

With a cold, merciless gaze alighting on the battered face below him, he let his fists rise and fall, his shoulders driving them downwards pummelling the frail form into submission. Over and over they rose and fell like pistons in an engine, their speed increasing with every revolution as he watched the blood arc through the air, splattering across his face... the floor... the walls. Slowly, he dragged the life from the man so bent on revenge, he had eked it out on the souls of the two people in this world Derek would gladly give all for.

Images of her flashed through his mind as he continued to pound out his broken fury into the mass of pulped fleshed beneath him. Her smiling face bathed in the setting summer sun as they wound their way through the golden fields of the French farmlands, the look of stunned joy as she gazed upon the diamond ring encircling her finger the day Derek proposed.

The sight of her walking towards him, the white silk dress hugging her slim form as he gazed upon her glowing visage on their wedding day, the sweat-stained and tired look of pride on her face as she held their new-born daughter.

That last memory gave him pause, his arms locking in place as he thought of their daughter growing up without a mother's love, without the all-forgiving warmth of her mother's arms to comfort her or hold her close while her daddy was away. Something inside Baker snapped, breaking away completely as he held that image in his mind—the smiling face of his wife and the small fragile form of his new-born daughter enshrouded in the soft towelling blanket as she was slowly rocked to sleep and how close he had come to losing it all.

Baker's arms dove down mercilessly, his tears flowing free as he snapped his head forwards, smashing his forehead into Ridgmont's face. He felt the bones of the man's nose splinter and vanish as he crushed it into a paste of powdered bone and pulped flesh. Driving his thumbs into Ridgmont's eye sockets, Derek pushed slowly, ploughing deeper and deeper into the putrid, filth-filled orbs, pulverising them into a mass of puss and slime as he curled his fingers round the sides of Ridgmont's skull and pulled.

Ridgmont screamed, blood pulsing from his eyes and nose as Baker clawed at the sides of his face, Derek's fingers tearing into the pulverised skin that framed the man's cranium, nails tore at bone, scrapping through cartilage and muscle with a savage lust for vengeance. He tore the flesh from his skull as his thumbs began to bore through the back of Ridgmont's eye sockets.

Then as soon as it had arrived, it was gone. Baker pushed himself up and away, the tangled mess of blood and flesh repulsing him as he staggered towards the door, the silent corridors carrying him through the cold, lifeless hospital. Derek's eyes shifted in and out of focus as he bounced off the wall, his weight dragging him around the corner as he stumbled into the cavernous atrium, the jumbled mass of overturned seats and smashed tables ensnaring his every step as he fell through the open doorway.

Cold seared through him as he sank to his knees. The cold brick paving beneath him bathed his battered skin as he slumped, exhausted and weary to the floor as blood began to pour from his scalp.

Derek's eyes drifted in and out of focus as he watched them approach, their grasping black-coloured hands snatching at him as they lifted him from the floor, bright flashes of orange filling the sky as he felt himself rise from the uncaring stone. A flash of red silk snatched at his eyes as a calm accented voice filled his ears.

'We have you, my friend; we have you, rest easy.'

The Teams

Team One

Derek Baker: Aged 38, 6 foot 3 inches, bald (partially shaven), often has a full beard—a habit from spending long operational periods in Arabic and Middle Eastern countries.
Blue eyes, missing his left ear. Has the SBS sword tattooed onto his forearm
Royal Marines Commando and SBS operative
Commander of Broadhead and assault team one leader Unflinching, pragmatic, and unerringly loyal, he will go above and beyond to complete his mission, no matter the cost to himself.

Richard 'Splinter' Sharp: Aged 30, 6 foot exactly, close-cut hair (shaven to within a millimetre of his scalp)
Paratrooper and SAS operative
Second in command of team one
Multi-skilled operative, marksman and guerrilla warfare specialist. Self-assured, confident and slightly cocky, he is not afraid to bend the rules to achieve his goals but will always let reason and sound judgment guide him above all else.

Dean Roberts: Aged 26
Royal Marines Commando and SBS operative
Skilled soldier and Marksman and demolitions specialist
Quiet and observant, he will go beyond the limits for a friend even if it means giving his life to save theirs.

Charles Hooper: Aged 27
Infantry soldier and SAS operative
Skilled soldier and tracker
Outspoken and loyal, a well-adjusted team player and valued member of team one.

Damien Colins: Aged 24
Royal Marines commando

Mountain warfare specialist and close quarters battle and light support specialist

Trained as a martial artist from a very young age and took his training through when training as a Marines commando.

Like all commandos, he is as blunt as a brick when it comes to honesty and is not afraid to back up his assertions with whatever means is deemed necessary.

Sam Fisher: Aged 25
Irish Guards
P Company and Pathfinder group attached
Highly opinionated and rough spoken, he is proud of his heritage and his family's long-standing connection to the Irish Guards and served and qualified in the same regimental areas and expertise as his father.

Nicholas Mariani: Aged 25
Irish Guards
Light support specialist
Soft spoken and reserved, he keeps to himself and can be seen as a little aloof by the men he serves with but is not one to shy away from combat and will always bring to bear all he can give.

Team Two

John Davies: Aged 29
1st Regiment the Rifles and SAS Operative
Team Two commander
Tattoo of the both regimental badges on his right shoulder blade
Highly trained and proficient killer with a deep moral compass, will
go above and beyond the call of duty to achieve what he thinks is the
right and most morally clean outcome.

Chris Jones: Aged 23
Princess of Wales Royal Regiment
Team Two second in command
Darkly sarcastic and regularly speaks his mind, regardless of whom
it upsets.

Rory Hamilton: Aged 25
Princess of Wales Royal Regiment
Light Support Specialist

James Clarkenwell: Aged 27
Infantry soldier SAS operative

Maximilian (Max) Reiley: Aged 26
Royal Marines Commando

David Baxter: Aged 27
Royal Marines Commando
Light support specialist

Team Three

Andre Patterson: Team Commander: Aged 29
Scots Guards
Highly Intelligent with a wit to match.
Uncompromising in all aspects and carries it through to the battlefield.

Ibrahim "Token" Kweku: Aged 31
Team Three second in command
Drone and explosives specialist

Dean King: Aged 30
1st Battalion Royal Irish Regiment
Spotter/Sniper

Carter Lucas: Aged 27
1st Battalion Royal Irish Regiment
Spotter/Sniper

Dominic Walters
Mercian Regiment
Light Support Specialist

Carl Sooker
Royal Welsh
Light Support Specialist

Derrek Carlstook
Royal Signals

Simeon Carruthers
The Rifles
Spotter/Sniper

Charlie Hampson
The Rifles
Spotter/Sniper

Team Four

Rufus Shaw: Team Commander: Age 29
Grenadier Guards
Highly Intelligent and clean spoken with an innate grasp of field tactics

Charles Kane
Second in Command
Royal Regiment of Fusiliers

Miles Pepper
Royal Anglian Regiment
Spotter/Sniper

Michael Faux
Royal Anglian Regiment
Spotter/Sniper

Simeon Stepps
Yorkshire Regiment
Light Support Specialist

Leroy Stoors
Duke of Lancaster's Regiment
Light Support Specialist

Marcus Bridgewater
Black Watch

Kenny Wilding
Black Watch
Spotter/sniper

Dean Movington
Black Watch
Spotter/Sniper

Rapid Reaction Team

By the nature of its insertion method, all team members are active Paratroopers.

Kevin Woodwrow
Team Leader
Five foot Ten
Black Hair
Short spoken and blunt
Honest to a fault and not afraid to call a situation as he sees it, which at times has caused minor friction between him and the other team commanders.

Richard Kerr
RRT Second in Command
Five Foot Eight
Blonde
Affable and easy going

Dominic Williams

Scott Sheperd
Light Support Specialist

James Clarkson
Light Support Specialist

Robert Brooks
Light Support Specialist

Air Wing

All members of the air wing are fully qualified pilots of both Rotary and Jet aircraft.

Jenniffer Lincruster
Brown Hair
Brown eyes
Soft spoken and honest
Qualified translator

Carla Westing
Blonde
Blue eyes
Flirty and outspoken
Part of the TRiM teams and qualified translator

Notable Civilians.

Janet Baker
Derek's wife and certified doctor of Medicine

Kevin Newcroft
Janet's Staff nurse and long-time friend

Jimmy O'Hara
Hospital Maintenance technician

Russian Members.

Fadei Bogatir

Andrey Gervasii

American Members

Sergeant Alexander "Rook" Richards

Corporal Jonathan "Hawk" Stabbler

Other works by the author

The Designated Series:
Designated: Infected
Designated: Quarantined

With Tania Cooper

The Heaven's Scent Series:
Heaven's Scent Book 1

Love, Life and Naughty Bits

Proof

Made in the USA
Charleston, SC
07 July 2015